Ann Dayleview

A TALE OF FROST

Book Two

Onyx Fire Press

Onyx Fire Press, LLC

ISBN: 978-1-7363705-4-4

Printed in the United States of America

Design by Jessica Pierce

For Lola,

My fluffy writing buddy who will never read my
books but is still my number one fan.

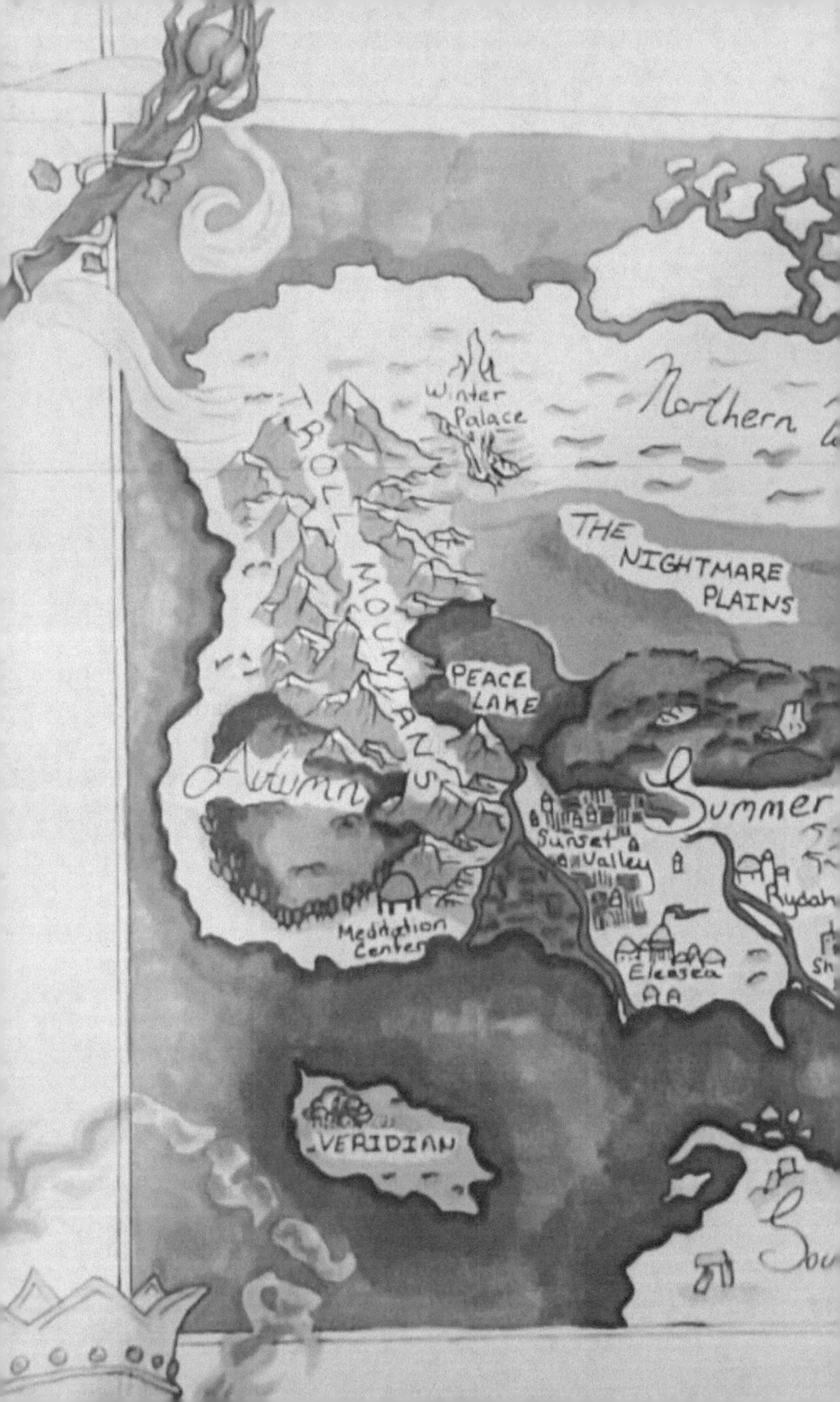

Winter Palace
Northern
TROLL MOUNTAINS
THE NIGHTMARE PLAINS
PEACE LAKE
Autumn
Summer
Sunset Valley
Rydah
Meditation Center
Eleasea
VERIDIAN

THE REALMS
OF
FAIRY
CRYSTAL MOUNTAINS
Vale
Spring
LAKE LAPIS
N
W
E
S
Winter Palace
Winter

CHAPTER I

Aiden

Aiden grit his teeth, fighting through the blaze skittering across his skin. It burned. It had never been this bad before. Was this to be his life now? His flesh flayed, then left until his skin grew back enough for Mab to return and start the agonizing cycle again? The thought sent lightning shivers across his body.

As if the life debt which kept him bound to their Majesties wasn't bad enough—at least then he had some glimmers of freedom. And despite their nightly drainings of his magic, he still had the opportunity to chase his revenge against the Summer Prince. Aiden closed his eyes; the familiar pain of the drainings barely phased him anymore—not with his skin so raw.

How many days had passed? He'd lost track the third time he'd been held under Mab's knife. Pleading had been useless—it'd been his fault they'd lost the Crown of Flames, his fault Summer still stood strong against them. And he had known this would be the consequence. Still… even in his worst nightmares he couldn't have fathomed the extent. Now he needed to find a way to block out the pain and accept his new existence.

Silence pressed in on Aiden like a wili's veil. Had the dungeon in the Winter Palace always been so quiet? Where were the screams of the tortured captives? The chatter of bored guardsmen and soldiers? Perhaps the war was going poorly without him and there were no new prisoners to interrogate. Or he was just being arrogant and their Majesties were keeping him in isolation from the others.

After all, it was arrogance that got him into this torture in the first place. If he hadn't been so overconfident that those in his inner circle wouldn't dare betray him… if he had just returned to the Winter Palace rather than spend the day with Wyn. No, he wouldn't regret the moments he'd spent with her; she was the only person who'd cared about who he truly was, at least after his parent's death. Aiden bowed his head; he'd likely never see her again. Who knew how long their Majesties would keep him down here?

Anger flashed through him, pressing his flames against his arms; their usually soft warmth seared his flesh. It was that vampire's fault… and the prince's. He'd known not to trust that Jefferson, but had been forced to keep him close. Dek, the closest person he'd had to a brother, was now dead because of him. If the vampire's lies hadn't drawn him out into the open when he was weak — if the prince hadn't ambushed them — the crown would still be theirs and perhaps Summer would have fallen by now.

A breeze whisked in, washing over his tormented skin, and a scream clawed its way out of his aching throat.

"Hello, Pet."

Ice flooded Aiden's stomach. No… it couldn't be. It was too soon; his skin had hardly healed.

The pattering of tiny pearls brushing against one another like rain drew closer as Mab entered the room. His heart pounded in his throat, and Aiden's muscles screamed at him to back away, but fear and pain stilled him.

She crouched down, her glowing violet eyes surveying him as one might a new blade. Aiden swallowed as she reached out a finger and stopped a mere hair's breadth from his chin — raising it so he lifted his head. The warmth of her burned like a candle against his skin as her lips quirked ever so slightly. His stomach churned, and he took a deep breath, refusing to vomit.

"You're still quite raw… strange. I could've sworn it didn't take as long for you to heal the last time." She cocked her head to the side. "Perhaps your body is weakening — how annoying."

Aiden's brow crinkled in confusion. Was she truly annoyed that the time it took between skinnings was longer? She'd seemed to relish in his renewed fear each time he'd lain before her, well healed and ready to be cut into again. What was a few more days?

"I have a mission for you. A chance to redeem yourself, but you can't go like this. You'll need your strength to carry it out. Perhaps I'll send Mare instead… for the first part anyway."

He longed to ask more about the mission, but his throat was far too raw for words, and he dared not tempt Mab with a reaction.

She straightened and stared down at him as though he were nothing more than a puddle. "Come, Pet. Perhaps healing in your room will speed the process. There is an element of timeliness to my plan."

Aiden winced through the pain and struggled to stand. Swaying, he caught himself just before he hit the floor. He tried and failed again. Mab let out a low growl, and his stomach dropped. His freedom was so close; he'd do anything not to have to suffer under her blade again. And now his cursed body failed him.

"Don't linger here too long," she said. Mab folded her arms and made her way to the door. "I need you in fighting shape within the next three days."

The door clicked shut, but there was no scrape of the lock dragging across it. A breeze raked across his skin. He groaned. The pain… it was nothing compared to the relief that washed through him. Freedom. Thank the sweet rain they still needed him.

He took a deep breath, crouching like an animal on the dungeon floor. He'd lost hope he'd ever see his old room again: the dim lights, rough sheets and beat up mattress, the books and few reminders of his parents beneath his bed. Tears welled in his eyes as the thought of returning to his old life filled his chest with hope. Perhaps it hadn't been good, forced to do their Majesties' bidding, but it'd been better than the endless cycle of torture.

Trying to stand again, dots flashed across his vision, and he fell back to his knees. Perhaps another hour of this place was for the best.

After several failed attempts, he rose, avoiding the mold-covered walls and limping carefully across the slippery floor. Bracing himself against the door, he hauled it open, and the damp dungeon air washed over him.

Aiden lumbered up the stairs to the frost-covered halls of the Winter Palace. Goblin soldiers snickered as he passed. What a monster he must look like, with his silver-streaked flesh on display so they all might see his failure. Their whispers pierced him like needles: "their Majesties' pet," "useless failure," "practically human."

The last one didn't hurt as much — he knew, and perhaps they knew too, just how powerful he truly was. He might look human, and his wing stubs were too caked in blood and loose flaps of flesh to make out what he truly was, but his magic was undeniably fae. Still, if he was human, if he could live in the Human Realm and practice human magic, what a blessed life that would be.

As he made his way through the glittering hall, he sensed the pulse of his own magic calling to him. Oberon must have used what he'd pulled from Aiden to reinforce the barrier and keep out Summer. Afterall, why should the king use his own magic when he could hoard Aiden's? Still, despite the cruel way it was ripped from him, the feeling of the barrier was a comfort — a constant reminder that, with his full strength, he had the power to take on the gold fae of Summer. One day he'd make them pay for the death of his parents and how they'd treated him.

His clenched fists trembled as he entered one of the smaller halls. The walls glinted with the pale green glow of the icy chandeliers. Shrunken green fae pounded on the sides of the bulbs — they must be recently captured, spies perhaps. The ones who'd been there longer had long given up their pounding in favor of pitiful glares. He rounded a corner and stopped to stare at the grand staircase leading to the ballroom.

Typically it was stark, the base made of ice clear enough to see the floor below and the railing coated in spikey shards of frost. But now green-capped elves wrapped pine garlands around the frost and hung bows and silver bells along the hallway. Lanterns lit with actual candles floated up the stairs in a spell-induced trance—no doubt forcibly controlled by one, or a few, of the captured green fae.

Could it be Solstice already? His heart leapt into his throat. It'd been near the end of autumn when he'd entered the dungeon. Had two months really passed?

A hag, a magic-less brown fae courtier, slowed as she spotted Aiden. He didn't have the strength to flare his blue flames menacingly to deter her from speaking to him. Instead, he kept his head down and picked up his pace, hoping to avoid any direct taunts.

"Tell me, will their Majesties have you dance at next week's festivities?" she cackled, recalling a previous punishment when their Majesties had forced him to wear iron slippers and dance before the court.

Aiden grit his teeth and glared at her, but she only laughed harder as she swept past. Tears pricked the corners of his eyes as he struggled to hurry to his room. Save for his nightly drainings, he hoped never to leave.

Stopping in front of his door, Aiden waved a hand and pulled on the wisp of magic at his core. Black flashed across his vision, and he stumbled back, catching himself before he hit the floor. Half crawling, he made his way into the bed and collapsed into its welcoming folds.

Sleep didn't come easily. Sharp pains from the sheets rubbing against his skin kept him from true rest. He needed to think of something to put his mind at ease. Wyn's laughing face materialized in his mind. The way she teased him each time he expressed his fascination over her human rituals, the way it felt to have her head tucked against his chest, and the flames that ignited within him when she kissed his lips swarmed through him.

It'd been nearly two months since he'd felt the heat of her lips against his. And now? Did she think him dead? Had she moved on? It wasn't fair of him to think she could be his forever… He could give her nothing, not even himself. It wasn't worth dwelling on things that could never be.

When exhaustion no longer clung to him like the twisting vines of Luching, Aiden peeled his eyes open and stared up at the dark ceiling. With a snap of his fingers, tiny fires burst to life around the room, bobbing mid-air. He tensed as the sounds of shuffling feet grew closer to his door.

"This plan of yours could easily get him killed. If you recall the last time…" Oberon's voice sounded just a little ways away.

"You worry too much." Mab's voice this time. "It's a trap; we'll lure him in and weaken his magic. And besides, our pet should be healed enough by then."

"I just don't wish to lose such a great source of power."

Mab scoffed. "You have plenty of his magic stored and more than enough green fae to sacrifice in his place."

The door swung open, and Aiden sucked in a breath as their Majesties approached his bedside. Mab wore her traditional white and pearls while the metallic tips of Oberon's antler glamour shone menacingly down at him.

Aiden swallowed as the king produced a crystal wand from the sleeve of his silver robe.

"At least you're awake this time." He placed the wand to Aiden's forehead, and the world exploded in pain.

Aiden wasn't sure how much time had passed when he woke again. The small room had no windows, and his internal clock was hardly reliable anymore. Aiden walked to his bathroom and inspected his reflection. A red- and pink-skinned monster stared back at him. He resisted the urge to scowl.

His mind flicked back to their Majesties' conversation — perhaps it didn't matter what he looked like if Mab's mission would likely end in his death. Though perhaps his instincts would lead him to wend away to Wyn like when the Summer Prince had nearly killed him. He didn't want her to remember him as a dying monster — he didn't want her to see him dying at all. Still, he could at least give her something to remember him by.

Aiden closed his eyes and thought of where he could go to

find an appropriate Solstice gift. There was the glass mountain in Autumn; the flowers there were beautiful. Though if one of the flowers should break or the wind blew too fierce and whipped up any stray shards, he'd suffer even more. If he could still go to Spring, he might be able to bring her back water from a wishing well. One sip and jewels could fall from her lips when she spoke, or whatever it was humans wished for. And what would Wyn want with jewels anyway?

Each idea that came to mind was more foolish or risky than the next. He might as well try to steal the Summer Prince's crown for her. It would probably cost him his life, and he'd likely ruin Mab's plans, but it was no more valid than his other thoughts. He sighed and sat on the edge of the bed. Reaching beneath it, he pulled out his father's book on human inventions. Perhaps there was something human she'd like. Not that he could build any of the complex contraptions he read about.

After several minutes of flipping aimlessly through the book, he stood and dressed in the loose black shirt and pants he used to sleep — the fabric much more gentle on his skin than his fighting leathers. He rubbed his chest, the place where his mother's ring had hung. There had been a story she had once told him, about the twelve Summer princesses who'd been lured to an underground kingdom by an encantado who'd impregnated and drowned them all.

He shuddered at the dark story. His mother always had a knack for telling terrifying stories when the family spent the night in starlit fields. His never came close to hers. But there was something in the tale which gave him pause. It'd been true; the Summer queen had been the only one of the twelve to escape. She'd seen to it that the encantado had been executed, and his river diverted, but the trove where he'd lured the princesses still existed. And it was said to have trees made of gold and silver. Perhaps a few leaves from one of those trees would be a good gift for Wyn. He could probably fashion them into some sort of jewelry.

Yes, it would be perfect. Pulling at the magic in his chest,

Aiden wended. His limbs shook and exhaustion hit him as though he were slammed into a wall. He hit the ground hard and cried out at his bruised and burning flesh. Cold raced through his body as he lay in snow, waiting for the pain to die down. When it finally did, he pulled himself up and shivered, staring out at the desolate wasteland.

This was certainly not Summer.

Streaks of violet, gold, and green illuminated the night sky, coated in a speckling of stars. The wind howled as it tore through his thin clothing, making his bones ache. He must still be too weak to wend. Freezing frosts. The irony of his failing blue fairy power would've made him laugh if he wasn't so cold. He should be able to easily wend to Summer, but still, he remained in Winter. The palace should be close. Aiden looked at the sky, hoping to recognize one of the constellations that would point him in the right direction. His father had taught him to navigate by the stars long ago, but now the memory, like that of his parents' faces, was warped and blurred.

He sighed and began walking. At least if he kept moving he was bound to come across something, hopefully. Trudging through the hard snow, Aiden spied three spikes just beyond one of the white dunes. As he drew closer, the brilliant colors of the sky above shimmered within the ice castle's graceful form.

Reaching out, Aiden felt for the familiar tug of his magic within the barriers, but it felt strange, almost as though the magic were not his, yet still familiar. His chest tightened, and he picked up his pace. Triglav, the three-headed frost giant who guarded the entrance, was nowhere to be seen. By the time Aiden reached the ice bridge, he was running. There were no sounds of their Majesties' beloved raucous revels, no howls of the drekavacs, just the wind as it blew swirls of snow into the ravine.

Had Summer attacked in the short time he'd been away? Surely he would've felt it if they'd managed to break his barriers. Aiden scarcely breathed as he crept across the bridge, barely extending any magic to keep his footing on the slippery surface.

The door opened for him, and he stepped inside. Nothing. Halls usually packed with brown fae bragging on their conquests against the greenies were empty. He hurried to the ballroom; perhaps the summertons had gathered all the people... bodies... there—it was the only place that could fit all of them. But when he reached it, like everywhere else, it was empty.

Heart racing, Aiden dared to call out, "Hello?" His voice echoed against the ice walls.

Perhaps he could go to where the green fae were forced to work? Surely Summer wouldn't have captured them. His footsteps crunched against the frosty ground as he raced toward the kitchens. Someone had to be there. Throwing the door open, three fire-salamanders spun to stare at him, their dark eyes widening. Orange and red slimy skin coated their bodies. Two stood on their hind legs, peering into a cauldron.

"Meat?" The one on the ground said, flicking its tongue at him.

Aiden took a step back. Today was not a day to fight them. He couldn't afford to use what little magic he had built up on them. Not until he found the others.

"Blue fairy..." another whispered. "We feed." The other two glared at their companion, then turned back to Aiden.

He tensed. How could they have known what type of fae he was? Surely this wasn't an aspect of typical fire-salamander magic. Then again, these creatures usually inhabited the inside of volcanoes—little was known about their powers.

"Come," the fire-salamander said and led him through the door he'd entered through.

Aiden's jaw fell slack. Where was the hall? Before him was the elaborate dining room where Mab and Oberon hosted important members of the brown fae community. As though they cared for the plight of brown fae. They were just a means to an end—power was all they craved.

The fire-salamander tugged him into one of the chairs, but he shook his head.

"We feed," they said.

Aiden glanced dubiously at the grand table. What would Mab do to him if she found him at her table? The last two months flashed through his mind, tearing through his chest and sucking the air from his lungs. Aiden doubled over, catching the back of a chair. A sticky hand rested on his shoulder, and he looked up. The fire-salamander held out a glass of wine, but there was no pitcher in sight.

"Drink."

Aiden took the glass and pretended to sip the red liquid. The rare times he'd been in a position to taste alcohol, he'd loathed the flavor. Wiping his red-stained lips with his sleeve, he looked sidelong at the flame-colored creature.

"Sit," it urged.

Taking a deep breath, Aiden took a seat in the chair to the right of the head. "Where is everyone?" While fire-salamanders were native to Summer, it struck him as odd that the army would abandon them here.

"Gone. Many, many years." It nodded solemnly.

"Years? But that's not possible, I—" His power was substantial, but even he couldn't travel through time… at least, he hadn't thought so.

A loud groaning noise sounded from beyond the door, followed by a click. Something tugged at his chest, almost like the sensation of being near the barriers but stronger, older.

"What was that?"

The fire-salamander shifted back. "Just moving." It nudged the wine glass closer to Aiden, and said, "Drink. Feed." He grabbed the glass, and the fire-salamander waddled from the room.

Magic pulsed from beyond the adjacent door, different from the one the salamander had passed through. Aiden rose, following the pull. His fingers trembled on the handle as he pulled it down and drew open the door.

He gasped. The room was filled with glittering snow under a pale blue light. Stepping inside, a cool breeze washed over him. Aiden flinched, bracing for pain, but there was nothing. Not even the slightest tingle. He rolled up his sleeve—his skin was no longer pink from Mab's cruel ministrations. Instead, it boasted a dark olive color he hadn't seen in months. Even his magic felt strong and natural. What was this place?

Walking through the snow, Aiden followed the pull of the magic. Fist-sized pearls scattered throughout the snow in all the shades of the aurora sky. Perhaps Wyn would like one of these. He stooped to grab a pale pink one when a blue twinkle caught his eye. A few feet away, a pearl filled with a bright blue glow seemed to call to him. Aiden dropped the pink pearl and reached for the blue. It flickered as he touched it, holding it up as the light reflected off the snow.

What was this? He pushed a bit of his power into it, testing its magical properties. The light flickered, but nothing else happened. Turning it over, he searched for any inscription and rubbed the sphere between his hands. Still, nothing. Perhaps it was just an unusually beautiful pearl.

"You didn't stay!"

Aiden whirled to see the three fire-salamanders engulfed in flames behind him. His own blue fire ignited down his arms, and he crouched, ready for a fight.

"What are you doing? What is this place?" Everything here was wrong—no, not wrong, just incredibly different from the Winter Palace he knew. But this room… this didn't exist in Mab and Oberon's court.

Liquid fire spewed out toward him, and Aiden gasped, throwing up his flames. The salamanders hissed, ignoring his question as their fire nearly rolled over his barrier and spilled out towards him. He leapt out of the way, tumbling into the snow.

Pausing, he took in the glittering frost-scape. Something like this shouldn't be guarded by creatures of Summer. One of them scrambled forward, and Aiden huffed a laugh. "I thought you wanted to feed me."

"Yes," it said. "We feed. We take." It opened its mouth revealing a row of jagged teeth. Aiden lept back. How could such creatures exist, and what did they want to take?

His heart pounded as the fire-salamanders divided up, crawling across the walls and racing toward him. Swallowing hard, he reached to his magic. The fire-salamanders' bodies glowed, and the liquid fire shot at him from three directions. Aiden wended, thinking of his room — even if he were somehow in the past or wherever… he could figure everything out from there.

Again, he hit a wall and stumbled backward, hitting the ice-covered ground. Groaning, he sat up, rubbing the back of his head. What was wrong with his magic? The ice burned his skin as he tried several times to push himself to his feet. When he was finally able to stand, he panted, struggling to see through his semi-blurred vision. The same ice palace stood before him, but now Triglav slouched against the entryway. How? Taking a step forward, the familiar tingle of his magic washed over him as he stepped through the wards — his wards.

If this was the Winter Palace, where had he been? He looked down; the blue sphere was still clutched in his hand. Had this been what those salamanders had wanted to take? It didn't even do anything. Perhaps, like Oberon, they'd hungered for his magic. Shuddering, Aiden slipped the orb into his pocket and made his way casually to the entrance.

"Cutting it close tonight, Dog," Triglav spat.

Aiden flinched at the nickname. "What is the hour?"

"Three minutes to midnight." The frost giant rumbled a laugh.

Freezing frosts. Aiden moved past him and entered the palace. It was full of chattering fae, just as he remembered. None of this made sense. Hurrying down the hall, he patted his pocket. At least he now had a gift for Wyn. The more he thought about it, the less likely it seemed the salamanders wanted an unmagical ball. After all, they'd known him to be a blue fairy, and they'd wanted to feed on him. No, this was a good, safe present for Wyn — a goodbye present, he reminded himself. He couldn't keep torturing himself by wanting her and hurting her by not being what she needed. He couldn't be.

The door to their Majesties' study was slightly ajar. Aiden pushed it open and froze in the entryway. Mab sat perched on the desk filing her nails — the image of her with a knife flashed through his mind. Her approaching; the knife sinking into his flesh.

"We don't have all night," Oberon said, stepping in front of his wife and sauntering to the center of the room.

Cold trailed from Aiden's face, down his body as he shakily closed the door and tripped into the room. He knelt before the king and closed his eyes, trying to ignore Mab's cold stare as he fought to keep the horrific memories at bay

Today, I'm free of that prison, and tomorrow, I'll see Wyn.

Oberon placed the tip of the crystal wand to his forehead and ripped Aiden's magic out.

CHAPTER 2

Freddie

The phone rang and Freddie blinked, rolling over to stare at the clock. Two in the morning... Who would call at this ungodly hour? Not that she'd been sleeping; her thoughts buzzed of her failure to secure a single byline in two months of interning for the New Wall Inquirer. And the ever-haunting image of the vampire's body as he's writhed in agony after she'd staked him with a red sole.

Hauling herself from bed, she padded downstairs to the kitchen and lifted the old-fashioned cord phone.

"Hello?" she croaked.

An official-sounding voice responded. "May I speak to the parents of Wynifred Jones?"

"This is Wynifred. They are..." She frowned; it was the middle of the night. "Who is this?"

Hesitation hung on the line, then she responded slowly. "This is Officer Carin from Northampton County Prison." She paused again, and Freddie's pulse picked up — all traces of sleep gone. "My parents are sleeping, can I —? I can pass along the message."

"I — I'm not sure. Can't you get your parents?"

She tightened her grip on the phone as the hair on her arms

prickled; nothing good could come of this call—she was sure. "I can't. They keep their door locked, and they're heavy sleepers."

The lie slipped from her lips with ease. Whatever this news, there was no guarantee her parents would share it with her. She swallowed hard, shoving back memories of Aiden's careful dances with truths as he failed to lie.

Several heavy moments passed until, finally, the officer cleared her throat. "I suppose it wouldn't do too much harm. You're nearly eighteen, and this does concern you…" She hummed a bit, and the sound of tapping fingers came through the speaker. "You were involved in a kidnapping attempt by one Dion Goatherd?"

If the officer's voice hadn't sounded so serious, Freddie might have laughed. She'd never been able to get over the fact that the faun's last name had been Goatherd. But now a tightness formed around her throat as she responded. "Yes."

"We're calling to inform you he's no longer in prison custody, and we caution you to stay inside or with large groups until he's apprehended."

"You mean… he's escaped?" She swallowed hard.

It had only been a couple of months since she'd revealed him as a serial kidnapper—far too soon for him to be released. What if he wanted revenge? The first time had been luck… fending off his vampire henchman with the heel of Amanda's shoe. Near death escapes were sometimes just part of the job of being a journalist, but she needed to survive long enough to be an official one.

"Yes, but don't worry. The police are working on the case as we speak."

Freddie pressed her lips together. At least before, she'd been the one to go after him, but now, she had no idea where he'd strike. "Do they have any leads?"

"I'm not privy to the case details. Just stay safe and let the police take care of everything. The majority of prisoners who escape are returned."

"Fae prisoners?"

"He's only a brown fae; he doesn't have any magic."

Freddie frowned. Dion wasn't completely harmless, nor was

he a brown fae. He was a satyr, a type of green fae, albeit with horns so short he could be a faun — an actual brown fae. Once he got his hands on a flute — and those weren't exactly hard to come by — he'd be dangerous. Or at least a bit more dangerous than the average human. She needed to find him before he found her. But this time she'd bring Raul and Jefferson, too. Maybe even Pelrin… maybe. Perhaps it'd been a tad reckless to try and corner a fae kidnapper with no fae backup.

"Thanks, I'll do my best to stay safe."

"We'll call your parents back in the morning and let you know of any updates," the officer said and hung up.

Freddie leaned back against the wall and glanced over her shoulder at the stairs. Her parents would probably try to force her to stay home for the last week of the semester once they found out. And if Dion truly was after her, his magic wouldn't harm her while she had Aiden's ring… but he might try to attack Amanda again. There'd definitely be no sleeping now. Where would the satyr go? Did he have anyone else in the city who would help him? Perhaps that werewolf girl, but she was locked up. Surely the police would increase security around her now.

Nerves buzzing with energy, she trooped back to her room to grab her laptop. If she got to him first, she could ask about Freya and the other students who hadn't been found — now all likely turned to vampires and werewolves like Dion and his cronies had tried to do to her. She shivered at the memory. The police probably already interrogated him, but they didn't have gold fae magic backing them up. And Pelrin was still trying to get on her good side… surely he'd use his magic to help her with this. Maybe he could enchant the truth from the goat-man's lips. To help save the students. Freddie pressed her lips together; the police seemed to have all but forgotten about them — but she wouldn't.

The first thing the satyr would need was a weapon. She searched for music stores near Easton — there were so many. She made a note to call them in the morning to find out which ones carried flutes. But then what? Would he try to take more people… or would he try to take her?

The hours passed slowly as she sat at her desk searching for useless things: places for fauns, where do escaped criminals go, goat herding tactics… Her eyelids drooped as the sun crested the horizon, filling her room with its golden glow. The events of that night played out in her mind for the hundredth time, as though she were reliving them.

She had followed Amanda into the dark office building as a cold dread she didn't remember having washed over her. A vampire stepped out of the shadows, his fangs flashing in the low light of the street lamps outside. Then a werewolf appeared, her yellow eyes glowing bright… and hungry. Freddie's stomach turned as she eyed the two red fae; perhaps her friendship with Raul, who was also a werewolf, comforted her slightly, but it was the vampire who turned her heart to ice.

He smirked and moved toward her but paused when the satyr called his name. She let out a breath. Despite being in charge, the satyr was scarcely a threat without the others. Still… His familiar words came back to her: "I'll even give you a choice: vampire or werewolf." The thought still gave her chills; she'd never want to give up such a huge part of herself. Knocking out Amanda first, then trying and failing to knock out Freddie, the vampire carried them off to the conference room they would later escape from. Aiden's ring had protected her.

She twisted it on her middle finger; the tiny leaf carvings glowed in the soft dawn light. Aiden… they'd been talking about him that night. The satyr had wanted him dead, or at least hoped Mab and Oberon would kill him. Her chest tightened. There hadn't been a day she hadn't thought of him… hadn't wondered if he still lived. What if the satyr was going to Fairy to see Aiden's fate for himself? What she wouldn't give to know, too.

Bowing her head into her hands, Freddie let her eyes close. She couldn't let herself remain hung up on him. They'd only gone on a couple of dates, but she couldn't stop her heart from pounding at their memory. It was stupid. Aiden was likely dead. Even if he was alive, their relationship was a constant risk to them both. Pelrin already wanted to kill him, and there was no telling what Mab and

Oberon would do if they found out about her and Aiden. Shaking her head, Freddie pushed away thoughts of him and picked up her phone. She had a faun, or satyr rather, to track down.

###

"Hot on a story?"

Freddie ground her teeth as the tip of a red braid brushed the table in front of her. A week had passed, and there'd been no word on the satyr. The last thing she needed was her archrival to rub it in.

"Don't you have someplace better to be, Mal?"

The girl above her twisted, leaning with her back against the upper school library's bench. "It's Mallory, and I was just checking on you. Especially with the news and all…" She trailed off, batting her eyes innocently.

"How—That information is supposed to be confidential."

Mallory held up her phone. "A journalist has her ways."

"Your dad told you, huh?" Despite his position as a sergeant in the Fullerton police department, Mallory's father didn't seem to be able to keep important information to himself. Pursing her lips, Freddie folded her arms over her keyboard. "What do you even want, Mal?"

"Well, Wynifred." Malloy's lips quirked as Freddie winced at the use of her full name. Couldn't her parents have come up with something more modern? "I know you're looking into that fae's escape, and since we both have journalistic internships now, I thought we could share leads."

Freddie scoffed. "Working for Chattable is hardly journalism." The site had grown in popularity over the past year with its five hundred character posts on world news. But in its rush to grow, its hiring processes had gotten sloppy. Now, near anyone could become a "journalist," and fact checkers were a fantasy. It was no more than a glorified social media platform.

"At least my posts actually get published." Mallory tossed her braid over her shoulder, and Freddie winced. Save for the article on the kidnappings, all her pitches had been passed along to senior journalists.

When she finally found the other students, she could write the follow-up to her original article — no one would be able to take that from her. But so far, the leads had been few and far between.

"Just leave me alone, Mal," Freddie sighed. She'd barely made a dent in calling all the music stores in the area, and so far five fauns had purchased woodwind instruments… and she had thirty more stores to go. Maybe she'd started calling too soon… maybe she should start over. Mallory peered over her shoulder, and Freddie turned her laptop out of view.

"Hmmm, I'm looking into all faun-owned businesses, too. He'd likely want to link up with his own kind. You know how fae are."

Freddie pressed two fingers to her temple. "How exactly are fae?"

"You should know, you shack up with them all the time." Mallory sniffed, and it took everything in Freddie not to stab her pale hand with her pen. "They have no regard for our laws or people. If they want something, they take it. Just like that faun tried to take you."

Freddie slammed her computer shut and got to her feet. "Just because one fae did something wrong doesn't mean all fae are bad. How can you be so — so heartless? Humans do awful things all the time, does that make us bad, too?"

"Fae are our natural predators. What we do in self defense cannot be compared to vampires craving our blood or fairies stealing our children."

Shaking her head, Freddie raised her voice. "Vampires have blood banks and synthetics, and fairies don't even do that anymore. And besides, are you trying to say humans don't take advantage of other humans?"

"That's different," Mallory said. "Fae on fae crime is much higher than that of human on human."

"Maybe that's because we hold most of them in poverty in this realm. There's barely a chance to escape."

"Please, there are plenty of well-to-do fae. The rest of them are just lazy."

Freddie opened her mouth to shout back, but a stony chill stiffened her limbs and strangled her throat. She gasped and saw Mallory in a similar frozen state of horror.

"There will be no shouting in this library," Ms. Euryale, the librarian on campus, said in a low, steady voice. Her flashing green eyes, hissing bun, and use of magic betrayed her green fae heritage. Freddie struggled against the magic holding her. "S-sorry, ma'am," she said in a hoarse voice. Mallory just glared at the woman as the grip of the magic lessened.

"I'm going to have to ask you both to leave. This is a place for quiet study, not a shouting match," the librarian said.

"How dare you use magic on me," Mallory snapped. Despite her seeming disdain, even she had dropped her voice. "I'm pretty sure that's assault, and I can report you."

Ms. Euryale shrugged. "You can report me after you leave. You're lucky I don't ban you for life."

Freddie shot a glare at Mallory, shoved her laptop and notebook into her backpack, and snatched up her coat. Striding out of the building, she left Mallory behind to gather her things at the other end of the table, not looking back.

Outside, the winter air bit into her cheeks as she marched across the upper school campus towards the shuttle stop. Other students passed her, bundled into thick jackets with their heads down so it was impossible to tell if they were fae or human. Wrenching her phone from her pocket, she texted her best friend, Amanda.

[5:03 PM] Movie night?

The reply was immediate.

[5:03 PM] Sure. I'll tell Raul and Jefferson.

Letting out a breath, Freddie joined the cluster of students waiting for the shuttle to New Wall's lower school. In just one more year… less than that… a few months, she'd graduate, and the upper school would be her home. Her chest swelled recalling the intense joy and relief of receiving her acceptance.

When the bus arrived, she piled in with the other students, watching the beautiful blend of gravity-defying fae structures mingling with the red-brick human ones whisk past. A movie night would be the perfect way to get everyone together and catch that satyr. She'd yet to tell any of them her plan. Amanda would worry if she knew their would-be kidnapper had escaped and would betray her — likely accidentally — to Jefferson. And Jefferson was dead loyal to Pelrin.

No, Pelrin couldn't know yet. She didn't need him sending one of his guards to follow her every move. Not that Ginny hadn't grown on her, but it was a relief when the little pixie had resumed her duties in Fairy now that Freddie was "safe."

Freddie jumped off the bus and headed across the Bailey, the open courtyard between the two lower school dorms. Warm air greeted her as she stepped into the building and trooped up the stairs. As she approached her room at the end of the hall, Amanda and Raul looked up from where they sat. Amanda, a short, Korean girl with pin-straight black hair stood up, her ponytail lopped over her shoulder.

"Jefferson's outside," she said, then pointed to the door across from Freddie's. "She put that up again."

Freddie's eyes narrowed as she approached Mallory's door, a simple wooden cross hanging from it. It was hardly a statement of piety. Freddie sincerely doubted Mallory even knew what the cross was supposed to represent. No, it was designed specifically to keep away vampires, aka to make Freddie's life more difficult. Striding to the window between the two doors, she hauled it open, letting a blast of wintery air blow through the dorm.

"Dios," Raul cursed and pulled the hood of his sweatshirt over his freshly buzzed head.

Freddie ripped the cross from the door and hurled it out the window before shutting the window again. "Tell Jefferson he can come up," she snapped and shoved into her door.

Raul and Amanda followed her in a bit of stunned silence. Freddie had never actually damaged anything of Mallory's before, and her stomach clenched as she glanced back out the door. Maybe she should pick it up later, but now she had to focus on finding the satyr.

Sinking onto the bed, Amanda flicked on the TV. "How 'bout Hallmark since it's the holidays and all?"

Raul groaned, sinking into the couch. "How about Die Hard? That's a Christmas movie."

"That is a stupid action movie, we're not watching that." Amanda's phone buzzed, and she strode to the door and pulled it open to reveal a pale, blond vampire grinning down at her, his red eyes glowing.

Instinctively, Freddie drew back, then inwardly cursed herself. Only one vampire had ever tried to hurt her. There was no reason to be afraid of all of them—especially not Jefferson. He bent down nearly in half to plant a kiss on Amanda's lips before stepping inside.

"What are we watching?" he asked, nudging Raul over to take a seat next to him. Raul's nose wrinkled, but ever since Jefferson had risked his life to steal back Pelrin's crown, the only thing keeping Fairy from falling to the Dark Fae Army, he'd all but dropped their feigned rivalry.

"Amanda wants something holiday related. What do you think about Die Hard?"

Jefferson grinned, but his face drooped when he caught Amanda's glare. Before he could suggest an alternative, Freddie cleared her throat.

"Hey guys… I kinda have something to tell you."

Amanda looked up from her phone while the others stared at Freddie curiously. "You're not getting back together with Pelrin are you?" Amanda asked.

"What? No!" Freddie folded her arms. "Why was that the first thing—nevermind. I really wanted to ask you all for help. You know I've been working on that story to find the other missing students, and I think I finally caught a break. The faun, er satyr, escaped from prison!"

"You say that like it's a good thing, Fred," Raul said.

Jefferson frowned. "How long has he been out?"

"Just under a week." Freddie shrugged.

Amanda slapped a hand to her forehead. "And you're just

now telling us? Do you at least have any leads?"

"Amanda! Freddie knows this is a dangerous matter. I'm sure she's just been scared and staying inside as much as possible, especially after what happened last time." Jefferson gave Freddie a pointed look as Raul struggled to disguise a snort.

Freddie sighed and took a seat next to her friend on the bed. "I've called a ton of music stores in the area. A few have sold to fauns Dion's age, but even if I did find out he bought one, I don't know where to go next."

Amanda reached out her hand. "Let me see your notes. Maybe I'll see something you've missed."

"No, you guys can't be serious about trying to track down the guy who nearly killed you," Jefferson said.

"There's no stopping Freddie, man." Raul slapped him on the back as Freddie passed her notebook over to Amanda.

"But you were nearly kidnapped, killed, and dragged off to Fairy!" Jefferson ran a hand through his chin length locks.

"Technically, they wouldn't have been killed, just turned into red fae like us," Raul said.

"It's the same thing!"

"Maybe for you…"

"Even if they didn't die that night, they would've died on the front lines of the war. It's brutal out there."

Freddie sighed, trying to tune out the boys' argument. "See anything?" she asked Amanda.

Pursing her lips, Amanda frowned at the five stores who'd said a faun Dion's age had purchased flutes, but there were countless others that had said they couldn't remember or had just laughed and hung up. Her finger hovered over the name of one location: Bethlehem.

"I think—" She tapped her phone. "Yeah, my mom sent me this." Pulling up her texts with her mom, Amanda showed Freddie her phone, and Raul leaned over to get a glimpse. It was a picture of her mom's computer screen where she could just make out a flier for a holiday woodwind competition. "My brother's entering."

"And maybe Dion is, too," Freddie muttered. It would make

sense if Dion was after her, or at least trying to get to Amanda. She pressed her lips together, not daring to speak her theory aloud.

"It's tomorrow night if you want to go with me."

"No, no—" Jefferson started but stopped as a blinding gold light filled the room.

"What are we watching? Titanic?" The light faded revealing a handsome fairy with gold wings and blond hair trailing down his embroidered gray jacket. "You look nice, Fred."

Freddie glanced down at her worn jeans and red hoodie and frowned. "I wear this pretty much every day, Pelrin."

He grinned. "And it suits you so well." Turning back to the boys, he angled himself to where Jefferson had been sitting. "Soooo we decided on a movie?"

"Die Hard—" Raul said just as Jefferson cut him off.

"They want to go hunting down an escaped criminal." The vampire's usually white face flushed red, the blood from his last meal still circulating in his veins. "Tell them that's crazy!"

Pelrin's turquoise eyes flashed as he turned to Freddie. "What criminal?"

Her stomach sank. Next time she'd just tell Raul. "Look, Pel, it's not as bad as Jefferson says. It's just a faun… for a story."

"You mean the faun who tried to kidnap you?" His voice shook, and Freddie drew back, fearing for the cardboard box she used as a coffee table. "He escaped?"

"Everything's fine. I just want to ask him some questions. We have to find those other students. You can even go with me if you want." She bit her lip, unsure if she actually wanted Pelrin there.

"No." Pelrin got to his feet. "You're not going. Where is he?"

"We—we don't know exactly…"

He turned to Raul, who shrank back. "Where?"

"I mean there's a woodwind contest the next town over, but Pel, it's just a hunch. No need to get all upset," Raul said.

Pelrin pressed his lips together. "I'll go, just in case."

"Pelrin, this is my story. I'm going." Freddie stepped in front of him, arms folded across her chest.

"I'll get someone to stay with you. If he's on the loose…" Pelrin stepped around her. "When's the concert? Jefferson, show me where it is."

The vampire glanced back at Amanda, who clutched her phone close to her chest. He gave her a half smile. "Come on, if your brother's in danger, isn't it more important than a story?"

Amanda flicked a glance at Freddie. "You're right — it is my brother. We should all go."

"That's not what I meant!"

Amanda shrugged, and Freddie smiled. "The more of us there are, the safer it'll be. Especially if you're there, Pel."

Gritting his teeth, Pelrin clutched at a bunch of his long golden hair and glared at Freddie. "Fine, but I'll lead, and you do exactly as I say. I suppose he's only a faun…"

Jefferson let out an exasperated sigh. "This is going to be a disaster."

They settled in, and Raul put on Die Hard. Freddie pored over her phone, scrutinizing photos of Freya, Daniel, and the other missing students for the millionth time. There had to be something she was missing, Aiden would know. She swallowed down the painful thought. Aiden wasn't here; she'd have to do this on her own. With the information she got from Dion tomorrow, she'd finally have a lead… she hoped.

###

The next evening, they met in the crowded Bailey. It was the last day before break, and the sea of students was flooding through the courtyard to get home. Amanda and Raul hauled their bags into Freddie's trunk, and they piled into her tiny Toyota Corolla and took off toward Bethlehem. Jefferson begged them to turn back the entire way while Raul tried to distract him by hounding him with questions about his Agera. But as much as Jefferson loved to talk about his car, it seemed the threat of Amanda in danger, once again, was too great to deter him from his argument.

Amanda's brother attended a private school for musically gifted kids. It suddenly struck Freddie as implausible that the satyr might have tricked his way in just to steal away a couple people. It seemed like more effort than he'd put in before, but then again, he

25

might not have anyone helping him this time. She pursed her lips as they parked and followed the slow stream of people into the auditorium.

Taking a pamphlet from one of the ushers, Freddie skimmed the student roster. Her gaze caught Amanda's brother's name, James Lee, then moved on to the instruments. Obos, fifes, several clarinets, and a french horn were positioned above a slew of flute players—no doubt this concert would last for hours. Sighing, she turned her attention to the students' last names, not truly believing Dion would keep his name while entering. But it looked as though several of the students came from a faun heritage with names like Ramsey, Nanny, and Pan. He could be posing as one of those...

"See anything?"

Freddie jumped and looked up to see Pelrin's handsome face hovering just inches above her own. She cleared her throat and shook her head. Passing the pamphlet to him, Freddie led her friends around back to find the stage door.

"I'm starting to think this is a bad idea," Raul hissed. "What if he's not here and we just embarrass ourselves by accusing some random guy?"

"And what if he is here and we miss our chance?"

"Yes, our chance to put him back where he belongs," Pelrin said.

Freddie glared. "Don't you care about the missing students? They're somewhere in Fairy. You could've sent people to look for them."

"I'm not sending my people to roam the four realms in search of people who don't even belong to Summer. We're in the middle of a war. Once you come up with a concrete location, maybe I'll send some of my people in to get them out."

"And maybe I won't sneak across the border to rescue them myself." Freddie flicked a curl from her face and darted backstage.

They scanned the flurry of students and faculty shuffling around. Freddie and Amanda did their best to stay out of the way as Pelrin headed over to the dressing rooms, and Raul and Jefferson moved to the opposite side of the stage to get a better view of the performers. Time slipped by as the musicians played one after another. Finally the first of the fauns stepped onstage — it wasn't Dion, though this faun's flute had a haunting melody that made the audience sway in their seats. Freddie frowned. What a cheater.

"Look there." Amanda pointed into the audience. Leaning against the back wall was Mallory, her narrow blue eyes scrutinizing the satyr as he stepped off stage. What was she doing here? Unless...

Freddie did a quick search on her phone for the background on the school. Sure enough, it'd been founded by a satyr and had been run by the same family for years. Now, a satyr and his nymph wife served as the school governors. Of course, Mallory would think they were guilty.

She grit her teeth, but her heart stuttered as a familiar melody floated across the stage. The audience stared blankly forward, mouths hanging open. Beside her, even Amanda's eyes glazed over in a trance.

Crap. Freddie twisted Aiden's ring on her finger, grateful for the protection it gave against magic. Ignoring the ache in her heart, she knelt down and pried off her boot. Well, if it worked once... She charged across the stage and swung it right at the satyr's head. He dropped the flute, and it rolled across the stage.

"Don't you dare!" Freddie raised her boot threateningly, and he backed away, but a grin spread across his face.

"I had been hoping you'd find me... though I'll admit, I didn't expect it to be this soon. You really know how to land yourself into trouble." The satyr huffed a laugh.

Freddie lunged forward, bringing the boot down on his head again. "Shut up."

"Ow! Will you just stop hitting me? I —"

"Police!" Mallory's shrill voice rang out, and almost instantly, several black-clad officers and plain-clothes people mobbed the stage.

"Wait!" Freddie cried as they shoved her back. "I just need to ask him some questions!"

"Looks like he was after the girl again, but we have him in

custody," an officer said into a communicator on her shoulder.

"Filthy human, you don't even know what's after you!" Dion cried as the police hauled him off-stage.

"Are you okay?" A policewoman put an arm on Freddie's shoulder. She shook it off.

"F-fine." What could he possibly mean? Had Dion found new henchmen so soon?

"Do you need a ride home? It must be terrifying that he came after you again. Good thing your friend was looking out for you." She jerked her chin at Mallory, and Freddie's face flushed red.

"I'm fine." Backing away, Freddie returned to her true friends. They were gathered together just off the side of the stage and looked up when they saw Freddie, their expressions strained. "What's wrong?"

"Have you seen Pelrin?" Jefferson asked.

Freddie shrugged. "No. Pelrin!" They waited — Pelrin always came when she called him. But he didn't. "Pelrin?" Nothing.

"We looked everywhere for him and couldn't find him anywhere backstage," Amanda said.

Raul held out a bit of fabric. "We found this by the dressing rooms."

Freddie took it and examined the embroidered dark gray material. It was definitely fae-made and looked to be terribly expensive — just like what Pelrin had been wearing earlier. She swallowed hard and looked up at them. "But Dion's just a faun... satyr; he can't really do anything to Pelrin. I mean, Pel's a gold fae."

Jefferson shrugged. "Maybe he got urgently pulled away for the war or something. I'm going to go look for him in Summer, just in case."

She nodded. "Keep us posted."

Bending down, Jefferson kissed Amanda, promising he'd be back soon. She nuzzled his cheek, just before he shrank into bat form and flew out of the auditorium. Freddie's stomach twisted as she watched him go. Tomorrow was Christmas Eve, and the fae celebrated it as Solstice, too. Hopefully Jefferson was right and Pelrin would be able to spend the holiday safe with his family.

Her chance at a story gone and Pelrin nowhere to be found, Freddie wrung her hands and headed back to her car. At least tomorrow would be better; she'd be home with her parents spending the holiday with her mom's special hot cocoa. She could figure out her next steps safe with them.

CHAPTER 3

Aiden

That plan of yours could easily get him killed. Oberon's ominous words played over and over in Aiden's head as he paced outside the study. His heart roared in his ears; what task could Mab impose upon him now? The orb he'd stolen for Wyn burned in his inner jacket pocket. Tomorrow would be the morning after Solstice when humans would have their big celebrations, or at least his father had told him so when Aiden was small. He swallowed — tomorrow he'd see Wyn, if he survived today.

A woman in a deep gray jumpsuit glided down the hall. Stray wisps of black hair escaped the waist-length braid to brush across her dark skin. Her jaw tightened as her eyes locked on Aiden. He stiffened in reply — Mare.

"Aiden," she said. Her voice was strained, as though someone were pulling the words from her throat with iron.

He gave her a curt nod, then turned away, his heart pounding for an entirely different reason now. Mare had been the one who'd abandoned him and Dek to the Summer Prince's mercy. Perhaps if she hadn't left them, Dek would still be alive. Aiden's throat tightened as he recalled Dek's body crumbling to ash in his arms. He'd always thought the three of them had been like siblings, but

Mare had apparently only thought of herself.

"You look better." She stared at the opposite wall, her arms folded over her chest.

Aiden frowned. "Not being skinned alive helps."

"I'm glad that even the harshest lessons don't seem to resonate with you." Mare rolled her neck, as though her eyes weren't strong enough to express her disdain.

"You think I deserved that?"

"Your selfishness and stupidity nearly got me killed. I would think your punishment might have instilled some sense of accountability in you, but I guess a shadow's source remains constant."

Pain twisted in the pit of his stomach. She wasn't entirely wrong; if he hadn't trusted the vampire that night… Aiden's hand tightened into a fist. But Mare also wasn't entirely innocent. "Do you truly think it was me who betrayed us? It was that vampire, and the prince."

"What did you think would happen if you led us into battle weak and unprepared? I begged you to let us leave, and your stupid pride kept us there—kept me there. It's your fault Dek's dead."

Heat flooded through Aiden's veins, pushing his flames against his arms. No, that wasn't his fault… it couldn't be. Blue fire erupted from his fingertips as he lifted his hand and shot them across the hall at Mare.

She blocked it with a billowing wall of darkness. "How dare you!" Shadows snaked from her shield to shoot out like sharp daggers toward him.

A wall of flame sprang up before Aiden, rendering the daggers harmless. "It was a trap. If you're so smart, why didn't you see it coming? Aren't you supposed to be the spy?"

Mare scoffed and tossed her braid over her shoulder. "You could've waited until you were stronger. We relied on your magic to protect us."

Aiden grit his teeth. As much as he hated to admit it, Mare was right; he should have waited. If he had, Dek would've still been alive. He'd still have been there to tease Aiden about the pitiful state of his love life and to comfort him after their Majesties' punishments. But Mare, even before this, had been nothing like Dek. And without him, their family was broken.

Chest tightening, Aiden took a step toward her. How could he have known it was a trap? A small voice in the back of his mind hissed, *your instincts told you not to trust that vampire.*

Sharp shadows sliced by him so quickly he barely had time to dodge. Rather than stabbing him in the shoulder, they merely sliced a shallow line across his upper arm, tearing his thin jacket. Beneath the tear, silver trickled down to stain his sleeve. He hissed, gritting his teeth as he looked up at Mare. She stared back at him with shock written across her dark features.

"I—" She mouthed, but no more words came out.

"It seems you're quite capable of defending yourself without my help," Aiden said. He let out a humorless laugh as the flames on his arms died down. What were they even doing? Going at each other like this wouldn't bring Dek back, no matter how hard they wished for it.

Mare shook her head. "Those flames weren't exactly soft and fluffy, Aiden." Though she glared, her words no longer held the same venom as they had earlier.

"What is going on here, dears?" Mab's delicate voice rang out as she and Oberon stepped around the corner. Oberon continued towards the study while Mab hung back, her eyes scrutinizing every inch of Aiden, then Mare. "No use wasting your energy on one another. You'll both need your strength for this task."

Aiden and Mare exchanged glances as their Majesties opened the door to the study and passed through. Settling herself on the desk with Oberon leaning back in the chair behind her, Mab stared at the two young fae with a hungry ferocity. Flashes of kneeling on the ground, Oberon tearing Aiden's magic from his body with the crystal wand, pulsed through Aiden's mind, nearly bringing him to his knees. Would they do it before Mare this time? Would she share in his magic? His breath came in short bursts as he stared at the spot on the floor where he'd collapsed so many times.

"What's wrong with you?" Mare muttered under her breath.

Aiden shot her a weak glare. "Nothing. Leave me be."

Before Mare could respond, Mab cleared her throat. "Now dears, I need you to fetch something very special for me: a curse of great power." Color drained from Mare's face, making the horrific memories melt from Aiden's mind like a spring thaw. He knew little about curses; he'd always thought they were created by powerful fae, not found. "Of course, bottled curses aren't easy to come by. In fact, there's only one person in all of Fairy who performs such a service. Do you know who that might be, Mare?"

Mare nodded numbly. "Y-yes, my Queen."

"Good, because I need the curse this evening. You two should prepare and leave quickly. From what I understand, the journey is long and hard."

"But—" Mare's mouth moved, but sound failed to follow. What was she so frightened of? She'd never acted this way before. Her lack of fear had been a source of continual frustration for Aiden when Mab would threaten them as children. "Please, Your Majesty, it'll take much more than a day to cross The Plains and back."

Mab got to her feet and crossed the room until she was a breath away from Mare. Her violet eyes flashed as she stroked Mare's cheek—Mare shuddered. "Very well. You have until midnight. Now you better hurry, time is wasting."

The queen straightened as Mare lowered her gaze. Glancing back at Aiden, Mare beckoned as she took off toward the door. He looked between Mab and Mare, a growing sense of dread clawing at his heart. His feet refused to move as thoughts of what Mab could possibly have in store for them churned his stomach.

"Run along, Pet. You don't want to be late." The queen grinned, her pearlescent teeth gleaming maliciously in the icy-warped light.

Aiden swallowed, Mabs words snapped him out of the terror-filled paralyzation like shattering ice, and he hurried from the room. Whatever this mission was, they couldn't fail. He couldn't go back to the dungeons. Mare stood a little ways down the hall, one hand pressed to her head.

"What's wrong? Where do we have to go?" Aiden asked.

She shook her head and mumbled to herself. "It's impossible. She's not going to just hand over a curse, even if it's Mab asking. There's always a price, and we don't have time..."

"Mare!"

"S-sorry. There's this... witch. She makes curses, but not without terrible costs. If Mab wants us to collect a curse from her, it won't be easy."

Aiden frowned. "A witch?" He'd heard of the humans who'd long ago stole fae magic and used it for themselves, but they'd been killed centuries ago. And if Mare was this terrified of her, could she possibly be worse than Mab? He studied her face, searching for some clue as to what lay in store for them.

"It's the closest thing I can think of to what she is." Mare shrugged. "She's definitely not human though."

A knot twisted in Aiden's stomach. What type of payment would this creature demand? It must be terrible if Oberon was concerned he might die. "Where must we go?"

"The Nightmare Plains."

He stared at her, mouth agape. He'd heard stories of people going to the Nightmare Plains and being driven mad by visions and consumed by the monsters that wandered the desolate place. Never had he heard of someone living there until he met Mare, and even she never spoke of her homeland.

Mare's hands were ice cold as she laced her fingers between his own. "Ready?"

Aiden jerked them away. "What, now? Don't we need weapons? Supplies?"

"We'll be okay with our magic. The Plains are not as bad as the stories make them out to be..." Something about the look in her eyes made him suspect that statement wasn't entirely true.

Still, Aiden closed his fingers around Mare's. Shadows peeled themselves from the walls to wrap around her. He pulled at the familiar sensation of magic and wended, following her essence as they moved through the nothingness. A dull ache crept over his body, similar to being too close to iron, as they materialized at the edge of a dark beach.

Black water lapped gently against orange sand that glowed with a dull light. When he looked up, there was nothing but black — no sun, no moon, no stars, just darkness. The water stretched out to meet the horizon on one side while the sand extended into the distance on the other. The air was devoid of any sounds of life, yet filled with a weighty silence. It sent chills across Aiden's skin as he followed Mare away from the water.

"Keep focused on the path and don't let anything distract you, no matter what. And stay alert; we may have to use our magic," she said.

Beyond the first dune, a small gray path cut through the orange. His chest tightened as they stepped onto it. A strange, unbidden fear seeped into his bones and sent goosebumps running across his arms and back. Panic rose in the back of his throat, and Aiden pulled on his magic, trying desperately to wend back to the beach… but failed.

"Wha — my magic?" He blinked; Mare was already several paces in front of him. When had he stopped walking?

"You can't wend out of here. This place was designed as a prison for the realms' trash," she said, a hint of bitterness tainting her words.

Aiden stiffened. If Summer ever caught him, they'd likely send him here — if they didn't execute him first.

As they walked, gray tufts of grass appeared on the edges of the path, waving in a nonexistent breeze. Rock formations rose in the distance, not quite mountains but more like giant ant hills.

Aiden pointed. "What are those?"

"That's where people live," Mare said.

"So you grew up in a place like that?"

"No."

He waited for her to offer more, but she remained silent. A voice, soft and barely audible, prickled at his ear. Aiden looked around, but the plains were as empty as ever. The voice sounded again; this time slightly louder. He slowed his pace, but there was still no one. The voice was too soft for him to make out what it was saying.

A scream let loose behind them. Aiden spun just as the voice cried out his name. He knew that voice... His eyes darted across the barren landscape, desperate to catch a glimpse of the source. Rounding the dune they'd just climbed was Mab in a black chariot pulled by two horses, seemingly made of shadow. Before her were several centaurs racing toward a lone figure.

Aiden's breath caught in his chest as he made out the familiar features. "Wyn."

It wasn't her. It couldn't be. Still, her eyes bulged as she skidded down the sand in her torn jeans and faded red jacket. Her face had smudges of blood on it, though he couldn't tell if she was truly injured. He took half a step forward and stopped. It was just a vision — Wyn was home, not here.

Mab's cold laugh cut through the dry silence, sending icy tingles racing across Aiden's skin. "Come back, dear. I won't hurt you." The chariot was catching up to Wyn fast.

Mab had to be an illusion too, a cursed trick of the sands. Aiden's chest squeezed as he searched the path for Mare, but she'd vanished. Had she been corrupted by visions too? Glancing over his shoulder, he noticed the path was several feet to the left of where he stood. But he hadn't moved...

Could this be another trick? A mirage to make him leave the safety of the trail, if you could call anything safe in this place. Wyn screamed again, and Aiden shut his eyes, turning away from the awful sound. He couldn't let himself believe it was real. It was no wonder people went mad here.

"Please, Aiden. Don't let her get me —" Wyn's words cut off as Mab let out another chilling laugh.

"Now, now, now. You can tell me all about your relationship with our sweet pet," the queen said in a sickeningly charming voice. Aiden inched forward, desperate to feel the hard stone of the trail beneath his feet.

"Mare?" he called out. A gust of wind washed over him, blowing sand into his throat and eyes. He shielded his face with his arm and ducked his head.

"Oh come now, pet. Don't turn away from us. The fun is just

beginning."

Aiden dared to look up. Mab's lips parted into a smile that betrayed the limits of her mouth. Several rows of needle-sharp silver teeth flashed menacingly as she brought Wyn's face close to hers.

Wyn whimpered, her eyes fixed on Aiden. "P-Puh-lease." Her voice broke alongside his heart.

What if it was Wyn? He hadn't seen her in months. What if she wasn't safe at home?

"Wyn," Aiden said, the word tearing from his throat. "Is it—I know it's not really you."

"It is me! We had pasta for dinner on our first date... We... We danced together... You read out of that stupid book."

He hesitated, looking from the grinning monster that was Mab to Wyn's trembling form. How could anyone from these lands know about what he and Wyn did? Again, he searched for Mare but found nothing except the path wavering in the distance. It was a trick. He couldn't possibly have gone that far out.

"Aiden, help me."

He stiffened. This couldn't be her; Mare had said this place would confuse the mind. His fists shook at his sides; if he was wrong it could mean his life to try and save her... Who knew what the creatures of the Nightmare Plains were capable of? He could end up eaten by the Mab-monster.

But if it were for Wyn, he would do anything.

"Mare!"

Still no response. It was as though she'd drifted away with the sands. He gritted his teeth as Wyn screamed again—Mab dragged deep red gouges down the side of her cheek.

"No!" Aiden shot a jet of blue flame at Mab's feet.

She screamed, dropping Wyn, unconscious, on the ground as flames licked up Mab's sides. Stumbling back, Aiden doubled over as the scents of charred flesh met his nose. A sharp pang of sorrow-tinged guilt stabbed through his chest, but he wouldn't be sad to see Mab go. Still, she had given him a home and a taste of revenge; it was who he was now. What would he even be without her fueling that flame?

He took half a step forward, hands trembling as the char melted off the queen. The world seemed to float past him in dizzying swirls. This wasn't real. Mab wasn't real, and Wyn…

Aiden clenched and unclenched his fists. "W-Wyn?" he called out, his voice hoarse.

But she lay still.

It didn't matter if she were dead, he told himself. She wasn't real. Just a mad vision — they both were. His heartbeat slowed as Wyn's form vanished. Whatever was causing him to see things was gone now. Perhaps it'd been hiding in Mab's form, though he'd no way of knowing what manner of creatures roamed these plains.

Endless stretches of orange sand and funnel-shaped rock formation lay in every direction. Aiden took a breath to shout for Mare again, but a foul-smelling breeze washed over him. Shuddering, he took a hesitant step toward one of the "houses." Perhaps one of the people inside would know the way out, but Mare hadn't said what kinds of people they were.

Something hard slammed into him, knocking him to the sand with a high-pitched growl. The putrid wind bore down on him, and he squinted back to see a gigantic, cavernous mouth filled with rows and rows of dagger-like teeth.

Mare stood above him, arms outstretched, a cloud of swirling shadows stretching behind her. Beyond her barrier a worm-like creature the width of a giant's head reared up before them. "One thing. I told you not to do ONE THING!"

Aiden scrambled to his feet. "What is that?"

"A nightmare. They mess with your mind and feed on your fear until you're just a husk of a person," she said. The barrier dropped, and she withdrew two daggers from the belt around her hips. "Are you going to just stand there, or are you going to help me?"

The creature dove at them, and Mare leapt, daggers poised for its head. Slime glistened off its pink-ribbed back as it crashed into the sand, speeding toward Aiden at an alarming rate. Flames so hot they were nearly white shot from his hands into the worm's gaping mouth. It screamed and writhed as Mare hit its back and dug her daggers into its skin.

Blood, thick and black, oozed from where Mare dangled, her feet slipping as she tried to find purchase. Her fingers slid off the dagger, and she tumbled down the creature's side. Aiden raced toward her, shooting weak blasts of flame at the worm to keep it from rolling over her.

"Mare, are you all right?" She was flat on the ground, covered in black blood amongst the sand, but her eyes were open and breath steady.

"You always act without thinking! You're going to get us — me — killed." She sat up and gripped her head.

An ear-splitting roar coated in the stench of decay shattered the palpable stillness of the Plains. Aiden longed to crouch and cover his ears but was forced to throw up a fiery barrier as the worm's head struck out towards them. Freezing frosts.

The scent of burning garbage clogged Aiden's senses as his flames hit the worm. Its tail whipped around, flinging Aiden against the ground. He sucked in several breaths. This was nothing like blasting through rows of green fae soldiers — their pitiful magics were hardly a match for his own. This singular creature seemed to hold the power of a gold fae or greater.

"Run!" Mare gripped his hand as they took off across the sand, distancing themselves as much as possible from the creature. When it was out of sight, Aiden slowed, but Mare kept pulling him onward.

"It's all right. It can't see us anymore," he said.

"It doesn't have eyes, you idiot. Of course it can't see us. It tracks by —"

The ground shook, and Mare's eyes bulged. From beneath their feet, the creature burst through the earth, showering them with sand. It let loose a roar, bringing both of them to their knees. Mare's barrier sprang up around them as she huddled by Aiden's side.

"How do we defeat this thing?" Aiden gasped as the creature thrashed against the barrier.

"You can't defeat nightmares. You either get away or you die." Sweat beaded on Mare's brow as she strained against the creature's power.

Drawing in a shaky breath, Aiden glanced around for something, anything, that would at least render the creature briefly unconscious while they fled. But there was nothing but sand. Sand…

"Mare, we need to get the creature back into the hole."

"Why, so it can jump back out again?" She shook her head, the barrier growing darker as she redoubled her efforts.

"I have an idea, but you have to trust me."

"And why would I do that? This is the second time your stupidity has nearly gotten me killed."

"You didn't have to come after me." Heat flared in Aiden's chest. He couldn't focus on trapping the nightmare when all Mare wanted to do was argue.

She snarled and dropped the barrier as the creature reared back. Threads of shadow shot from her fingers toward the beast. "Drive it into my net!"

Aiden nodded and pushed his flames toward the back of the creature's head. Its mouth and rows of teeth plunged into Mare's shadow net. For a moment, Aiden thought it would hold as she dragged its struggling form just over the hole. But the head burst through the shadows, and the rest of the body spasmed, shrinking back down. Aiden's eyes widened, and he blasted the worm again and again, driving it deeper underground.

When only the tip of its tail remained, Aiden took a deep breath and let loose a torrent of white-hot flame around it, the hole, and the surrounding area. Mare jumped back, racing away from the glassy surface spreading across the melting sands. The creature made to surface again, but Aiden shot flames at where the ground rumbled. Mare cried out as the sands tossed and tumbled, while the glassy surface and Aiden's flames remained steady. Soon, the shaking stopped, and the area where the worm had been was a slick glass. Aiden took several steps over to it and peered down. Like looking into a frozen lake, the nightmare's head and rows of teeth were still beneath the shiny surface.

"That won't hold it long. Those things are forces of nature. Nothing can kill them."

"What do you mean?"

Mare grabbed Aiden's arm. "Autumn has tornados, Spring has hailstorms, Winter has blizzards, Summer has hurricanes, and we have nightmares. Just trust me. We need to get back to the path."

He nodded. "But how will we find —" The path was only a few feet in front of them. Aiden stared at it incredulously; how had he not seen it before?

"The nightmares will play tricks on you," Mare said as they returned to the safety of the hard ground. "Just keep walking here, and we'll be fine. I should probably keep holding on to you, so you don't go wandering off shouting my name again."

"If you heard me, why didn't you respond?" Aiden rounded on her, but Mare continued to drag him onwards.

"I did, the first time. That thing really got into your head. And it wasn't just me you were calling. Who's Wyn?"

"None of your business." Aiden grit his teeth and shook Mare off, but she recaptured his hand.

"No, I'm not trusting you on your own again."

He huffed, and they continued down the path in silence until a rock formation, larger than any they'd seen before, rose up in front of them.

He glanced at Mare, but she remained silent as she led them toward the giant structure. The path ended at the base of it, but rather than climbing or searching for holes, Mare walked right through as though passing through air. Taking a shuddering breath, Aiden did the same.

"Hello?" Mare's voice rang out in the darkness.

This was no ordinary dark — it moved. He rubbed at the spot where his mother's ring once lay to keep from shivering. It wasn't cold, yet there was a slithering sensation that coated his body in a thick sheen of fear.

The air wavered as the space lit up, though the slithering sensation remained. Aiden blinked his eyes, adjusting to the familiar living room of Wyn's parents' house. He cast a glance at Mare. Did she see the same thing? Would she even suspect this vision came from him? If she did, she gave no reaction, her face expressionless.

"Mare dear, how nice. You brought a boy home for dinner." A woman, who looked to be an older version of her, descended the stairs in a green robe, identical to the one Wyn's mother had worn when he'd first met her. She smiled when she met his gaze, her teeth sharp. Almost like the nightmare's.

"Mother, this is Aiden, and neither he, nor I, am for dinner," Mare said.

Mother?

"Oh, but dear, his soul is so deliciously tormented." The woman sucked on her fingers one by one as she fixed her gaze on Aiden. A sharp tug at his chest brought him to his knees, and he gasped. This magic was nearly as strong as Oberon's cursed wand and miles beyond that of Mare's gentle prickling.

"Mother!"

"Not even a taste?"

"Leave him be."

Aiden flicked a glance at Mare and slowly got to his feet. "Mare, you have a mother?" he muttered to her.

"Of course she has a mother," the woman said, tossing her hand back as she twirled closer to Aiden. Mare put an arm out in front of him, pushing him back. "Though she abandoned me for that troll woman. What an ungrateful brat, don't you think... my pet?"

Aiden stiffened.

"Don't call him that. You tried to eat me countless times. If it weren't for that troll woman, I'd be dead."

"We all have our faults, dear." Mare's mom glided across the room to perch on the back of the couch. "You're not perfect either."

Mare let out a low growl, inching in front of Aiden. "We've come to get the curse Mab ordered — nothing more."

"You're not even going to introduce me to your boyfriend?"

"He is not my boyfriend. And you do not need to know him."

The woman pouted and crossed her hands over her chest. "What a cruel creature you've become." After a second passed, her pout smoothed, and she dropped her arms. "I suppose you are your mother's daughter."

"Mother, we're short on time. The curse?"

Aiden shook off what felt like an eel sliding around his waist and up his back. Everything in him screamed to run. But he couldn't, not until they completed Mab's task.

Mare's mother surged towards them and gripped Aiden's arm. He cried out as her nails dug into his flesh and silver leaked down her fingers. "Blood of the enemy," she muttered.

"Stop! Just give us what we came for." One of Mare's shadow's entwined around her mother's wrist.

The woman released him and shot her daughter a glare. "And what will you give me in return? Surely you know none of my curses are free." She drifted across the room as part of the wall melted away to reveal a bubbling cauldron. Aiden's stomach clenched as he watched her shake his blood into it.

"What's the cost?" Aiden asked through gritted teeth. He clutched his wound as he watched her murmur over the pale liquid.

She hummed, her eyes dancing as she looked the two of them over. "I do love torment." The light flickered and she was within an inch of Aiden. "How about the pain of the death of your last hope?" She dangled a round potion bottle before him.

"Mother, no. He doesn't need any more pain." Mare attempted to step between them, but several tendrils of shadow dragged her back.

"Silence, dear. It's his choice."

Aiden swallowed. "I — I fear you come to collect too late. I hope for little in this life."

"Little isn't nothing. And the last hope is the sweetest. If you agree, your last hope will die in just a few months, and your pain will be mine." She ran an icy finger down his cheek. "So, do we have a deal?"

Aiden nodded. What hope did he have to lose? And even if by some chance she managed to find some minor bright spot, having

Mare's mother take his pain didn't sound so bad. It couldn't be worse than what he endured with Mad and Oberon each night.

"Excellent." She pressed her lips to his. Aiden's eyes flew wide, and he struggled back. But her shadows held him firm until she pulled away. Then, she was back at the cauldron, spooning its creamy white contents into a small vial. "I can't wait to taste your pain. Now take your curse. You don't have much time. Do you, Mare?"

"No, we must go." Mare snatched the vial away from her mother and looped Aiden's arm in hers.

"Until next time, Dear Heart." Her mother waved as the livingroom and cauldron faded to blackness.

Just before the darkness closed around them, Mare dragged Aiden outside to the desolate plains. "If we don't hurry, we'll be late." They took off jogging down the path, and Aiden's concentration fixated on the bit of gray before him.

"That wasn't as bad as I'd thought," he said.

Mare's lips twitched into a grimace. "You won't say that when she comes to collect."

CHAPTER 4

Freddie

Freddie tried calling Pelrin several times over the course of the day, and still there was no response. A tingle on the back of her neck whispered all the terrible things that could've happened to him: captured by the Dark Fae Army, killed in battle, or any of the other countless horrors that could harm him in Fairy. Though, she'd be lying if a full day without Pelrin butting into her life wasn't something she'd longed for. Still… she didn't want him hurt… or worse.

"Wyn! Are you almost ready?" her mom called up the stairs.

Freddie scowled down at her sweats. It was Christmas Eve — they should be spending it together as a family, not with those human warts, the Falluses. "I told you, I'm not going."

"Oh, Wyn." The sound of chunky heels stomping up stairs drew closer as Freddie took several deep breaths — preparing for battle. "Wynifred Jones! I told you to get ready an hour ago. The Falluses are extremely important to your father's career."

"Not for long. The only good thing about Mr. Fallus winning the election is that he'll be moving far away from here, and we can go back to how things were."

Her mother bit her lip. "Please just get dressed, Hon."

"They don't even want me there. I'm just some know-nothing kid to them." She squared her stance and folded her arms across her chest.

With a sniffle, her mother lifted her chin. "You know what? Fine. Don't come. I just thought it would be nice for all of us to be together on Christmas Eve."

"You guys could always stay home. No one is forcing you to go."

"Are you so selfish that you don't care at all about your father's job? This is important to him, to us. Wyn, you know it is."

"As long as Dad is working for that racist di—" Freddie hesitated, her mother's expression growing intensely stern. "—racist dolt, I'll not lift a finger to support him. Can't you see how awful he is? Think of all the people his words are hurting. People have nearly killed fae in his name."

"Oh honey, those are radicals. Senator Fallus never asked them to do those terrible things. He just wants fae to come here in a safe and legal manner, rather than flooding over the borders lawlessly. He's speaking for the people who haven't had the types of privileges you've had."

Freddie scoffed. "So you're siding with the uneducated. That sounds smart."

"Watch it, Wyn. I'm merely saying that people who don't have the money to live in areas like this and go to good schools like yours deserve to have a voice too. Just because many of them didn't go to college doesn't mean they're stupid; there are many ways to be smart."

Freddie grit her teeth. She'd never meant to sound arrogant, but it was so hard when so many people swallowed the hate Mr. Fallus spewed without question. Were there just that many bad people in this country? Who knew how many of them existed in the world. Surely being stupid was better than being evil...

"I'm sorry, Mom. I can't go. This is against everything I believe in."

Her mother pulled her lips into a tight line but didn't respond. Instead, she turned on her heel and shuffled out of the room, struggling with her long evening dress as she left. Freddie let out a sigh and sank onto her bed. Being home alone wouldn't be so bad. She could make her mom's special blend of rich cayenne hot cocoa, watch all the cheesy Christmas movies, and sleep on the couch to maximize the guilt factor when her parents came home.

A small smile tugged at her lips as she trooped down the stairs to say goodbye and make her first mug of cocoa.

Freddie breathed in the silence as she waited for the milk to heat. She supposed her family wasn't the only one separated for the holidays. After all, no one had found Freya or Daniel or any of the missing kids from the other schools. Freddie swallowed. Were they dead? Her chest tightened at the thought. Forced to kill and die in the civil war in Fairy? That's what Dion had said their fate was. She pressed her lips together — so much for her promise to help them. Without so much as a lead after losing the satyr to the police, she was right back where she started. Nowhere. The only thing she knew about the students was that they'd been taken to Fairy, but they could be anywhere in the six realms... well, likely anywhere in the four seasonal realms.

The hiss of bubbling milk hitting the burner made Freddie turn, and she rushed over to the stove. It was most likely the students were in Autumn or Winter, the two realms that had been conquered by the Dark Fae Army. But still, it was impossible to search an entire realm, nevertheless two.

If Aiden... Freddie shook her head and stirred in the thick chocolate. She couldn't let herself keep thinking of him. Even when they were together, the only possible outcome was disaster. Aiden wasn't free to stay with her, and she didn't have the power to free him even if staying with her was what he wanted. That stupid life debt would only break if Mab and Oberon were dead. Freddie took a furious sip of hot chocolate and choked at the heat and spice. She couldn't free Aiden, couldn't find any leads on the missing students, and couldn't even get one other article published; maybe journalism wasn't for her; all it brought was frustration and heartache.

Even as the thought fluttered across her mind, Freddie knew

it was a lie. Journalism was for her — she just needed to find a way to make it work. Tiptoeing over to the couch, she resolved to lose herself in some cheesy movie about the "magic of the season." Just as she turned on the TV, her phone rang.

"Hi, Mom," Freddie said.

"Umm, I don't remember giving birth to you, Fred, but cool." Amanda's voice came from the other end. Freddie looked at the screen — sure enough, it was Amanda.

"What's up? Is Jefferson back? Did you just get home from a date?" As much as she usually hated Amanda's post-date breakdowns, hearing all about her friend's too cute boyfriend might just be the distraction she needed.

"Sorry, it's not that. I heard from Jefferson this morning though. He's still in Fairy, and he can't find Pelrin."

"You mean he's not in the palace, or they sent him on a mission or something?"

"Jefferson's not sure. But Pelrin doesn't usually just shut him out."

Freddie's heart pounded in her throat — she'd thought... hoped Pelrin had just needed to rush back to Fairy. But what if something had happened to him at the theater? Pelrin was a gold fae, the most, or at least the second most, powerful kind of fae. He could surely fight off any threat that came near him, unless Aiden... No, that wasn't possible. Aiden wouldn't come back to the Human Realm without saying anything to her. Right? Besides, if something had attacked Pelrin, regardless of whether it was Aiden or not, they'd have heard it or seen some sign of it.

"I'm sure he's just busy. Is that what you called about?" Freddie let out a shaky breath. He was just busy.

"No, sorry, I know it's Christmas... although it doesn't sound like you're with your parents. Where are you?" Her tone was sharp as a dwarf's ax. Freddie snickered as she set her hot chocolate on the arm of the couch.

"At home. They went to a party at the Falluses."

"Gross. But you haven't heard from Raul, have you?"

"No, why? Were we supposed to do something today?"

"Nothing like that." Amanda hummed three short notes as she often did when she was worried. "His mom called me. He was supposed to be home for family dinner, but he went out and didn't come back — never called or anything. It's not like Raul to do that."

"Yeah, especially not on Christmas Eve. Have you tried calling?" Freddie lifted the mug shakily to her lips and splashed hot liquid against her chest. She suppressed a gasp.

"Like ten times. Do you think we should go to Alpha House?" Amanda hummed again.

"Why would he be on campus? Do you think he started drinking and passed out or something?"

Tears pricked at the backs of Freddie's eyes. She held the mug close and got up to stare out the window. Everything would be okay. Raul, like Pelrin, was probably fine. Where would he even go? They had to be fine.

"Maybe…" Amanda let her last word hang in the air for several heart-pounding moments. "Do you think —"

The mug slipped from Freddie's fingers, shattering across the hardwood, and she shrieked.

"Freddie! Freddie!"

Cursing at the mess, she held her phone with her shoulder as she scampered to the kitchen to find a towel. "I'm fine, Amanda. Sorry."

"What the hell? Don't do that to me, especially not with everyone going missing. What happened?"

"Nothing, I just dropped this stupid mug."

"You screamed like you were getting murdered just for a fallen mug?"

"Well, it was filled with hot chocolate, which is now all over me and the floor, and it's shattered. I gotta go. I need to clean this up." Freddie grabbed the whole roll of paper towels and headed back into the family room.

"Alright, I'll keep trying to get ahold of Raul, and keep me posted if you hear anything. First Pelrin, now Raul… I'm getting worried, Fred."

"I know, me too. But I'm sure they're fine. Raul's phone

could've died; it could be no big deal." Freddie moved the paper towels to soak up the mess; most of the hot chocolate appeared to have landed on her. Thankfully it wasn't piping hot anymore, but her skin tingled and itched uncomfortably.

"Well, Merry Christmas. I'll talk to you tomorrow, but please text me if you hear from Raul." Amanda's voice shook, and Freddie's heart squeezed, longing to comfort her friend.

"Night, Amanda. Enjoy your Christmas with your family. Everyone will be okay — I promise."

Putting her phone aside, Freddie picked up the shards of her mug. Her hands shook as she moved quickly through the pieces; her fingers fumbled over a large one, and it sliced into her hand.

"Mother Christmas." She grit her teeth as blood mingled with the hot chocolate on her clothes.

Freddie stripped off her sweatshirt and used it to soak up the remaining hot chocolate, then hurried upstairs to bandage her hand. She must've been truly bad this year for everything to fall apart on Christmas Eve. Changing into a new pair of sweats and gingerly wrapping her hand in gauze, she headed back downstairs and flicked on the TV — anything to keep out the pulsing pain in her hand. Did she need stitches? What a perfect gift, another sweatshirt ruined. It was almost hard to tell where the bloodstains ended and the cocoa stains began. But at least the bleeding didn't look serious.

She leaned her head against one of the cushions, closing her eyes. Whooville's greatest hits were humming from the TV when she jerked — something scratched at the door. It must be a racoon — they always went through the trash, and it would be cold enough that one would want to come inside. The look on her mom's face if she brought in a creature like that. She smirked. Maybe it would serve her right; a racoon was better company than the Falluses.

The scratch at the door came again, this time followed by a yelp. Could it be a dog? Frowning, Freddie peered out the large living room window, but she couldn't quite see the door. Tip-toeing, she slowly unlocked the door and pulled it open a crack. Her jaw fell agape as she stared at a large gray wolf.

"Oh, Freddie, thank God you answered. You've gotta help

me," the wolf said.

Wut… Her brain was breaking; that was the only explanation. "Sorry, I think you have the wrong address." She inched the door closed. Animals didn't talk… well, unless they were people cursed by fae, but that was just in stories; no one had actually ever seen that happen.

"Fred, please, it's me. Look at me. I can't go home like this!" The wolf slid a paw into the door to block her from closing it. Its voice sounded familiar…

She frowned. "Raul?"

He nodded. "Just let me in."

Opening the door a bit wider, she breathed out. At least he was here and not spirited off to parts unknown. Raul lumbered in. His back brushed against her hip as he made his way to the sofa and sprawled out.

"So, um, why are you in wolf form?" Her eyes traveled nervously from his oversized snout to the gigantic brush of his tail. "You don't shed, do you?"

"Come on, Fred. It's been a hard day." Raul paused and sniffed the air. "Where are your parents?"

"They're out. Speaking of hard days, want to tell me what happened? It's not a full moon."

Raul sighed, the scent of his dog-breath made her nostrils flare. But despite his smell, he was kinda cute, in a dog-like way. Resisting the urge to scratch him behind the ear, Freddie squeezed into the small remaining space on the couch and sat crossed-legged… waiting.

"All right, so I really wanted to get my mom this bracelet for Navidad, but it was kinda expensive. So, I needed a way to make some extra cash."

"So, you did something incredibly stupid?" Freddie crossed her arms over her chest.

Raul growled. "I don't need you to judge me."

"Sorry, sorry. Go ahead."

"I saw a sign for this drug test to help weres stay lucid during the transformation. If it worked, great. If not, I just made an easy hundred bucks. Win-win, right?"

"You're saying they wanted to put chemicals in you that messed with the magic in your blood, and you went along with this for only a hundred dollars?"

"You think I should've asked for more?"

"I think you should've used that college-boy brain of yours and figured out that taking strange chemicals, especially ones that affect your change, is a bad idea."

"Well, I know that now." He let out a little whine.

Freddie reached out and scratched him behind his ear. "So they just left you as a wolf? They didn't even try to turn you back?"

"Well, they said it would wear off…"

"When?"

"Eventually. They said maybe with the full moon." Raul covered his nose with his paw and stared up at Freddie.

She returned it with a blank stare—how dare he use his cuteness against her. "Raul, that's a month from now. What are you going to do in the meantime?"

"I figured your parents would be more likely to be okay with you getting a dog… or fostering…"

Freddie raised an eyebrow.

"I can't explain this to my mom. She'd murder me! Can't I just crash here for the night? Maybe going home on Christmas might soften her up a bit."

She sighed. "Fine, but my mom isn't going to be feeding you human food."

"Thanks, Fred, but I'll be fine. I stayed with my aunt for two summers as a kid, and let's just say she didn't inherit the family gift for cooking."

Freddie laughed, but Raul went still, sniffing the air. His fur bristled.

"Do you—"

The door slammed open, and the blood drained from Freddie's face. Just visible beyond the shadowed doorway was a bear. Its white fur snagged against the frame as it forced its way in. She screamed, squeezing her arms around Raul's neck until he yelped.

"Can you fight it?"

"It's a bear, Fred. You try fighting that thing."

"Freddie Jones," the bear said in a low voice. "Come with me."

"He talks?" Freddie looked from the bear to Raul. "Please tell me this is one of your buddies from the drug test."

"It's a bear, a giant polar bear who just barged into your house. I think I would have told you if I had met a psycho like this."

Freddie's heart throbbed in her throat, and she tried to swallow but couldn't. Her brain was slower than usual — the only thing it seemed to say was run.

"Go away!" she shouted.

The bear snarled. "You have no power to send me away."

"Wha-what if I don't go with you?"

The bear chuckled — a dark ominous tone. Raul scooted closer to her. "That wasn't a question. You are coming with me." He lumbered closer to them.

Freddie clung to Raul so tightly that he yelped again. Letting out a deafening roar, the bear caught the edge of the couch and dragged them toward him. The last thing Freddie remembered before her world was engulfed in black were the bear's oddly cerulean eyes staring back at her."

CHAPTER 5

Aiden

Aiden wended to the street where he'd last met Wyn. He couldn't sense her though… she must be wearing his mother's ring. The thought warmed him, giving him comfort that she hadn't forgotten him. Soon they'd be together, she'd love her Solstice gift, and everything would be better, if not good, for a few blessed hours — then he would have to say goodbye. For good this time. He swallowed hard, shoving all thoughts of their inevitable parting from his mind. It was for the best; it was too dangerous for them to stay together, he told himself.

He patted the orb in his pocket and changed his glamour into the same one he'd worn the last time he'd been with her parents. It was cold, but no snow coated the ground as he walked toward the house. A car with merrily sparkling red and blue lights rushed past, nearly knocking him over. Aiden frowned. Humans could be so reckless sometimes, no doubt someone drunk on the excitement of the holiday. Sighing, he moved down the street admiring the houses decked with colorful lights.

His heart squeezed as his mind flicked back to before the war when his parents would take him to the Human Realm. His father's eyes would light up as he would explain all about the electricity and how each of the tiny bulbs works while his mother would revel in the snow they never had in Spring. She'd teach him how to pack it into tight balls and hurl them at his father. Tears pressed against the corners of his eyes. The streets were devoid of snow, yet the frost still lingered in the late morning haze. It didn't detract from the beauty of the human homes and the flashing car in front of Wyn's. Perhaps she would explain how the lights on the cars functioned.

A group of people gathered outside her house. Perhaps this was how the humans were to exchange gifts. If so, he was right on time. Aiden jogged over, scanning for Wyn, but he couldn't spot her.

Two men in dark suits stepped out from the decorated car. Aiden watched as they strode over and exchanged words with a man in a blue uniform decorating the house in a yellow ribbon. One of the suits entered while the other one made his way straight to Wyn's parents. Aiden held back as he watched them talk; there was something wrong about this scene. No one seemed to be smiling, there should be food and drinks, and it was near silent except for low murmurs from the crowd.

Wyn's mom looked up from the suit — her eyes meeting his. "Oh! Aiden!" The waver in her voice made Aiden's heart clench.

"You're Wynifred Jones's boyfriend?" the man in the suit asked.

The word "boyfriend" sent a tingle down his spine. Was that what he was? Did he dare call himself that in front of her parents?

"Yes, he is," her mom said. "Aiden, dear, I know Wyn said you were out of town, but have you seen her?"

"She-she's missing?" Ice, colder than the flats surrounding the Winter Palace, frosted over his skin. Had he been wrong? Could that possibly have been her in the Nightmare Plains? No. It couldn't be. He'd seen the nightmare change with his own eyes. But if she wasn't here...

"Yes. She hasn't been seen since last night," the man said. He gestured to the house. "The door was ripped off its hinges, and there was furniture overturned. It looks like some sort of animal broke in."

"Was there… blood?" he asked, barely controlling the tremble in his voice.

The man frowned and looked to Wyn's mom, who broke down into tears.

"Her sweatshirt was covered in it. I don't —" Sobs shook the woman's body, and Wyn's father put an arm around her shoulders.

Aiden couldn't keep his limbs from shaking as he looked up at the house. "I need to see." He raced forward, up the porch stairs, and through the doorway where a hard arm slammed him back. A goblin, dressed in a blue uniform, held him against the door shaking his head.

"Only police inside. We can't have you tainting the crime scene."

Aiden's eyes hastily darted throughout the room, landing on Wyn's red sweatshirt, crumpled and stained a dark reddish brown. "No," he mouthed. The man pushed him outside as Aiden's jaw fell open in horror. Wherever Wyn was, she was gravely injured, but he refused to believe she might be dead. He had to find her… He had to go, now.

The man in the suit marched over to him with Wyn's mother trailing behind. "We weren't finished."

"My daughter has been kidnapped by fae, and you're sitting here telling me it's important to interrogate her human boyfriend who she hasn't seen in months?"

"Please ma'am, he's obviously fae," the man gestured to Aiden's face. Aiden looked down; he'd nearly forgotten Wyn's lie to her parents that he just had "some fae ancestry." How was he supposed to keep that up without her?

"He's not fae. He just has some fae in his family's past that makes his eyes like that. You're wasting your time with him. Besides, even if he was, he couldn't have done that to the door."

"We need to make sure we are covering our bases ma'am I —"

"Just find our daughter and stop interrogating people who obviously didn't take her." Her mother put a hand to her head. "I'm honestly beginning to see why Wyn thinks you people are useless."

The man sighed. "Just don't go far," he said to Aiden. "I may have some questions for you later."

"Of course," Aiden said.

He looked back at the house. The door permitted entry only to the swirling winter wind as a group of people crowded around the base of the porch. Could this be his fault? If Oberon or Mab had found out about her, or worse, the prince... He needed to find Wyn and fast.

"Come on, Aiden. The house is a crime scene; we won't be able to go back inside for a while. We're staying in the city with the Falluses." Wyn's mom touched his shoulder, and Aiden jerked. "Are you going to go back home with your family?"

"What about Wyn?" He took a step toward the house.

"The police will find her. I have to believe they will. There's nothing we can do."

"I—" Aiden stared back up at the house, the image of her bloody sweatshirt flashing in his mind. He tried again to sense her, but there was only nothingness.

Wyn's mom looked so frightened, and her eyes were glassy as she shivered, looking back at her husband who was talking to another man in casual clothing. Aiden's chest tightened.

He couldn't just leave her; her eyes, so like Wyn's, pleaded with him to stay. "I don't have to go back yet," he said. He at least had to wait until all the people in uniform left to sneak back into the house and look for some hint as to where Wyn had gone.

The woman's expression softened. "Then come stay with us for a little. We can try and distract our minds from all this." She held onto his arm and pulled him toward a silver car. Taking the cue from his wife, Wyn's dad jogged over and gave Aiden a curt nod as he slid into the driver's seat.

"Sit in the back, dear," her mother said.

Aiden climbed into the back seat, and the orb pressed against his thigh. He needed to look for Wyn. The humans wouldn't cross into Fairy—they didn't know of her ties to him. A vision of Mab, her pale fingers clutching Wyn's arm, passed before his eyes. He dropped his head into his hands. Hadn't he been punished enough? He'd been so careful; they couldn't have found out. Even Emmerick and Irina hadn't known, and Wyn had faced both of them.

The memory of her story stabbed at his chest. She was so brave. A human staking a vampire and fending off a werewolf, armed only with a shoe.

"They'll find her. She'll be fine. They are thinking it might have been a rabid werewolf." The voice of Wyn's dad cut through Aiden's misery.

He looked up. "The one she imprisoned?"

"No, the police already called. That one is still locked up tight." He let out a shaky sigh. "But she has a friend —"

Wyn's mom slid into the passenger seat and her dad looked up, his eyes wet and shining.

She shook her head. "I called Raul's mother. She is beside herself — it seems Raul went missing, too."

"So they are probably together," her dad said.

"There was no sign of a struggle at Raul's. The police said they are going to look into them as a possible link."

"Were they close? Wyn and this… Raul?" Aiden didn't like the way heat blazed in his chest. He shouldn't feel angry. It'd been he who'd left her. If she was with this werewolf now, he should only want her happiness.

"They were friends. Don't worry, she'd have said something if they'd started dating. She wouldn't have run away with him and not told us, or you."

"You think he kidnapped her?"

"Well, he's never been aggressive before. Perhaps someone came after him and took them both?"

Aiden bit his lip. If it was a werewolf who'd kidnapped Wyn, they'd be easy enough to sense and track down once he was able to examine the house. And when he found them, that creature would rue so much as looking at Wyn.

The car started, and he clenched his fists in his lap, thinking of all the things he would do to the werewolf when he found them. They drove out of the neighborhoods and onto a highway. Soon the familiar buildings of New Wall rose up alongside the frozen banks of the river. What if Wyn was hurt or suffering right now? He was wasting time when he could be searching for her.

If he wended… if he wended, her parents would know he was fae and would forbid Wyn from seeing him. The police would likely suspect him if he just popped into their crime scene. But surely that was all worth saving Wyn…

A sickening feeling twisted in his gut. If he revealed himself to the police, it would only be a short amount of time before Mab and Oberon found out about her. If they knew he was risking himself for a human, Wyn would be killed, or worse. He ground his teeth as the car swerved around a turn and skidded to a stop at a red light.

"S—Sorry. I shouldn't be driving like this," Wyn's dad said. "But it's only a little farther now." They continued on several sidestreets, early afternoon sun melting the frost-tipped grass as they pulled up to a large drive.

The Falluses lived in a twin house that overlooked the river. It had a white facade framed by two columns, reminding Aiden of the styles of homes in the Summer Isles. A garage and driveway off to the side had a slick, black car parked in front of it. He stared up at the building as Wyn's dad parked the car, and they got out. Wyn's mother seemed to share in his awe as her head turned from the cars to the house and the river beyond.

Her father pressed a button on the doorframe, and a bell rang from somewhere inside. There was a long pause, then a shuffling of feet, and Mrs. Fallus answered the door. Aiden remembered her from their brief meeting. Her too-tight face, blond hair, and deep black eyes made her look almost inhuman.

"Judy, how are you!" She tottered forward to kiss Wyn's mom's cheek and embrace her. She put a hand on Wyn's father's arm. "I'm sure they'll find her."

Wyn's mother let out a little sob. "You—you remember Aiden, Wyn's boyfriend."

"The one who looks kinda fae?" Richard Fallus stepped up beside his wife. "You don't know where she's been spirited off to, do you?"

"No," Aiden said. For once he was glad for his inability to lie.

"He came to surprise Wyn for Christmas but…" Wyn's mom put a hand over her mouth. Her father wrapped his wife in a one-armed hug.

Aiden shifted, waiting like the others for her cries to die down. He needed to go, but Wyn would want him to look after her parents… wouldn't she?

Mr. Fallus shot him another skeptical look but gestured into the house. "Come out of the cold. We didn't make up a room for the boy though…"

"I'm not staying," Aiden said.

He followed Wyn's parents into a house more opulent than the Winter Palace. A gold railing curled down a spiraling marble staircase. The foyer was lit by a bubble shaped chandelier that cast an iridescent light on the sparkles in Mrs. Fallus's dress. Everything from the glossy piano in the living room to the floor tiles that melted seamlessly into polished hardwood gleamed with a blinding light.

"Are you hungry?" Mrs. Fallus asked. "We can order some food."

The Joneses shook their heads. Aiden pursed his lips. How could anyone think of food when Wyn was gone? Nevertheless, they followed the family into the dining room and sat at the long table.

No one spoke for a long minute until Mr. Fallus cleared his throat. "When your daughter gets back, you'll be able to send her to a non-mixed school in DC; it should be better for her. No more of this fae nonsense. I did try to warn the kids on how dangerous they are."

Wyn's dad nodded, but didn't respond.

A knock on the doorframe made everyone, save for Aiden, jump. Aiden merely tensed, his eyes flicking towards the newcomer.

It was as though all the air had been sucked out of the room. Aiden's tanned skin turned ashen as he stared at the man shuffling forward. Balding and wearing a pair of thin-rimmed glasses, Oberon inched toward Mr. Fallus.

"Excuse me, brother," he said.

Mr. Fallus glared. "Now is not the time, Oscar. What have I told you about interrupting meeting times?"

"Apologies, but I thought you might want to know that Carolyn Banks has accepted your offer as your chief of staff."

"Excellent. It will be nice to have a woman on board, right Minge?"

Mrs. Fallus beamed up at her husband. "You're so inclusive, Rich."

Aiden's heart raced as he stared hard at the man. If Oberon was here, did that mean he had Wyn? Was this a threat? Had he come to summon Aiden back?

The man glanced around the table, and his glowing green eyes met Aiden's amber ones. But Oberon's eyes were brown, and they never glowed.

CHAPTER 6

Freddie

A gentle snore made Freddie jerk. She pulled her knees to her chest as she took in the room around her. A fire crackled merrily in a translucent hearth beyond the fur-cloaked bed while the walls were covered in what looked like glittering frost… but it couldn't be. Freddie ran her fingers across the impossibly soft texture of the fur, which shone like molten copper. What type of creature had this been from? This must be a dream. Places like this didn't exist outside the North Pole… or Fairy…

The snore sounded again, this time louder, and her gaze flicked to the foot of the bed where a large, gray wolf lay on its side. She shuddered, her heartbeat picking up. Where was she? How had she gotten here? Her head hurt as she tried to untangle the knot of impossibilities. Had Raul really been stuck as a wolf? Had she really been kidnapped by a polar bear? No. That was crazy. Freddie gripped her curls and let out a low groan. This isn't real, this isn't real.

The wolf yawned, its pink tongue nearly touching its nose. "Morning, Fred."

"Ohhhh no. You really are a wolf." Freddie let out a shaky

breath.

If Raul was a wolf, then was the rest of her mad dream true, too? No. That was impossible. Polar bears didn't just wander the suburbs of Pennsylvania kidnapping people.

"Uhhh, yeah?" Raul blinked, his brown eyes flashing yellow in the firelight. "Where are we?"

"I—I don't know. Hopefully we are still in the Human Realm?" She patted her side for her cell and groaned. She'd left it on the couch, and apparently the polar bear didn't see fit to bring it with her.

He sniffed, then pulled back his lips, and his fur bristled. "This place smells wrong."

"What do you mean?" She sniffed but nothing seemed to stand out from their surroundings.

"It's like blood… or violence. I can't really explain it."

She pressed her lips together and scanned the room again, hoping to find something, anything that could orient her. Her eyes lingered on the window reflecting the inside of the room with a dark mirror-like quality. Tiptoeing out of the bed, she crossed to the window and cupped her hand so she could see beyond the glass.

A frozen tundra stretched to the horizon, lit by the light of a fingernail moon and purple and green streaks arching across the sky—definitely not Pennsylvania.

"We must be in the North Pole… or Winter. I can see the northern lights."

Raul padded over to her and pressed his large snout against the window. "This isn't good. The last thing I remember, there was this polar bear, and… and…"

"And suddenly we were here? Yeah, me too." Freddie sighed. "There's a door over there. Do you think it's unlocked?" Before Raul could respond, she was across the room turning the handle.

"I don't think we should be trying random doors when we don't even know where we are."

"If we don't do anything, we'll just be stuck here." Adjusting the waistband of her sweatpants, she pushed the door open and stepped into an elegant sitting room with another great hearth giving out light and warmth. A figure stirred in one of the chairs, cast in the shadow of the firelight. They rose and rounded the chair to face her — their eyes flashing yellow like Raul's.

Freddie sucked in a breath, but raised her chin.

They moved their hands to their face. "Well it's about time you woke up. I was getting bored waiting for you," they said in a nasally voice.

Freddie took a step deeper inside, and Raul brushed against her, growling low. "Why were you waiting for me? Where am I? What—"

"Hey, tell your dog to settle down."

Freddie frowned. What type of werewolf couldn't sniff out one of their kin? As her eyes adjusted, she could make out a boy with a slender frame and large watery eyes hidden behind oversized glasses. He was so familiar.

"Daniel? Daniel Brown?"

"You—you know me? Who are you?" He moved closer, adjusting his glasses.

Freddie flicked a half smile. Fears of her disturbing new setting slipped from her mind. Now was her chance, a lead, finally! "I'm Freddie Jones—I go to New Wall too. Your posters were everywhere."

"Yeah, were you checking me out?"

Freddie's smile dropped, and Raul resumed growling. "I was hoping nothing bad happened to you. What are you doing here?"

Daniel looked around as though seeing the icy room for the first time. "I—I'm not sure. They just sent me here. Said I was useless." He shrugged.

"Who sent you?" She inwardly kicked herself for not bringing her phone to take notes. It's not like she'd planned on coming. "How long have you been here?"

"Hard to tell; it's always night here." Daniel rubbed his arm. "It could be a few days… maybe a week or two? I've eaten and slept several times."

Her gaze narrowed, taking note to circle back to her first question. "It's been a little over two months since you vanished, and if you've only been here two weeks, you must've been somewhere else for the rest of that time, right?"

"Look, I don't think I'm supposed to talk about that. Don't you want me to take you to get food or something? You've been sleeping for over a day."

"A day?" Freddie's stomach growled in response. Her heart pounded. "Do you know why I'm here?" Could Dion have had something to do with this? He was only free for such a short time; surely it wasn't enough to recruit a talking polar bear into helping him.

Daniel shifted. "How should I know?"

"I — really? How are we supposed to get home? We can't stay here!" She gestured at Raul.

"Oh please, you wake up in the lap of luxury and you're complaining? Trust me, you could be waking up in much worse."

A sinking feeling ran through Freddie's stomach. Where had Daniel woken up? She needed to get home… or at the very least get answers for her article and then to find a way home.

"I don't even know who took me or how I got here." She strode towards Daniel as anger flared in her chest. "I want answers, Daniel. I want them now."

"Well, you're not going to get them from me. I barely know how I got here!"

"But you know who sent you."

"That information won't help you."

"I'll be the judge of that." What if all the missing students were here? Could she find a way to get them back home, too?

Daniel sighed and ran a hand through his hair. "Let's just go and get something to eat. Maybe then you'll think clearly and realize this isn't so bad."

"I haven't got Stockholm Syndrome just yet. Besides, I don't even know what this is! You haven't told me anything."

He didn't respond but led the way through the sitting room and out into a long hallway. Before Freddie could follow Daniel out the door, the hall gave a loud groan followed by a whirring. It broke free of the room, and the torches that lined the walls zipped past.

She blinked. "What was that?"

"This palace has some quirks. I'm starting to think it's on some type of schedule." The noise died down, and a door stopped in front of them in place of the hall. Daniel sighed and pulled it open.

Creeping after him to lean over his shoulder, Freddie peered into a small bathroom. "I really hope this isn't the only bathroom. How often does it stop by?"

"You have one attached to your room. Let's hurry before it moves again—the bathrooms never stay in one place long," he grumbled as though speaking from personal experience.

They crossed through the bathroom and into another bedroom. Door after door led them through studies, workshops, and a salon filled with plush cushions and a window that looked into a room filled with books. Freddie scrutinized each corner of the strange palace, as Daniel had called it. She'd never even heard of a place like this in Fairy. Where could they be? Somewhere in Winter; there seemed to be nothing but tundra for miles...

Walking down a staircase, they stopped abruptly as it ended in a pair of grand doors. Freddie stared up at the scene of Winter fae carved into the ice above them: snow women in bulky robes and frost fairies with spiky hair dancing and feasting. The way it shimmered in the bright sconces made it almost look as though the people were moving. Echoes of Daniel's tapping foot bounced off the ice. Pressing her lips together, Freddie looked to him and sighed.

"Well? I thought you were taking us to eat," she said.

"Yeah, about that... It's a bit complicated."

"How is food complicated?"

Again Freddie pressed her hand to her temple. Part of her wanted to forgo—breakfast, was it? And return to her room to sleep off the growing headache from all this ridiculousness of moving rooms, talking polar bears, and the strange, icy palace. Her stomach rumbled as if to provide a counter argument.

Daniel looked to the door, then back to Freddie. "So, I can't tell you details, but you'll be dining with someone else."

"Who?" She folded her arms over her chest.

"I – look, it's hard to say."

Another answerless question. Freddie threw open the door and marched into a grand dining room. Her eyes instantly fell to the silverware gleaming on the long table. Snatching up a fork, she rounded on Daniel. "Tell me what I'm doing here."

"You're threatening me with a fork?"

"A silver fork. I wonder what kind of damage it can do to one of your kind." She moved closer; fork poised to stab his shoulder. Raul opened his mouth, but Freddie shot him a look and he shut it. She didn't want to think what would happen to them if her captors found out he wasn't a dog – she couldn't bear this place on her own.

"Isn't it silver bullets that kill werewolves?"

Freddie frowned. Daniel had been a werewolf for at least two months – surely he'd picked up on some of their magic since then... then again, that girl who'd tried to kidnap her was in jail. Maybe there was no one else to teach him. He couldn't even sniff out Raul...

"It might not kill you, but there are plenty worse things I could do." Her eyes trailed down as she lowered the fork.

"Look, I'm sorry but I'm not supposed to tell you anything about the curse." Daniel stumbled back a few steps, nearly falling over his feet.

"What cur –"

"That's enough!" a voice boomed behind her, and Freddie whirled, dropping the fork. Ten feet tall and hulking muscles covered in cream-colored fur, stood the polar bear.

Freddie's chest squeezed, and a silent scream scrambled to get free of her throat. "Wha-wha-," was all she was able to say.

"Just sit down, will you?" The polar bear sat in a seat toward the end of the table and gestured at the place across from him.

Freddie shook her head. She'd thought she'd come to accept her situation, but seeing the bear reminded her how impossible this all was. "Nope. This is just some horrible nightmare. I did not just get kidnapped and dragged to a mad castle in the middle of nowhere by a talking polar bear."

"I know this might be a bit startling for you but –"

"Startling! You think startled is how I feel?" Beside Freddie, Raul growled, lips pulled back to reveal his sharp fangs to the bear. "We—I feel horrified! This isn't even a normal fae kidnapping. Is there even a changeling?"

"You weren't kidnapped."

"Oh really?" Fury burned through Freddie's body, flushing her face. She wanted to hurl something at the bear as she strode across the room to glare into his turquoise eyes.

"Well, technically I suppose you could call it kidnapping, but you were needed here."

"I was needed right where I was." She picked up a plate, and the bear ducked down as she threw it at where his head had been.

"Why are you so violent?"

Freddie panted, her breath coming in short bursts. "This can't be happening…"

She closed her eyes. At least she could focus on the positives, she had her first lead on the missing students. Maybe the rest of them were here, too. Her door didn't seem to be locked, so maybe she could explore this place to find them, even if she risked getting hopelessly lost. And once she confirmed where they were, where she was, then she could plan their escape. Breaths slowly came easier to her as she sank into the seat across from the bear. Just stay calm and make a plan.

"Are you alright?" he asked.

"Not really. Tell me more about this place. Daniel said it was cursed?" She could at least try to get answers out of the bear, if Daniel was being so tight lipped. Glancing over her shoulder, she searched for the bespectacled were, but there was only Raul sitting beside her glaring daggers at the bear. "Where—"

"Daniel wasn't supposed to say anything about the curse," the bear said.

Freddie frowned and got to her feet. "Did something happen to him?"

"I… don't know." The bear rose too and lumbered towards where Daniel had been standing. Freddie followed him while Raul sniffed the floor around them.

"Daniel?" Freddie called into the deserted hallway. "Are you there?"

The bear called for him too as they took several hesitant steps out of the room. Perhaps he'd tried to leave and got whisked away to some far part of the palace. Raul barked and Freddie whirled. Both she and the bear hurried back through the entrance to the dining room as Raul skidded out of their way.

"You found something?" Freddie stepped in front of the bear, and Raul looked down. He nudged a pair of oversized glasses towards her.

Wherever Daniel had gone, there was no way he'd gone by choice.

CHAPTER 7

Aiden

Aiden's heart stuttered as he stared at Oscar Fallus. If this man was Oberon's fae twin, that meant Oberon was human—surviving off of stolen magic… Aiden's magic. He swallowed hard and leaned back in his chair.

"Ah, I see you've noticed Oscar's eyes," Mr. Fallus said. "Don't worry, most people have that reaction when they see him."

Oberon's twin lowered his gaze, an act the real Oberon would never do.

"You're a changeling?" Wyn's mom asked.

Oscar looked up. "That's right, ma'am. My brother's been kind enough to give me work on his campaign. Finding work is hard for—"

"That's enough Oscar," Mr. Fallus said. "They don't want to hear you complain about the state of the economy." He turned to Wyn's father. "I always say, there's plenty of work back in Fairy. Joining the military is a perfectly respectable career choice, but he insists on staying here."

Another emotion Aiden had never seen on Oberon's face flickered through Oscar Fallus's eyes—hurt. He must have been young when he was switched to have such an attachment to the

Human Realm. From the little Aiden had learned about changelings, it seemed the brown fae never fit in much in Fairy either. Like wingless fairies without magic of their own to protect them, he'd seen them shoved into the lowliest work in the Summer Realm. There weren't even changelings in Mab and Oberon's court — perhaps, though, this was why.

"Rich is very kind, giving Oscar work," Mrs. Fallus said. She smiled, her pink lips stretching across her face in the most unnatural way.

"Yeah, well, it was Mother's pleading that got to me." Mr. Fallus patted his wife's hand. "Go away, Oscar, unless there is something else you need to tell me? These folks are distraught, and they don't need you hovering around making them feel worse."

Oscar's shoulders slumped, and he headed back out the door he'd come through without a word. Aiden watched him go — there was no way a man like that could be a spy for Oberon. But if their Majesties weren't behind Wyn's disappearance, who was?

"Sorry about him," Mr. Fallus said. "He's been with the family since I was ten. It's actually quite an interesting story. Terrible, but interesting."

Wyn's parents exchanged glances. No doubt they were hoping to steer the conversation back to Wyn and how the Fallus's could help find her.

"When I was a boy, my older brother and I would fight a lot. He was only two years older than me, but I can still remember him taking all my toys and picking on me with his friends." Mr. Fallus chuckled. "Brother stuff, you know?"

Wyn's father shrugged. Aiden grit his teeth; this was such a waste of time, but Mr. Fallus continued regardless.

"Well anyway, one day we were playing in the woods behind our house, and as usual, Oscar and his friends left me behind, and I came across this old well. I threw a stone in it and when I looked up there was this hideous old woman standing there. She asked me to fetch her some water, and of course, like all children, I listened to my parents. I knew what the fae were like."

Aiden closed his eyes and massaged his temples. He already

could see where this story was going. If Oberon was switched by a hag, he was more than your average fairy changeling. It didn't matter to hags how old the fae or human was; they fed off sorrow and pain. Unlike other fae who'd switched infants, hags chose children old enough to miss their parents back in Fairy yet young enough to be helpless to return. The wretched creatures had flocked to him when their majesties first built up their court and pulled in creatures like that as their nobility — feeding on his misery. But as his powers grew, they'd made their presence scarce like every other fae at court save for Dek and Mare. Pain struck his heart at thoughts of Dek, but he clenched his fists, easing the hurt back as he tried to focus on Mr. Fallus's story.

"So I fetched the crone her water, thinking she'd turn into some blue fairy. I was still a kid, mind. I didn't know any better." Mr. Fallus cleared his throat. "She didn't change or anything, but she said she'd grant my deepest wish. I'd forgotten at that point what I'd wished for when I threw that pebble into the well. But if I'd recalled, I'd have taken it back." He shook his head and dabbed at it with his napkin. "That night I woke to someone sobbing. At first I tried to ignore it, thinking my parents left the TV on. Finally, I got up to check. It was coming from my brother's room. The window was open and there was a figure on the bed crying. I thought it was my brother, so I asked what the matter was. Imagine my horror when that creature looked up with those glowing eyes."

"Oh, Rich, that must have been terrible," his wife said.

"Yes. With Wyn gone, I can imagine the pain your parents went through," Wyn's mom said with a sniff.

"They called the police and everything. This was back before the war, and they even sent a force over into Fairy to work with the Summer Guard. But no luck. The creature couldn't tell us where he was from, and the hag was long gone. My parents suffered only a little. My mom insisted on caring for the new Oscar as though he were my actual brother. I never forgot though. And I won't. A fae stealing my brother. That's why I work so hard to make sure these things don't happen again. What happened to your daughter is a perfect example of why humans shouldn't live among these dangerous creatures."

"Here, here, dear." Mrs. Fallus banged a fist on the table.

Wyn's dad jumped. "Are you talking about complete segregation?"

"I'm saying we should do what they're discussing over in Britain now. Rounding them up and sending them back where they came from."

Aiden glanced at Wyn's father. If Wyn were here, he could imagine her outrage over the man's cruel comments towards fae. Some of those people had lived in the Human Realm for generations.

Her father shifted in his seat. "Maybe we should just focus on getting a strategy together to find Wyn."

"You're right, enough of this troubling talk. I'll go find us some dinner," Mrs. Fallus said and left the room.

All the while, Mr. Fallus talked about the terrible things the fae did to those they took. Aiden's stomach churned as he watched the dining room clock as though it would get up and fly away. Part of him knew Mr. Fallus's stories were just nonsense, but a small voice whispered what if they were true? There'd been so much blood on Wyn's shirt... How could her parents just sit here and do nothing? Every nerve in his body burned to race out, burst into her parent's home, and search for clues as to who or what stole Wyn.

Aiden could barely eat any of the rich food Mrs. Fallus served as thoughts of Wyn consumed his mind. The sky outside was already hinting at orange; it would be dark before long. But he couldn't wend out of here without causing a disastrous stir. He would find Wyn again, and he couldn't risk her parents hating him because he was fae.

"You, boy," Mr. Fallus said through a mouthful of sausage.

Aiden blinked. His thoughts of Wyn shattered like bits of mirror.

"You haven't said anything all night. Perhaps you know where Wyn is. Can't you use that residual fae blood of yours to sense her?"

He swallowed, choosing his words carefully. "If only I could."

He hadn't been in school long enough to learn the double speak with which most fairies lied. "I miss her greatly."

"Sure, sure," the man said. "You sure you're not a changeling? Your eyes are bright enough."

Wyn's mother's grip tightened on her husband's arm as they all stared at Aiden.

"I'm sure. My parents wouldn't have given me away." Though they'd been forced to abandon him anyway, once the Summer King burnt them to ash. He clenched his fist, his food untouched on his plate.

"And where are they now? I'd like to see if their eyes are as unique as yours."

"Rich, please," Wyn's father said.

"I'm just making sure. For all we know, he's the fae that spirited your daughter off." Mr. Fallus waved a hand as a few grains of rice dribbled from his chin.

"They're dead." Aiden stared blankly back at the man. Years of practice with Mab and Oberon had taught him well how to hide his feelings.

"How did they die? Some fae got to them?"

Even Mrs. Fallus shot her husband an uneasy look.

"Fire," Aiden said. Keeping his answers short had always worked with their Majesties.

"Oh, Aiden, I'm so sorry," Wyn's mom said. "That must have been terrible for you."

Aiden nodded.

Mr. Fallus rocked back in his seat. "Yeah, I'm sure it was." He cleared his throat. "Well, about your daughter, I'm sure it was fae. There's not a whole lot we can do tonight. For now, let the police concentrate on the werewolf. I'll talk about it tomorrow, when I'm on with Bruce Carter. His radio show has a broad audience."

"Thanks, Rich." A relieved look spread across Wyn's father's face. "Any mentions of her disappearance will be a blessing."

"Anything for my best advisor. Now let's talk about your move to Washington."

Aiden only half listened as the Falluses and Wyn's parents

droned on about going to some foreign city. How could they be talking about things like that when Wyn was missing?

Again, he watched the clock as it ticked passed three, four, five…

Aiden cursed. If he didn't get back soon, he'd be missed. Mab had mentioned something about another mission, and he didn't want to wait until they drained him and he was lying half dead to receive instructions. Though there was one thought that gave him pause, that filled him with dread just picturing the Winter Palace. Oberon. Seeing Oscar and knowing that it was a human dragging out his magic and using it as his own made Aiden shudder.

It was one thing thinking Oberon was a fae using Aiden's magic as additional stores for the war, just in case the palace was attacked. But it was entirely different if the man's sole source of magic was Aiden.

"Please, excuse me," Aiden said, getting up. "I must return home." He couldn't stand waiting anymore, even if Oberon was back there. The sooner he fulfilled Mab's mission, the sooner he could return to his search for Wyn.

"Of course," Wyn's mother said. She rose from her seat and hugged him. "Thank you for staying with us. Come visit soon. I know Wyn will be glad to see you when she's back." Her eyes were still glassy with unshed tears.

Aiden inclined his head. "I will return as soon as I am able."

Mr. Fallus grunted as Wyn's father stood and shook Aiden's hand. Making his way back to the front door, Aiden studied again the opulence of the home. Such beauty disguised such ugliness within. No wonder Wyn fought so hard to tell the fae's stories. Humans needed to know that not all fae were evil; there was evil within their own people as well.

He wended to the back entrance of the Winter Palace, desperate to avoid Triglav. As soon as he had a free moment, he'd return to search Wyn's house and pick up her trail. Frustration burned in his chest. If only he could get away, just for a day, to search when no one was there. But no, he was forced to return here, the cursed life debt making him acquiesce to every one of their

Majesties' whims. Yet, Wyn needed him. He would follow her across the Seven Realms if he could. And when he found those that took her, his fire would make quick work of them.

Aiden entered the palace and crunched through the frost-covered halls. Green fae servants stared and darted out of his way. He hated seeing the looks on the elves' tiny faces. Their eyes were wide and lips drawn as if to say, you're one of our kind — how dare you betray us. Or perhaps they fearfully wondered instead what manner of monster he was.

As he headed toward the throne room, the servants grew scarce, replaced by brown fae guards and courtiers. Their expressions were little changed from those of the elves, however, perhaps holding less fear and more disgust. A figure in a black slip dress glided into the throne room ahead of him, and he jogged to keep up with her.

Mare sniffed. "Where've you been all day?"

"The day isn't over." Aiden shrugged his shoulders, his body instinctively shrinking into itself as he entered the opulent room. The glares of the fairy soldiers, trapped in the crystal bubbles that made up the chandelier, made his spine tingle as he approached their Majesties' dais.

"That's not an answer."

Three thrones gleamed in the fairy-light, carved from the purest white ice. Mab beckoned Aiden and Mare over to her. Beside her, Oberon's bored gaze raised goosebumps across Aiden's skin. Now that he knew, he couldn't unsee Oberon's humanity: his dull brown eyes, the ever so slight wrinkles indicating Aiden's magic was fading. He grit his teeth and approached, trying not to look at the fae king whose power was built on a lie.

What about Mab? Did she know her husband wasn't fae? Their goal of conquering Fairy with the army of brown and red fae, without true magic of their own, could that be some kind of sick revenge against the green fae who'd never have accepted him? And what of the Human Realm? Would Oberon want to reclaim the realm that failed him?

Aiden's head pounded as he kneeled before Mab while Mare

remained standing; her favor with their Majesties was never in question.

"Aiden, Pet, I haven't seen you all Solstice." Mab smiled, her usually pearly teeth now a pebble gray.

"He's a soldier, dear. There is no place for him at our galas." Oberon took a sip of his wine, looking a perfect younger image of his twin.

Aiden bowed his head. Better not to respond. After all, he was only their tool: to suck the magic from and use in battle. Their cause of bringing liberation to the brown and red fae, allowing them equal rights amongst the greenies, was a lie. Oberon was just using them for power. Aiden sucked in a breath as he lifted his chin. Had he been stupid enough to believe Oberon wanted the best for the brown fae? No, he'd always known deep down, but their cause should've been led by a brown fae. A changeling at the least. Humans had no part in this war. At least not yet.

"We have a new mission for you two," Oberon said.

"You worked so well together on the last mission, we figured you'd do so again." Mab laughed like tinkling bells at the distaste on Mare's face. "Come now, Mare, sweetheart. He's not that bad. If I remember correctly, you used to be quite fond of him."

Mare glanced at Aiden, then back to Mab. "I of course will do whatever your Majesty asks of me." She smiled, and Aiden ground his teeth.

"I remember the four of you as children, Mare and Tati always chasing around Aiden and Dek to get them to join them for tea."

Tati? Tatiana? He'd not heard anyone speak of their Majesties' daughter in ages. When the battle in Autumn had grown fierce, their Majesties had sent her off to the Human Realm, but where he did not know. He looked to see if Mare shared his surprise, but she stood stiffly, staring at the wall as though the mere mention of Tatiana had been a gorgon's glare.

"Please, my dear. The boys needed to train — they had no time for tea; and neither did you, Mare." Oberon set his wine down and looked sharply at her, and she ducked her head.

"Tatiana needed a friend." Mab's lip quirked.

"Perhaps I should've put her in training too. At least then she'd know how to defend herself. But it is no matter; this mission does not concern her."

Mab sniffed and turned her cheek to her husband.

"Mare, you and Aiden will be traveling to Sunset Valley. I want that territory for our army in three days' time." Oberon's voice was gruff and betrayed none of the tiredness hidden behind his eyes.

"But that's in Summer," Aiden blurted out. And though he didn't dare say it out loud, Mare was hardly a fit partner. She was a spy, not a soldier. What did she know of commanding troops?

"Look, my dear, the boy knows geography," Oberon said, his voice dry.

Aiden swallowed hard. "The Summer Prince has the Crown of Flames. I was barely an even match for him the last time, and his forces outnumber our own. I—"

"Then it's a good thing we are sending you both."

Mab laughed again. "I have the utmost confidence that you two will be able to take the Valley. And Pet, you already know the consequences of disappointing us."

Aiden shuddered, bile creeping up his throat. He couldn't go back there—he'd die first. He bowed his head, and Mare did the same. "Yes, Your Majesties."

"Go then and prepare. You leave tomorrow." Oberon waved a hand.

Aiden bowed again and left the throne room. As he walked, pinpricks of pain stabbed through his boots and chest. He gritted his teeth against the inevitable increased intensity of Mare's energy-draining shadows, but it didn't come.

"What in the seven realms was that? Acting like you're afraid of the Summer Prince is exactly why their Majesties are so hard on you. Look at you, you can barely walk."

Aiden put a hand to his temple. "That's because your shadows are sapping away my energy."

"Oh…" Mare twisted her wrists, and the shadows withdrew. She looked away, the closest thing to an apology Aiden had ever seen her give.

"You were afraid, too."

"Yes, but I try harder not to show it. Just give in — it could always be worse." She rubbed at her arms. "They aren't as hard on me because I try to show enthusiasm."

Aiden scoffed. "And you're the princess's friend."

"We're all friends," she muttered. "Besides, your family was murdered by Summer. You should enjoy this too."

"We slaughter people. Sometimes innocents."

Mare's dark hair slipped from behind her ear to curtain her dark face. "No one's innocent."

For not the first time, Aiden wondered what her life had been like before she'd joined Mab. The Nightmare Plains were terrible, but what had happened for Mare to come here? He never dared ask, and she never offered anything. Swallowing his curiosity, Aiden said nothing as they continued down the stairs.

"I'm not like that — I can't just kill for enjoyment," he said.

She held up a hand as they reached the bottom and leaned so close her lips nearly touched his ear. "You're too good for this place, Aiden. Why are you here?"

He lowered his gaze.

Mare sighed and turned off to her room while Aiden made it to his own dark chambers. He wished he could enjoy the cruelties, like she did. Perhaps it was his blue fae nature preserving what little was left of his soul.

He sat on the edge of his bed and breathed out a sigh. Dropping his head into his hands, he closed his eyes; the weight of all the forces conspiring to drag him into deeper misery swirled in his head. In the morning he'd have to go back to battle, Oberon was a human changeling, Wyn was gone, and he was helpless to do anything about any of it. He needed to find her; she was the only goodness in his sea of misery. She couldn't be dead. If she was — if it was his fault… Tears pressed against Aiden's eyes, and he pushed them back. He couldn't fight Oberon's order no matter how badly he wanted to. No, he could only hope to survive the fight in Sunset Valley long enough to return to the Human Realm and search for

ANN DAYLEVIEW

Wyn.

CHAPTER 8

Freddie

Freddie didn't remember falling asleep. The soft furs enveloped her, yet an icy chill resonated within her veins. Thoughts of Daniel still prickled in her mind. Where could he be? Despite all the moving rooms, she, Raul, and the bear had searched most of the castle only to find it deserted save for the four fire salamanders who'd prepared their dinner. Shutting her eyes, she tried to picture herself back home, longing to fall asleep, but to no avail.

The chance to find the missing students had been so close, but now Daniel was gone, and she was right back where she started. And there weren't even any clues as to where he had gone. Everything she'd worked for seemed just out of her grasp, and now what? She was hopelessly trapped here, for God knew how long. What if she couldn't find a way out? She'd never publish another article, never impact the anti-fae sentiment with her stories, and never see her parents or Amanda again. Freddie pulled the blanket tighter, tossed to her other side, and froze. Something warm and smooth like flesh met her arm as it flopped to the other side of the bed. Nope.

Maybe it was just Raul turned back into a human. He

probably changed when he was asleep and hadn't realized he was himself again. She breathed out slowly and peeled her eyes open.

The pale silver, green, and purple light that came through the window gave the room a dull glow. Freddie peered to her side, but she couldn't make out anything but the outline of a figure.

Something stirred by her feet, nearly making her jump. Reaching down, her stomach dropped when her hand met fur. If Raul was still a wolf and sleeping at the foot of her bed, then who… The self-defense classes she'd taken in school hadn't prepared her for this. If the figure beside her was attacking, sure, but they were just laying there, sleeping.

She prodded them with her finger, retracting it quickly when they began to stir. The figure groaned and let out a deep sigh, falling easily back into steady slumber. Her heartbeat picked up. Again, she prodded them, this time with her whole hand. They groaned again, and their eyelids fluttered open revealing two glowing turquoise eyes staring back at her. Both Freddie and her bedmate shrieked.

Scrambling back, Freddie pulled the fur up to her neck.

"What? Who?"

"C-can you see me?" he asked in a much too familiar voice.

Heat flooded Freddie's body as fury burned through her. She ripped aside the fur. All thoughts of the kidnapping, being trapped in the middle of nowhere in Fairy, and her lack of leads to find the missing students built into one frustration narrowing in on the figure.

"What. The. Hell. Pelrin?"

"You can see me? No… not good… you can't." There was fear in his voice, not just the slight tremor he sometimes used to garner her sympathy. No, he was genuinely afraid of something.

Freddie squinted, but she could see nothing but his outline. "Why are you here? What's going on?"

"Look, Freddie, I may not have much time to explain. You weren't supposed to see me."

"I can't really see you. Well not most of you. I can only see your eyes, and a bit of your shadow, but I can hear you just fine."

Pelrin let out a breath. "We might be all right then."

"All right from what? What's going on? Are you behind all of this?" She waved her hand, gesturing at the dark room.

"What? No, I didn't do this. I mean I did bring you here, but this curse isn't my fault." Pelrin's voice cracked, and Freddie's gaze narrowed. He might not be able to see her in the dark, but he could feel her. She drew her fist back and slammed it into what felt like his arm—not hard enough to hurt her hand, but hard enough to bruise a human... though maybe not a fairy prince.

"Ow, that hurt."

"Good. Now take me home." She crossed her arms, staring at the moving shadow on the other side of the bed.

"I can't do that. You don't understand." Pelrin reached for her, but she jerked away.

"Enlighten me."

He lowered his voice as though afraid of being overheard.

"I-I'm under a curse. I have to stay here with a human for a full year without letting them see my face, and then we can both go free. Please—"

"Any human?"

"Well, I didn't want to be stuck with a stranger. And Jefferson would have murdered me if I took Amanda, so there's only one human left..."

Freddie growled. "You could've chosen anyone, anyone at all, but you chose to rip me from my perfectly good life to trap me here with you?"

"Freddie, please. I didn't have a choice."

"Save it, Pel. It's a good thing I'm not supposed to see you anyway. I couldn't stand to look at you. Now, get out of my bed, or I promise I'll make it a very unpleasant night."

"Look, I'm sorry, but I really can't leave."

"Oh no?" Freddie kicked him just as he scooted farther from her. She heard him flailing as he reached the utmost edge of the bed, but he didn't fall.

"It's part of the curse. You have to have dinner with me each night, and I must sleep beside you in my true form."

"Fairy curses," Freddie grumbled under her breath. She pressed her fingers to her forehead and breathed out slowly. "So, you're the bear, too?"

"Of course, who did you think the bear was?"

"Oh, I don't know, some random talking bear? It's hard to think critically when you're constantly being traumatized."

"Yeah, sorry about that. I didn't mean to be so dramatic."

"Get over yourself, Pelrin." Scooting back down in the bed, Freddie turned her back to him. "Think long and hard tonight on how you can return me home. If you were able to drag me here, I'm sure you'll find a way to take me back."

"Freddie…"

"Good night." She tossed the fur back over her shoulder and shut her eyes, though sleep was a far-off fantasy.

Pelrin too seemed to be settling back into bed. It took mere moments before his heavy breathing turned regular, and Freddie sighed. Something sparked in her mind. How had Raul slept through that? She'd practically been shouting, and they had been anything but still. Stretching out her toes, she met Raul's hulking form; still fast asleep. He'd make a terrible guard dog… unless there was something wrong with him. She leaned over to press a hand to his side; he was still breathing. Perhaps the stress of this messed up experience had exhausted him. If only she could sleep that well. Hours passed as Freddie stared into the darkness. Eventually her body shut off her mind, and she fell into a deep sleep.

When she finally had the energy to reopen her eyes, it was to see the room illuminated by the crackling fire in the hearth and several other sconces giving off dim white light. How long had she slept? It was impossible to tell with the forever nightscape beyond the window. She rolled over to ask Pelrin, but he was gone.

Swallowing hard, Freddie sat up. Raul thumped his tail and looked at her from his place at her feet.

"Finally. I was beginning to think you died," he said.

Freddie scoffed. If only he'd seen himself last night. "How long did I sleep in?"

"Not sure, but my stomach is telling me it's past breakfast."

A soft gurgling from her own belly mirrored Raul's sentiment. "Let's go find the kitchens then. I'm sure those salamanders would be happy to whip us up something to eat."

"Maybe we should find that bear first. The salamanders seemed more keen in whipping us up into something to eat."

"Oh please, you're exaggerating. They're just lizards."

"Fire amphibians who live in volcanoes and apparently can survive just fine in the dead of Winter and look at me like I'm food!"

Freddie rolled her eyes. "Fine, let's go find Pelrin."

"What?"

"Wha — oh, right. The bear is actually Pelrin under a curse."

Raul's eyelids dipped into an unamused stare. "Right. Did he do a drug test, too?"

"Can you imagine? I mean he totally would!" She snorted. "He's cursed. I found out last night while you were passed out like a log."

"So you really want me to believe that the bear is Pel?"

Freddie nodded; the realities of the situation settling back in. She didn't know much about breaking curses, other than it was extremely hard to do.

"Well, I guess that's even more of a reason to find him before we go find food — gold fae magic and all. Maybe he can break it."

Pulling her lips in a tight grimace, Freddie swung her legs over the side of the bed and scooted out. She was still wearing her sweats and couldn't ignore her own smell. Wrinkling her nose, she held up a finger to Raul who padded into the sitting room. There were two other doors within her room, Freddie tried the first and was relieved to find a small bathroom, just as Daniel had said. Twinkling gold highlighted the ice-white fixtures as she stepped inside. Eagerly she ran a bath and took care of her other necessities. It felt nice to relax in the warm water and pretend, just for a little while, that she was back home in her parent's house.

After she bathed, she wrapped herself in a towel and tiptoed back into the room. The next door held what she'd hoped it would. It was a closet the size of her bedroom back home. A plush bench sat in the middle, so one might look out at the dark tundra as they tried on the delicate slippers and boots that lined one of the many shelves.

Freddie dressed herself in a pair of moccasins, loose gray pants and a fairy-made fur-trimmed tunic that hung to her knees. There was even a wide toothed comb so she could detangle her curls. It was almost as if the closet had adapted to her; everything fit so perfectly. Pulling her hair back into two french braids, Freddie admired her reflection in the mirror. Perhaps she could pass for a snow woman or some type of Winter princess. The thought would have made her smile if not for the direness of her situation. Did the closet want to make her comfortable here so she'd forget about her old life? If this place was cursed like Pelrin, everything in it likely had a sinister motive.

Her stomach let out a yowl; she patted it and hurried to meet Raul. Hopefully the salamanders had something readily on hand. He looked up as she approached, his eyes roving over her clothes.

"Well, you smell better."

"Gee, thanks. It's not like I've had a ton of time to bathe since we got here."

Raul padded towards the door. "The smell of this place overpowered most of what I was getting from you anyways. It wasn't that bad."

Freddie pulled her lips tight and braced herself to navigate the palace's ever-moving halls. Yanking open the door, she yelped as a vampire girl gasped back at her. Raul sat with a soft huff of fur as the girl's red eyes roved over them.

"H-hi, I'm—"

"Freya, Freya Park, right?" Freddie frowned. First Daniel, now Freya. Perhaps all the missing students really were here? Maybe they were part of the curse like she was, but then again, Pelrin probably didn't spend his nights going to sleep in each of their beds.

"How do you know my name?" She bit her lip, revealing one of her sharp fangs. Freddie drew back. Ever since she'd staked that vampire, she couldn't shake the little chill she got from being around their kind — even Jefferson made her chest tighten.

"We went to school together." Freddie glanced down. "I'm friends with Raul." He looked up at Freddie and gave her a wolfish glare. She supposed he wasn't in an ideal form to greet his crush.

"Oh… Oh! How is he? Does he —" She looked down, her pale cheeks flushing ruby. "Nevermind."

"He's good, just worried about you."

Raul made a strained sneezing noise.

"Oh! What a cute puppy!" Freya crouched to Raul's eye level. He blinked back at her. "Can I pet him?"

"I'm sure he would love that." Freddie smirked. "Do you think you could walk and pet though? We were just about to grab some food."

Freya beamed. "Of course! I'd love to see more of this place. Did you know the hallways move?"

"Yeah, I found that out the hard way yesterday. You didn't come across a boy with brown hair, maybe looking for a pair of glasses did you?"

Freya pressed her lips together and looked away. "No, but we should find you something to eat."

Freddie frowned, she'd have to do some more prodding later, but for now, she needed a clear head. Leading the way into the unnervingly still hall, Freddie headed towards where she hoped the kitchens would be. Perhaps the palace was like her closet, working based on intention. Though, she'd intended for hours to find Daniel and all it did was bring her back to the dining room with Pelrin.

After what seemed like hours, but admittedly could've been ten minutes, the girls met the same ice carving which led into the dining room. This time it was at the end of a long hallway. Freddie pushed the doors open wide revealing Pelrin, his face buried in a bowl of something white and creamy.

He looked up. "What are you doing here?"

"Aren't we supposed to eat our meals together?" she asked.

"Yeah, dinner. It's lunchtime… I think."

Freddie cringed. How late had she slept in? "Well, I need to eat too."

Pelrin swiped at his face with his paws, a fruitless effort to remove the bits of sauce clinging to his fur. "You should at least give me some warning."

"Like you did, before you kidnapped me?"

"You know my people depend on me. I have to see this curse through." He glanced meaningfully at Freya who raised a brow.

"Shouldn't you want to find a way out of here if they need you so bad?"

"It's too dangerous. If I fail…" He shook his head.

Freddie sighed. "Look, Pelrin, I, at least, am going to work on finding a way out of this. Right after I eat." If she searched the palace again, perhaps she could find some clue or map that could guide her home and the rest of them to freedom.

"You can't!" Pelrin and Freya said together. An orange salamander skittered across the dining room and placed a piece of chicken breast, smothered in a creamy mushroom sauce, in front of Freddie. It shot a look at Raul and licked its lips before scampering back into the kitchens. Raul shuddered and lifted his nose to sniff at the dish as Freddie speared the meat and cut away a buttery-smooth slice.

"You guys didn't think I'd just sit here for a year, did you?" She said through her mouthful. The sauce was incredible, she could only imagine what the salamanders could do with a waffle iron.

"You don't have a choice," Freya said as another salamander appeared and shoved a metallic bottle into her hands. She sniffed it, hesitantly, then took a large swig.

"There's always a choice."

"Yes, there's the smart one, and the stupid one that Freddie always seems to choose," Pelrin growled. "Just stick it out for a year, follow the rules, and we'll be fine."

"I have class and articles to write. I can't just stay here for a year. I could lose my internship." Freddie's fork scraped against the bottom of her plate, making Raul flick his ears back. She wouldn't be able to help any of the students either if she couldn't get back soon—someone had to tell the Human Realm how bad things were getting in Fairy.

Freya looked down. "You'll get used to missing your old life..." Raul trotted over to her and rubbed his side against Freya's legs.

How long had it been for her? Two, three months since she'd been taken by Dion's gang. But how had she ended up here? They'd said the students were taken to be soldiers on the front lines, but this was hardly the center of the war. Freddie's appetite evaporated. If Freya was here... and Daniel... that had to mean Mab and Oberon were behind this place. Perhaps she could handle three rogue fae, but the rulers of the Dark Fae Army... how was she supposed to overcome them?

Every curse has a backdoor; she just needed to find this one, somehow. Her head pounded as the ridiculousness of that thought raced through her head. She'd never broken a curse before, and from what little she knew about them, even the strongest fae struggled with undoing the magic.

"When I said I'm not staying for a year, I meant we. We are finding Daniel, breaking this curse, and leaving." Her voice trembled as she tried to sound confident. But she'd already tried and failed to find Daniel. And if this place was guarded by Mab and Oberon's magic, there was no hope in her overcoming it. They had an army, and she had nothing.

Freya and Pelrin stared back at her blankly. Revealing her bloody teeth, Freya opened her mouth and shut it again. No doubt stunned by the sheer stupidity of Freddie's statement.

"Yeah, not happening. We're not going anywhere or breaking anything. It's too dangerous, especially for you." Pelrin shoved his plate away, averting his eyes from Freddie.

"But what if we can find the way out?" She stared pleadingly at him. Perhaps she wasn't strong enough to get out of this on her own, but surely Pelrin was. He could at least try.

"Freddie, you don't know who's behind this."

Her throat tightened at the fear in Pelrin's voice. "You're

the Summer Prince. Can't you just—"

The sconces lining the walls shattered one by one, leaving them in a terrible darkness. Raul let out a bark while Freya screamed, and Pelrin's turquoise eyes darted about. Heartbeat picking up, Freddie tried to make out something, anything other than the three fae's eyes, but there was just blackness.

"What's happening?" she said.

"I-I don't know, this has never happened before." Pelrin's voice shook as the sounds of him lumbering towards them drew nearer.

Freya shut her eyes, making her invisible in the darkness. "I s-swear we didn't break any rules."

"Rules?" Freddie began. "What—"

The air turned icy, and she shuddered, wrapping her arms around her shoulders. Blue light burst from the center of the room, followed by an ear-splitting scream. Freddie couldn't help but echo the noise. It faded as her own scream died down, and they waited several long moments for the next horror to arise.

But there was only the dark and silence.

CHAPTER 9

Aiden

Dry grass crunched beneath Aiden's feet as he climbed a familiar hill. He hadn't been here since he was a child, since Oberon brought him here to get his first taste of murder—it'd been sickening. But it was as close as he could get to Elessea without drawing the attention of the Summer army.

Scents of ripe strawberries made his mouth water, and he pushed back the memories of Mab, before she'd been queen, just a bitter fae servant. She'd bring him the berries while she tended to his damaged wings. A strange lump grew in his throat at the memory. Had it been some long buried inkling of kindness motivating her to do that? Or perhaps she was just saving him from the brink of death so he'd be indebted to her and she could control him utterly... It didn't matter, nothing of his past in Summer mattered. His orders were to capture the valley, and that's what he would do.

He surveyed the village beneath them. In the distance, the golden spires of the Summer capital flashed in the sunlight. The village had guards, but not enough to defend against the small force at the base of the hill. With their Majesties sending troops to engage in skirmishes all along the borders, the Summer forces were spread too thin, forcing this village to rely on aid from the larger army in Elessea. But their attack wouldn't give the Elesseans the time needed to mobilize the army. No. The prince would have no choice but to negotiate the freedom of this place himself.

Mare placed a hand on Aiden's shoulder, her long, black hair braided down her back. "Do you think he'll come?"

Aiden tensed. "Who?"

"The prince, of course. Are you ready to take him on?" Mare's grip tightened. Was she frightened, or just annoyed about his failure the last time they'd taken on the prince together?

"I'm ready," he replied stiffly. "Are you prepared to handle everything else?"

She huffed and shot him a glare, but her eyes betrayed her fear. "I'll have to be."

With a nod, Aiden pointed to one of the village's three stone towers. "Let's take the lodestones. It's almost sunset."

"I say we ignore the stones and make the attack quick and brutal."

He shook his head. "If we do that, the prince will be here in seconds. We need more time to force Summer to negotiate. The last thing we need is a fight behind and before us. We take those out carefully, and then we attack—no warning."

Mare frowned. "Isn't that how you lost last time? Playing by the same, predictable strategy? If we attack now, head on, the prince won't have time to rally his forces. He'll have to come alone."

"Or with an elite group of gold fae. I don't want to lose, Mare. We need to play it safe; it's my skin we're risking, not yours."

Mare's sharp features showed the ghost of softening. "You know they only torment you because they know you hate things like this."

Aiden let out a harsh laugh.

"I'll prove it to you. Be the hero of today, and I guarantee they won't do anything but give you praise. Fail, following my plan, and I'll take full responsibility."

"I doubt anything you say will have any sway over them."

"We're trying to win a war, Aiden. You heard how Oberon

spoke to me. Any weakness, by anyone, needs to be dealt with swiftly and harshly. And you're just full of weak —"

"Fine! You think you're so great, lead the charge head on. You'll only fall back on me to wipe out half this place." Aiden's flames flared to life down his arms, and Mare jumped back. At least this time the Summer Prince would be facing him at his best. Even with Mare's reckless plan, their odds of victory were still good… not great, but good. "Just don't lose."

Mare flashed her teeth as she faded into the shadows. "We won't, so long as you take care of the prince," she hissed.

Angry streaks of magenta crossed the sky as though foreshadowing the blood to be shed that night. Aiden's nerves buzzed — the vampires would just be waking up, and the trolls would be at their strongest. This battle had to be won, and fast. He needed to return to the palace before midnight. He grit his teeth, desperately pushing back thoughts of the impending pain. No matter how well he did in battle, Oberon wouldn't spare him — the human king needed Aiden's magic to maintain his lies.

Aiden stared down into the village and flexed his fingers, suppressing the shudder racing up his back. When he'd stood on this hill before, it'd been the one year anniversary of his parents' deaths. He'd thought he'd been ready to kill, but he'd been weak. Aiden closed his eyes. Screams, burning flesh clogging his nose, charred bones beneath his boots. No. That was the past; he was stronger now. This time the attack would be his choice — his revenge.

Mare brushed past him, the clanking of armor and the pungent scent of troll following her as the rest of the army marched past. He sucked in a breath; this had to work. Mab would call him back to the dungeon if he failed, and madness would surely overtake him if he had to suffer under her knife again. The thought of the pain and the sight of his silver blood splattered throughout the dungeon sent bile rising in his throat.

Horns blasted a thunderous note, and the blinding flash of the lodestones signified his people crossing into the village. Aiden squared his stance and raced into the fray; the Elessean forces would be here within the hour. Could they secure the city before then? A roar from a minotaur made him turn just in time to see the bullish man lift a fairy, clinging to a pitchfork, and throw him into a ransacked building. Aiden sucked in a breath; his heart squeezed as a fairy couple raced past, struggling to hold one another's hands.

People shrieked and ran in chaotic patterns. Burning buildings filled his nose and throat with their smoke, but he was well used to pushing through such sensations. Many of the fairy villagers, however, were choking, crouched on the ground or furiously swiping at their eyes. Werewolves, more animal than human, descended on them and tore them to pieces. Aiden turned away as silver spilled out along the dry earth. He couldn't, wouldn't, let himself feel for these people. They were standing between him and the freedom to search for Wyn, and she was more important than all of them. Dek, though, would have loved a battle this chaotic…

Memories of his pseudo-brother teaching him how to spar, showing him the best way to use a blade, and bandaging him when he'd been hurt came flooding back. Clenching his fist, Aiden hurled a blue fireball at the wall of a shattered store. The prince, and that traitorous vampire, had murdered Dek and caused his own torture. When the prince showed his face, Aiden would make him pay.

Aiden's hands shook with fury as he moved through the battling crowds. The ground thundered, and Aiden danced out of the path of a charging troll — a fairy woman caught on the rock-creature's spear. Cringing, he pressed onward, dancing around the warring groups. A nymph raced past, a Summer soldier leading her toward a break in the smoke. Several Summer guards lay glassy-eyed along the cobbled streets. Perhaps this was too much; he could've shown at least the citizens mercy, given them time to run. Did Summer show your family mercy?

The image of his parents' charred corpses pressed to the front of his mind, reigniting the flames down his arms. He thrust a fist at a row of houses. A torrent of blue fire rushed from him and engulfed the buildings. Again and again, he burned more and more until the heat of his blaze drove even some of his own soldiers to flee.

Aiden blinked. It'd been more than long enough for the prince to be summoned. Did he not care about even his own people? Surely he wasn't vain or stupid enough to think they could fend for themselves. The villagers, save for the few guards, were mostly farmers. Farmers who didn't deserve to be slaughtered without consequence. His chest tightened as he stared at the carnage around him.

"Watch it, Aiden. It's nearly an inferno in here!" Mare jogged over, silver and black smudges painting her sweat-soaked face. "This town is nearly ours. Let's make you the hero and me the winner of our bet!"

"Are you not concerned the prince isn't here?"

"I am, but it's lucky," her voice held a slight tremor as she glanced around. "We should take advantage of this opportunity. Their Majesties will be so pleased we've captured a town so close to the capital. Now what boon shall you gift me..." She gave him a half smile, and the guilt in Aiden's heart grew sharp like a blade cutting into him. "Look, if you don't show them you're enjoying yourself, Mab will keep picking on you. Do you want that?"

He tensed. "No, but—"

"They blame you for every misstep, every loss, no matter the cause. She knows you've no stomach for battle." Aiden swallowed hard. As a child, Mab had occasionally given Dek, Mare, and him sweets. Her constant doting on Tatiana had made her heart soft and full of joy. But after the war came too close and their Majesties were forced to send their daughter away, Mab had become a creature that reveled in vanity and cruelty.

"You know nothing of my desires," he snapped.

"I know you cringe at the thought of attacking humans and find every way possible to give the civilians a chance of escape with your overly cautious plans."

He turned from her. Mare was right. He'd have shown these people mercy, even though Summer had taken everything from him. Even when he lived there, they'd spared him no compassion. They'd just used him for his power under the guise of honor. Aiden grit his teeth, suppressing the urge to burn yet again. "I have no interest in sparing Summer."

She patted his back. "We'll be out of here soon. Just pretend slaughtering these pathetic people is your favorite thing to do. They'd have done the same to you given the chance. You'll see — their Majesties will be thrilled."

As if to solidify her point, a group of undines shot a blast of water at them. Aiden blocked with a jet of blue flames, turning the water to steam. The undines' skin turned red as angry boils bubbled across their flesh. The screams were terrible, but he forced his face into a neutral expression — no mercy.

"Nice work. Now, let's end this."

As more and more of the summertons fell, the scents of their blood made Aiden want to gag. He sucked in air and breathed through his mouth and continued on. Darkness had just swallowed up the sun when the horns sounded again. This time their trill was familiar; victory. Mare wrapped her arms around him.

"We did it!" she squealed.

Aiden let out a slow breath. "It's over."

But where was the prince? How could he not have come? Aiden followed Mare to the top of the hill and stared at the once thriving village. Cool blue flames rose up, creating a haze of black smoke. Shops, homes, and fields of crops burned, destroyed as though they'd never meant anything. How many lives had been taken that night? Burned to ash, just like his own. When the fire died down and the smoke cleared, there'd be little more than ruins of this place.

He shuddered. Mare took his hand, and together they wended back to the Winter Palace, leaving the troops to guard their new territory.

Aiden took his time showering and changing. At least he could be comfortable for a few hours before he had to see Mab and Oberon. While drying his hair, someone knocked at his door, and he paused. If it was their Majesties, they wouldn't knock, and servants' knocks were much more timid. Who... The knock sounded again.

He pulled on a black, wool tunic and opened the door. Mare stood there with two plates of steaming food in her hands. Aiden's stomach growled as he looked them over. It was so rare he was given hot food. A memory of Wyn pushing him to eat the incredible, garlicky pasta flashed in his mind — he needed to find her.

"I brought you dinner, since you never come eat with us," she said.

"I'm not permitted."

"Says who?" she said. Aiden arched a brow. "Well, they aren't here. Never did understand why you and Dek stayed in the kitchen. Can I come in?"

Aiden looked over his shoulder. His room was empty but for the unmade bed in the center. "I —"

He was going to say no when Mare ducked beneath his arm and strode inside.

Mare paused, frowning. "Is this it?" Aiden glared at her. "I suppose this is why we always used my room." He cringed as she crossed to sit and set the two plates down on the bed.

Mare patted the space beside her and gave him a weak smile — her expression notably drawn.

Aiden sat and braced himself for her inevitable drain of his magic. "What do you want?"

"To feed you." She held out the plate.

He took it and prodded a chunk of meat with his fork. "Why?"

"Oh, come on," Mare said. "I'm hardly going to poison you."

Pressing his lips together, Aiden could no longer ignore the tantalizing aromas. He dug into the venison sausage and roasted vegetables. Hunger fought a war against his taste buds as he tried, and failed, to savor the meal.

"Calm down, now," Mare said. She patted his knee.

Aiden finished the last bite and set the plate aside. "Thank you, Mare. Why are you being kind?"

"You think I'm typically not?"

"You're typically a stuck up energy leech." He leaned back and stared at the frost-covered ceiling.

"And yet you love me anyway." She kissed his cheek and took his plate from the bed. "Their Majesties are so pleased you got into the battle spirit. I've come to collect my debt."

Aiden flinched as one of her shadow tentacles teased out a bit of his energy. "I have yet to speak to their Majesties. Just because they told you they were pleased with me doesn't mean they'll be gentle in my treatment." There would never be a day when their Majesties would skip their nightly draining, not so long as Oberon was human.

"Fine, go see them. I'll be listening." Sauntering out of the room, Mare waved one hand over her shoulder.

Alone, and full, he fell back onto the bed and slept, knowing that when he woke, it was to suffer beneath Oberon's wand.

He woke five minutes to midnight, as though his body knew his schedule, but it was probably fear that dragged him from his peace. Ignoring the stares of the guards, he made his way to the study.

Someone whispered. "...right outside Elessea."

"...only a matter of time now before the Seasonal Realms are ours," another voice said.

Aiden swallowed. Never had the guards observed him with anything more than suppressed disdain. Was it possible this victory had swayed people? Was he the hero Mare had teased? He entered the study with a deliberate slowness.

"Good work today, boy," Oberon said. "I hear we were quite successful, and so quickly." The king glanced at Mab, who smiled in a cat-like manner.

Aiden bowed. Mab watched him cooly from her chair, her expression giving away nothing of her true emotions.

"Let's get this over with, so we can all go back to celebrating, dear," she said to Oberon.

He nodded and approached with the wand. As the crystal touched Aiden's head, the pain didn't fade — it didn't allow him to get used to it, but simply tore through his body, ripping out his magic. He screamed, his body already weak from the battle throbbing in an even deeper agony than usual. When they were done, Aiden fell forward and laid panting on the floor, his brow glistening with sweat.

"See you later, Pet," Mab said, stepping over him as she led the way out of the study.

Aiden pushed himself to his feet. His legs held the familiar wobble as they threatened to give way. Stumbling, he walked as best he could back to his room, the stares of the guards following him as he passed. When he finally returned to the barren space, he stumbled towards the bed.

"Why did they do that to you?" The soft voice seemed to come from the darkness itself.

"Please, go away, Mare," Aiden said, not bothering to open his eyes.

"You did everything they asked. You didn't even complain, they had no right —"

" — they have every right."

"You're too good for this place, Aiden," she said. "Why don't you leave?"

"I can't."

Darkness solidified into arms which wrapped themselves around him. He sighed and closed his eyes, sinking into her embrace.

###

Wyn's hand curled into his as they walked through the empty halls of the Winter Palace. Aiden flinched before allowing her fingers to fit between his. His heart pounded faster than a stampeding snow-zaan.

She pointed to a blank-eyed portrait of a snow woman. "What type of fae is that?"

He grinned. For once, he was the expert on their date, and she was the bumbling questioner. "Snow women are green fae. Well, some can be gold fae… they're like fairies, but not quite." Freezing frosts. Why was he stumbling over his words? He knew these answers. "It's said they ruled Winter a hundred years ago." Or at least his mother's bedtime stories had told him of their rule; there'd been little evidence here to suggest they'd ever reigned.

"What happened to them?"

"No one knows, though I'm sure if anyone were to find out it'd be you."

She beamed and leaned into his side. His breath hitched, and he let it out, relaxing into their closeness. Breathing in, Aiden savored her scent of paper and something sweet and homey he couldn't quite place.

"What's this door, Aiden?" She pointed to the icy door of the study.

Air sucked out of the space around him, and Aiden struggled to draw a breath while Wyn remained unphased. How had he not realized? This was dangerous. She couldn't be here, especially not with him. Had he lost his mind? Had she lost hers?

The study door opened. Dressed in red and glowing in golden glory, the prince stepped through. He smiled slowly and extended a hand to Wyn. She pulled away from Aiden's side and took it.

His heart thundered as he looked between the two of them. What was happening? Why was she staring at the prince with doey eyes as though she knew him?

"Wyn," he hissed. "He's dangerous." She smiled back at him and shook her head.

The prince chuckled, meeting Aiden's broken stare. "It would seem she prefers me."

CHAPTER 10

Aiden

"My God, Pelrin, what did you do?" Freddie hissed. A creepy tingle ran up her spine as she blinked in the complete blackness.

"Me? You were the one shouting!" Pelrin's voice sounded from across the room.

"Will you two shut up?" Freya said. "Something's obviously not right here. I don't think this is part of the you-know-what."

Freddie shuddered. If this wasn't part of the curse, then what could it be? A soft thing brushed against her leg, and she jerked. Raul's cold nose nudged her hand, and slowly Freddie squatted to meet what she hoped was face to face.

"I smell blood," he whispered.

"What do you mean? I don't smell anything."

"I don't know, it's almost like it's somewhere else... it's hard to explain."

"But how—"

"Freddie?" Pelrin called. "What are you doing?"

"Uh, nothing." She straightened. "Just looking for the switch." Crawling across the floor, Freddie felt cautiously for any of the broken glass from the shattered sconces.

"You know you're in Fairy, right?" Freya's voice held strong notes of sarcasm.

"Right." Freddie got to her feet and blinked, hoping for something other than darkness. Maybe a sliver of firelight from the salamanders in the kitchen or from under the door that led back out to the castle. But there was none.

This had to be some type of magic, but what kind of creature could cause this? Her thoughts drifted to Pelrin. He was the only one powerful enough to cast a spell to snuff out all light. She pressed her lips together and moved along the table.

"Freya, keep talking. We should stay together," she said.

Pelrin scoffed. "Yeah, especially after what happened to that last guy."

"Daniel. His name was Daniel," Freya said. "I'm here, Freddie."

Raul clung close to her side as Freddie inched forward. Freya began to hum, and she followed the sound until Freddie's hand closed on the girl's icy wrist.

"Can't we just leave him?" she said. It seemed Pelrin's slight towards Daniel had struck a nerve with Freya. What had their relationship been like? Did she know what had happened to him?

"We can't just leave him, unfortunately. Something dangerous could be in here."

"Why are you so against me? I'd do anything for you, Fred." Pelrin's hulking footsteps moved closer to them.

Freddie sucked in a breath. "Don't play stupid." Pelrin didn't respond, but it didn't take long for his fur to brush against her outstretched hands. Good, they were all together, but now what? "Pelrin, do you know what this is?"

"I thought it was part of this curse. Some weird twist..."

"Or maybe this place is haunted." Freya pressed into Freddie's side and stepped on one of Raul's paws, making him yelp. "Sorry, sorry."

"That's ridiculous," Pelrin said. "That's just human superstition. There's no such thing as ghosts. The closest thing is residual magic, but even then the creature that died would have to be super powerful and die violently."

"So, if I decided to murder you for kidnapping me and

trapping me in a haunted castle, you'd become a ghost?" Freddie snapped.

Pelrin growled low. "If you were so inclined, I'd become residual magic. But you don't really hate me that much, do you?"

"You're lucky I'm still standing next to you."

They waited in the dark for several long minutes, but nothing happened, nor were there any sounds from the outside — not even the groaning of the castle. Freddie cautiously nudged them towards the door. They made it all of two steps before a blast of bitterly cold wind washed over them, and she gasped.

Flames burned throughout the dining room, and everything was visible again. A woman with white spiky hair raced through the flames, cradling something in her arms. She pressed a hand against the wall, and blue light erupted from her fingers, trailing up her arms, and illuminating her bright blue wings. Freddie's eyes widened as a door appeared in the wall, and the woman vanished into the room beyond.

She blinked and darkness faded, returning the light in the sconces as though they'd never been shattered. There was no fire — not even the scent of smoke — the door the woman had entered was just a normal door, and Pelrin, Freya, and Raul huddled around her. What had been with those flames? A vision?

"What — um? I-It looks like that's over," Pelrin said. He shook out his cream coat and padded, a little too quickly, to the door.

"We should try to figure out what that was before it happens again," Freddie said, staring at the door the fairy had gone through.

"Are you insane?" Pelrin rounded on her. "You can't go sticking your nose into everything dangerous just because you think I'll come to your rescue."

Heat surged up through Freddie's chest to blaze in her eyes. She'd lived a perfectly fine life up until the year they'd dated. "I don't do dangerous things because I think you'll come to my rescue. I can handle myself."

"Oh? What would you have done the last time if I hadn't saved you?"

"I would've been fine! I killed the vampire, I knocked out the faun, I called the police. You just showed up!" Freddie screamed as she stood nose to nose with him. In any other situation, being this close to an angry polar bear would be downright terrifying, but Freddie was done being coddled. Her fists trembled at her sides. She'd done all those things without Pelrin's help, surely she could find a way home, too.

"You don't know anything. Humans are fragile. You're lucky I'm willing to protect you."

"You really don't have to do that, Pel." Tears pricked at the corners of her eyes as Freddie pushed past him and flung open the door to the hall. Raul bounded after her.

"Where are you going?" Pelrin roared after her.

"None of your business." She moved as fast as she could up the staircase and through the moving halls. Red thoughts of fury swam through her head as she marched towards her room. She needed to do something. There had to be a way to escape without relying on Pelrin. When she reached the frost covered walls, she slammed the door, nearly catching Raul's tail. "Sorry," she grumbled as she made her way to the bed.

"I guess that really is Pelrin." Raul looked back towards the door as Freddie flopped onto the soft furs. "He's being such a tool."

"I really hate him sometimes." Tears spilled from her eyes as she rolled over and stared at the ceiling. Pelrin could be controlling, but holding her captive was taking it too far. Freddie wanted to scream, to punch the windows, but that wouldn't help her escape. How was she supposed to spend a year in a haunted castle? She didn't even like horror movies.

"Don't worry, Fred, I'll protect you — he won't get into bed with you again."

"Thanks, Raul, but we can't stay. I have to get out of here." The idea burned through her mind, erasing all other thoughts. She couldn't spend one more night in the castle with Pelrin; she'd go mad.

"What do you mean you're not staying? The curse —" Raul nudged her with his cold nose. Freddie got up and threw open the closet. A thick coat in white fur hung in the front — it reminded her of Pelrin. With a smug satisfaction, she snatched it off the hanger and pulled it on. "Where are you going?"

"I'm leaving." She strode back to the door. She couldn't be trapped. If Pelrin was able to carry her here in bear form, then she could walk to the Human Realm. How far was it really?

"We're in the middle of nowhere. Think this through, please!"

The castle, for once, seemed to be aligned with what she was thinking and moved so she could easily find the main door. Raul's moaning and pleading was drowned out by the rush of blood pounding in her ears. Pelrin could wait out the year in this castle by himself—she was going home. It'd be nice to have a full year without him harassing her.

"Freddie, this is a bad idea," Raul said as she dragged open the main door. Icy wind bit into her cheeks as she braced herself to enter the frigid tundra.

"I'm not staying here. I won't."

The cold enveloped her as she descended the slippery steps. The wind had prevented the snow from getting too deep, and it only came a little below her ankles. It wasn't too bad. It was Winter; it was supposed to be cold. And the fur was keeping her warm.

Freddie tucked her hands into her sleeves and ducked her head so the wind wouldn't burn her cheeks as bad. Her heart sank as she looked ahead and saw a black ravine. The only way across was a delicate bridge of clear ice. Would it magically be like normal ground or would it be slippery?

"No, Freddie. It's too dangerous. What if you fall?" Raul whined as he trotted beside her.

"It's probably enchanted. I at least have to try." She headed for the bridge, heart pounding with each wavering step. "Let me try first, and I'll tell you if it's safe."

"Why are you being the hero? Maybe I should go first," Raul said. He sniffed the edge of the bridge and glanced balefully up at her.

Freddie shook her head. "I have thumbs; I can hold the railing."

She withdrew her hands from her sleeves and cringed as she

grabbed hold of the ice. It was cold… and felt real, unlike the enchanted ice in the castle. Crap. Ignoring her fluttering heart, Freddie stepped onto the bridge, and her foot slid across the ice. Of course it was slippery. But if she could ignore the pain in her hands, perhaps she could make it. Taking slow, deliberate steps, she inched her way across the crevasse.

The wind buffeted her thick furs. She stumbled and screamed as her foot slipped. No, no, no. Struggling to regain her footing, Freddie let out a slow breath. She moved a few more steps forward, now in the middle of the bridge. If she kept on the way she was going, she might actually cross this thing. But what of Raul? Pelrin would probably take him home once he realized it was him. It'd be fine, as long as she escaped — everything would be fine.

One step at a time, she neared the other side. The wind picked up ferocity again. Freddie tightened her fingers on the railing, but they were so numb she could barely move them. She looked over her shoulder and gasped as her feet slipped from under her.

Screaming, Freddie tried desperately to get them back under her but they fell instead into the nothing beneath. She clung to the railing, her fingers burning from the cold. Tears welled in her eyes as she thought of her friends, her parents… Aiden… if she called him, would he come?

"Aiden," she sobbed. "Please help." Nothing happened. Her heart increased its pounding — she could try again, but Aiden had never said he could hear her calls. There was only one person who'd ever come like that. Hating every bit of herself, but knowing her fingers wouldn't hold out much longer, Freddie called out.

"Pelrin!"

CHAPTER 11

Aiden

Aiden slammed a fist on the table and gritted his teeth against the pain reverberating from his knuckles and up his arm. He'd attacked five Summer towns. They'd taken a quarter of the northernmost province, and still the prince hadn't come to defend his people.

"Calm down. We're winning." Mare crossed to his side. Her presence was a reminder of the time before he'd been ordered to steal the prince's crown — things were different now. It was strange how empty the palace was without Dek or the others. But he didn't dare put his trust in anyone new, not after Jefferson. Not after losing the crown had cost him his freedom, his skin, Wyn… No, he'd failed too many times to trust the uncertain.

Her disappearance still gnawed at his chest. What if she was already dead? There'd been so much blood. But he hadn't been free to search for her, and he had no leads.

"It's not that. I'm worried about what Summer could be planning. The prince hasn't been in any of the battles."

"Mab and Oberon don't seem too concerned. Maybe they did something to him."

" And would they tell us if they had done something? We need to know for sure. It's too much of a risk to keep attacking like this."

He curled his fingers into fists. Why would they hide it if they had captured the prince? Or perhaps he and Mare didn't matter enough to share such delicate information. But he needed to know; he'd carelessly let his guard down during the last battle and led the army to surround the village, entering on all sides. If the prince had shown up, they'd have been far too spread out for a victory.

"I can ask. Oberon has been a bit more civil to me."

Aiden turned his head away from her. "Let me know what they say."

She gave him a mock bow and vanished into the shadows.

The dream of Wyn and the prince played over in his mind. He shook his head; no, they weren't together… there was nothing connecting them. Nothing, at least, besides him. But nobody knew that. Surely neither side would've taken Wyn to get to him. He would have had to know about it by now.

Aiden paced between the table and the wall. What if Wyn was being tortured for information about him? She didn't know anything. But if Summer had her. If he had hurt her… The flames on Aiden's arms leaped to life. Blue light filled the room, casting harsh shadows along the walls.

Mare reappeared, he jumped, and the flames died out.

"What did they say?" he asked, hoping Mare wouldn't notice the desperation in his voice.

"I only found Mab, and she thought I was joking. I think they know where he is, so we shouldn't worry."

Aiden shook his head. "I need to see him for myself. Did she at least give you an idea of where they've taken him? We can search the dungeon first…"

"No. All she said was to keep focusing on the attack and leave the prince to her."

A sinking feeling moved from Aiden's chest to his stomach. Part of him wanted to see the Prince, to face him in battle and finally get revenge. But if their Majesties had him, there was hardly any reason to keep it secret. Nothing good could come of it.

"What do you think they have planned?"

Mare shrugged. "Whatever it is, it doesn't concern us. The

prince killed Dek — you should be happy their Majesties will make him suffer."

"Unless they are holding him for some other reason…"

"Like what?"

"I don't know, nevermind."

"You're acting strange. Are you alright?"

"Fine." He pressed his lips together, not daring to let his true fears slip.

"Right. I'm going to get food. I suggest you do the same before our next briefing." She tossed her loose hair and strode off down the hall. Aiden watched her go, nerves still clawing at his stomach.

Thoughts of the horrid plans their Majesties might have in store, not just for the prince but for him, burned in his mind. Would they pit him and the prince against one another and make them fight to the death? It'd be great to finally defeat the scum… but would their Majesties let Aiden win? He swallowed — he couldn't die, not now. There were more important things to worry about, like Wyn.

His heart ached for her, but their Majesties' tight hold over him made it near impossible to aid her. Still, there was hope, perhaps not to free himself from the life debt, but he would not let Wyn succumb to whatever fate lay in store for her. Even though he couldn't sense her, he knew she was alive — she must be.

There were still several hours to midnight, and their Majesties had yet to tell him where to attack next. Surely they wouldn't notice him missing. Squaring his shoulders, Aiden left the room and headed towards the palace's front entrance. If he didn't go search for clues now, he might lose any leads that may be left.

###

Wind rushed past, biting into Aiden's cheeks as he made his way down the snowy street toward Wyn's house. The lights on the homes were still up, but none lit like the last time he'd visited. Solstice was over, and everything was now cold and bleak. Wyn's house looked more hollow than the other houses, as though someone had sucked the soul from it — perhaps it was her absence.

He approached, nearly forgetting to glamour his clothes.

Glancing around for prying eyes, he transformed his black jerkin to a deep green sweater and his pants to jeans. Hurriedly, he jogged up the steps and knocked on the door. Don't bow. At first, no sounds came from inside… What if they weren't home? Maybe that was better. He could examine the house without dancing around questions and investigate fully. Footsteps sounded just beyond the door. There was a pause, and Wyn's father opened it.

Aiden straightened, lifting his chin as he met the man's stare — it was not stern this time, but surprised perhaps?

"Aiden, we weren't, uh… expecting you."

Aiden gripped his wrist behind his back. "I can leave if it's an inconvenience." Please don't be. He couldn't return to Winter with nothing.

"No, no. It's fine. The house is a bit of a mess, but come on in." He stood back and beckoned Aiden inside.

Her father hadn't been joking. Boxes and papers lay scattered throughout the living room while the furniture had been pushed askew as though to make room for more mess.

"We're actually moving. I know the timing is horrible with Wyn missing, but the Lees across the street have promised to keep watch for her if she does turn up. And we don't plan on selling." He looked everywhere but at Aiden as he spoke.

Aiden curled his fingers into a fist. How could they leave when Wyn could be anywhere? Though she was likely in Fairy, the humans would've — or at least should've — found her by now if she were in the Human Realm. Still, he'd have searched the world in its entirety had he been in their place. He cleared his throat to rid it of any venom. "Where, uh, how far are you moving?"

"DC," her father said. Aiden tried to recall if any of the cities he'd visited with Emerick and Irina had gone by that name. "It's only a couple hours from here. My job — the offer was just too good to pass up, you know?" His breathing picked up, and he fiddled with his wedding ring.

"Who is it?" Footsteps pattered down the stairs, and Wyn's mom poked her head into the living room. Aiden tensed, bracing himself for her questions. "Oh Aiden, how wonderful to see you!

As you can see we're a bit hectic right now."

Pressing his lips together, he glanced up at the landing behind her. Perhaps he could gather more information upstairs on who, or what, took Wyn. "I could help you with Wyn's things."

Her mother smiled. "Come upstairs then. Earl told you about the move then?"

"Yes, we were just talking about it." Wyn's dad flashed him a weak smile, but Aiden couldn't bring himself to return it.

Following Wyn's mother up to the second floor, Aiden scanned the living room, his eyes pausing on the front door. Gouges remained along the wall as grim reminders of the creature who'd taken Wyn, but most of the damage had been well repaired. What type of beast could have done that? Surely they were too big for a werewolf, and wendigos didn't live in this area. Aiden's stomach turned.

"Have you heard anything from the police?" he asked. "Did they check the faun and the werewolf who kidnapped her?"

Wyn's mom pulled her lips tight. "They recaptured the faun the day before she went missing. I know the police questioned him again, but..." She shook her head, staring at a far-off nothing. "There aren't even any clues so far."

"Recaptured him?" A chill washed over him. The faun had been working for their Majesties. What if he told them about Wyn? What if their Majesties wanted revenge?

"He escaped a few weeks before she was taken, but I guess she wouldn't have had a chance to tell you. He's back in prison, and he didn't hurt her."

Aiden pulled his lips thin. The faun was probably harmless alone, but if he'd reached their Majesties, there was no telling what had been done to Wyn. "And the werewolf?"

"Still locked up, thank goodness. Our Wyn is a bit of a reckless one." Her mom gave him half a smile and continued up the stairs towards Wyn's room. Aiden's chest tightened as he thought of the last time he'd been there. It'd been Wyn he'd come to when he thought he was going to die. Without her clever human treatments, he might not have made it.

Her mom opened the door, and the pink glow greeted him like a whisper of Wyn herself. A pain shot through his chest as he remembered the keen look in her eyes when she'd studied the clues for her article. He could nearly feel the warmth of her body. She'd been so close, trusting him easily as he pointed out the new red fae soldiers in the Dark Fae Army. It'd been almost too easy to forget who he was.

But here, like downstairs, was in disarray. Her mother made her way over to the closet where clothes lay in several piles on the floor.

"Do you want to do that side of the room? It's mostly her pictures and trinkets. Just wrap them in paper and use that box over there." She pointed, and Aiden crossed the room to grab the box. "Just… be careful." Her voice trembled on the last words, and she busied herself with folding Wyn's clothes. Aiden nodded to himself and surveyed the items around him. Her bookshelf, dresser, and desk held pictures and small objects of various origin.

He took a bit of packing paper and grabbed a picture of Wyn and a dark-haired girl standing next to what could only be a vampire judging by the blurred form. He squinted, trying to make out any noticeable features. Both girls wore lovely gowns, but Wyn's was breathtaking. The bright blue taffeta clung tight to her chest before hanging loose at her hips, and pearls decorated everything from her hair to her ears and neck. Aiden touched the image, then frowned. There had once been someone standing next to her. Their hand was still visible on the other side of her hip.

Heat burned in his chest. Likely this photo had been taken before he'd met Wyn, but what he wouldn't give to have a moment like that with her. They'd danced together once, but it'd been nothing so elegant.

"That was Wyn's junior prom," her mom said, making Aiden jump. "She went with that horrid fairy boy."

Aiden tensed at her words. Would he be a horrid fairy boy too if she found out, or did his crime have to go beyond his fae blood? Though perhaps, if the Summer King hadn't murdered his parents, he could've been the fairy in the picture, and he'd never have done anything to earn her mother's hateful title. Remaining silent, his mind lost in what-ifs, he wrapped the picture and placed it into the box. Aiden made his way through several more items, the thoughts of Wyn pressing even more deeply on his mind. Was she scared or hurt? Surely she missed her home. Every second he spent not looking for her could cost her another minute. Freezing frosts.

Nonetheless, he continued to pack away Wyn's things: a green fairy figurine, a pink notebook covered in butterfly stickers, and a mini pink typewriter. Each item brought images of Wyn scribbling in the notebook or fiddling with the typewriter to his mind. He moved on to Wyn's collection of clothing magazines, and an article titled 5 Ways to Make Fae Boys Notice You made his cheeks flame. Something silver caught his eye. He turned to see Wyn's mom holding a pair of shoes with what looked to be a smattering of silver jewels on the tips.

"What are those?" They looked far too similar to the stardust light crystals that only grew near his home in Spring.

Her mother looked at the shoes as though surprised she was holding them. "Oh these are Wyn's; a gift from that horrid fairy." She scowled and tossed them into the box.

Aiden swallowed. "Might I see them?"

With a look of pity, the woman slid the box across the floor. "She wore them with you?"

He said nothing and reached inside, careful not to lift the shoe over the rim. A slight pulse raced down his wrist as he pushed magic into it, and the crystal at the top of the shoe twinkled, confirming his suspicions. He gritted his teeth. It was hardly likely that some other fairy from Spring had crossed the now-closed border, somehow found Wyn, and dated her. But how would he ask her mother without betraying his own parentage? Aiden put the shoe back and passed the box back to Wyn's mother.

She gave him a weak smile and returned to packing clothes. Several of Wyn's trinkets stared back at him from her bookshelf; an old doll covered in dust, a teacup, and a vase of fabric flowers. Something among them must have some hint, some clue as to who the fairy was before him. But perhaps he already knew. It wasn't possible, it couldn't be.

Each item he packed away was more useless than the last. A small voice in his head nagged that he should be focused on clues, and not who Wyn had dated, but perhaps they could be connected. Old plastic cameras, like the ones used across the border, pots of makeup, and books about Fairy—nothing. He shifted and felt something press against his skin, reminding him of the fist-sized sphere in his pocket. It had been a reminder of his search for Wyn; a hope that when he found her, he could greet her with a gift. He placed it in a box with her other decorations—his present was just as useless as they were. She'd hardly be impressed by it, so it'd be better off among the other items she likely kept out of pity.

Aiden shuffled over to the little table at the side of Wyn's bed. He busied himself with pulling out the endless fancy pens, notebooks, and… Something was stuck in the crack between the base of the drawer and the side. He frowned and picked at the corner of a slip of paper. Likely nothing other than trash, but what if it wasn't? His pulse raced.

The paper slowly inched out of the crack, its slick surface scraping along the side of the drawer. He paused as he pulled it halfway free. What if it was one of Wyn's secrets? He shouldn't be going through her things, but she was missing and he'd yet to find any clues—he had to know.

Finally, it came free, and Aiden's heart stopped. He stared at an image of two people, a sunny beach stretched out behind them. No—it couldn't be. Wyn wouldn't—he'd never even bother with a human, but here they were. Nausea tore at his stomach. The Summer Prince and Wyn beamed out of the photograph—they looked happy. Had Wyn ever been that happy with him?

Heat thrashed against his arms, demanding release and searing his flesh as he struggled to keep his flames in check. Pain as though he'd been speared by a minotaur pierced his chest.

"Is this…" He held up the image, his voice barely a whisper.

Wyn's mother looked up, and her eyes narrowed on the paper in his hands. "I thought she'd gotten rid of all of those pictures of him. Give it to me, and I'll toss it."

Aiden's hand trembled as he handed the photograph to her mother. Perhaps Wyn's disappearance wasn't his fault. Mab and Oberon might not have her after all. It could be some personal vendetta the prince had against her. What if he was hurting her? Maybe that's why he hadn't attended any of the battles. Or worse, if he had stolen her to convince her to return to him, to rekindle their love. Thinking of Wyn and the prince together churned his stomach. The prince had stolen everything from him; he couldn't let him take Wyn, too.

CHAPTER 12

Freddie

reddie's heart pounded. She could barely breathe from her nose, and her throat felt as though she'd been eating sand. She groaned and opened her eyes to see a bear looming above her. The bear — Pelrin. Ugh.

"You're alright," he said in a low soothing voice.

"No, I'm not," she rasped.

He bristled. "What? What hurts? You have a slight fever, but it's nothing that should kill you."

"There's a talking bear standing over me, and I'm trapped in a haunted castle. How is that alright?"

Pelrin sighed. "The castle isn't haunted."

"Yes, it most definitely is." Footsteps approached the bed, and Freya peered over at her. "You look in really bad shape. I wouldn't even drink from you if you offered."

Freddie blinked up at her. "Gee, thanks, Freya." A coughing fit overtook her, and she rolled to her side, head spinning.

Pelrin hunched down. "You're sick. You shouldn't have gone out there. What were you thin —"

"Shut up." Freddie knew he was right. Despite being buried under a pile of furs, she shivered. How was it possible she was freezing? It didn't help that the room looked like a winter wonderland, playing tricks on her mind.

It'd been stupid to try and run away. Raul had been right; they were in the middle of nowhere — and in Winter, no less. Even if she had made it across the bridge, she'd likely have died wandering around the tundra. But there was no way of crossing the ravine without slipping to her death. There had to be a safer way to get back home… but it seemed fulfilling, or breaking, the curse was the only way. And she just couldn't wait here for a year doing nothing.

Raul padded to her side and rested his head on her chest. She stroked his head and stopped, reminding herself he wasn't actually a dog. Her chest ached as she coughed and shuddered deeper under the blankets.

"You almost died, you know. What if I hadn't gotten there in time? You could've at least called me. My magic is weaker, but I still would've heard you." Pelrin got up and stared down at her.

She frowned. "I thought I did?"

"I saw you struggling across the bridge from the window and ran like a zuowu to get to you." He shook his head. "I can't lose you, Freddie." He lowered his head towards her, then paused as though he thought better of it. "Just feel better."

Freddie didn't hear him leave before she fell asleep. She tossed and turned as dreams so real she could almost touch them swarmed her mind — long falls and sharp rocks.

Aiden stood with his back turned to her. Was he even alive? Something tugged at Freddie's chest — no, he couldn't be dead. He looked back, that gentle joy glittering in his amber eyes. Relief flooded her as she ran to him, but it was as though she were wading through mud. He frowned and made to move towards her; a blast of orange flames engulfed him.

Noooo! She was screaming, but it was muted. Tears ran down Freddie's cheeks. No, he couldn't be dead. He would come back to her… if he could find her. Swallowing, Freddie looked at the spot where Aiden had stood. It was only ash now.

Pelrin stepped into view and smiled. "Don't worry, Fred. You're safe now."

Similar nightmares plagued her every time she closed her eyes.

Why hadn't Aiden come when she called him? Surely he was powerful enough to hear her between realms... but Pelrin hadn't heard her either. She fiddled with the silver ring on her middle finger. Could that be why? Maybe she should try taking it off, but if this place was truly haunted, or had "residual magic," maybe it was best to leave it on. At least for now.

It wasn't like she could call Aiden right in front of Pelrin anyway. She shuddered at the thought of seeing them face off against one another. The last time Aiden had nearly died. But when he turned himself over to Mab and Oberon, they might have actually killed him.

She stared at the dark ceiling as tears slid down her cheeks. Pelrin's warm figure did nothing to comfort her. The Dark Fae Army's stronghold was supposed to be in Winter, but she had no way of getting there. And it wasn't like she could just walk up to them and ask for Aiden. It was almost laughable to ask Pelrin if he could go check on him, but maybe Freya knew something. Reminding herself to ask, Freddie's exhaustion took her again.

Days slipped by as she passed her time between the bed and the bathroom. Pelrin always brought dinner to eat with her. It was almost sweet, save for the curse forcing him to do it. Freya, always trailed by Raul, would turn up during the afternoons to sit and chat. They shared stories about New Wall and things they would do if they could go home. Freya always got choked up whenever Freddie mentioned going home. Her parents had never looked too kindly upon fae, and if they rejected her, she'd have nowhere to go.

Freddie huddled in one of the armchairs in the sitting room beneath a pile of furs while Freya sat opposite her, Raul at her feet. They stared into the roaring fire, Freddie finding it more comforting than Freya's watery red eyes.

"I'm not just getting myself out, Freya. We're all going home. Even Pelrin." Freddie said. Even if she wasn't sure how yet, she'd find a way to break the curse. She had to.

"You have no plan. We can't just walk out of here, and you know who is always watching us." Freya shuddered at the thought of Mab and Oberon's looming presence as Raul slid his head into her lap. Freddie stared at him. What would Freya think when he was human again? Vampires weren't typically the greatest fans of werewolves… then again, Freya didn't seem to take issue with him now.

"I'll figure something out." Coughing, Freddie put a hand to her warm head. The worst of her fever had broken days ago, but she still felt like crap—not good enough to drag herself through room after room inside the moving castle. "Can I ask you something?"

Freya's brow wrinkled. "Sure, but I don't know anything more than you do."

"It's not about that, it's…" She hesitated. Did she dare ask Freya about Aiden? She'd talked herself out of it for weeks, and here was her chance yet again. Freya and Pelrin weren't close; there wasn't too much risk in her telling him about Freddie's question. Freddie's eyes flicked to Raul; his eyes were closed as his chest steadily rose and fell. "I… you were—are—in the Dark Fae Army, right?"

Freya rubbed a hand along her arm and nodded, not meeting Freddie's eyes.

"Do you know a fae called Aiden? I know the army is big but—"

"Of course. I mean I know of him, at least. Everyone does."

Freddie studied Freya's face for any hint of how she might feel about Aiden, but she couldn't make out anything definitive. She bit her lip as she thought through how to phrase her next sentence. "Have you seen him recently?"

Freya shrugged, though her shoulders quivered slightly. "I've been here. Besides, I'm the lowest of the low. It's not like I'm invited into their Majesties' war briefings." She flinched as though someone were about to hit her. Freddie looked around, but nothing happened, and Freya relaxed. Had she been afraid of the same thing that happened to Daniel happening to her?

"Oh, sorry, I was just curious. Do you know what happened to Daniel?" Part of Freddie wished Freya had been a fairy so that her answers were guaranteed to be honest, but she'd take what she could get.

"I can't talk about that." She pressed her lips together and stared down tenderly at Raul. "Please, just stop asking about us. Why don't we go back to talking about school again? Did you ever have Mr. Barker for English?"

Freddie sighed and nodded. Freya obviously knew more than she was letting on, but Freddie didn't have the energy to pry. Laying in bed wasn't getting her anywhere — she needed to be back on her feet to look for clues. There had to be some clues on the curse's source or loopholes. Or, if there was a library here, maybe she could find a record of a similar curse. "I think I need a bit more rest. We can talk in the morning… afternoon… whatever time I wake up."

When she woke, it was to Raul nudging her with his nose. "Hey, now that Pelrin's gone, are you going to tell me what all those questions about Aiden were about?"

Freddie cringed. "Pelrin came? And left already? What time is it?"

"Don't change the subject."

"I was just wondering. Pelrin always says he's so dangerous, but Jefferon didn't think he was so bad. Maybe Freya had some thoughts." She shrugged.

"Jefferson never said he wasn't dangerous. He's bad news bears, Fred. Why do you have to go sticking your nose into everything that can, and wants to, kill you?"

"What can I say, I'm just a curious soul."

Raul growled low, but stopped and leaned closer. "How are you feeling today? I think you've been in bed for two weeks."

"Weeks?"

"I've been trying to count the number of times I fall asleep — I think Pelrin's been knocking me out. Que puto."

"I wouldn't be surprised." She spun the ring with her thumb. Raul just thought it was a gift from her grandmother; thank God he didn't press her on Aiden. Stretching out her toes, Freddie took a deep breath and was shocked she could breathe through her nose. "Much better. I feel alive again."

"Then let's make a plan to break this curse." Raul leapt off the bed and looked back at Freddie.

"Um... Let me shower first. And since when did you want to break the curse?"

"I don't want to stay trapped here. Do you know what my mother would do to me if I was missing for a year?"

Freddie snickered, a guilty twinge pinching her stomach. Her own parents must be worried sick. "All right, consider this curse broken... almost."

Dressing herself in a soft, knee-length leather tunic and linen pants, Freddie led Raul to the door, and they peered out into the hallway. The bathroom whizzed by, and Freya, looking a little frazzled, stepped out.

"Well, I never thought I'd ride a bathroom to visit anyone, but here we are."

Freddie smirked. "We were just about to look for clues about the curse. Care to join us?"

"I wish you wouldn't do that." Freya pressed her lips together. "What if they try to stop us?"

"They can't watch us all the time. And what would they do about us finding a loophole in their curse? Even the most powerful fae can't mess with the rules of a curse."

"I suppose you're right... Alright, I'll go."

Waiting for the rooms to stop moving, the three finally stepped into a deserted bedroom. Freya made to move to the other end, but Freddie held up a hand. "There could be clues here. We need to find out more about who slept here." She looked down at Raul. "See if you can sniff anything out."

A canopy bed, dressed in fine linens, sat on one side while opposite was a roaring fireplace with a plush chair before it. The pictures on the walls were all snowscapes, and there was nothing personal about this place. Perhaps it was a guest bedroom?

Raul barked, and both girls rushed over to him. He scratched at the wall. Beneath the frost was black. Freya rubbed around the spot, revealing a scorch mark. Strange. Why would there be scorch marks in Winter?

Freya shrugged. "Maybe we should check the other rooms."

They stepped out into a long hall and opened the first door they came across. It was the bathroom again, as if to taunt them with its uselessness. Freddie slammed the door, and they continued on. The next room was a cigar room. Portraits of yetis and frost fairies in ancient Winter soldier uniforms lined the walls. There was still a faint scent of tobacco within the dark leather, which couldn't help but contrast the white surrounding them.

Freya moved to rub at the wall nearest them. Sure enough, there were more scorch marks.

"Do you think a battle happened here?" Freya asked.

"I've never heard of any war in Winter, save for when the Dark Fae took over, and there's none of them in sight. Well, besides you."

Freya shuddered and looked around. "This is a different place. I feel like I would know if we were still in that palace."

Questions burned in Freddie. She longed to ask about the palace she was talking about, and where the other students were kept, but it wasn't the time. There was something important about the scorch marks; they needed to find out more. After, she'd circle back to Freya; the two had to be connected somehow. She led them down a staircase, her eyes constantly scanning her surroundings for anything out of place.

"What if Mab and Oberon killed everyone in this castle and left us here?"

Freya flinched. "That's not possible. They don't have weapons that would leave scorch marks."

"There's one person in their army who can leave scorch marks." Pelrin lumbered down the stairs to catch up with them. Under his breath, Freddie could've sworn she heard him complain about oversized bear paws. "What are you all doing? I saw Freddie's room empty and went to look for you."

"We're trying to find clues to break this curse, Pel. We searched some of the rooms and found scorch marks on the walls, so we figured…"

"You think he did this?" Pelrin shook his head. "The Winter Palace is where the Dark Fae Army is stationed. Mab and Oberon rule it as though it's rightfully theirs." The notes of disgust in his voice almost made Freddie believe he'd swallowed something foul. "There's only one palace in Winter; this has to be something else."

"Can a curse build a replica palace, maybe? And the scorch marks are leftovers from the curse?"

"I've never heard of anything like that, but whatever this is, it's a strong curse. There aren't too many fae that could cast something like this."

Freddie swallowed. Was it possible Aiden had created this? He hated Pelrin just as much as Pelrin hated him, but would he really trap him like this at the expense of a human girl? Even if he didn't know it was going to be her, it was still a cruel thing to do.

"Well, maybe the army moved?" Freddie looked from Pelrin to Freya.

"Unlikely," Freya said.

"Show me these marks." Pelrin was already halfway up the stairs as they jogged after him.

They stepped into another bedroom, and Freya rubbed at the wall—sure enough, there were more scorch marks. The room itself was small and simple, likely the bedroom of a high-ranking servant. Images lay across a frost-covered dresser. Freddie dusted one off, revealing a small child with silver hair and translucent wings. They reminded her of the vision she'd seen of the blue fairy. How had she not pieced it together before? There had to be a clue in the dining room. Why else would whatever was haunting this place give her a vision there?

Pelrin peered at the mark Freya revealed by the bed. "These look old... and they aren't caused by fae of any significant power. A sundiva could've easily done this."

"So, this could've been caused by Summertons?" Freya asked.

"Maybe, but there's never been a war between Winter and Summer. We're too far apart... and what would be the point?"

"We need to go to the dining room," Freddie said. Looking at the black marks on the walls wasn't going to help anything. They needed to move on to the next lead. "I think there's a clue." Both Pelrin and Freya gave her odd looks, and she pinched the bridge of her nose. "Just trust me."

The room jerked and moved down a hall and up a flight of stairs. Freddie and Freya clung to one another, and gripped the doorframe, while Pelrin slid haplessly to the back of the room. When it stopped, they faced the elegantly carved doors of the dining room. Freddie pushed them open and made her way over to the door beside the long table. Her heart pounded as she approached. This held the answers they were looking for — she could feel it. Placing a hand on the knob, she slowly pulled the door open and stared into a room filled with glittering snow under a pale blue light. Beautiful.

"Stand back, Fred. It's probably dangerous. Let me go first." Pelrin pushed her out of the way and stretched out a paw towards the door. Blue flame leapt up before him, and he roared.

Freddie stumbled back, the carnal noise reverberating in her heart. "What was that?"

"A protection spell," he gritted out. "There's something in there someone doesn't want us to get."

"A-are you alright?"

Pelrin stood on his hind legs and waddled back toward the entrance. "Don't worry about me. I'll heal in a bit. Just don't try anything foolish with that room."

Freddie shut the door. Obviously she wasn't going to stick her hand in the room after what she saw it do to Pelrin. Why would the palace show them a vision, though, if they weren't meant to get inside? A thought flitted across her mind, and her stomach sank. "Do you think that's what happened to Daniel? He tried to get in that room?"

"No, he got sent back. They weren't too happy he told you guys —" Freya clasped her hands over her mouth. "Crap. Why…"

"Freya, it's okay. We're not going to let anything happen to you." Freddie crossed the room, her hand outstretched for Freya's. "We already know who's holding us captive and the details of the curse. We just need to find the loophole, and you don't know that either."

Pelrin cleared his throat. "There's nothing you can tell us we don't already know."

"Except where we are… or I guess where we are not. You and the other students are in the Winter Palace, the real one, right?" Freddie gripped Freya's trembling hands as she nodded slightly. Letting out a breath, Freddie smiled — finally, an answer. Now she just needed to find a way to get to the real Winter Palace. Did Freya know that, too?

Before Freddie could ask, cold whipped out of nowhere. She tightened her grip on Freya's hands and shivered as it swirled, forming snow and shards of ice in its depths. Her heart squeezed in her chest as the wind twisted until it formed a vortex behind Freya. No.

Freya's jaw dropped in mute horror as she stared into the icy depths. "They're taking me back," she gasped.

"Who — I won't let them hurt you." Freddie desperately tried to drag her back, but the swirl of ice and snow grew faster and darker as it yanked Freya off her feet.

She screamed. "No! Please, help me!"

Freddie held fast, but the vortex was too strong. Already, her grip was loosening.

Pelrin held the back of Freddie's tunic with his teeth, and Freya inched out of the vortex. Freddie's heart lifted. They were almost there. This time Mab and Oberon wouldn't take one of her classmates; they'd already taken too much from Freya.

But Freya's skin was so cold, and Freddie's hands slipped. Freya screamed again.

"Where are they taking you? I won't leave you." Tears blurred Freddie's vision as she tried to double her grip on Freya's other hand. Pelrin slowly pulled them back, but just as Freddie reached for her arm, Freya's hand slipped, and she fell back into the swirl. With one last look of terror in her ruby eyes, the snow swallowed her up.

And she was gone.

CHAPTER 13

Aiden

Aiden rubbed his hands on his pants as though to rid them of the photograph's lingering chills. The prince knew Wyn. What if she'd let something slip? What if he took her in revenge for their ended relationship?

Aiden swallowed hard, desperate to rid himself of the horrible image of them together. "I must go."

"So soon?" Wyn's mother got to her feet. "Earl!" she called down the hall. Footsteps approached them, and Wyn's father stuck his head into the bedroom. "Aiden has to leave."

"Oh, already? I guess you probably only stopped by for news on Wyn," he said.

Aiden nodded — and what news he had learned. "Do the… Are there any new suspects or clues?" He couldn't stay in the house any longer, not when there was a chance the prince had taken Wyn. He'd burn down all of Summer searching for her — starting with the capital.

"No." Her father shook his head and stared out the window.

"The police still won't go look for her in Fairy," her mother said, a slight tremor in her voice.

Aiden pulled his lips tight. The police might not ever find her, but he would. His parents' burnt corpses and the cold grin of the

Summer King as he stepped over them clouded Aiden's mind. He wouldn't let that happen to Wyn. Again, his flames pushed against his arms as his magic churned with his fury. His control over them was shaky at best. If he didn't leave soon, he might burn their house to the ground.

"Forgive me, I have another engagement." Aiden stopped mid bow and straightened. Wyn's parents were staring at the boxes cluttering their daughter's room, oblivious to Aiden's error in human courtesy.

"Don't worry about us," her mother said, the tremor in her voice hinting at tears. "I'll write down the new address for you in case you want to visit or if you hear from…" Her voice trailed off as she scuttled over to the desk and scribbled on a pink square of paper.

Her father looked down, avoiding Aiden's gaze. How could they think leaving at a time like this was a good idea? What would Wyn think when she came back to an empty house? When he brought her back?

"I shall visit again," Aiden said and took the slip of paper. In shaky writing was an address somewhere in Washington, DC. At least now he'd know where he should take her — not here. She didn't need to see evidence of who her parents valued more. He carefully tucked the paper into his pocket and followed Wyn's father down the stairs.

"It was good to see you as always, Aiden." He patted Aiden's shoulder, making him stiffen.

Taking one last look around the living room and seeing nothing more hinting at Wyn's whereabouts, he gave her father a curt nod. "Until next time."

The man waved, and Aiden jogged down the steps, back into the crisp winter air. He took a deep breath, soothing the fires beneath his skin, and hurried down the street.

When he was far out of sight, he unleashed the flames along his arms, burning every bit of fury he felt toward the prince. There would be no mercy when he saw him next, especially not if he'd hurt Wyn. There'd been blood on her sweatshirt — red blood.

For several minutes, he leaned against a streetlamp, letting his rage course through him until the fire dimmed. He couldn't greet their Majesties battling with so much anger. No, he needed to be as perfect as possible.

He wended and crossed the bridge to the palace. Triglav glared down at him as he passed.

"And where have you been, dog?" he spat.

"My whereabouts are my own business." Aiden tried to step past him, but the giant blocked his path. Gritting his teeth, his earlier rage reignited, and blue fire broke free along his arms. "Do not make me remind you of your place."

Triglav laughed deep and loud enough to send vibrations through the ground. "My place? I am not the one everyone calls 'dog,' at the beck and call of their Majesties' whims. Nor am I the one who grovels in front of them before the entire court."

"No, you're not." The anger in Aiden built until he held his arm up and swiped it before him, lashing out with an arc of fire. "You're just the one chained up in the yard who barks at intruders." Ignoring the screams of the frost giant, Aiden passed through the door and entered the glittering main hall.

There was no time to argue with Triglav; he needed to tell their Majesties to attack Elessea now. Every second Wyn was with the prince, he could be hurting her. They needed to… Aiden slowed his pace as the holes in his theory revealed themselves. If Mare was right, the prince was being held by their Majesties—Wyn couldn't be with them unless… Unless they'd been together. But her mother had said the prince was in her past, and besides, their Majesties wouldn't send a creature after the prince. But they might send one after Wyn to lure the prince into a trap.

A sick feeling overtook him as he stopped, halfway to where their Majesties held court. What would they do with Wyn once the prince had been captured? Would they torture her to hurt him, to keep him compliant? Or would they dispose of her? He clenched his fists, trying to put aside horrific images of what they might be doing to Wyn.

"Aiden!"

A voice cut through his thoughts, and he jerked. Mare walked alongside him, an annoyed expression tugging her lips straight.

Shaking his head, he met her dark gaze. "S-sorry."

"Right. We don't have time for your daydreaming. Their Majesties have put you on another mission."

"We're going somewhere else?" The capital? Surely it was too soon — their army was spread thin across the rest of Summer.

"No, not me. Just you." Mare led him into the throne room where Oberon slouched in his chair, observing his court of brown fae.

A temor ran through Aiden's body. Please don't let them have Wyn. But if they hadn't been the ones to capture her, who had?

Mab smiled when she spotted them approaching, and Oberon sat up. "Well, that was fast."

"He was in the hall." Mare shrugged, and Aiden sank to one knee before them. Triglav's comment about groveling gnawed at the back of his mind.

"Rise, Pet," Mab said. "We need you to take a quick trip to the Human Realm."

Aiden cleared his throat. "The Human Realm?" Could they be sending him to check on Wyn? Could they be hiding her there?

"You know it best out of anyone, and we need someone to escort our daughter home from school."

Aiden's heart sank. "You want me to return Tatiana here?"

"Yes, boy!" Oberon slammed a fist on the arm of his throne. "And if you keep asking stupid questions we'll send you to the Human Realm skinless."

Aiden's eyes widened, and he stumbled back, too shaken by the king's outburst to apologize.

Mab's smile curled like a cat who'd cornered a mouse. "Here's the address, and a note from me to give to the school." She handed him two slips of paper. "We'll see you this evening."

Aiden bowed low, his gaze flicking to Oberon. But the king was ignoring him once more; looking bored as he stared out at the court. Straightening, Aiden left the room with a nod to Mare. He passed out the servants' door, avoiding another confrontation with

Triglav, and wended to the city where Tatiana was supposed to be located. He took off towards the main street, but how was he supposed to know where this address was?

It'd been years since he'd last seen her, and he couldn't remember if she'd been particularly unpleasant. If he didn't remember, that was a good thing… wasn't it?

Stepping onto the street, he yelped as a car swerved around him. He stumbled, another car narrowly missing him. Aiden scrambled to get out of the road and looked at the place he crossed. Herds of cars were moving in two even lines. Perhaps he should call one of those "taxi" things Wyn had told him about… but how? He scanned the lines of people pushing past him. None of them looked to be calling a taxi, though some were just waiting. Perhaps he should wait too, but he didn't have the time.

Pulling a bit of magic into his throat, Aiden leaned into the street. "Come, taxi!" he shouted. Several people, both human and fae, gave him odd looks. Aiden cleared his throat and shrank in on himself. Wyn had been so bold when she'd done it. She hadn't even needed to use the car's name.

"You new or something?"

Aiden looked down to see an elf man, no taller than his knee, clutching a pretzel. "I—"

"You gotta hold out your hand like you mean it. You're calling a cab, not a dog."

Aiden's face heated. How was it that he'd read countless books on the Human Realm but managed to humiliate himself every time he was here? Swallowing hard, Aiden stepped back up to the curb and stuck out his hand.

"Like you mean it!" the elf said. Aiden scowled but lifted his chin and straightened his arm. The elf pushed him aside. "Hey, taxi!"

Almost immediately, an orange car pulled away from the flow of traffic to stop before Aiden. "You did it," he said, beholding the magnificent vehicle. It was covered in a fine mist of salt but gleamed like a fresh, Summer citrus beneath. Its rounded body and glowing light on top spoke of finery surpassing all of the other cars along the road.

"You're welcome," the elf said as he strode away. "Tourists, I tell you…"

"You getting in?" the taxi driver asked.

Fumbling with the door handle, Aiden scrambled inside. The scents of smoke and alcohol clung to the cracked seats as Aiden examined the inside. A screen, like that of Wyn's phone but bigger, clung to the back of the front seat. He ran a finger across it, and the picture reacted, lighting up. Fascinating!

"Hey buddy, you gonna tell me where we're going?"

"Oh, um," Aiden passed him the paper Mab had given him.

The driver gave it a quick look and handed it back. "Posh place." He studied Aiden from the rearview mirror. "You applying for a job?"

"No." Was making conversation with this man part of the cost of being taken to one's location? Perhaps he should've asked their Majesties for more information and gained a better understanding of the location to be able to wend there.

They drove through crowded, unfamiliar streets. Aiden watched the parade of cars on either side, each so different and filled with all types of humans and fae. Perhaps one day, once he found Wyn, he could learn to operate one of these for himself. How hard could it be if so many others were doing it?

As the cars grew fewer, the buildings grew grander, shifting from plain, glassy facades of gray and black to ornately carved ivory and crystalline. The taxi slowed and stopped before a structure shaped like a diamond bubble. Could this truly be Tatiana's school? It was far more elegant than Wyn's.

"This is it." The taxi driver held out a hand in front of Aiden and stared expectantly.

Right, the man needed to be paid… but how much? Reaching into his pocket, Aiden glamoured several leaves into human money and handed it to the man, hoping it was enough.

The taxi driver's eyes widened. "D-do you need change?"

"No, keep it." Aiden slid out of the car. At least his glamours lasted years rather than the minutes that most green fae cast. The man might at least get some use from it.

Aiden approached the building in awe of its beauty. Iridescent windows glistened at the point of the diamond, forming a door which opened automatically as he approached. Aiden paused to inspect it. There was no tingle of fae magic; this door's craft was human. There must be some mechanism or lever making it open. The door jerked as if to close, and Aiden jumped inside the building as it shut behind him. He blinked. Perhaps next time he saw Wyn she could explain how the doors worked.

"Can I help you?" a dwarf woman said from behind a long white desk. Behind her on a wood slat wall were the words "Berrypine Academy." She stroked her long, braided beard as he approached.

Aiden cleared his throat. "I'm here to take Tatiana home." He handed the woman the note Mab had given him.

"And does she know you?" the woman asked.

"I think so—yes."

The dwarf raised an eyebrow and pressed a button on a white machine. "Is Tatiana ready to go? There is someone here to collect her."

There was a long pause, and for a moment, Aiden thought the strange device wouldn't respond. "She'll be right down," a voice came from the machine.

Aiden's eyes went wide. What he wouldn't give to take the device apart and study it. How did the sound carry without magic?

The dwarf woman looked up. "You're from Fairy?"

Aiden nodded.

"It's an intercom," she said. "We prefer to use a mix of technology and magic here so the students aren't so jarred when they graduate and go off to whatever realm."

A fairy woman floated down the stairs, followed by three luggage trunks. Aiden frowned. Tatiana hadn't been a fairy the last time she'd seen her. Then, behind the luggage, came a girl vaguely resembling the scraggly child he remembered. She had dirty blond hair braided into one plait down her back. Bushy eyebrows straining to meet in the center of her forehead hovered atop eyes nearly as dull as a human's—nearly. Aiden reminded himself that she was half human. Did she even know?

"So, they sent you?" she said when they reached the bottom stair.

Aiden bowed, unsure of what to say.

Luckily, the fairy spoke before he was forced to. "Please don't go, Tatiana. At least finish the year and get your diploma."

"I don't really have a choice," Tatiana said. "Staying here is much preferable to being in Fairy. But mother says." She rolled her eyes at Aiden.

The fairy woman wrapped Tatiana in a tight hug and closed her eyes. "We're going to miss you so much, dear one..." Aiden's chest tightened. He doubted Mab was capable of showing half the affection this woman had.

Tatiana returned the hug and rested her cheek against the woman's shoulder. "I'm going to miss you, too."

They separated, and the woman kissed Tatiana's cheek. "Be a good girl and stay in touch."

Tatiana didn't meet her eyes. Instead, she looked to Aiden. "Come on then, let's go."

The woman let the luggage sink to the ground. Aiden snapped his fingers, and it rose back into the air to follow them. He didn't miss the fairy's narrowed gaze as if to ask, as most did, what type of fae he was.

Rather than answer her unspoken question, he led the way back out the mesmerizing door, Tatiana following him in silence. She wore a light jacket of fleece. The city where the school was located was just as cold as it had been at Wyn's parent's house, but it was nothing compared to the tundra of the Winter Realm.

"Do you have a warmer jacket?" he asked.

"The cold doesn't bother me."

Aiden frowned. He'd noticed Mab didn't change from her glamorous gowns when she deigned to go outside. Perhaps Tatiana inherited her mother's imperviousness to temperature. "If you wish." He groped in his jacket pocket and withdrew a small pouch of fairy wing powder. Cringing, he took a pinch and glanced over to Tatiana. As he tossed it into the air, he could have sworn he heard her say something about it being barbaric. But that wasn't possible; she was Mab and Oberon's daughter.

He wended to the edge of the bridge and took the girl's hand as he guided her across the slippery ice. By some miracle, she seemed to have little trouble gliding across the slick surface.

Triglav bowed and said nothing to Aiden as they passed through the doors. Tatiana gasped as they stepped inside the warm palace. Her eyes trailed up to the green fae soldiers captured and displayed within the chandelier. For a moment, Aiden thought she would remark on it, but she turned back to the entrance and frowned.

"Who was that?"

"Triglav. He was a lord of Winter before we took it."

"Why is he a guard if he was an enemy? Shouldn't he be locked up?"

There it was, the mentality of her parents. Triglav was a Winter fae, so he should be locked up. Typical. Aiden forced his features to be neutral. "He betrayed Winter early on. This is his reward."

"Seems like a pretty crappy reward." Her gaze flicked again to the chandelier, but she said nothing.

Aiden blinked; her language was like Wyn's, so… human. Who could this girl be now? Their Majesties saw Triglav's fate as amusingly cruel, but she seemed to think the dungeon was a mercy—perhaps it was.

He picked up his pace; he didn't have time to worry about Tatiana's character. The faster he got rid of her, the faster he could go off in search of Wyn. Perhaps he would try the dungeons first. If he could just find the prince… but his magic wasn't strong enough to sense gold fae.

Tatiana gazed around the palace. The frost-covered walls glittered in the fairy light illuminating the series of elegantly crafted arches and pillars leading to the pale doors to the ballroom. She hadn't been there for the conquest of Winter or the fall of Autumn. It must have been a welcomed change from the troll caves they'd stayed in before.

"This place is…" She continued to stare. "This place is too grand. I miss Grandfather's cave in the mountains."

Oh. He squirmed as she turned her intent gaze on him. His mind flicked back to the time they'd spent in the Troll Mountains just before the first attack. Aiden had quickly grown sick of sleeping on the hard ground and training in the frigid mountain climate. But Tatiana hadn't experienced such hardships there. Her expression now was soft, almost as though she were on the verge of tears. The troll chief had died in the first battle of Winter. Had Mab not told her? "He's—"

"Dead. I know. I miss it—that's all. Do I have a room in this place?" She gestured to a staircase gilded with sparkling ice diamonds.

"Of course, yes," Aiden said, leading her up the stairs and to the wing of the palace he rarely visited, where their Majesties slept. Mab had designated a room for Tatiana when they'd first conquered this palace. Why hadn't they sent for her then?

"You don't talk as much as I remember." Tatiana's eyes still roved the halls, occasionally resting on the magically warped portraits of the green fae, as she followed him.

Aiden stopped himself from saying he'd learned to train his tongue, so it wouldn't get him in trouble. "Much has changed. I've been involved in the war efforts."

She wrapped her arms around herself. "I suppose that would quiet a person. What about Mare and Dek? Are they as silent as you?"

"Dek… died." The words fell flat like heavy stones weighing on his chest. What did she even know about Dek? She was hardly close enough to grieve him. She'd been living comfortably in a fancy human school while he and Dek had been forced into battle.

"Oh, Mother didn't say. I'm so sorry." She looked down. Despite all of them being around the same age, it was always made clear that he, Mare, and Dek were less than Tatiana. Mare had been the only one who hadn't distanced herself from Tatiana. Perhaps to have the company of another girl. "What about Mare? She was always chatty."

"She's still around," Aiden said. He nearly pitied the soft mewling in her voice. Almost. The undertones of loneliness were painfully familiar. He knew too well what it was like to be ripped from a happy life and forced into something new and ominous. But Tatiana wouldn't suffer as he had.

"Perhaps you could ask her to visit me? Or I will go see her…" Tatiana trailed off. "This place is so eerie. I've been terrified of coming back here, to be honest."

"Oh?" Aiden couldn't help the curiosity creeping into his voice. She was the princess; what did she have to fear from Mab and Oberon?

"Of course, the news always shows Mother and Father as the bad guys. The horrible rebels destroying Fairy. I don't want to be associated with that. But I also don't want to be treated as a lower-class citizen just because I'm not a green or gold fae."

"I understand," Aiden said as they passed through the ballroom and entered the far hall leading into the palace's royal wing.

"Do you? I never got the impression that you were truly passionate about the cause."

Aiden shrugged. "I am still here." He opened a door gilded with icy roses and guided her luggage inside.

Tatiana stepped into the room and gaped. A fire blazed in an icy hearth while two plush, red armchairs invited them to watch it. Beyond the sitting room, a large bed covered in furs sprawled in the center of a large bedroom. "This place is huge. Far bigger than anything we had back at school. Still… I'd rather be there with my friends and Mrs. Fox." She gazed pleadingly up at him, and Aiden took a step back.

"Then why are you here?" He pressed his lips together, not meaning for the question to slip out.

"Didn't my parents tell you? I'm supposed to be married off to the Summer Prince. End the war and all. I'm trying to do the right thing."

Choking on his breath, Aiden stared at her, eyes wide. "You're—the prince?" The Summer royals would never agree to marry their son to Tatiana, no matter how powerful the Dark Fae were. How was this possible?

"I know. Wild, right? At least I've heard he's cute. What girl wouldn't want to marry him?" She rolled her eyes.

Before he could suppress them, flames sprung to life along Aiden's arms. "I can think of at least one," he gritted out.

Tatiana jumped back. "Are you all right?"

"Fine. I just…" Aiden trailed off. He needed a plan to get into Elessea and confront the prince himself. Tiny skirmishes along the border to draw him out weren't going to cut it. If their Majesties and the prince were somehow working together, then Wyn was in more danger than he'd initially thought. "I need to go."

"Wait." Tatiana reached for his arm but stopped short at the flames.

"Forgive me, I must —"

"There you are." Mare stuck her head into the room, her gaze fixed on Aiden.

"Mare! It's so good to see you!" Tatiana rushed over to her, but Mare stiffened.

"Your Highness," she said, dipping her head.

"Mare, it's me. You don't have to be like that."

Mare didn't seem to take notice of the heartbreak in Tatiana's eyes and turned back to Aiden. "You're needed. Summer attacked the town we took… and they brought the crown."

CHAPTER 14

Freddie

Freddie stared at the spot in the dining room where Freya had been standing. All had returned to normal as though she'd never been there. Her body trembled as she looked to Pelrin, whose expression was just as horrified as hers. How had this happened? Was this the same thing that took Daniel? Raul growled, his fur on end, racing forward towards the spot where Freya had vanished. Throwing herself in front of him, Freddie stopped her friend just before the now empty space.

"Careful," Pelrin said as he followed after her. "Whatever magic took her could still be active."

Freddie bit her lip and inched forward, Raul close at her heels. Would Aiden's ring be powerful enough to protect her? He was a blue fae after all… But Raul wasn't safe, and even Pelrin could be taken at a moment's notice; she couldn't be trapped here alone.

"There's nothing here." She held out a hand, feeling the spot on the floor, her throat tight. Turning around to face Pelrin, Freddie clenched and unclenched her fists. "Can you sense anything?"

He shook his head. "It seems whatever was here is gone now."

"Do you think she said too much? It seems like —" She pointed to the ceiling and Pelrin looked up. "Doesn't want us to know what happened to everyone else." Freya had been so afraid of them taking her back. What had happened to Daniel? Freya seemed to know. Gritting her teeth, Freddie pressed her palms against the table.

"It's more likely they don't want us to know where we are. If Freya and Daniel are in the true Winter Palace, maybe the vortex was a good thing. If we'd followed after her, maybe there'd be a way to get there and break the curse."

"Or it could be a trap. We have no idea what was waiting for Freya. And even if we did, you'd still be a bear, and I — I wouldn't be able to fight Mab and Oberon." She glanced back at the door. There was something about it; perhaps something that could help them. But without being able to go inside, she wouldn't even know what to look for.

"Pel, what do you know about curses? What typically breaks them?" Maybe it was too risky to talk about this specific curse, but surely curses in general wouldn't activate the vortex.

Pelrin looked around, his expression grim. "I — I'm not sure we should keep talking about this. Freya just got sucked up, and you're right, the two of us are no match for the Dark Fae — at least not in this condition." Raul sneezed, and Pelrin looked down at him, eyes narrowed.

"Please, Pel, we're so close. We know who cursed us, and it's not too hard to figure out they wanted you out of the way. They're using Freya and Daniel, and perhaps the other students, to keep watch on us. I mean they vanish them whenever we get too close. Be vague if you have to, but I just need to know what I'm looking for to get out of this place, to get us all out."

"Even if you know how to break a curse, I doubt it would help you, Fred. There's nothing we can do so long as we're trapped in this castle."

"Then just tell me, please."

He huffed a sigh and sat. "You could destroy the magical item that is the source of the curse. But it doesn't necessarily need to be near the impacted party to work, so it could be anywhere in Fairy. I doubt they'd keep it here where we can get to it. Then there's always killing the caster, but since we have no way of leaving, there's probably a small chance we'd be able to get to them and an even smaller chance I'd be able to kill them on my own."

Freddie pressed her lips together. Killing Mab and Oberon would be near impossible, and Pelrin was right; they wouldn't store the object of the curse here. Her chest squeezed — then they were trapped, and there was nothing they could do but wait. Even if they were able to open a vortex to the Winter Palace, Mab and Oberon could easily order Aiden to defend them, and he'd be helpless to stand aside. And if by some miracle, Pelrin — in bear form — won, it would mean losing Aiden, if he wasn't dead already.

Tears pricked the corners of her eyes. It was hopeless.

"Oh," Pelrin's lips quirked as he looked at Freddie. "There's also true love's kiss."

"I don't think so, seal breath." She swiped at her face and turned to glare at him — despair erupting to fury. "Even if there was a chance that would work, there's no true love here."

Pelrin looked down. "Some of us have held onto true love…" he muttered.

She scowled. Pelrin knew what he did. There was a time when a kiss may have worked, but now she'd just be grateful if Pelrin stopped chasing her. Besides, he didn't have to sleep with that fae girl. He made his choice — a human just wasn't enough for him.

It was another useless solution.

"I'm going back to my room," she sighed.

"Freddie, wait," Pelrin called after her, but she couldn't look at him. Old anger burned in her chest as she stomped up the staircase, Raul following behind.

They stepped out into a bedroom; no doubt the walls in this one were charred too. A thought prickled in the back of her mind. Even if Mab and Oberon were holding them captive here, it didn't explain the vision, the flickering lights, and the moving rooms. Maybe whatever was haunting this place was trying to give her a clue on how to get out. But how were they connected to the students? The Dark Fae curse? As though it read her thoughts, the lights flickered again.

"Fred, run. We've gotta get out of here," Raul said as he

bounded to the door.

"I think—just wait a moment. It might be trying to tell us something."

A cool wind washed over them, and there was the blue fae woman again. The bedroom melted into the hall that sometimes resided outside Freddie's door as the woman strode down it. Eyes widening, Freddie stared as the woman knocked on the familiar door to her room.

A soft voice beckoned her to enter, and Freddie and Raul followed her inside.

"We shouldn't be doing this." Raul glared up at her.

She put a finger to her lips. "Quiet, they'll hear." They tiptoed behind the woman as she stood in the doorway, but she didn't seem to notice them. Raul leaned his head out to sniff her and sneezed. Freddie jumped but the woman didn't react.

"I think this is just a mirage," Raul said, creeping forward. Freddie followed after him, and the woman turned as though looking right at them but said nothing as they rushed into the room and closed the door.

"Eira." Another woman, with gold wings, leapt from the chair and raced over to the blue fairy. She must be a royal. Wrapping her arms around her neck, the gold fairy beamed up at her companion. "I'm so glad you're home."

"With bad news I'm afraid," the blue fairy said as she buried her face into the other woman's long, dark hair.

"What is it? What's wrong?" Backing away, the gold fae broke the embrace and stared up into the other woman's face. "You've never looked so troubled."

"You may wish to sit." She gestured at the chairs, and the gold fae sat.

Freddie looked to Raul. "Do you have any idea what's going on?"

"Of course not, why would I know anything about Winter?" He hissed.

"I think…" Freddie looked around the room; it was much the same as her room now, but decorated with portraits of other dark haired gold fae. On the ornate tables were images of the two women, smiling and laughing. Where had they all gone? "I think this might be the past."

"Well that would explain how there's a blue fairy here. This must be a really long time ago."

The gold fairy sat back in her arm chair, her brow creased. The blue fairy crossed over to her.

"My Queen," she began.

"Eira, stop. Sit with me." The queen held out a hand, and Eira took it.

"Dani, we're not safe. My trip to Summer did not go well. We found out some troubling things about the king."

"Troubling how?" The queen's voice trembled as she tightened her grip.

"He showed us the army — it's growing more powerful by the day. He's even drafting his own people by will or no. At first, we thought he feared an attack from the Sea Realm; it's so close, and they are so easily offended. Then the spies found this." She held out a slip of paper depicting three of the four objects of power: the Staff of Wind, the Crown of Flames, and the Orb of Ice. There was a question mark where the fourth, the object of Spring, should've been.

Freddie pulled her lips tight. Even back then Spring had kept their object a secret. Perhaps Summer was just curious as to what it was. Although the king and queen had always been a tad haughty, it was just to humans and brown fae, which the other realms looked down upon too... at least she thought they did. Besides, they had a strong army now, but they only used it in defense.

"This doesn't mean anything. It could be a coincidence." The queen placed a kiss on Eira's cheek. "Stop your worrying. We'll be fine."

Eira shook her head. "I thought much the same at first, but I followed him just to be sure. He was talking to his generals about going after our orb. We're not far by sea. I came back here as soon as I could, but they're coming. We need to get our people out. Now."

"They're attacking? But the other realms…"

"Spring would rather flee, and their army is weak. They only focus on defense. And all of Autumn has taken the 'path of peace.' They don't even have an army."

"What about the North?"

"They would never get here in time."

The queen's face crumpled. Fat tears rolled from her eyes, and the blue fairy pulled her close. "We can send our people to the isles, Lo and Veridian. They won't look for them there."

Eira shook her head. "That's Summer territory. The king would hunt them down. There's a portal not too far that leads to the Human Realm. They'll be safe there — Summer wouldn't think to attack the humans."

"Then we shall do it. What about the orb?"

"The king has no blue fairy to sense it. If I hide it with strong wards, it'll be impossible for anyone but another with blue magic to enter."

The queen nodded, and the blue fairy turned, looking straight at Freddie and Raul. Freddie stiffened, reminding herself that the woman probably couldn't see her. Behind the fairy, the queen vanished in a cloud of gold dust. Freddie blinked up at the woman whose expression softened.

"Let me help you," she said and walked over to the window. Freddie glanced back at where the queen had been. There was no one behind her. Her eyes widened as realization dawned.

"How?" Freddie croaked, her voice all but gone in shock. She glanced at Raul who was staring, jaw open at the woman.

The blue fairy smiled and cupped her hands beneath her mouth. She blew and what looked like glittering snowflakes left her hands and snaked out between the curtains. "Like this." Throwing open the drapes, the woman disappeared in a flood of moonlight.

Freddie threw up her hands to shield her face as her eyes adjusted to the brilliance. Beside her, Raul let out a long cry. Freddie dropped her hands to squint at him.

"Do you have a towel?" he whined. Crouching on the floor, Raul— human Raul—covered himself, his expression pitiful.

"Oh, dear." Freddie raced off to the bedroom and returned with a large nightgown from her closet—no, the queen's. Apparently, it didn't produce men's clothing. Raul had just tugged it on when there was a knock at the door, and it burst open.

She let out an exasperated sigh. "Pelrin, what do you want?"

Pelrin's jaw dropped as he stared from Freddie to Raul. "How did you—what—when—for how long? Why did you bring Raul here?"

"Really? That is what you ask. Why I brought Raul here... well, Pelrin, I didn't bring Raul here. We were KIDNAPPED."

Pelrin's eyes widened. "I just thought you'd got a dog, and it'd be nice... oh no."

She got to her feet, all hints of the fear and confusion from the vision gone, replaced by the anger that had been building throughout the curse. Pelrin fought against Mab and Oberon all the time; he should at least have the guts to try and get out of here.

"You stole me from my life and what, expected me to play Scooby Doo with you for the next year? I have a life Pelrin, those students are still missing, and no one cares because they're in Fairy. Someone has to help them."

"And why does that someone have to be you? Think of how hard it was for me being trapped here alone, with no one I knew."

"I asked you countless times to look for them, and you refused."

"My people are dying out there in the war, and I'm not able to protect them. I couldn't just send my soldiers to roam Fairy looking for some humans. And besides, even if I knew they were in the Winter Palace, it's not like I could just fly up and knock on the front door."

"You selfish prick. I find it funny you just wanted to wait out the curse, rather than search for a solution, since you care for your people so much."

Pelrin growled, and the sheer ferocity of the sound and the yellowing teeth of the polar bear made her take a step back, the pace of her heartbeat doubling.

"How did you even end up in this mess?"

He scoffed. "I got caught because I was chasing that faun for you. It was a trap, and he was ready with wing powder to drag me back to Mab and Oberon. If it wasn't for me, it'd be you under this curse."

Freddie stumbled back as though she'd been slapped. No, she wouldn't have fallen for the satyr's trap. It was Pelrin's fault he was here… Still, the reasoning sounded false no matter how often she replayed it in her mind.

Unshed tears glistened in her eyes. Pelrin was wrong. The words she'd been longing to say for the past year bubbled up to her throat. "If you didn't try so hard to protect me all the time, maybe you wouldn't have fallen into the trap. The satyr was caught, and I was fine. I'm always fine. I don't need you, Pelrin. I never did."

Pelrin flinched, and his face crumpled. "I — I'm sorry."

Freddie blinked, her jaw trembled as the words swam in her head like wisps on a breeze. "That's really human of you…"

Fae never gave pleasantries: pleases, thank yous, and sorrys were not in their vocabulary. Still her heart blazed even as guilt clawed at it. Pelrin bowed his head; the words were true, but she hadn't wanted to hurt him. Perhaps some leftover feelings for him had held her tongue, but he needed to know, and he wasn't taking any of her hints.

Sinking into an armchair, she let out a breath as her anger cooled. "All right, Pel, let's just figure out where we go from here."

He buried his head in his paws. "I — this curse, Fred. I didn't want to drag you in, but… I was scared."

Her heart clenched. "Is there something you're not telling me? I can help, just trust me."

"I won't let them hurt you. Please, just wait it out; just you and me. Raul needs to go."

"Go? As in…"

"Go home. Geeze, Fred, you don't think I would —"

Freddie let out a breath. She wasn't sure what she thought Pelrin might do. The situation was so dire, and they'd already lost two people. They were trapped, weren't they?

"In that case, it'd be my pleasure," Raul said as he gave a mock curtsy in his nightgown. "Whenever you're ready, I'm happy to leave this loco place."

"And how is he supposed to get back?"

"I can take you to the Human Realm tomorrow," Pelrin said.

Freddie's eyes widened. "The Human Realm? This whole time—"

"I need to take Raul home. It could mess with the curse if he stays."

"And you're taking me home, too?" Freddie asked.

"No." Pelrin's voice quieted. "I can only be away from the castle for a week. If you go home for longer, I'll die."

A dull pain pulsed through Freddie's chest—of course she didn't want Pelrin to die. But her chest ached with homesickness. "And you chose now to tell me? Where else can you go? Why haven't you summoned an army to break us out?"

"Mab and Oberon threatened to attack Elessea if I returned to Summer. As long as I stay here and no one sees my true face. I'm sorry I didn't tell you."

Freddie frowned. "And you think they would tell the truth?"

"I can't afford to sacrifice my people on the chance they might not be honest."

She supposed, if it was for his people, Pelrin was doing the right thing. And if she stayed with him, she'd be saving lives, too. Pulling her lips tight, she rounded on Raul.

"And what about you? You're fine just leaving?"

"Hey, I love you, Fred, but if I stay here with the two of you, I might just sacrifice myself to the ghosts."

Freddie rolled her eyes. It wasn't fair to him, and if Raul stayed, it would only make things more dangerous.

"Don't worry, Freddie, I'll pro—" Pelrin stopped short. "I'll keep you company." He got to his feet and cocked his head. "Come on, Raul, let's just go to bed. We'll leave in the morning." The two of them headed off to the bedroom, and Freddie leapt from her chair.

"Uhhh, what are you two doing?"

"This bed is huge," Raul said, gesturing at the Alaskan sized mattress. "We can all fit."

Freddie sighed. "Fine, but I'm not sleeping with a bear. Sorry, Pel."

"I won't be a bear; you know that. And anyway I've been sleeping with you every night. There's room in here for three."

"Fine. I don't want you to die, and I suppose there's room... But you both stay on the edges, and no pervy dreams."

Pelrin chuckled, and Freddie shot him a glare. On the other end of the bed, Raul was already curled up, his eyes closed. Pelrin waved a paw, and even the moonlight was snuffed out. Laying back on her pillow, Freddie listened to him rustle around next to her and batted away his wing tip. Finally, he stilled, tucking his wings at his back. She jerked as a familiar hand closed around hers.

"See, it's me. It's really me."

"Save it, Pel. I'm tired." Tears welled in her eyes. At least tomorrow she'd be able to go home, for a little while. But how would she explain all this to her parents? Maybe it wasn't even worth going to see them, breaking their hearts all over again when she left. Freddie closed her eyes as her mind drifted between her mother's tears, castles filled with beasts, and the strange blue fairy.

CHAPTER 15

Aiden

Mab brushed past them as Aiden followed Mare into the throne room. Her face glowed as she all but ran towards Tatiana's room. The familiar pang of homesickness struck at Aiden's heart; but his mother and his home were gone.

Oberon's eyes narrowed as they approached, and though he leaned back in his throne, his body was tense. Aiden couldn't help but suppress the flare of rage in his chest as he gazed upon the king's adorned antlers. A vain waste of magic, his magic, that he could be using in the war.

Aiden gave Oberon a curt bow. Unlike Mab, Oberon didn't require the dramatic display of loyalty—he knew Aiden had no choice.

"I have missions for the two of you, and they need to be executed quickly. You'll need to leave now." Oberon sat up and scrutinized Mare and Aiden. Mare cast her eyes away from him, and a muscle flexed in Oberon's jaw. "Summer has finally fought back in the Sunset Valley. It seems the lives of their people were less important than territory—it's good to know."

"We can go and organize the troops," Aiden said, but Oberon shook his head.

"They'll be fine for the time being. What I need you to do is hunt down a way to destroy Summer for good."

Aiden's brow creased, and he opened his mouth to reply but shut it again. How was he supposed to do that? If Summer had the Crown like Mare had said, there was little else he could do than confront the prince head on. And unless their Majesties had done something to him, Aiden feared he might not survive the encounter.

"I see your confusion, but worry not. I don't expect you to think." Oberon's lips curled into a cruel smile. "Boy, you will return to the Nightmare Plains and have the witch brew me a curse. One that will render Summer useless."

A sick feeling ran through Aiden's stomach. The idea of returning to the Plains without Mare made his skin itch. How was he supposed to get past the nightmares and convince her mother to brew him something on his own? But he didn't voice his concerns aloud. From the look on Oberon's face, their Majesties would expect him to come up with the payment on his own.

"And you, Mare," Oberon said with a sly grin. "You will spy on Elessea. Find me their weaknesses and the best place to release the curse. It, of course, won't be your first time there."

Mare swallowed hard and nodded. She looked as though she were going to throw up...

"Go."

Aiden took a step towards the door, but Oberon ordered him to stop. Body going rigid, Aiden inwardly cursed the life debt that gave their Majesties complete control over him.

"The wards are down — leave right now."

Mare shot a worried glance at Aiden as shadows enclosed around her body. He bit his lip and wended. Oberon might not show it, but he was likely worried about Summer. They had the Crown, and their Majesties merely had Mare and him. There was still a chance they could win.

Black water lapped gently against the orange sands as he reappeared. A breeze wafted past, and although it wasn't cold, he shuddered. Just stay on the path. He'd be fine if he focused on his feet and ignored his surroundings. At least he hoped that was how this realm worked. Gritting his teeth, Aiden took off down the path.

Screams and growls surrounded him, but he remained focused on the road in front of him. Wyn's voice called out to him, and he froze. He'd longed to hear her voice, now even moreso after discovering her past with the prince. Was she all right? He looked up to see a Nightmare hovering above her, but she didn't seem to notice. Aiden's heart lurched, and his muscles screamed at him to save her, but he told himself it wasn't real. Wherever Wyn was, it wasn't in the Nightmare Plains.

The nightmare attacked, and Aiden turned his head as Wyn screamed. Taking a shuddering breath, he returned his attention to the path and took small steps onward. The rock where Mare's mom lived rose up from the horizon, and he sighed. As he grew closer, his heart pounded faster. The wrongness of the air was to be expected, but it felt no more comfortable as he approached, and this time he was alone.

Aiden stepped into the dark of the entrance to Mare's mom's home. He tried to conjure his flames to his hand to light the way, but nothing happened. Again and again he tried, panic building in his throat.

"Now, now, let's not have any of that." With a snap of her fingers Mare's mom appeared in a pool of slowly spreading light. "Ahhh, it's the suffering one. Welcome back, love." She smiled, revealing her pointed teeth.

He swallowed and bowed to her. "I've come with a request from King Oberon."

"I bet you have." She circled him, licking her lips. Aiden eyed her. If she could turn off his magic, what else could she do? Would she attack? "And what curse would the false king want me to brew up?"

"H-he would like something that would bring down Summer. Something he can use to attack Elessea."

She wrinkled her nose. "I never did like those Summertons; always dumping their rubbish here. But I think another trade is warranted for this curse. Don't you?"

"I have nothing to offer. My life is not even mine to give."

Speaking the words aloud, solidifying their truth, stung more than he expected.

"There will come a time where you will have to make a choice. If you use this curse, you'll take the path of the greatest pain. Then, I will come and feed." She grinned, and Aiden stumbled a step back.

"You mean, you can leave here?"

She chuckled. "Of course, as easily as Mare. Well, even easier. I don't have to trudge to the lake. Do we have an agreement?"

"What will happen to me when you…"

"Nothing worse than what you already experience each night, though it might take you longer to wake after I'm done with you."

"And if I don't make the painful choice?"

"This curse will ensure you will."

He blinked back tears. Had he not suffered enough these months? Though it was not as if he had any other option. Oberon had ordered a curse, and a curse Aiden would deliver.

"Do we have a bargain?" Mare's mom held out a small silver dagger.

Aiden nodded and extended his hand.

Quick as a water sprite, she swiped the blade across his palm. He hissed and clenched his fist, silver trickling through his fingers. What new horror had he brought unto himself?

Mare's mom dropped the dagger into her cauldron and snapped her fingers. A black flame flared up around it as she added an assortment of liquids and powders into it. "Tell me, love, what do you want this curse to do?"

"I-I'm not sure. Just something that disables all of Elessea."

She put a black-tipped finger to her chin. "I've made this one a couple times before, but it's always a favorite of mine. And the activation is so fun!"

Aiden grimaced. What would Wyn think of him cursing so many people? Did this go beyond her forgiveness?

Dropping something into the cauldron, she danced over to Aiden. "There is something troubling you."

"I'm fine."

"You're worried. I can taste it, not as good as your fear, but —
"

Aiden doubled over as a spike of pain pierced his chest. Sinking to his knees, he stared up, eyes wide at Mare's mom.

"Oops." She put a hand to her mouth, and the pain eased. "I didn't mean to get so excited. But tell me where you think she is, and maybe I'll tell you where she really is."

"You know where—" Aiden stopped himself. What if it was a trap? What if she wanted to go after Wyn to cause him more pain?

"Yes, I know where your precious Wyn is, and I bet it will make you even more delicious."

Aiden grit his teeth. "Why don't you just tell me?"

She smirked and peered into the potion. "Nearly there. Your sweet love is with one who shares your greatest weakness."

"She's with a fairy? There are hundreds of thousands of fairies. How is that supposed to help?"

"Hmmm... I thought you were brighter than that. Perhaps it would help if you knew she was with someone who wishes to keep her safe."

Aiden folded his arms across his chest. "Her sweatshirt was covered in blood. I sincerely doubt they were concerned about her safety."

She shrugged and reached a hand into the cauldron, pulling out what looked like a large silver needle. "This is how you are to defeat Summer."

Aiden took it from her, examining the length of the thin blade. "How does it work?"

"You only have to draw blood from a gold fae, and all of Elessea will fall under an enchanted sleep. It'll be beautiful."

Taking the needle, he placed it into the pocket inside his jacket. "Now, tell me of Wyn."

A dark laugh erupted from the woman's chest. "She's where you least want her to be, with your greatest enemy."

Aiden's eyes widened. "The prince? But how? Mab and Oberon are supposed to have the prince now."

"Yes, they got a plaything for the bear they tamed. But Wyn is not under the spell of your rulers. There's still hope. I know you'll make the wrong choice."

Heart drumming, a roaring sounded in his ears. Wyn couldn't be with the prince, not with their history, not knowing how cruel the prince truly was.

"I must go," he muttered.

Mare's mom laughed, once again dousing the cavern in darkness. He hastened back down the path. If any of the nightmares called out to him, he didn't hear them. As soon as he showed the curse to Oberon he'd search for the prince. This time he'd go through any lengths to find him, even if he had to confront Mab directly. If their Majesties and the prince were close to Wyn, he needed to get to her, and fast.

CHAPTER 16

Freddie

Icy wind whipped across Freddie's face as she let the soothing sleep spell overtake her. Aiden's ring tucked safely in her pocket, she buried herself into Pelrin's thick fur, not wanting him to grow suspicious if his magic failed to affect her yet again. Around them, the snow-dusted tundra blurred past underneath the glow of the green and purple lights. Pelrin had said it would take three full days to reach her parents' and another three to return. But a day back home was better than being trapped in the haunted ice castle alone while he returned Raul.

Closing her eyes, she dreamed of the home she'd known all her life — the welcoming pale pink walls of her room. Everything in its place, as though she'd never been dragged off.

How would her parents feel when they saw her again? Would they be angry or worried? Both? Freddie tried to picture their faces, the microfiber of her mom's favorite robe brushing against her cheek as she sank into a hug, and her father's stiff face melting into a smile as it so rarely did.

Raul whooped, waking her up. They were in the wooded part of her back yard. Darkness covered the street, save for the moonlight making the grass glitter with frost.

"We're home!" he said, swinging himself off Pelrin's back. He cursed as he hit the cold ground in his slippers — the only shoes the wardrobe would produce for him. Her own efforts had been more successful with her white, hip-length tunic, enchanted fur coat, and fur lined leggings — warm boots covered her feet, protecting her from the cold.

Freddie, too, slid off Pelrin, crept up to the back door window, and peered through. The house looked dead as though abandoned, not sleeping as it should be. Lights still brightened the windows of the other homes on the street, so it couldn't possibly be that late.

"Pel, what time is it?" she asked as she rounded the darkened house to the front door to find the spare key.

"Bears can't wear watches," Raul said as Pelrin cleared his throat; he glared at Raul, and Freddie rolled her eyes.

"It's best if your neighbors don't see a polar bear on their street. I'll find you tomorrow evening."

What would her parents think of her leaving again after only one day? They'd likely rather Pelrin die and have her return. She looked through one of the front windows. The furniture was gone — every trace of her family removed from existence. Her stomach sank. Where were they? The key usually tucked under the front mat was gone, but even worse, there was a realtor's lock on the front door.

Her parents couldn't possibly have moved. She'd only been gone a month at most… right? It was certainly not a year. She'd heard stories of people waiting years for their missing kids to come back. Surely her parents wouldn't just pack up and go.

"Where…" Freddie bit her lip. Her dad had vaguely mentioned DC if Mr. Fallus won the election, but it was never a sure thing. They wouldn't have left her, not unless… But surely her parents weren't so heartless as to abandon her simply because the Falluses said so? They wouldn't have done that.

Freddie took a deep breath, letting it out slowly between her teeth. She looked to Raul. "Let's go see Amanda. Maybe she'll know where they've gone. They can't have just disappeared."

"Like this?" Raul pointed between their fae garbs. Amanda's

parents were much more liberal than her own, but even they were wary about having their daughter date a vampire. Two missing kids showing up at their door looking at though they'd come from Fairy would surely be a shock.

"Amanda's brother might have something you can borrow. Besides, would you rather go home looking like that?"

Raul swallowed, looking down at the nightgown. His mother was the type to murder him for disappearing, and the thought he went to Fairy would be another thing to add fuel to her loving rage. "Fine. Let's just get there quick, and you go first. You at least could pass for a lady politician."

Pelrin poked his head around the side of the house. "Just one day, don't forget."

She sighed and raised her pinky finger. Across the street, Amanda's house cast a warm glow onto the sidewalk. Gone were the glittering holiday lights her mother had so meticulously put up. Raul moved behind Freddie, and she knocked.

When the door flew open, Amanda's mom glanced at her and half turned back inside. "Oh, Freddie, come on in. Amanda's upstairs." She started walking away, stopped, and rushed back to the door, locking her into a tight embrace. "Freddie, my God. You're back! Where have you been? We've all been so worried. Have you seen your parents?"

Freddie coughed and struggled in the woman's tight grasp. "It's good to see you too, Mrs. Lee. Have you seen my parents?"

"Of course, of course. Amanda! Get down here!"

"Why?" Amanda screamed from upstairs.

"Just get down here." Mrs. Lee was already smudging her eyeliner onto Freddie's face with her tears.

"Mom, I—" Amanda stopped at the top of the stairs. "Fred? Is that really you?"

"Hey, Buddy," Freddie said, finally escaping Mrs. Lee's grasp.

Amanda raced down the stairs and launched herself at Freddie. She squeezed her nearly as tight as her mother had, then pulled back and punched Freddie hard in the arm. "How dare you come back here like everything's okay. We thought you were kidnapped."

"Ow. I was." Freddie rubbed the spot on her arm that was no doubt going to bruise. "But I'm okay. It's complicated; I'll tell you everything later." Surely when Pelrin had said not to tell people about him, he didn't mean Amanda. It wasn't betraying a secret if she just told her bestie.

"Let me call your mom, Freddie. Your parents have been frantic without you. Have you eaten? Let me get you some food." She bustled off to the kitchen.

As soon as she was gone, Amanda rounded on Freddie. "Tell me everything, now. Everyone thinks Raul kidnapped you. Well, not everyone, but it's a pretty big theory."

Raul stepped out from behind the door. "Why am I blamed for everything?"

"Raul!" Amanda threw her arms around him. "What — what are you wearing? What are both of you wearing?"

"Can we go upstairs and explain?" Freddie asked.

"Yeah, of course, of course. My dad and brother are at the game, so we'll have all night. At least until my mom gets back." Amanda led them to her room and ran out to grab clothes from her brother's closet.

Freddie collapsed onto Amanda's bed. She hadn't thought about how hard it would be to return and have everyone want an explanation of where she'd been. Perhaps coming home had been a bad idea. Her mother, Amanda, everyone would be absolutely livid when she told them she would have to leave again tomorrow.

Amanda tossed a bundle of clothes at Raul.

"Thank you!" He turned his back to them and changed.

"So where have you guys been? Why were you together?"

"You don't want to know," Raul said, hopping into one leg of his sweats.

"Would you believe we were both kidnapped by a talking bear?" Freddie grinned as Amanda raised her fist, and she flinched away from her punch. "Okay, okay." Sitting up on the bed, Freddie told her everything, with Raul chiming in every so often to add the occasional forgotten detail. When they were finished, the room was quiet, and Amanda looked from one to the other as though expecting one of them to reveal a punchline.

"So Pelrin turned into a talking bear and thought it was a good idea to kidnap you both?" she said as though Freddie had been babbling nonsense. "And you've both been in Fairy?"

They nodded.

Freddie couldn't help but feel relieved. At least Amanda believed her. Maybe it wouldn't be so hard to explain to her parents and anyone else who asked.

"And you think Pelrin is actually this bear… Have you seen him? Like really seen him? You said he turns back each night and sleeps in your bed. That's really creepy."

"Well, he acts like him," Raul said.

"And I've felt his body, not in a weird way, but it's definitely a fairy sleeping next to me," Freddie said. "Why would he lie?"

Amanda frowned. "Lots of fae can lie. It could be Mab and Oberon getting revenge on you for hurting their recruiting efforts. Especially with that faun escaping and if Freya was there."

"It's a weird way to get revenge. They could've just killed me." Unless Aiden somehow talked them out of it. If he even could…

"Well, Jefferson will be relieved to hear Pelrin's all right… kinda. He's been in Summer since you left. Apparently, they kept saying Pelrin was too busy to see him. I figured he was off frantically looking for you and the guards were covering for him. But kidnapping you for his own selfish reasons does sound more like him."

"I never thought he'd be this extreme though."

"Well, now that you're back, we'll figure out a way for you to stay in the Human Realm."

"I can't just let Pelrin die!"

"All I was going to say was we need to break the curse and find an excuse for you going back. You know, for your parents." Amanda rested her cheek on her hand. "You could always say you're chasing a story. Everyone would believe that."

"That is true, but how would we explain the claw marks?"

"Maybe you can link it to side effects from those drugs I took,"

Raul said. "Tell your mom you're investigating the company, but it needs to be kept quiet. Then when you get back, you can actually investigate them." Raul clenched his hand into a fist.

"That's not a bad idea," Amanda said. "Make sure your parents don't tell the Falluses, though. They've been parading you around TV like some kind of conservative martyr."

"They what?" Heat flooded through Freddie. Surely her parents knew, even if she was dead, she wanted nothing to do with the Falluses.

"It's for a new bill he's trying to push through."

"What bill? What does it say?"

"The Human Protection Right, or the Fairy Ban. It pretty much says no matter the circumstance, no fae can cross the border from Fairy, and any fae suspected of crossing illegally will be sent back." Amanda took a deep breath and laced her fingers together while Freddie pressed her fingers to her temples, her jaw hanging open. "But let's focus on your issues right now. You saved Raul from some crazy lab people who wanted to experiment on werewolves."

"But they followed us back to your place and tried to kidnap us, and we only just escaped," Raul said.

"Guys, wait. What about Freya and the others? They wouldn't be able to cross the border, and they'll have to be sent back."

Amanda bit her lip. "Probably. I mean the bill says under no circumstance."

"But that's unreasonable. There's a war going on! People need a safe place to flee to. And all those students were kidnapped — going to Fairy wasn't their choice. I'm sure if people saw them and heard their story they would see how racist this bill really is." Freddie looked from Amanda to Raul.

"Well you better get them back fast; they're voting on it next month," Amanda said. "Let's just focus on one problem at a time, Fred. Make sure to stick to the story — my mom is like a truffle pig with lies." She got up and dug into a drawer, handing a pair of pajamas to Freddie.

"Thanks, Bud," Freddie said, taking the cartoon bird-printed bundle from her and changing.

As soon as she tugged the shirt over her head, the door burst open. Amanda's mom stood clutching her phone in both hands. "It's your mom, Freddie." She held out the phone and paused. "Raul, when did you get here?"

"Freddie just told me what happened, Mom," Amanda said. "Let's go downstairs and get Raul something to eat."

Her mom nodded. "Amanda, did you go through your brother's clothes without his permission?" Amanda rolled her eyes, and they followed her mom down the stairs.

"Heh, yeah what are the odds..." Raul took the lead out the door with Amanda ushering her mom after him. As they made their way down, she muttered about needing to call Raul's mom, too.

Freddie took the phone and held it up to her ear. "Mom?"

"Wyn? Is that really you? It's so good to hear your voice. I miss you so much."

"It's good to hear you, too, Mom. I—I missed you." Her throat ached as she pushed out the words. Even though she left her, all Freddie wanted was her mom. A hot tear slid down her face.

"Where have you been? We've been frantic."

"I—it's a long story, Mom. And it's late—"

"I know you need your rest, but your father and I will be up first thing in the morning. I promise."

"Where are you guys?"

"In Washington. Your father got a job opportunity here he couldn't pass up, and you're going to love the new house. And you'll go to a new school, a nicer one!"

"Wait, Mom. Dad took a job with those people, and you just moved... without me?" Tears pressed against the edges of her eyes.

"Well, Richard said it would be better to take the job and then have more resources to look for you later. We hired a private eye, but even they couldn't find any clues. And we knew if you came home, Amanda was right across the street..." Her mom's voice rose in octaves as she spoke and cracked on the last word.

Freddie's head pounded. How could they just follow Dick Fallus blindly? She cleared her throat, swallowing the homesick lump. "It's fine, Mom," she said, even though it wasn't. "I can't wait to see you guys tomorrow."

"We can drive up tonight if you want, Wyn."

"No, tomorrow's fine. I'm really tired. I just want to sleep."

"I'm glad you're safe, and you sound all right?"

"I'm fine, Mom." How could they just move without her — she hadn't even been gone that long. They apparently cared more about getting in good with the Falluses than her. Maybe it wouldn't be so bad to return to Pelrin… at least he cared.

"I love you, Wyn," her mother said, her voice still pitched with what Freddie could only guess was guilt.

"Love you too." They exchanged their goodbyes, and her mother hung up. With a groan Freddie heaved herself off Amanda's bed and followed her friends downstairs. Her limbs seemed to grow heavier with every step.

Sliding into a seat at the kitchen island, she replayed the conversation with her mom in her head. Her parents were completely brainwashed by that anti-fae fear-monger. And she couldn't even be their tiny voice of reason. How bad would they be when she returned after a year if they'd abandoned their own daughter after a month?

Wiping the tears from her eyes, she looked over to see Mrs. Lee with Raul in a strangle hug, preventing him from accessing a plate of spaghetti and meatballs.

"They did experiments on you? You poor, poor, baby boy," she said as Raul attempted to inch his fork closer to the food. "Don't you worry — I'm calling your mom next." She passed the phone to Raul who picked it up with trembling fingers.

As soon as he said hello, an angry tirade of Spanish spilled through the speaker from the other side.

"I know, Mama. Lo siento. Lo siento," Raul said, his face ashen and his lips drawn tight. "Te amo?" Rage seemed to radiate from the phone again.

Freddie picked at her leftover spaghetti while Raul attempted to quell his mother. When he was finished, they trooped back upstairs to find their usual sleepover spots in Amanda's bedroom. She had only a few days to break the curse and find those missing students — she couldn't let that bill get passed.

CHAPTER 17

Freddie

Two days had passed, and Aiden had yet to find a hint or trace of Wyn and the prince. He cursed himself for not prodding Mare's mom for more answers, but he doubted she'd give them to him anyway. No, now he had to find the words to ask Mab. His fear wouldn't be the reason he let Wyn down.

Swallowing hard, he stepped into the throne room. Oberon gave him a cruel smile as he entered, and Aiden's stomach sank.

"We were just about to summon you, boy," the king said.

Aiden bowed, his hands in tight fists.

"The attack on the Sunset Valley is not going well. They've brought out the crown." His lips pulled into a thin line, and his stare turned icy. "You'll need to confront them."

"The prince is in the Sunset Valley?" Confusion swirled in Aiden's head. If the prince was there, it meant Wyn was close by, but how was that possible if they were cursed?

"Enough of your foolish questions. Go now."

Aiden nodded and wended from where he stood, materializing on the hill overlooking the valley. Wind whipped his dark hair around his face as he stared out at the blazing town and the shining city beyond. What a contrast between the peace of Elessea and the chaos below — it wouldn't be that way for long.

Summer had taken his parents, Wyn, everything from him. Now it was his turn to be the thief.

The wings of the green fae flashed as they hurled spells at the Dark Fae's remaining forces. A few times, Aiden thought he caught a glimpse of gold, but it could've been a trick of the light.

He raised an arm and raced down the hill into the fray. The flames on his arms ignited, and excitement rumbled in his chest. Revenge. He could practically taste it. If the prince was here and wielding the Crown, Aiden would dedicate his full power to ending him.

Ducking a half-hearted barrage of arrows, he entered the city. Scanning the town through its arched entrance, Aiden saw nothing hinting at the prince's presence, but it was so cluttered with debris and fighting.

A scream made him turn, and three naga kids slithered toward a blackened doorway — no doubt part of a Rydahn family escaping the madness only to find more destruction here. This wasn't a war for the brown fae; they'd suffered enough. Now it was the green fae's turn to feel the proverbial boot on their necks. Aiden looked away. This war had been centuries in the making, and oppressing people for that long never brought about good consequences.

He swerved a barrage of a nymph's water blasts and ducked behind a charred ruin. If he'd never tasted Summer's wrath, would he be on the other side of the war? His parents surely couldn't have supported the brown fae's oppression — though he recalled little of Spring's culture. They were holed away, barred from the fighting by the great white wall. Did they even know of the horrors beyond?

Flame, hot and orange, erupted from the town square, and several blackened bodies dropped from the sky. Some of them were goblins, but there were fairies among them. It appeared the prince no longer cared who he hurt in his pursuit of victory.

Aiden rushed toward the source of the flames, arms ready to throw up a shield of his own, but when the glittering gold wings came in sight, it wasn't the prince… but the king. A knot of pain and horror burned in Aiden's gut as he stared at his parents' murderer. Like the prince, the man had brilliant gold hair tied back in a braid to his lower back. His eyes, a lighter blue, glared out at the chaotic scene before him.

This was the man who haunted his dreams when Mab failed to show, his laugh often echoing in Aiden's ears when fear seeped into his bones or when exhaustion brought an inescapable blackness to his vision. How he longed to wipe this man from the realms, but the Summer King had centuries of battle experience, the crown, and the finest army behind him.

Aiden hesitated. He could avoid him, perhaps organize the others to ambush the king so he wasn't forced to attack alone. But the remainder of his army was too far to be of any aid.

"There you are." The cold voice sent chills down Aiden's spine. "You've become quite the splinter in my finger. It's about time you joined your parents."

Red and searing flame shot toward him, and Aiden rolled out of the way, sending a blue blast at the man. All thoughts faded from his head, and he saw only fire. It burned through his body as he shot quick jets around the man's impossible inferno. Green fae and goblins alike fell around them, caught in the surrounding blaze. It seemed no life was precious to the king, perhaps save his own.

"My boy, I used to want to preserve you. Can you imagine a blue fairy soldier in the Summer army? We'd be unstoppable." His cadence, so like Oberon's, but Aiden was not indebted to the Summer King.

"I am not your boy," Aiden said. He shot more flames at the man who ducked, narrowly missing his strike. "And I'll have no part of your army, unless it is to crush it."

Flame licked around Aiden's wrist, and he cried out. It was nothing like getting grazed by the prince's flames; those were far more manageable. This… This was as though the fire never left his skin, as though it continued to melt away at his flesh even though it was well gone. Gritting his teeth, he sent a burst so pale blue it was nearly white down his good arm and into the dirt beneath the King's feet. It turned red and bubbled as the man screamed and leapt into the air. Cursed fairy wings. Panting and clutching his wrist, Aiden glared up at him.

"Don't think you can defeat me, young one; your power may have grown, but the Crown of Flames makes me invincible." He laughed a cold, sharp bark. "How about I invite you home? You will be punished for your crimes of course, but in time, you could be forgiven. All will be as it was."

Fury raged inside Aiden like a living being. He couldn't speak, couldn't see beyond the fire blazing before him. His arms moved without his bidding as a roaring rose within his ears. Despite having his magic drained, he'd give a thousand lifetimes in service to their Majesties if it meant never returning to serve his parents' murderer. How could he think Aiden would be willing to stand by his side after he and his had ripped everything, everything he'd ever loved away?

With a scream, Aiden hurled all the fire his fury could conjure at the fairy. The air smelled of flesh and ash as the man came crashing to the earth. Aiden's heart beat a little too hard in his chest, surging with triumph. Smoke blocked the King from view, but it'd been a powerful, if not deadly, hit.

The king's cold laughter rang out as he swayed to his feet and circled Aiden like a hunting chimera. He pulled back his lip and let out a feral snarl. Sweat ran down Aiden's back and sealed his hair to his face. Around him, the battle had fanned out, both sides evenly matched, the ground littered with too many bodies and stained in metallic scented streaks of silver and red.

"Hesitating like your parents."

Fire rushed down Aiden's arms as he spun to face the king. A drumming, starting in Aiden's pulse, rose to pound in his ears. "Don't you dare."

"I already dared." The man gave a manic laugh, tossing back his head. His wings were charred halves of what they once were — he would never fly again. Aiden flinched, knowing all too well what it was like to lose that part of himself.

Another blast from the king grazed Aiden's shoulder before he could dodge. The king took the momentary distraction to lunge at him, tackling Aiden to the ground. "If I can't have the power of a blue fae, then no one can."

Aiden kicked the man squarely in the face, sending him reeling, but he'd grasped hold of Aiden's ankle.

The smell of smoke and flesh. A hand grabbing his ankle as his wings beat with every ounce of his strength. Being pulled back to the ground... no.

Rage coiled around Aiden's heart and lungs, squeezing the breath from him.

"Give up. Come back with me, and I promise your punishment will be brief." The king's voice was ragged, his eyes unfocused.

"I would die first." Blue light crackled down his body like blazing lightning and shot toward the king.

He screamed as it bit into his arms and lit his insides. Power rippled beneath Aiden's skin as he pushed more and more strength into the attack. The king released him and rolled away, panting on the black earth. Aiden got to his feet and pushed his wet hair from his eyes.

"I saved you from living a life of poverty on the streets of Spring, gave you a home in my palace and a respectable job. You owe me," the King rasped.

Fire blazed in Aiden's mind so bright it nearly blinded him. Owed? He was not in the debt of Summer, but it was their fault he was bound to their Majesties. The only thing Aiden owed the Summer King was death. With his hands raised, Aiden brought a ray of white hot flame lancing out toward the king. The man screamed as the heat engulfed him. Golden ash scattered across the ground—all that was left of the man who'd stolen every hope Aiden had for a life of freedom.

He swayed and stumbled forward, unaware if he moved toward or away from the battle. Something flipped over Aiden's boot, causing him to fall. When he looked down, he stared in mild disbelief—the crown. It was the weapon of monsters, and now it was his. Tucking it close to his chest, he straightened.

A pulse of magic made him shiver, and an owl screeched as a familiar woman materialized from nothing. The sounds of the battle stilled with a twitch of her fingers. Her dark skin seemed to glow beneath her ragged black and red gown as she approached. It was the woman who'd spoken to him of impossible freedoms at Shell Bay.

"What do you want?" he asked, his fingers twitching at his sides, unable to summon his flames. His heartbeat picked up. Was she coming to avenge the King? But no, a fae with her power wouldn't bow to King of Summer…unless they were allies.

"To guide you to freedom, dark one." Her voice seemed to echo in his bones. "You are so close to the right path; you just need to give in."

"Give in to what? I don't need riddles. If there is truly a way to get my freedom, then tell me." He cleared his throat. "Please."

"You're not yet ready. Vengeance remains in your heart. You've murdered today, and you are unsure if you feel remorse." She shook her head.

Aiden's blood heated, and he glared back at the woman. Why couldn't she just be straightforward? "You don't even know what they did to me. They deserve to die. Every last gold fae in Summer."

"I know many things about you, Aiden."

He flinched; the mention of his name stabbed at his heart like a dull spear. "Then you know they stole everything from me. I can't let him — them — live."

"The prince has remorse for what he did."

"Does he? He's tried to kill me every time he's seen me."

The woman shook her head. Tiny bones clinked at the tips of her shoulder length locs. "You're losing sight of what is truly important."

"He stole Wyn from her home, and you think that's not important!"

The woman raised a brow. "Remember what I said. Let it go and give into love. Only then will you be on the path to freedom."

"Do — do you know where she is then?" Aiden looked up into the woman's glowing brown eyes.

She raised her chin and tilted her head, scrutinizing him. "You must find her on your own, but I will tell you the place she was taken is a place you have been."

Frustration grew in the back of Aiden's throat. He'd been all over Winter and Autumn in search of where their Majesties might be hiding the Prince and Wyn. But before he could demand more answers, she was gone. A screech owl flew into the night, and he cringed as the sounds of the battle slammed back into life.

The king was dead, and Aiden was nowhere closer to finding Wyn than he had been before. Perhaps that woman was right... at least about some things. His revenge had gotten him nowhere.

Around him, minotaurs charged at ifrits who pounded on their shields with torrents of flame, undines caught werewolves in bubbles filled with water until they drowned, and forest nymphs dragged Dark Fae soldiers beneath the earth with thick vines. Despite losing their ruler, the green fae battled as strong as ever. Did they even know?

A goblin shouted just as an arrow struck his wing, and he was forced to the ground. "There's a gold fae leading the attack by the gate. We need your help."

CHAPTER 18

Freddie

Morning came with piles of bacon, grocery store fried chicken, and pancakes. Amanda's mom fretted over them as they ate. Tucking hair behind their ears and pouring pools of syrup on their plates. The doorbell rang, and she raced to open it. Both Freddie and Raul leaned back to get a better view.

"Wyn?"

Freddie flinched at her mom's voice.

"Wyn!" She raced into the kitchen and scooped Freddie up in a tight hug. Freddie melted into it, savoring the smell of cocoa butter from her mother's lotion.

"I missed you, Mom," Freddie mumbled into the fur of her mom's hood. Tears welled in her eyes. Where was the mom who loved her more than politics and certainly more than money?

"Baby, we were so worried. Have you eaten enough? Your father's in the car. We can stay a bit, if you want." She glanced at Mrs. Lee, who nodded.

Freddie shrugged. "I'm full, and I want to see Dad." Even if he did care more about his job than her.

"Oh, good." Her mom thanked Mrs. Lee and ushered Freddie to the door. "Your boyfriend's been by a couple times. He's been just as frantic as we've been."

"My boyfriend?"

"Yes." Amanda said. "Your boyfriend?" Raul paused midway through tearing apart his chicken.

"Yes, the one you brought home, or did you two…"

Freddie flushed, her heart pounding faster than hummingbird wings. "No, we're still together." I think. Amanda glowered from behind Freddie's mom. "Let's go see Dad."

"Who's this boyfriend, Fred?"

"No one important." Freddie dragged her mom toward the door. Now was neither the time nor place to reveal her relationship with Aiden.

"You better text me details, Wynifred," Amanda said.

"No phone!"

Amanda caught her by the arm. "Seriously, Fred. We need to keep in touch. When am I going to see you again?"

Raul followed after them.

Freddie paused. "Mom, can you give me a moment?"

"Your dad's really eager to see you."

"I know, I'll be quick." She let Amanda pull her to the base of the stairs. "I don't know if I can make it back before… you know."

Amanda pulled her lips tight. "Just message me before you leave."

"Be careful," Raul said.

"I promise Pel and I are going to keep trying to break the curse."

"We'll work on a way to get you out here, too, but there's only two days until the realms shift, and you won't be able to get back until next winter." Amanda tightened her grip on the railing. "Be safe, buddy… And tell me about your boyfriend."

A smile quirked the edge of Freddie's lips. "Gotta go!"

"Freddie, you'd better tell us when you get home." Raul pulled her into a hug, and Freddie sagged into his arms.

She pulled away. "I'll see you guys soon." Amanda looked at her teary eyed as Freddie walked back to her mother. "Let's go, Mom."

With a last goodbye to Amanda's parents, they stepped into the harsh winter sunlight.

Her mom stared at her. "I don't know why you haven't told Amanda about Aiden. He's really a lovely boy."

Before she could respond, her dad rounded the car and snatched her up into a rib-aching hug. "I thought I'd lost you," he whispered.

Tears formed in Freddie's eyes. She wanted to yell and cry — why had he chosen Dick Fallus over her? More than anything, she wanted to pretend her father was the same man she'd known before the Falluses came and ruined her life. When her dad finally let her go, Freddie felt the absence of his warmth as though someone had scooped out a part of her. She plunked down in the back seat and stared out the window as they pulled away from Amanda's house.

"So Aiden was here? He asked about me?"

"He came for Christmas," her mom said. "Poor boy looked devastated; we all were, Wyn. Where have you been? You hardly look upset."

Freddie told them the story she'd concocted with Raul: the scientist testing on werewolves, their attack of the house, and the article. When she was done, she braced herself for her parents to poke holes in the story, for them to ask her questions she couldn't answer, but there was only silence.

Finally, her mom said, "Well that sounds like a thrilling adventure. In that whole time you couldn't get access to a phone to call us?"

"Mom, they kidnapped Raul and me. When I got loose, I had to find a way to free him. I couldn't risk being found out." Freddie cringed at her lame excuse.

"Well, I hope you write a vicious article Wyn, and the police shut them down. I'm sure they'll want to talk to you."

Freddie stiffened. "Can it wait? I'm still settling in, and I haven't even taken notes yet."

"We'll hold them off as long as we can, but they'll still want to talk to you soon."

Freddie nodded and slouched against the seat as the car sped toward DC. Her dad put on the Latin Artists Top Forty, and she fell asleep to trumpets and bass. When she woke, they were pulling into the driveway of a small house where a group of people stood outside holding a banner.

"Welcome home!" they screamed as the car came to a stop.

Freddie scanned the crowd, looking for familiar faces. There were a couple people from her dad's office she'd seen before but couldn't name. Most of the people appeared to be strangers, though her eyes narrowed in on one red-headed girl with two braided plaits and a very preppy outfit.

"Oh, Wyn, look. Your friend from school is here," her mother said.

A ball of ice plunged into Freddie's stomach and boiled. "Mallory." Locking herself inside the car and staying there until all these people left seemed like a good idea. But she knew her parents would pry her out. As though preparing to walk through the Southernmost part of Winter naked, she braced herself and stepped outside.

Mallory was the first to rush toward her and wrap her in a hug. Freddie stiffened, but she leaned in close. "I'm so glad you're back. Come find me after. We should talk." Pulling away, Mallory gave her a shy smile and stepped toward the back of the crowd.

After a couple other hugs from her dad's half-remembered work friends, Freddie glanced back to the unfamiliar house, wondering how much longer until they could go inside and see what was left of her things.

"Wyn, dear, look who came to make sure you're okay. They've been a big part in trying to help find you." Freddie's mom came over, leading a woman in spikey heels and a man melting into his suit.

Her upper lip curled as she stared at the Falluses.

"It's so good to see you safe," Minge said in her baby voice.

"Yes, your parents have been worried. We sent the best private eye I could find to search all the fae groups. But it takes true agility to escape on your own." Mr. Fallus held out a hand.

Freddie raised an eyebrow at his use of agility, but ignored his offer of peace. In the corner of her eye, Freddie caught her mom chewing on her bottom lip and inching closer. Good. Inviting them should make her uncomfortable.

"Too bad I wasn't kidnapped by fae," Freddie said. "Your detective was looking in the wrong places."

A man in a rumpled brown suit who resembled a younger Mr. Fallus, save for his messy hair, thin frame, and glowing green eyes, hurried up to them. "Brother, we need your approval of the second clause regarding the removal of fae from elderly caregivers employment," he said, holding out a stapled pack of papers.

What was Mr. Fallus doing employing a fae? Freddie stared at him, and he caught her eye.

"Oh, hello, I'm Oscar Fallus. Welcome home."

Dick Fallus cleared his throat and gave Oscar a pointed stare.

"Just Oscar, really." Oscar lowered his eyes.

"My assistant here is a changeling. My real brother was kidnapped, like you, as a child and replaced by him." Hurt shot through Oscar's gaze, and he hunched his shoulders, digging in his coat pocket and pulling out a pen. He passed it to his brother.

"I wasn't kidnapped by fae, and I'm sure he didn't choose to switch places with your brother," Freddie said.

Mr. Fallus laughed and signed the papers, and Oscar hurried away back to an old beat-up Dodge before Freddie could say more to him. "Changelings are worse than most fae; they make you forget those they replaced. The liberals will have you think they're so innocent with no magic, but they brainwash people like my parents."

"Oh, we're not brainwashed, we just —"

"I think that's enough, Wynifred," her mom said. Freddie shut her mouth and glared at the Falluses. "Why don't we get you in the house to rest. Thanks for coming, Minge, Richard."

They nodded, and Mr. Fallus shot her a glare back. One day, she would bring him down. First, she had to make her parents see how truly evil they were. Her mom led her into the split level and up a short flight of stairs to the end of the hall.

"Our room is just across." She pointed. "But here's yours."

Freddie stepped inside. The room was a near perfect replica of her room at home, everything in the same place as it had been, save for the walls; they were bright white rather than tinged with pink.

She sighed. "Thanks, Mom. I'm gonna stay here for a while. If that's okay?"

"Of course, dear." Her mom hesitated. "Do you want me to stay with you?"

"No, I'm good."

Freddie sat down on the bed. She wasn't particularly tired, but she needed to figure out her next move. Tomorrow, she would have to leave, and she was no closer to figuring out how to break this curse than when she'd first been kidnapped. All curses had an out, a way to break them without begging the caster. She just needed to find this one.

A tap at the door made her look up. What could her mom possibly want? She scowled as she shouted, "Come in." Mallory waved to her from the entrance as she tiptoed inside.

"Freddie? I—I just want to say I'm sorry. Not just for interrupting you when I knew you were trying to get a story, but for everything. I've been jealous of you wanting to be a journalist for so long. You're able to find these great stories, and I can't find anything."

Freddie bit the inside of her cheek. Was she awake? Not only would Mallory never apologize, but she never called Freddie by her nickname—it was always Wynifred. "Are you... okay?"

She laughed. "Yeah, I'm fine. I was just worried about you. You're so great at this, and I didn't want you to get hurt chasing a story." Freddie arched a brow. This wasn't happening. "Who'd be my rival?" Mallory grinned, and Freddie wondered if the castles' magic had addled her ability to tell the difference between being awake and asleep. The Mallory she knew didn't know how to talk like this.

"What do you want, Mal? This is..."

"I know I'm acting weird. It's just I'm tired of fighting with you all the time. Can we call a truce?" She took a seat on Freddie's desk chair.

"A truce? Uh, sure?" Mallory was the one who started everything with her ignorance. If she was willing to give that up, Freddie wouldn't retaliate.

"So what really happened to you? I thought you'd be a lot more banged up and haunted."

Freddie gave her a sly smile. Maybe she wasn't the worst journalist. "I was kidnapped by a talking polar bear," she said, pushing as much sarcasm as she could muster into her voice.

"Like a fae curse?"

"You believe that?" Freddie frowned, but Mallory looked wholly sincere.

"Of course. Should I not?"

"It's the truth…" Hesitating, she debated what harm it would do to tell Mallory the truth of what happened. On the one hand, no one would believe her about the talking polar bear. And if Mallory did go blabbing, Freddie at least would know for sure this whole friendship nonsense was an act. But on the other, if her mom at all suspected Pelrin had a hand in this, she'd feed it right to Mr. Fallus who could now do real harm to fae communities. Running her tongue over her chapped lips, Freddie told Mallory of the ice castle, leaving out everything about Freya, Raul, and Pelrin. Most of it was a lie, but she slipped in a few nuggets of truth here and there.

"And this guy who claims to be a cursed fae has to sleep next to you every night?"

Freddie nodded.

"Well if I were you, I'd have gotten a good look at his face."

"I can't. I told you, bad things will happen."

"What bad things?"

"He didn't say, but you know how curses are."

Mallory scratched her chin. "Right, but how do you know he didn't just create the curse?"

Freddie opened her mouth and shut it. What if Mab and Oberon were making her think she was trapped with Pelrin for revenge…Could they even do that? And Amanda was right, lots of fae could lie… What if some fae creature was taking advantage of her memories to torment her and keep Pelrin looking for her, distracted from the war?

"You could be on to something, Mal... lory," she said. "Why don't you tell me what you've been up to? Any great stories?" The subject needed to change. Freddie needed to think. Maybe she should try and sneak a peek at Pelrin... just a quick one to be sure it was him.

Mallory went on a tangent, talking between Freddie's nods and uh huhs. Hours passed until her mom called them down for dinner, and Freddie realized how ravenous she was.

Freddie shot her mother a look as she followed Mallory down the stairs. Her parents deserved to feel hurt and guilty for giving up on her and moving after only a month, but her heart missed them so much.

Mallory took the lead during the dinner conversation. The awkwardness seemed not to bother her. When they were finished, she gave Freddie another hug and promised to come back soon.

Freddie gave her half a smile. It wasn't the worst afternoon she'd ever had. Maybe there was hope for the two of them. Weird. Mallory left, and Freddie's mom leaned out of the kitchen.

"Wyn, we should talk. You have to understand with the move we didn't have much of a choice."

Freddie glared at her. "You mean you didn't want to give up working with those racist dicks."

"Wyn," her father said in his warning tone.

"I don't—" Her voice caught in a half sob. "I don't even know who you guys are any more." She raced up the stairs to shut herself in her room, letting the tears fall down her cheeks. Sitting on the floor, in the dark, she listened to the muffled murmur of their voices as they cleaned up and headed into the living room. Finally, Freddie got up and crossed to her desk. Soon it would be time for her to leave, and as much as it would serve them right to vanish without a trace again, she wasn't that cruel.

Her hand trembled on the pen as she held it above the printer paper. A tear splashed onto the page, and Freddie smeared it away. What if Amanda hadn't been home the night she'd returned? Her parents just up and left her to move two states away.

Pen touched paper as she scribbled out her note apologizing for following her story and leaving them again. Would they think she ran away because of their argument? Well, good if they did. Maybe it would make them realize how crazy Mr. Fallus's ideas really were.

She hesitated, afraid to note when she'd be back. Amanda had said she only had two days. But she had no plan and no clues on how to break the curse. Freddie shook her head as she packed her bag. She'd found her phone in its charger and safely tucked in the pocket of her puffer. The magic in Fairy might prevent her from calling anyone, but the flashlight would work just fine. And if it were some evil fae banished to the castle, she had to know. The thought sent chills through her. But he sounded, acted, and felt like Pelrin…

"I love you both," she wrote, and signed the letter.

Zipping up her parka, Freddie opened the window. It wasn't a long jump, but the tree leaning toward the house served as a strong guide. She walked to the end of the street where an entrance to Rock Creek Park welcomed joggers, pot-smoking teens, and human girls looking to run away with polar bears.

"Pelrin?" she called. Was it possible some other fae could intercept summons like this? Was calling a fairy's name like cell phone waves that could be blocked and rerouted? "Pelrin," she said a bit louder.

"I'm here." A shadow shifted among the trees and stepped onto the jogging path. His massive form blotted out what little dusky light filtered through the branches. "Did you have a good visit?"

"It was too short," Freddie said and looked back toward the house.

"I'm sorry." Pelrin stepped closer and bowed his head, so she could get on.

Freddie mounted, and soon they were off at an inhuman speed, racing through the streets and past the highways. She nearly screamed as Pelrin leapt a massive river in one bound. They were at the border before she could catch her breath, then they were through it. Freddie buried her face into Pelrin's fur as the cold intensified. She slept on and off, waking only to see white mounds and moonlight reflecting back at her.

It was still dark as they crossed the ice bridge, and Pelrin let her down onto the stairs leading up to their palace. She was back, trapped with Pelrin, or a demon, and she intended to find out for sure. That night.

CHAPTER 19

Aiden

Aiden's heart picked up, and he glanced back at gold ash marking where the Summer King had been. Who could the gold fae be? Ducking around warring groups, he made his way to the gate. Despite the green fae magic, they appeared to be evenly matched. What a knock to the greenie's pride to see the red and brown fae facing them like equals.

A fairy dove at him, a slender silver wand glowing in her hand. Aiden moved to blast her out of their path, but froze. Oberon's crystal wand flashed in his mind. Though she grew closer, there was nothing he could do. No. It pounded in his mind, the inability to refuse, to fight back. Darkness surrounded him, and someone smacked the back of his head.

"You moron," Mare said, holding out her arms as she projected a shield of shadow around them. "Were you planning on just watching as she cursed us?"

"S-sorry." Aiden bowed his head, his face hot. How could he let himself succumb to fear so easily? Oberon had drained his magic hundreds of times, so he ought to be used to it. "How are you here?"

Mare shrugged. "I was following the Summer King, but I guess I don't have to do that anymore." A small smile played about her lips, and he couldn't help but return it. The king was a monster;

he deserved to die.

Mare jerked her chin at the cluster of brown and red fae encroaching on a singular spot. It was almost impressive how the newcomer managed to fend off so many on his own.

"He's there. I think the others will pull back once he falls," Mare said.

Above them, scores of fairies moved in organized patterns, fighting the goblins out of the sky. They were skilled, but there was no denying their need for a leader. While they were neat and organized, the goblins battered any fairy who got too close — striking down as many of them as were killed.

A gap formed in the crowd, and Aiden sucked in a breath as he recognized a familiar face. The king's brother, the fairy general who'd helped take him from his home and cared for him during Aiden's brief stay in Summer. Unlike the king, the general had been as kind as was possible for Summer royals. He'd given Aiden a home, toys as well as weapons. But the general also knew what it took to win wars and would push Aiden in his service to the king.

Magic pulsed along Aiden's arms, but they had yet to ignite. Did he truly dare to take this man on? The general might not have the crown, but he had hundreds of years of experience.

Mare looked to Aiden and then the general. "He's just one gold fae. He'll fall to you easily."

Aiden wanted to scoff, but he was too tired. Battling with the king had drained him both physically and magically. His vision blurred, and all he wanted to do was to collapse into his bed. Time to get this over with.

"I'll be all right once he's dead." Aiden squared his shoulders, he might feel guilt for this kill… if he survived.

Letting out a jet of flame, Aiden slammed the gold fae back, and the man hit the hard ground with a sickening smack. He cringed but rushed closer. The other fae parted to let him through while the general got back to his feet, a ball of yellow light forming between his fingertips.

"Aiden?" he said. A note of uncertainty trembled in his voice.

"Who else do you know who shoots blue flames?" Aiden

hurled another ball of fire at the man, but he dodged it.

"I'd hoped never to see you like this. You've fallen so far. I wish I could help you." Another ray of light shot toward Aiden, but it was sloppily aimed. It took barely any effort to side step it.

"I do not seek your kind of help." Memories of his time in Summer sent flames racing down his arms and out toward the general. "Unless you wish to turn traitor."

"You know I won't do that."

Aiden smirked. "Your king is dead. Loyalty to those tyrants has gotten you nowhere." He aimed a jet of icy blue flames at the man's head. The scent of burnt hair made Aiden's nostrils flare. While the fairy general had managed to dodge the flames, they'd singed off his ponytail, leaving his charred, blond hair to tangle about his face.

"You murdered..." A brokenness flickered in the man's green eyes. "You murdered my brother? How they have corrupted you." He shook his head and sent shards of light pulsing out, forcing Aiden to dance around them. One shard struck Aiden in the arm, and he stumbled, barely managing to stay upright as it burned his flesh. Silver welled around the wound, and he hissed, looking back at the general.

With a scream, Aiden charged at the man, fire blazing around his fist. The punch struck the man's shoulder despite his attempt to move out of the way. Tumbling, the fairy rolled away from Aiden and jumped into the air. Aiden swallowed as shards of light rained down upon him. He ran, casting a pale blue shield over his head, but knowing it was not enough. Perhaps if his parents were still alive, they would've been able to train him in the true might of blue fae magic. The Summer King had taken them by surprise; otherwise, they'd never have fallen to him.

"I pity you, Aiden. You should've never had to turn to Mab and Oberon. I've blamed myself for not protecting you against the court's cruelty."

"My parents were murdered by your king," Aiden snarled. "There would never have been happiness for me in Summer."

The general pressed his lips together and sank back to the

ground. "My brother… he did some terrible things. But I always saw you as a son, no matter what he'd done in the past." He stared at Aiden with a look of sickening pity.

Aiden shook his head. He needed a plan of attack, something that would force the general to let his guard down. Even now, the man had his arms ready to summon a shield, but there had to be some way…

"Please. If my brother is truly dead as you say —" The general choked on the words, and Aiden fought his lip from curling. "If he's dead, perhaps I can find a place for you at court. I have sway with the queen, and if you helped in the war, you'd be viewed as a hero rather than a villain."

Aiden raised his chin, the beginnings of an idea formulating in his head. "You would take me back? I'd live with you and the prince?"

A muscle twitched in the side of the man's forehead. "That's right."

"And you would have me fight in the war to what? Spare the prince of his fears?"

"The prince has no fear of protecting his people."

"Then why isn't he here? His father instead comes to do his dirty work." Aiden crept closer to the fae, forcing his features neutral. The general just needed to hold still, his defenses down just a little bit longer.

The prince is elsewhere occupied." The general's eyes shifted to the left, the closest he could do to lie.

"Yes, I'm sure he has more important responsibilities than caring for the lives of his people." He let the white hot magic flow to the tips of his fingers.

"I know the prince cares for his people —"

"Then where is he? You would ask me to care more for Summer than her prince?"

"I don't know, I — What are you doing?"

Aiden snapped his fingers, and fire so blue it was nearly white surrounded the general. The man threw up his hands, crying out as his wings were singed.

"I would never return to fight for Summer. Especially to fight side by side with the prince who—" Aiden grit his teeth and looked away. He couldn't face the general's eyes as he finished him. The man had made the best of an impossible situation; he had no part in the death of his parents. Yet still, he'd stood by idly while the royals tormented him. Aiden's fingers twitched, and the flames moved closer to the man. Around him, sounds of the surrounding battle seemed to die down, but Aiden didn't dare distract himself by looking.

"Forgive me, Aiden. I truly failed you if the teachings of Mab and Oberon have sunk into your heart. Never would I have imagined you were the heartless killer the rumors spoke of. I always thought they had something over you, or you were driven by fear of returning." He stared at Aiden, his eyes welling with tears.

Aiden's jaw ached from grinding his teeth, but he couldn't look away. "I don't do this by choice. I was driven to this by your prince."

Shaking his head, the general dropped to his knees. "Then do as you must."

Hands trembling, Aiden inched the flames closer to the man, then they flickered. What would killing this man bring him? Mab and Oberon would scarcely spare him any kindness for his actions, and it would bring him nowhere closer to finding the prince. No, killing the general would only add to the dull emptiness in his chest. Pulling back the flames, Aiden stared down at the man kneeling before him.

"Retreat. Now. Before I change my mind," Aiden said.

The general met his gaze. "Please, Aiden. Let me help you, don't become the monster they say you are."

"I fear it's too late for that." A joyless smile spread across Aiden's face. "I am exactly who they say I am."

Getting to his feet, the man reached for Aiden, but he took a jerky step back. "I don't believe it. One day, others will see the kind-hearted boy I knew. He's there, beneath this mask, though perhaps even you have forgotten."

Aiden opened his mouth, but no response came out. That had been so long ago — only Wyn had brought that out in him. And now the prince had taken her from him too.

The general sprung into the air. Crouching on the edge of the wall, he let a nearby fairy help him straighten.

"Eleasseans, retreat!" The general shouted with a magically enhanced boom.

The green fae took to the air, and those that could not fly slowly drifted towards the gate. Aiden wandered through the streets, taking inventory of the dead. By some miracle, it was mostly green fae. Several brown fae, likely forced by desperation to attend to the high ranking green fae soldiers, stood over their former masters, clutching silver splattered knives. Summer still hadn't learned how to treat their brown fae citizens it seemed. If they lost this war… when they lost this war, they would have brought this doom upon their own heads. Mab and Oberon might have unsavory methods, but they had expertly manipulated the green and gold fae cruelty to their advantage.

A shadow figure raced, along with the retreating green fae, toward him.

"We did it!" Mare wrapped her arms around him. "The king is dead, and we have the crown. Summer is nearly ours!" Her black eyes glittered as they dodged out of the way of an undine's last-ditch attack. "Aiden! What happened to your arms?"

He looked down. The pain adrenaline had let him ignore now came cascading back, and he choked down a cry. The angry red twist from where the king's flames had touched him and the silver ooze from the general's light pulsed on either side of him. He stumbled, and Mare caught him.

"Go back to the palace and rest. This battle is over." Mare patted his back. For a moment, Aiden thought to protest, that this was another of her cruel tricks and she would betray him to their Majesties. But perhaps not. They'd saved each other countless times over the past month. Maybe he could trust her. The battle was truly over.

"Come find me if you need me." He wended back to Winter,

creeping in through the palace door as Triglav dozed, the lazy fool.

It felt as though he'd trekked through the frost-covered halls for hours before reaching his room and collapsing into his bed. His thoughts turned back to Wyn and the prince as his eyelids drooped closed. As soon as he healed, he'd return to his search for Wyn and the prince—one more Summer royal to turn to ash.

CHAPTER 20

Aiden

Dreams of snow and fire dragged Aiden from deep sleep. His body still pleaded with him not to move. He looked down; both his sheets and his black uniform were smeared with silver. He waved a hand, and the grime vanished in a waft of soap-scented wind. The world spun, and his vision dimmed — how stupid was he to use magic when he couldn't even stand? Turning his face up to the ceiling, he closed his eyes and tried to picture Wyn's face.

She smiled at him, that warm beam of excitement that always crossed her features when he saw her. He didn't deserve it though; he'd failed her. If Mab and Oberon had her and the prince somewhere — she might already be dead. Hesitantly, Aiden reached out to sense her, but pain lanced through his forehead, threatening to plunge his thoughts into darkness.

A soft tap on the door pulled him out of his thoughts of Wyn. Aiden's eyes opened a crack, and he stared at it. Mare's knocks were hardly so timid. Who...? The knock sounded again, this time followed by a voice.

"Aiden, it's me, Tatiana. Are you in there or up to seeing anyone?" The last word wavered as though she were pleading. Why would she plead with him?

He cleared his throat. "Come in."

"I heard you were back," she said as the door opened. "Is Mare with you…" Her eyes flew wide. "I'm so sorry. I didn't realize you were sleeping!"

"I—I wasn't." Aiden struggled to sit up, biting back a groan as he put too much weight on his injured arm.

"And you're injured! What happened?" Tatiana stopped short at the foot of his bed and rocked back, wringing her hands.

"It was just the fight," he said, suddenly remembering the crown jabbing at his side. Only a few months ago, the crown had consumed his thoughts, but now, so much had changed. "We won though."

"And is Mare hurt, too? I can't believe my parents would let you guys do something so dangerous."

He pressed his lips together, not trusting himself to respond. Did she not know of her parent's cruelties? "Mare was fine last I saw. She's just finishing up."

"That's good. What can I do to help?"

"You want to help? With the war?"

"Well, it is my parent's initiative. If I'm going to be here, I should be more active, right?"

Aiden frowned. Was this some sort of trap? He didn't have time for these games; he had to figure out where the prince was. But if Tatiana was to marry the prince, then perhaps…

"Do you know where your betrothed is right now?"

A small frown tugged at her lips. "Does it matter? It's not like he needs to woo me."

"I—uh, surely he'll come to see you before the wedding? Maybe your parents have told you about him."

"All I know is in the next few months I need to show up in a white dress."

"You don't have a date?"

She shook her head. "The longer the better."

A laugh bubbled up out of his throat, and Aiden coughed to cover it.

"Do you know him?" she asked.

"He is the Summer prince." It was the best he could think of. Memories of the prince's cruelty when they were children pressed to the front of his mind. Thankfully he was still weak, and his flames remained dormant. Tatiana didn't need to see what thoughts of the prince brought out in him.

She crossed her arms. "I know what it sounds like when fae try to lie. He's horrible, isn't he? Pretty on the outside, rotten on the in?"

Aiden's jaw stiffened. "Perhaps he'll be different around you."

Her lips tightened, and she stared off into the corner of the room. "I hate this whole thing. Fae weddings have to be willing, but I..." she trailed off. "I'm sorry. I woke you up, and now I'm complaining about my life when you're injured. I'll just leave." She hurried to the door.

"You don't—"

The door shut, and Aiden stared at the spot she'd fled from. Did fae marriages truly have to be willing? He could hardly imagine the prince being willing to marry Tatiana. Their Majesties must have found some other way to force him to marry their daughter.... or to trick him. But what type of trick would involve Wyn?

Aiden curled in on himself. Silent tears streamed down his face. He was useless; Wyn was a pawn in some elaborate game orchestrated by their Majesties, and there was nothing he could do about it.

The only thing to do now was rest and wait for his body to heal. He waved his hand and winced as a bit more magic was pulled from him. A book, pages yellowed with age and smelling of ash, landed on his stomach. Gingerly, he lifted it and flipped through the pages of a book of poems he'd found in the ruins of his parents' house. His mother had read them to him as a child, but he hadn't had the heart to read them in years. He flipped through the pages and chose a poem at random.

Song for the South

East of the sun, west of the moon,
Through Autumn's breeze, behind Spring's bloom,

> *Over ice, and over snow,*
> *Beyond the skylights' glow!*
> *I dance though Winter's glory*
> *More graceful than the hunter's quarry;*
> *And I please the Winter court.*
> *To protect her orb, and serve escort;*
> *Her lips of red and hair of ebony,*
> *This fairy's heart, hers forever will be.*

A love poem to a Winter fae, perhaps even a royal. He flipped to the front of the book to find the name of the author but saw no one and frowned. Turning back to the page, he spotted a slip of paper stuck in the binding of the book and picked at it. It came free, and he pulled it out and unfolded it. His eyes skimmed over the paper and widened at the mention of his mother's name.

Eira, I can't wait to come home to you. These northern factions are the opposite of our home in the South Pole. Missing you every second. Dani

He'd never heard his mother speak of a Dani or of the South Pole. Did Winter even have a South Pole?

Letting out a slow breath, Aiden tried to remember any conversation, any story of Winter, but he couldn't recall any other than the one about the Lord of the North giving presents to the good children on Solstice. But something else pricked at the back of his mind: the deserted palace in Winter where he'd found the pearl for Wyn. Could it have been what remained of the South Pole? But it was hardly the opposite of their Majesties' palace; it had been nearly a mirror image… but a mirror was flipped.

Thoughts raced through his mind like shooting stars as his heartbeat quickened. If their Majesties were relying on his magic, they could only take the prince to places Aiden had been before. Well, he had been to the South Pole. It was the perfect place; no one would find them. He pushed himself up and cried out. Freezing Frosts. This was as close to finding Wyn he'd been, and he was too weak to even follow the lead. Laying back, he willed his body to heal. In the morning he'd see Wyn.

\###

Pulling a wisp of magic from his core, Aiden wended and disappeared into the frosty air.

As though he'd gone but a few steps away, Aiden stared up at the twin of the Winter Palace. Its spires stuck up like icicles in the green-streaked sky. He let out a cloudy breath and made his way across the ice bridge, nerves racing through his body. Hesitating, he put a hand on the carved ice door. What if he was wrong? What if there was still no one here… no prince, no Wyn, no hope of finding her?

But it was as though something inside was calling to his magic the way his mother's ring often did—but stronger. A gentle, comforting song that felt of home. He pushed open the door and stepped into the familiar hall. Loud groaning and scraping noises came from all sides of the castle. It hadn't sounded like this the last time he'd been here.

He came to the ballroom… or at least what should've been the ballroom. Behind the grand entrance a broom closet slid past, followed by a bedroom and a toilet, then finally the ballroom slid into place with a clank. Aiden stepped inside cautiously and looked behind him. Throughout the palace, clanks rang out. He shuddered. There was something not quite right about this place.

Aiden's feet nearly took him down the staircase leading to where his rooms would be. But the magical tug was coming from upstairs. Voices trickled down from the top floor, and he froze.

"Can't you just sleep on the floor?"

His heart lifted at Wyn's voice, and he raced up the stairs. She was here; all these months of searching were finally over. Soon, she'd be in his arms, traveling back home and then… And then nothing, he told himself. There was nothing he could give her, once he saved her, she could go back to her life, and he to his.

"That's not how this works," a gruff but vaguely familiar voice said.

Aiden frowned. A guard perhaps. Footsteps slowing, Aiden crept closer to the voices and the magic.

"Sometimes I feel like you're making up this curse for your advantage."

"Are you insinuating I enjoy being a bear, trapped in a barren frigid wasteland, in a haunted castle?"

A bear? Haunted? What was going on? Aiden paused. Should he knock? But if he did, the prince, or his guard, would be primed to attack without sufficient time for Wyn to seek cover. Taking a deep breath, he pushed open the door.

Wyn, dressed in a shimmering pair of loose white pants and a long-sleeved shirt, turned. Her eyes lit up, and the warm smile he'd ached for broke across her face. He couldn't help but return it, but as though there'd been some unspoken trigger, they both looked to the bear, and their jaw's dropped. Aiden's more for curiosity than anything else. Why was there a polar bear, and what did it have to do with Mab and Oberon or the prince?

The creature let out a low growl. "What are you doing here?"

Aiden's eyebrows shot up. "It talks."

"It can also rip you limb from limb." Turquoise blazed in its eyes, and Aiden took half a step back. Wyn's face had gone ashen and her limbs stiff as she looked from the bear to him.

Had it frightened her? Flames sprang to life down his arms as he rounded on the creature; his gaze met Wyn's, imploring her to hide. She did not.

"Come to fight me, dog? After all, it was your mistress who cursed me."

"Cursed?" He frowned, then a slyness quirked his lip. The turquoise eyes, the arrogance... How had he not guessed immediately? "I'd hoped to find you here, but I didn't expect..."

The bear rocked back onto his haunches, and flames appeared on either paw. "I may have been transformed, but I'm strong enough to break you."

"Let's see." Aiden tossed a small ball of flame at the bear, barely enough to singe fur. How would Wyn feel about him attacking her former beau?

The prince easily blocked it and countered with flames so strong they forced Aiden to roll across the floor so as to not hurt Wyn. He needed to get closer to her.

"Not fighting back, dog?" The prince rounded on him, fur

bristling as Aiden scrambled to his feet. Backing away, he drew the prince from his position in front of Wyn.

When she was just a few feet to his side, Aiden formed another fireball between his fingers while the prince did the same between his paws. "Thought you'd see the sights of Winter?" He raised an eyebrow at Wyn.

Her grin turned to fear when the prince hurled his fireball right at them. Aiden countered with his own flame, causing a blast which shook the room as they met in the middle. Wyn backed up towards the wall, and the bear snarled.

"Don't speak to her."

"If you care so much about her, perhaps you should mind your flames. Hoping to charm her with your ability to burn through her flesh?"

The bear growled, but he didn't shoot any more flames. "You know nothing about us!"

"Us?" Aiden fought to keep the hurt from his voice even as it swelled in his throat.

Wyn took half a step forward "There is no us. Especially not with Pelrin as a bear."

So, she knew who the prince was, yet denied loving him. Aiden's heart fluttered as he looked to her over his shoulder. "That must be a disappointment for you, Your Highness." Growling, the prince charged and swiped a massive paw at Aiden's head. He just barely dodged, the blow ruffling his hair. He hadn't planned on fighting a bear.

"Maybe you could help us out?" Wyn said.

"He won't help; he's part of the problem." The prince lunged at Aiden, forcing him back and closer to Wyn.

He held out his hand. "Tell me where it is you wish to go, fair maid."

"What did I say about talking to her!" The prince hurled flame at them. Reckless like his father. How would the prince react when he learned of the king's death?

Flame of the palest blue blazed in his hands, rebounding the prince's blast as he twisted them into an attack.

"No, stop! You'll hurt him!" Wyn put a hand on his shoulder.

Aiden tensed. How could she care about his welfare? "I won't kill him in front of you," he said under his breath.

"How about not killing him at all? What is wrong with you?" Wyn didn't conceal the fury in her voice, and the prince looked up.

"He's a murderer; that's what they do. Kill," the prince growled.

She stared as though looking at a stranger. Chills ran through Aiden's stomach, and he broke their gaze. It wasn't as though she didn't know he killed people; he'd told her about the war, but this… This was different. Perhaps —

A flame tore through the air, blasting him back and causing Wyn to shriek.

"Are you alright?" the prince said as he rushed to Wyn's side. She didn't respond.

Aiden sat up and scanned the room for her. She was laying by the door, her face scrunched, clutching her head. Around her the frosted ground was smooth from the heat of the prince's flame, but she didn't appear burned. Rage boiled in his chest. It mattered not if the prince attacked him, but Wyn… Did he know Aiden cared, or was it just foolishness? It took everything in Aiden not to shove the prince aside to care for her. But no one could know of his feelings except her.

"It appears I am not the only one you're trying to kill," Aiden's head throbbed only slightly from the blast; the heat behind the flames was nothing compared to what the prince used on the battlefield.

The bear whipped his head around. "I would never hurt her."

Nerves chewed at the inside of Aiden's skin. Did the prince know how to heal? Head wounds were serious; she could be more injured than she let on.

Wyn rolled away from the bear. "Oh? And who was it that just hurt me? Why don't you both just leave."

Aiden opened his mouth to protest, but thought better of it. "It seems you've upset her."

The prince reared up on his hind legs and roared. "You want

to fight, I'll give you a fight." He charged, and Aiden fled from the room into the hall.

It reminded him of the wing of the North Winter Palace, making it easy to lead the bear down twists and turns, farther and farther away from Wyn's room. Several times the prince made awkward leaps, causing him to scramble across the icy hall. Aiden resisted laughing as he continued to run, shooting out the occasional burst of flame behind him. It wasn't until they reached the ballroom that he realized the prince was trying to fly, but for once they were on equal footing.

Aiden skidded to a halt and turned, casting a wall of flame between them. The prince shot a jet of orange fire at him, but it barely wavered against his shield. Now was the time; the prince was weaker in this form. All of his fairy tricks depended on a body he was familiar with; all he had was his strength and his flame. And Aiden had no intention of getting close enough to be bothered by the prince's strength — not when his own flame could do so much damage from a distance. He pushed the flames forward, struggling for a moment, then the prince's jet of fire gave in, and Aiden's power crept a couple feet closer to the bear.

"It seems Your Highness is weakening. Has life as a bear made you lazy? Or should I say lazier?"

The prince let out a low rumble, but from the heaving of his body, Aiden could tell he was expending a good amount of strength in pushing back the blue flames. "My strength is enough to..."

Aiden quirked a brow. The prince couldn't even speak the lie that he was strong enough to defeat him. Flexing his fingers Aiden readied himself to move the barrier again. Wyn wouldn't have to see the prince's body. He could return to her after this, heal her, and take her home. Never again would she have to concern herself with the 'nasty fairy' her mother spoke of. And she could live out her days happy and free of Mab and Oberon's games. Free of the traps and the reckless danger the prince pulled her into. He pushed harder, and all light went out save for his flames.

"What did you do?" the prince hissed.

"I didn't—"

"Leave!" A wavering woman's voice echoed from all angles of the room. Chills raced down Aiden's spine, and his flames dimmed. A gust of wind pounded at him, blowing out the fire and lifting him off his feet. Aiden cried out and from far away a growl sounded.

The door at the entrance opened, letting in the moonlight just before the wind pushed him out into a bank of surprisingly soft snow. He panted, staring back at the door as it slammed closed. Did he dare go back inside? No. Not when he didn't know what attacked him. That magic had no feel of Summer; if anything, it was cold and prickly like Winter, though it'd been years since he faced any Winter fae in battle.

It was best that he left now, lest he lose track of time and be late for their Majesties' draining. He shuddered as he made his way across the ice bridge. Turning back to the palace, he could see the windows were once again filled with light. Wyn had been talking and moving, even if the prince didn't know how to heal her. She would be alright until he returned. Now that he knew she was here, he would try to steal a moment alone with her… though perhaps she no longer wished to see him. After all, she'd stopped him from attacking the prince. Was it possible Wyn lied and still felt something for the prince? The thought burned like a hot coal in the back of his mind.

First thing when he woke in the morning, he would return, find her, explain things, and take her home.

CHAPTER 21

Freddie

Freddie crawled to a chair and leaned back. Pelrin was so reckless with his magic, no wonder he so rarely used it. Or perhaps he was just out of practice. She reached back to touch the part of her head that throbbed. Good. At least there was no blood.

She sighed and stared up at the ceiling. The ghost of Raul's furry head brushing her hand made her chest ache. He would tell her what an ass Pelrin was, and Aiden… Her heart squeezed; he'd been nearly just as bad. Though at least he tried to avoid her with his spells and protect her from the worst of Pelrin's. Still, he seemed more intent on killing Pelrin than seeing her. But perhaps it was an act for Pelrin's sake. The fight replayed in her mind. There was no faking the fury in his eyes; it'd been as if they'd been on a battlefield. Their hatred ran so deep — but why?

Outside of the war, there was nothing personal in their fight. Aiden didn't even want to be there. And Pelrin was an ass, but he'd never intentionally or willingly go out of his way to hurt someone. Aiden seemed to be the only exception.

Pushing herself up, Freddie made her way over to the bathroom. She strained her ears for the sounds of their battle, but it had faded, and the groans of the castle drowned out all other noise.

Strange. She hadn't noticed the sounds of the castle when Aiden had been there, though perhaps she'd just been too distracted to hear it.

Perching on the edge of the tub, Freddie stared at the painting of the snow woman. There was something cursed here. It seemed the only way to find out more about it was to travel through a vortex like the one that took Freya… and perhaps Daniel, too. She bit her lip; so much could go wrong if she tried something like that though. And how would she even begin to open another vortex?

A thought tingled at the back of her mind… Did she dare? If she broke the rules again, if she looked at Pelrin, like Mallory had suggested, maybe the vortex would reopen, and they could jump through together. But what if Mab and Oberon were on the other side? She was hardly capable of fighting them off.

Freddie slipped on Aiden's ring, a pitiful armor for her terrible plan. Again, she strained her ears for the sounds of the two fighting—her nerves itched to seek them out. If one of them gravely hurt the other, how was she supposed to react?

Making her way out of the bathroom, the image of the relief in Aiden's eyes when he first saw her burned in her mind and brought heat to her cheeks. Maybe after she got home and rescued the students, she could look for a way to free him, and they could have a real relationship in the Human Realm. Pelrin would have to come around somehow. Surely their hatred of one another was just some misunderstanding. Or… they would murder each other when they found out. She bit her lip. That was a problem for the Freddie who survived this.

Scorch marks covered the walls and had even damaged the furniture. The rest of the palace must have looked like this… long ago. She couldn't just sit here and wait for one of them to return. Striding over to the door, she hauled it open and stepped out into the hallway.

Uncertain of exactly where she was headed, she walked forward and allowed the castle to guide her. Finally, she reached a dead end at the dining room. Glancing around, she made her way to the door. Both Freya and Daniel had vanished when she'd gotten too close, but there was no one here now. Perhaps she could open a vortex without risking Pelrin.

She placed a hand on the handle and pulled it open slowly. The glitter snowscape invited her in, but her mind drifted back to its rejection of Pelrin. Still, it'd been she who'd been given the vision about this place as though something wanted her here. Something that might be the key to this whole curse. She poked the barrier but met nothing but air. Trying two fingers, then three, nothing happened, and Freddie put her entire arm into the room. She stepped inside, breathing in the freshness. What was this place?

"I was hoping you'd come." The frost fairy from the vision, Eira, stood before her.

Freddie looked over her shoulder to see who she might be talking to. After all, she hadn't been able to see her the last time... or had she? She'd let in the moonlight that changed back Raul. "Hello?"

"Yes, I can see you. Or sense you, rather, as I no longer have a body." She gave Freddie a warm smile as though oblivious to her horrifying words.

"Y-you—"

"In life I was a powerful blue fairy, advisor and lover to the queen of Winter, but now I guard her most prized possession... or at least I did."

"Oh." Freddie frowned. "So you don't know a way out of this curse? There's no connection?"

She shook her head. "I've been watching you, and I like you, Freddie. I will do what I can to help, but I don't know a way out of this curse."

Freddie sighed. All this chasing visions had been a waste of her time. She didn't need yet another person theorizing with her, she needed answers. Time was running out. "Thanks, but I think I'm alright."

"But I know of something that will help you free your missing people," the fairy said. "Come." She brushed past Freddie in a waft of icy air and led her out of the room.

Freddie sucked in a breath and followed her. They exited the dining room and ended up at a staircase. The woman led her up and turned abruptly into the bathroom which seemed to follow her everywhere. Stepping into the small space, Freddie watched the fairy as she looked mournfully around the room. With a wave of her hand the scene changed.

A dark-haired gold fae hurled shards of ice from the doorway but was blasted back by a torrent of flame. Freddie gasped as a man she recognized stepped into the doorway — Pelrin's father.

"Give up, Dani, and just give me the orb. Maybe then I'll let you keep your miserable life," he snarled.

"Never!" The palace shook, and the hallway moved sideways, making the king lose his footing. The queen shot another round of ice spears at him, two of which punctured his arm and chest as he stumbled into the room.

"You're going to regret that."

Freddie's guide turned her head. Before the queen could defend herself, another blast of flame engulfed her, and she collapsed into a pile of glittering ash. The king roared, and the vision faded.

Tears glistened in the blue fairy's eyes as she pointed at the spot where the queen had fallen. "Pound your fist on the ice."

Freddie frowned but did as she instructed. It cracked, revealing the golden dust. She looked back up at the fairy, uncertain of how her dead girlfriend's ashes were supposed to help break this curse.

"The ashes of fairy wings carry the power of transportation. With those of a green fairy, you can transport small groups across any of the realms. However, with gold fae ashes you can transport an army."

"I'm not planning on leading any armies." Freddie's hand hovered over the glittering powder; at least it didn't look like dead person ashes.

"What about a large group of students?"

Freddie's eyes widened. "Oh. Oh!" If Mab and Oberon held the students captive, she'd have to move them away fast, before they got caught. This powder would make her mission much safer.

"Thank you!"

She looked around for the fairy, but she was gone. A soft voice echoed around her. "Take care of him."

How strange… At least now her plan to purposefully trigger a vortex to suck up Pelrin and herself was less risky. Although, why did the fairy want her to protect Pelrin so bad if his father was the one who murdered her lover? Perhaps it didn't matter. She'd fulfill the fairy's wishes and take care of Pelrin, herself, and the missing students, tonight.

Freddie bit her lip as she arrived back at her room. Pelrin was already there, pathetically trying to clean up the scorched ruins.

"What are you doing?" she asked, staring at him as he batted at a chair with his paw.

"I guess I should probably use magic to right this place," he said. "But the last time I did, I hurt you. How is your head?"

Freddie gingerly touched where she'd fallen; it was still sore. "Bruised. Painful. Can you heal it?"

He nodded and moved over to her. His paw hovered over the spot, and a burning sensation crept over the wound. When he released her, it was still a bit sore, but at least she would be able to lay on it.

"Better?"

She nodded. "Thanks." Sleep pressed heavy on her as she let out a breath. Maybe the pain of her injury had been driving her to avoid it. But now, she pictured the soft pillows and snug furs of her bed. And with Aiden's ring on her finger, the sleep could be none of Pelrin's enchantments.

But she couldn't fall asleep — not tonight. Gripping the phone in her pocket, she turned to Pelrin.

"I'm going up to bed. Are you…"

"You go first. I don't want this to be awkward."

Freddie rolled her eyes. She wished he'd been so considerate when he'd climbed into bed with her and Raul in full bear form. At least now Pelrin was trying to be decent.

She snuggled deep into the soft bed. With the move and her parents' new connection to the Falluses, this place felt more like home than the one in DC. Laying back in the warmth, Freddie told herself she would only take a quick power nap than peek at Pelrin, but even as she closed her eyes, she knew it was a lie.

Her bladder woke her. She hauled herself out of bed, only barely opening her eyes to make the quick trip. Fumbling her way back, Freddie ran her fingers against something thin and delicate. She followed what felt like a curved, hollow bone until it met warm flesh. A wing? Her mind finally caught up, and she plunged her hand into her pocket for her phone. Pelrin hadn't stirred; now was the perfect time.

The phone buzzed; coming to life as she carefully pulled it out. She shouldn't be doing this. It was too dangerous. But if it wasn't Pelrin sleeping next to her, she had to know, and if it was, this might be her only chance to rescue the students. She patted the handkerchief she'd used to store the fairy dust. Jump through the vortex, find the students, and escape. Easy peasey.

With a few taps she flicked on the flashlight. Her hand trembled as she raised the phone and held it high above her bedmate's head. She sucked in a breath. A boy with soft golden hair cut trailing down his back, his nose perfectly straight between high cheekbones slept peacefully beside her. Pelrin.

He groaned and looked up at her, holding up a hand to shield his face from the light. "What are you doing, Fred?" His voice was heavy with sleep.

"Sorry, I'll put this away," she said, lowering the phone.

Pelrin tensed. "Freddie, what did you do? I —"

A tinkling laugh cut him off as a vortex opened up, not unlike the one which swallowed up Freya. This was her chance. "I told you, little prince, human curiosity will always win out," a woman's voice said.

"Please, wait!" Pelrin grabbed hold of the bed as the vortex pulled at him. Freddie reached out to grab him, but it was as though his body were made of hourglass sand. Reaching a hand up she tried to pass through the vortex, but it wouldn't let her pass. No, no, no.

"Say goodbye to your love, human girl." The laughter

sounded again, and particles of Pelrin drifted away into the gaping hole. Freddie scrambled desperately after Pelrin, but it was useless.

Tears streamed down her face as the last of Pelrin slipped through her fingers.

"Just remember," he said. "I will always love you." And he was gone as though he'd never been there.

She sat for a moment on the bed, trying to process what had just happened. Pelrin couldn't be gone… she couldn't be here alone. Her heartbeat picked up as she fiddled with Aiden's ring, twisting it and sliding it up and down her finger. Had he known about the curse? It hadn't seemed like it… he'd been genuinely surprised to see Pelrin as a bear. She tugged the ring off as she thought out her next move. There was a flash of blue light, and the room faded.

Freddie screamed as she fell through nothingness, but it quickly gave way to darkness, and she hit something soft, bounced, and rolled onto something hard.

"Ow," Freddie said as she moved her hands about searching for something to get her bearings.

Her hand brushed a cord, and she followed it up to a switch and flicked it on. Light flooded the room, making her wince. She looked around and her heart stuttered… it was her room, in her parents' new house. Somehow, impossibly, she was back.

CHAPTER 22

Aiden

Few things could draw Aiden from his sleep after their Majesties drained his magic, but the commotion above followed by a familiar sensation pulsing in his magic made his eyes snap open.

Pain lanced across his body as he struggled off his lumpy mattress and tugged on his boots. His dark hair was still tousled as he stepped into the hall—but it was empty, devoid of all guards. Straining his senses as he made his way to the stairs, Aiden tried to decipher the source of the pulsing. It wasn't decidedly bad, though he couldn't say for sure it was the opposite. Whatever, or whoever, was here held strong magic.

Mare's black, satin nightdress swished around her ankles as she met him at the top of the stairs; Tatiana, in an old t-shirt and sweats, reminding him of Wyn, hurried behind her. His brow crinkled. Wasn't Mare's room on the opposite side of the palace from the princess's?

"What's going on? I sensed something strange." Mare's black eyes were wide as she stared in the direction of the throne room.

"And my parents aren't in their bedroom," Tatiana said.

Mare whirled. "I thought I told you to—"

"It could be dangerous." The princess put her hands on her

hips while Mare massaged her temples.

"Exactly."

"Well, I just sense power, not danger." Aiden took a step forward, and the other two followed him.

Another shout came from the throne room. "Hold him firm and fetch the iron crown!" Mab's voice.

The three of them parted as Tatiana stepped in front of Aiden and Mare and pushed open the doors. Mab and Oberon looked up as they entered; an amused smile painted Mab's lips as she surveyed them. Her violet eyes landed on her daughter.

"Dearest, I'd like you to meet your groom." She gestured at a man, struggling and held in place by four guards. Like them, he was dressed for sleep. His bare chest heaved as he glared at them with flaming turquoise eyes — the prince.

But if he was here… where was Wyn?

Aiden's heart beat in his throat — he needed to wend back to the castle. But he couldn't, not with their Majesties and the prince watching him.

Tatiana let out a small gasp. "I — What?" She stared at the prince, her eyes wide and filled with dread. Something pulsed behind Aiden, making him groan and press a hand to his temple. Several guards marched in, and the prince looked up, his own brow crinkling.

"This." Mab gestured at the prince. "Is Prince Pelrin of Summer, your future husband. Isn't that right?"

He spat on the ground in front of Mab's feet, and a twinge of fear raced down Aiden's spine. If he'd shown such disrespect, the punishment would be beyond imagining. Waves of pain wafted through his head. It'd been too soon for his magic to replenish completely, but something was making him feel as though he'd just left the study. Mab brushed past them to the soldiers and returned carrying an iron crown. Aiden bit back another groan as the prince's eyes flew wide.

"Now, son, I know how much you love crowns, so I had one made for you. Would you like to try it on?" Her pearlescent teeth gleamed as she grinned.

The prince shook his head.

"No? You must address me properly. After all, I am a queen."

"No, Your Majesty," the prince said through gritted teeth.

Mab laughed. "Excellent! You see, as long as you continue to be such an obedient son, we'll get along just fine."

Aiden swallowed, the iron's power making him sway. Someone grabbed him by the shoulder, steadying him, yet still he could not maintain focus.

"Just breathe, we'll get out of this soon," Mare hissed in his ear.

"Mom, I don't think you should be threatening him." Tatiana looked from her mother to the prince. Red marks formed on her hands as she wrung them.

"Don't worry. I know how to handle men like him — men who think they are better than us."

Lounging on his throne, seemingly unphased by anything his wife had said or done, Oberon snorted and winked at his daughter.

Tatiana bit her lip. "I don't even know what to say to him."

"He can speak for himself." The prince's lip curled back in a familiar sneer. Heat blossomed in Aiden's chest. How he'd longed to burn that look right off the prince's face.

"Sorry," Tatiana said to the prince. She lifted her chin and cleared her throat. "Welcome to the Winter Palace, Prince Pelrin."

"You welcome guests, girl, not prisoners." The prince's haughty facade melted as Mab raised the crown once again. The iron's power struck Aiden too, and he gripped Mare tighter.

Tatiana flicked a glance back at the two of them. How sorry did he look in her eyes, rendered near useless? "Well it's been great to meet you. But I have to go." She turned to the door, and Aiden took a stumbling step to follow her.

"We'll set up something more formal for the two of you to get acquainted." Mab wiggled her fingers at them. "But in the meantime, you will learn the price of disrespecting my daughter." She rounded on the fairy prince, the crown in one hand.

Aiden didn't look back as a scream erupted behind him. All the times he'd dreamed the prince would take his place here had never felt like this. The hatred in his heart no longer burned so bright. Had Wyn somehow dimmed the flames? Regardless, he needed to find her.

In the corridor, Mare leaned him against a pillar like a rolled rug. Letting out a slow breath, Aiden studied the way she stared at Tatiana. Was Mare's gaze always so intense?

"Well, this is…" Tatiana faltered and looked to Mare.

"A disaster. You shouldn't have to marry him. He should be rotting in the dungeon if anything. Or worse." Shadows smoldered in Mare's eyes. "Marrying you, Tati, should be an honor, not a punishment."

Tatiana pinked, and Aiden frowned. Had something been going on between them and Mare just hadn't bothered to mention it? Although, he'd hid Wyn from her.

Sucking on the end of one of her braids, Tatiana looked to Aiden. "Why do you look so awful?"

Aiden shook his head. "I'm fine."

"He's not fine," Mare said, brushing a hand past her face as though banishing the thought. "It's the iron. The fairy in him can't handle it."

"Oh, Aiden, I didn't know you were a fairy," Tatiana said.

He nodded. "I just — I just need some air."

"I'll help you outside." Mare moved to grab his arm but Aiden pushed her off.

"I'm fine." He needed to find Wyn, and he couldn't do that with Mare clinging to his arm.

"We'll be in my room then," Tatiana said. "If you're feeling up to it."

He shrugged and hobbled down the narrow servants' passage around the ballroom and out the main entrance. His legs shook as he crept past a bored-looking Triglav.

As soon as his feet touched the ice bridge, he heard a shout from behind him. "Their Majesties let you off your leash, dog?"

Aiden grit his teeth. Wyn, Wyn, Wyn pulsed in his blood. Besides, he was just barely strong enough to wend; he was in no condition to pick a fight with the frost giant. He continued walking across the bridge, blocking out the slew of insults Triglav slung at him. When he finally reached the end, he wended, crossed its twin, and headed back into the castle.

"Wyn?" he called out, stepping into the large atrium. Crossing to the ballroom, Aiden remained alert for the light that had thrown him out the first time. "Wyn?"

His voice echoed against the smooth ice walls as though mocking him. A small, dark voice whispered in the back of his mind. What if she hadn't recovered? But that was nonsense; she'd been moving and talking last he saw her.

Still his heartbeat raced as he followed the same path back up the stairs to her room. "Wyn?"

"Wyn?" the ice castle called back.

How could the prince just leave her here? If he'd been in his place, he'd have ensured her safety before their Majesties took him. Aiden shook his head. He'd given her the ring—magic wouldn't affect her—so she'd be fine. Perhaps whatever spell Mab had used to capture the prince had rolled right off her, and she was somewhere safe. Pausing, Aiden strained his weak magic to sense her… if she was in the castle, maybe he could find her. Again, nothing.

He reached the room and crumpled to his knees. Between the wend there and trying to sense Wyn, he could hardly go on. Staring at the contrast between his olive skin and the crystal white of the frosty floor, Aiden cursed himself. He'd abandoned her, and now she was gone again. The scent of warmth made him look up. A chair, slightly charred, no doubt from their fight earlier, sat before a crackling fire; a fur draped over it practically inviting him over. Aiden picked himself off the ground and collapsed into the chair, letting his eyes fall closed.

"You have so much worry. I never wanted any of this for you."

Aiden's eyes flew open— a woman with frost-white hair and glowing amber eyes stared back at him, her blue wings folded against her back. Air pulled from his lungs as he stared at the vision… it couldn't be real.

"M-mother?"

She shook her head. "I am, and I am not. I carry her memories, her thoughts, her feelings, but I'm just a remnant of her magic. She used quite a good deal to protect this place. It was her undoing."

He swallowed. "It was why the Summer King was able to murder her?"

She nodded. "At least it kept the orb from unwanted hands until some roguish blue fairy barged in, stole it, and gave it to a human to keep safe!"

"The orb?" Aiden sat up. What had he done?

"It is like the Crown of Flames you so covet, but for Winter. I placed an enchantment that only a blue fae might enter the room and touch it. Never did I think my own son would put Winter in such jeopardy."

The remnant of his mother glowered at him, reminding him of the times he'd run off to play in the woods without telling her.

"Winter has already fallen to the Dark Fae. Summer will fall soon, and the reign of the gold fae will be over."

"I never wished for my son to become a murderer."

Aiden flinched as though she'd smacked him across the face. "Your son was left with little choice. I thought you might be glad the man who killed you is now dead." Tears burned in his eyes as he looked at her through a glassy haze.

"I am never happy you thought you needed to hurt your soul for me."

"You sound like... never mind." He shook his head. The owl woman, his mother, why did they all act as though he'd chosen this? He was the monster this world created. At least Wyn didn't see him that way... or at least, she hadn't.

"Don't disregard those that would see you do well. I know you must kill, but don't do it with anger in your heart. Promise me."

Aiden opened his mouth to respond, but the sounds of something creeping along the frost made him sit up. His mother turned, and her eyes widened as four fire salamanders crept toward them.

"Freezing Frosts! The king left them here so I might never recover the orb before him."

Aiden struggled to his feet, a yawning ball of fear roiling in his gut. "I was able to get past them, and the king never showed."

"I doubt he was expecting to be defending so much of his realm when I returned. Things are much different now. Can you wend?"

Reaching into the pool of magic within him, Aiden stiffened as his power was so diminished. He doubted if he could even shoot sparks. Wending would be a challenge, but he might be able to manage it, once…

He cast a glance at his mother and nodded. "I think."

"Good. I'm going to drop the barrier around this place. On my say so, get yourself far away."

"But what will happen to you?" Aiden could only imagine what taking down a barrier that powerful would do to her. His own barrier around the Winter palace would leave him depleted for weeks if he was ever ordered to take it down.

She looked at him, her lips drawn thin, her amber eyes watery. "I'll be gone. I'm just the magic your mother left behind; I'm not her. You've already mourned her."

"No, there has to be another way. I have so many questions."

She shook her head. Flames, nearly as hot as the Summer King's, flooded the doorway. Aiden stepped back, his heart pounding in time with his head. If he could just push through his exhaustion, maybe he could save her. Maybe he could save them both.

His mother raised her hands, and a loud crack rang out across the palace. "Go, now Aiden."

"But —" The flames pushed closer to them, sucking away the air. In their midsts, the salamanders chittered, knowing their prey had nowhere to run.

"Now!"

Half on instinct, half on fear, Aiden wended, his knees hitting the ground hard when he arrived back at the Winter Palace. No. He had to go back. What had he been thinking? His mother… Reaching inside himself, Aiden tried to wend. Nothing happened but a deeper wave of exhaustion washed over him. No no no.

A hot tear splashed on his hand as he crawled toward the ice bridge. How many times had he ached to see his parents, only to have his mother ripped away? Again.

CHAPTER 23

Freddie

The unwelcoming chill of her parent's new house seeped into Freddie's bones. She stared at the ring and realized she was still gripping her cell phone. Her hand shook as she flicked off the flashlight.

What had she done? Pelrin was gone… and it was all her fault. What if Mab and Oberon used him against Summer somehow? She could've turned the tide of the war in their favor. And now, back here, she was no closer to saving anyone than she had been months ago. What had she done?

Freddie closed her eyes, pushing back tears. Crying wouldn't help Pelrin. And the question wasn't what had she done, but what would she do? Freddie drummed her fingers on the phone. If she was able to take down a vampire with only a shoe, surely she could figure out something to help Pelrin. Ugh. This was stupid. If Mab could capture Pelrin, she could easily kill Freddie. But, if she could get word to his parents, they could send a gold fae to save him.

She unlocked her phone. Several notifications popped up, some from her friends harassing her about her secret boyfriend, one from her mother imploring her to understand the Fallus's reasoning, but one from the Times stood out. Her face stared back at her, snipped from a family portrait. She frowned and tapped into it.

Twice Kidnapped and Deluded: The Wynifred Jones Story.

The byline read Mallory Sheppard. Freddie growled, flipped to her text messages, and punched out a message to Amanda. "I need you."

The response was almost immediate. "What did you do?" There was a pause, followed by another message. "Be there tomorrow."

Freddie sighed; Amanda was more level-headed. She would be able to figure out a way to get a message to Pelrin's parents. Maybe even Jefferson could help. Her head pounded with thoughts of Pelrin tortured or killed in Mab and Oberon's dark lair. She should've never tried to break the stupid curse — she wasn't strong enough.

Closing her eyes, Freddie tried to calm her mind enough to sleep, but it wouldn't come. She tossed and turned until the sun came up, then rose from bed with a pounding headache.

After a quick shower, she trooped downstairs to find her mom sitting at the kitchen table facing her. Shit.

"What on earth were you thinking? What were you trying to do to us with this note?" Her mom held up the letter Freddie had written them last night. It would've been better if she'd said nothing at all. "You want to go after them again? Have you lost your mind?"

"Mom, I'm practically an adult. I need to start thinking of my career."

"Honey, you're still in high school." Pinching the bridge of her nose, her mother shifted in her seat. "I'm just glad you came to your senses before you actually left."

"Mom, I need to stand out if I want to be a real journalist. Just because I didn't chase this story last night doesn't mean I won't."

"Charging head first into danger won't make you stand out — it'll only make you look foolish. Only a few months ago you were in the hospital for chasing one of your stories, then you were kidnapped. I don't want to think of what will happen next." Her mom's voice broke on the last word.

Freddie's chest tightened, and she grimaced. Hurting her

parents was never part of the plan, but neither was getting Pelrin captured by Mab. Recently it seemed everyone who came near her got hurt: Aiden, Freya, Pelrin, her parents… maybe she shouldn't have called Amanda.

"Mom, I can really make a difference in this world. I just need the space to figure things out on my own."

"Wynifred! When you figure things out, you're nearly killed. I won't lose a daughter just because you've romanticized the life of a journalist. Why can't you try to be a political reporter like your friend, Mallory? It's so much safer."

Freddie gritted her teeth. Why had she even told Mallory what she was going through in the first place? Mallory just wanted to discredit her. But they'd all see once she saved Pelrin and Freya and the others. Her story would be front page news. "My goal is to tell the truth, Mom, not whatever lie a politician wants us to believe. And Mallory is not my friend."

"Well she should be. You need friends who can talk some sense into you. Good, solid human friends."

"Do you have a problem with Raul and Jefferson now? If you remember, Raul was kidnapped, too."

Her mom flushed and averted her eyes. "I—I just think it might be healthier if you were around people who were more like you. Raul and Jefferson have different goals."

"They're interested in finance! You're starting to sound just like that DICK!" Freddie whirled and started back up the stairs. She slammed her bedroom door and leaned against the wall, slowly sliding to the floor.

The day passed by slowly. Freddie downloaded the untouched modules of homework she'd missed and tried to work her way through it. She needed a break, something, anything to keep her mind off the destruction she caused.

Eventually, savory scents of garlic and sage drifted up to her room. She walked down the stairs and sat awkwardly at the table with her parents. They ate in silence, her mom opening her mouth several times, only to shut it again. When dinner was over, her father took up his post in the dining room with his Bible while her mother returned to the kitchen to clean up. If it was a typical night, Freddie would offer to help her, but now she could barely tolerate being in the same room.

She checked her phone. Amanda had texted OMW three hours ago. Where was she? Freddie had just finished several more calc problems when the doorbell finally rang. She raced downstairs.

"Who's that?" her mom asked.

Freddie ignored her and jerked open the door. Amanda and Raul gave her hesitant smiles.

"Oh, Amanda, Raul, how um. Why are you here?" her mom asked, her face red as Freddie led her friends inside. Her father gave them a lackluster wave from his chair.

"Just here to hang with Fred," Amanda said.

"Mrs. Jones, you got anything to eat?" Raul drifted toward the kitchen, but Freddie grabbed the back of his hoodie.

"Raul, does your mother know you're here? She had some choice words to say to me after the incident." Freddie's mother blocked their path, her arms folded.

"I—uh, well. She thinks I'm at church," he said.

Her mother sighed. "I'm calling her."

"Wait, no!"

"You can deal with that later—we need to talk." Freddie shot a dark look at her mother and dragged Raul past her mother and up the stairs.

"I'm calling your mom, too, Amanda!" Her mother held the phone as though it were a weapon and shook it from the bottom of the stairs.

Amanda sat on the pink bedspread while Raul sank into an inflatable pink chair.

"Do you think this thing will hold me?" he asked.

"That's not important right now," Amanada said. "Why are you back, Freddie? Did you break the spell on Pelrin?"

"No." Freddie dropped beside her. "I've made things worse; I looked at him, and I think Mab took him." She buried her head in her hands. "It's all my fault."

"Oh Freddie, it's not." Amanda patted her shoulder.

"So is Pelrin… is he…" Raul squeaked in the chair, his face ashen.

"I don't think he's dead," Freddie said. "If she wanted him dead, she wouldn't have gone through the whole bear thing. I think he's her prisoner. We have to help him, don't we?"

"Do we?" Amanda's voice rose an octave.

"Couldn't you get word to Jefferson? He could warn Pelrin's parents," Freddie asked.

"Jefferson was told that Pelrin is in the palace and won't see him. He can't even get past the guards. How do you think he can warn Pelrin's parents?"

"He could tell them he knows me. I'm pretty sure Pelrin never told his parents we broke up."

"He tried that as soon as you went missing. It's no use. I don't want to say this but—"

"Then don't. He might be a stuck-up jerk, but Pelrin is our friend, and I got him into a heap of trouble. I need to find a way to get him out of it. And Freya too, none of this would've happened if I hadn't been so eager to break the curse."

Raul scooted closer; his face flushed. "Too bad you can't talk to his parents yourself."

"That's a great idea." Though Freddie's stomach sank as she spoke, a plan formed in her mind. "The border's not too far. We could just wait a couple days until spring and cross into Summer and warn his parents."

"You want us to just walk into Fairy like there isn't a war going on?" Amanda said.

"We'd avoid the war zones obviously. And there aren't any battles between Spring and Summer; those roads are perfectly safe."

"Relatively." Raul huffed and folded his arms. "And how are we going to get into Spring? It's supposed to be walled off."

"We have to at least try!"

Amanda ran a hand through her hair. "I don't like this plan, Freddie. So many things could go wrong. We have no idea how far it is to Summer—it's not like we could drive. There's no GPS. How will we even know where we're going?"

"Pelrin could die a horrible, horrible death if we don't help him. I—I understand if you don't want to go. It's my fault he was captured, and I'm the one who needs to make this right."

"Freddie, this wasn't your fault. Mab was the one who cursed them," Amanda said.

"But if it weren't for me, neither Pelrin nor Freya would've been vortexed."

"Or Mab would have taken you, too. You can't just go running into Fairy because Pelrin's been taken."

"No one else knows about Mab or the castle in Winter. We need to get word to Summer, and the only way to do that is to go ourselves. Or myself." Freddie looked imploringly at her friends.

Amanda glanced to Raul then back to Freddie. "No, no if you go, I go. My mom will probably murder me, but it's okay. The important thing is saving Pelrin."

Raul sighed. "I guess I can't let you girls go alone. And I won't just abandon Freya."

"We'll get Pelrin's parents to rescue them both... and the others I guess." Tears shone in Freddie's eyes. Maybe they could really do this. "Now what to pack?"

Raul's phone buzzed almost violently. He looked down at it, and his face paled. "You guys pack, I got to take this." Angry shouts came from the other end as Raul cringed.

Amanda laughed. "Now, where were we? We'll need shoes, clothes, tampons, hand sanitizer, batteries. Oh God, so many things."

"Tampons?" Raul put a hand over the speaker and raised a brow.

"Yes," they both said together.

"I'm more curious about the hand sanitizer," Freddie said.

"Well, nature." Amanda got up and dug out Freddie's backpack. Emptying it, she sorted through Freddie's clothes.

Raul finally hung up with a "lo siento" and moved to help Amanda. She shoved him aside, and he wandered around the room, inspecting a littering of trinkets on Freddie's desk and bookshelf.

"It's probably best to stay out of her way," Freddie said as she scrolled through her phone, trying to research anything else they might need.

He paused at the nightstand, picking up a weighted leather pouch with a paper tag. "What's this?"

Freddie looked up from her phone. "Toss it to me."

Raul held onto it and squinted at the tag. "It says… To Wyn, love Aiden. Aiden?"

"Give it!" Freddie's face heated as she launched herself across the room and snatched the pouch away. It was heavier than she expected. She reached inside and found a pearlescent ball a little bigger than her fist.

"It's from your secret boyfriend, isn't it?" Amanda crossed the room to inspect the present next to her. "What is it?"

"I don't know." Freddie turned the ball over, searching for some hint or inscription. Maybe it was just a pretty pearl; she knew the perfect place on her shelf for it.

"Fred, I only know one Aiden, and he's bad news. Please tell me it's not the same guy," Raul made his way over to the bed to roll Freddie's clothes and shove them into her backpack.

"How would she have even met him?" Amanda rolled her eyes and considered a pair of heels.

"No, Amanda, I won't need those." Freddie snatched them away from her and hurled them back into the closet.

Raul zipped up the bag, still with plenty of space for food, and sat down. "She did meet him that one time at Illusion."

"You said she was drunk."

"I was drunk." Freddie hastily slipped Aiden's gift into her bag besides the Winter queen's wing powder. They would need it to get home. Had Aiden been hurt, seeing her with Pelrin? Did he regret giving her this gift now?

"Freddie, just tell Raul you're dating some other Aiden. It is a rather common name, you know." She stared pointedly at Raul, and Freddie shrank in on herself. Lying would be easy, but when the truth of all this eventually came out, it would be doubly messy if they didn't know. Groaning, she buried her head in her arms.

"No, Freddie, tell me this isn't the same guy Jefferson defeated!" Amanda gripped her shoulder. "He's obviously using you for revenge. Maybe to get the crown back?"

"We were dating before that."

"You what?" Amanda spat out her hair. "How long has this been going on, and why didn't you tell me?"

"Since that night you tried to set me up. He was there, at the club, and we hit it off… kinda." A small smile crept across her face, remembering how terrified she'd been; it was hardly love at first sight. Was it even love now?

Amanda scowled. "How could you not tell us? Don't you trust us?"

"You're dating Jefferson! He'd go straight to Pelrin, and they'd kill each other, literally!"

"Well, killing people is what he does…" Amanda trailed off.

"It's a war. Pelrin kills people, too. Are you really going to say just because he's on the other side of the war, fighting for brown fae rights, he's evil?"

"This is going to end so bad, Fred," Raul said. "When Pelrin finds out…"

It was bad enough seeing them together the last time when they had no idea she knew them both. Putting her hands behind her back, she twisted Aiden's ring. She needed to talk to him, to explain things. He needed to know the truth and that she still cared about him.

"My love life isn't important right now. We need to finish packing and figure out something to do tomorrow." Freddie got to her feet and hauled her bag off the bed.

Raul sighed. "Why don't we just go tour DC and leave tomorrow at midnight? That way we'll arrive in Fairy just as the realms shift."

"You want us to navigate a magical warzone in the middle of the night?" Amanda looked at Raul. The phrase if looks could kill came to Freddie's mind.

"Okay, here's an idea," Freddie said. "We see the city, get

some waffles, and leave first thing in the morning?"

"Jeeze, Freddie, what is with you and the waffles?" Raul shook his head.

"No electricity in Fairy, remember? They don't have waffles. Gotta get 'em while I can." She grinned, though inwardly her mind buzzed. Things were getting dangerous. She couldn't go after Pelrin and the others on her own, but she loathed risking the lives of her friends too. At least it was just through Spring and to Elessea; the Dark Fae hadn't penetrated those areas yet. It was as safe as a trip to Fairy could be.

###

Freddie bounced her knee against the car door as the town melted into trees. Sunlight shone blindingly off the iced-over snow.

"Don't turn," she said when they reached the exit for the border.

"What? Why? I thought we wanted to cross." Raul frowned as they passed the sign.

"There's a gap farther up."

"Do I even want to know why you know that?" Amanda pressed a hand to her temple.

"Journalistic privilege," Freddie said.

"That's promising." Raul slowed as he reached the end of the highway and the road turned to gravel and trees. They got out of the car and crunched through the snow toward the forest. "So, where's the border?"

Freddie slipped her freezing hand into Amanda's. They stepped forward. A pressure settled on her shoulders as she took another step.

"I think this is…" Freddie stopped. Raul was no longer beside them. "Where's Raul?"

They stepped back. Raul was standing behind a tree.

"Where did you guys go?" He scratched his head. Amanda sighed and held out her hand.

The pressure came again as they moved forward, like walking through jello. One step, two steps, a gust of warm air blew past, and they stepped into Spring. Grass as green as turf covered the rolling hills before them. At their backs was a massive white wall; Freddie gasped as she tried to spy the top of the structure, but it disappeared amongst the clouds and to either side. They were trapped, but at least they were on the right side. Now they just needed to figure out how they were to get to Summer.

A light breeze blew by, ruffling her hair. Had Amanda packed for warmer weather? Shedding her coat, Freddie took several steps toward a grove of trees bursting with pink and white flowers, perfuming the air with their gentle scent.

"Well that was almost too easy," Raul said.

"We're not even halfway there yet, bud," Freddie said as they marched through the grass.

"We need to go south." Amanda glanced up and pointed. "Jefferson says that's how he gets to Summer."

"But Jefferson can't get back now, because of the wall, right?" Raul gestured at the wall. Amanda nodded. "So if we go south, how are we to get out?"

"Well, we're already stuck. Going farther in won't make things worse." Freddie flicked a look at her hand. The ring…Could it have let them enter? Was it powerful enough to pass through Spring's barriers?

They walked through an endless meadow for what seemed like hours, taking breaks to snack on the Oreos and Doritos Raul had packed for "sustenance." The sky was just becoming tinged with orange when he pointed at a castle like the ones the fae built in the forests of Europe after the first treaty had been passed.

Seven towers jutted into the air; the center one stood proud above the others. Large glass windows shimmered like bubbles from between intricately designed arches and frames. Below, tucked into the hill, she could just make out a myriad of buildings.

"Do you think that's the capital?" Amanda asked.

"There's only one way to find out." Freddie's heart lifted; perhaps they'd be able to find someone who could help them get a message to Summer faster. The fairy dust pressed against her leg from her jeans pocket, but she didn't dare use it yet. If Summer sent people in to rescue Pelrin, she'd slip away from Amanda and Raul and go with the soldiers. That way, everyone would get out safely.

They raced toward the city. As they drew closer, the meadow turned into farmland, then to cobblestones. Several green and brown fae stared at them as they slowed, entering the city surrounding the castle.

A gaggle of dryad children, their green skin patterned with leaves, shimmered in the evening light. One stumbled over a ball and sprawled out in front of Freddie.

"You're okay," she said and helped the child to his feet.

He gathered up his ball, eyes wide. "You're outsiders, aren't you?"

"That's right, we just came to visit," she said. A prickling sensation raced up her back as several other people turned to stare.

"Really just passing through." Raul put a hand on Freddie's shoulder and spoke loud enough so that those surrounding them could hear. "Not staying whatsoever."

"Where are you from?" the boy asked.

"The Human Realm," Freddie said. Raul nudged her hard in the ribs.

A man stepped forward. His torso was that of a chestnut horse, the brilliant coat matching his hair. "I — uh, I think you should see the queen. I could take you. She'll want to see anyone who breaches our borders." He beckoned, and Freddie and Amanda exchanged glances. They didn't have much of a choice now.

They walked up a winding cobblestone path past brightly painted buildings decorated with daffodils and tulips. A faun playing a flute paused mid-note to stare along with the other Spring citizens. Freddie flinched — an image of the satyr coming toward her flashed in her mind, then dissipated.

The polished quartz walls of the palace glowed a translucent pink. The three of them gaped as they passed fairy guards standing at attention. Several dwarves even stood at key intervals amongst them, battle axes at their hips. Freddie raised her brows. In Summer, dwarves and other brown fae were always in service positions, never as high ranking as a royal guard.

"Stay here," the centaur said as they stopped in an open

courtyard. Freddie nodded as he trotted off inside.

"Welp, it's been nice knowing you friends," Amanda said, her eyes trained on the group of staring guards across from them.

"What do you want to bet they throw us in the dungeon? They seem to be real unhappy that we 'outsiders' found our way in," Raul said.

"They're probably more concerned about their wards. We'll be fine." Freddie pulled free a curl from her french braid and twirled it around her finger. Hopefully. The more time they spent here the longer Pelrin suffered.

"Says the girl who nearly got us turned into vampires," Amanda said.

"We had a choice, vampires or werewolves. And I'd like to point out that we are neither."

"Dios mio, why did I agree to come with you guys?" Raul gripped his hair and whirled toward the castle entrance just as a woman in a shimmering gown of silver, gold wings tucked behind her, stepped out to greet them. But the gold fae's appearance wasn't what gave Freddie pause. Beside her, hunched with a face covered in wrinkles was another fairy woman — but her wings were blue.

CHAPTER 24

Freddie

Freddie sucked in a breath as she and Amanda curtsied. Raul attempted a bow, but the heavy bag on his shoulders forced him to flail his arms to keep his balance. The gold fae laughed as Raul fought to right himself.

"Welcome to Spring. I am Queen April Rain, and this is my advisor Delthuria. We heard you were passing through and had some questions about how you got to our realm." The queen waved a hand, and suddenly the courtyard filled with arm chairs and couches. Freddie, Amanda, and Raul squished together on one couch as the queen and the blue fairy took positions opposite them.

"Please, call me Nona." The blue fairy looked them over, her smile fading as her eyes landed on Freddie. Leaning forward, she grabbed her wrist. Though she tried to pull away, the old woman's grip was like iron as she examined the ring… Aiden's ring.

"Where in the seven realms did you get this? This is no human trinket." The woman ran a boney finger over it.

"It was a gift." Freddie finally yanked her arm away from the fairy.

"Oh God, Freddie, did he give it to you?" Amanda looked between Freddie and the fairy. "We are so sorry if it's offensive."

"Who is 'he,' and how did he come across this ring?" the fairy asked. The queen's brow was now furrowed too… crap.

Freddie bit her lip. "He's my boyfriend, kinda, and I have no idea how he got the ring but he said it would protect me."

"Or get you into a heap of trouble," Raul said under his breath. Freddie wanted to groan, but now was not the time.

"A human boy gave you this ring?"

"No, he's fae." She didn't dare give up Aiden's name. Mentioning that she was dating an infamous soldier in the Dark Fae army probably wouldn't go over well with these people.

"I see…" Nona frowned, eyes narrowing in on Freddie before she straightened. "It seems your boyfriend has somehow stumbled upon the Ring of Rains."

Freddie pulled her lips tight. She'd always known Aiden's gift was powerful, but surely she would have at least heard of the Ring of Rains… Pelrin had told her about the objects each realm held sacred, but Spring's was unknown. She bit her lip; if it came down to it, would she give up Aiden's ring for the chance to save Pelrin?

"I'm sorry, but we're in quite a hurry. We need to get to Elessea as fast as possible."

The blue fairy's smile dimmed. "You have no idea what you have there. It belongs to Spring."

She twisted the ring on her finger. Could it possibly be their object?

"Is this your object of power?" How had it fallen to Aiden? Surely he could've used it to escape his bond to Mab and Oberon…

"So you know about the objects of power." Nona leaned back and glanced at the queen. "April, dear, I can handle things from here."

The queen pressed her finger tips together, then rose from her seat. "I'll have some rooms prepared for you."

Freddie sucked in a breath. They couldn't stay here — they had to make it to Summer.

Nona watched the queen swan back into the palace, then turned to Freddie. "Do you know the story of how the objects were created?"

Freddie shook her head as Amanda creeped her hand into

Freddie's and squeezed.

"They were made centuries ago by blue fairies, to help the gold fae protect their realms. That's why only blue fae can sense the objects' powers, but only gold fae can use them. Each realm used to have a blue fairy protecting their objects, but other realms got greedy, and they hunted us down in search of the power we hid."

"Does that mean you were supposed to be protecting Freddie's ring?" Raul asked.

Nona shook her head. "Not me. My son and his wife. They were killed in a horrible fire along with their child. I searched for the ring for months, but it was to no avail. I feared it had been destroyed."

A fire... Hadn't that been how Aiden's parents had died? Could this be Aiden's grandmother? Her face burned at the thought.

What if Mab and Oberon had saved him and that was how he'd fallen into a life debt with them? Her heart squeezed at the thought of Aiden going from the horror of watching everything he loved burn to being forced to serve the Dark Fae.

"Well, at least you did your best to find it." Freddie got to her feet, Amanda and Raul following suit. Raul's stomach roared.

"Why, I often forget how hungry you young people get. And the sun is near set. Come along, and I'll get you something to eat." The blue fairy leapt into the air, and Raul jogged after her.

Freddie could have kicked him. They should be planning how to escape, and yet he was mesmerized at the mere mention of food. Flowers burst from overflowing pots from all angles of the palace, filling the room with a scent more suffocating than perfume.

"You'll understand now, of course, why we have to have the ring back," Nona said without looking back. "We'll give you a boon in compensation."

Freddie pulled her hand close to her chest. They weren't going to let them leave until they took her ring, and she had no intention of giving it up, not when she'd need it to get everyone home safely. The bag of the fairy wing powder pressed against her leg.

Something twisted in her gut. How much powder did she

have? If she used it now, what if there wasn't enough to get the students out? Her nerves buzzed—if they didn't get out of Spring there'd be no saving the students anyway. Summer was bound to have some way of rescuing the students, if it meant getting Pelrin out too. Biting her lip, Freddie turned to Amanda.

"Grab Raul," she said to Amanda. Freddie slipped her hand into her pocket and maneuvered out a pinch of the golden powder.

Amanda dragged Raul back, and he frowned. "What's wrong? Aren't you guys eager to see what they serve in a place like this?"

Eyes flying wide, Freddie pulled them back as Nona turned. "What are you humans up to?"

Freddie threw the powder into the air, picturing the golden domes and spires of Pelrin's home city. "Summer Palace," she whispered. One hand on Raul, the other on Amanda, the world before them blurred. Blue light shot at them, but as soon as she saw it, it was gone, replaced by the grand steps of the palace.

"That could have gotten us into some serious trouble, Fred," Raul said, a muscle in his temple throbbing.

"But she was right to do it." Amanda stepped between them. "That blue fairy wasn't about to let us leave." Raul looked from Amanda to Freddie and sighed.

"Sorry, Raul. I would've told you guys my plan, but I had to act fast or…" She drew her finger across her neck.

"I get it. It's just this whole thing. Everytime we meet someone nice they either get kidnapped or want to kill us."

"Welcome to life with Freddie." Amanda ribbed them both.

Freddie shook her head. "Come on, guys. Pelrin's counting on us."

They approached the palace without being questioned. Freddie eyed the guards as they passed—shouldn't they be stopping them? The realm was at war… The steps shone like polished ivory as they looked back from the entrance hall at the shimmering river, reflecting the lights of the city. A black-cloaked woman, head bowed, brushed past, muttering her apologies. Freddie frowned at two sneering leprechauns as they followed behind. How could a city so lovely hide so much ugliness? It was almost as though they were trying to cover up the war and their own suffering people.

They walked through halls open to courtyards bursting with flowers glowing white and blue in the twilight. She was so enraptured with the courtyard, she didn't see the faun before she crashed into him.

"Oh my God, I'm so sorry!"

He turned and looked her up and down. "Are you human? You don't even look like a changeling."

"Does it matter?" Heat flooded Freddie's face. Flashbacks from when Pelrin first brought her to the Summer court pressed to the front of her mind. His parents hadn't been too impressed with her humanity either.

"I suppose not… I guess we all need to petition the royals about something." He gave her a half smile and turned back around.

A fairy put a hand on Freddie's shoulder and wrenched it back. "Of course it matters — humans go to the back of the line."

"Says who?" She no longer had to play the part of Pelrin's doting human girlfriend. Who cared if they judged her now.

"Back down, Fred," Raul said. He shot the fairy a dark glare, and she folded her arms.

"Don't think you're any better, werewolf. You red fae are just as bad as the brownies and humans."

Amanda stepped around Raul and shot a kick at the fairy's ankle. "What did you say about red fae?"

"Jeeze, friend." Freddie pulled her back.

"Jefferson has been battling idiots like her for months to see Pelrin. I'm tired of these stupid faries treating him like crap."

"Why you little—" What looked like glowing, green sand materialized around the fairy's fingers. Something blurred before them, and the fairy shrieked as Jefferson gripped her wrist.

"Try it, and I'll snap your hand clean off." His red eyes flashed as the green light dissipated.

"Jefferson!" Amanda gasped.

For a moment she looked as though she'd back down, then,

with a wicked smile, she opened her mouth. "Guards!"

A man, with skin like tree bark, jogged towards them, a tiny pixie bobbing just behind. "What's the issue here?"

"Them." The fairy pointed at Freddie and her friends. "They tried to—"

"Freddie? Is that you?" The pixie cried as she drew closer.

"Ginnith?" Freddie made out the coily red hair and the overly bright green eyes of the guard Pelrin had stuck on her when she'd been investigating the kidnappings.

"What are you doing here? What are all of you doing here?"

"You, uh, know these… people?" the other guard asked.

"Excuse me!" The fairy put her hands on her hips. "Are you going to arrest them?"

Ginnith puffed up her chest. "They are personal guests of His Highness. You will do well not to cause problems."

She snarled at them, but stepped back in line.

The other guard shrugged. "That's on your shoulders now." He gave a half-hearted wave to Ginnith and strolled back down the line. They stood in silence as they watched him disappear amongst the crowd.

"Now tell me what you guys are doing here. Did His Highness send you?" Ginnith flitted in front of Freddie—her wings beating so fast they buzzed.

"Pelrin's in trouble, Ginni. Mab cursed and took him. We need to tell his parents so they can send someone after him."

Ginnith blinked. "You're sure it's Mab."

"Yes, and he might not have much time."

"I'll take you to see the queen, but the rest of you have to stay here. The other petitioners would lose their minds if they saw. The general's dealing with them all while the queen's in mourning."

"Over Pelrin?"

"And the king. That Dark Fae dog murdered him." Ginnith trembled, red tinging her face as she bared her teeth. "If I ever see him on the field, I'll do what it takes to bring him down."

Freddie swallowed and looked back at Amanda, Raul, and Jefferson. "Anything you want to add, Jefferson?"

He shook his head. "I was going to request a small party to search for Pelrin, but you seem to have a better lead than I do. Just tell the queen and come right back. Do not volunteer or try to sneak off and go look for him yourself."

"I want to be a journalist, not a casualty." Freddie scoffed as Ginnith led her down the hall.

"The Dark Fae have been getting closer with every attack. I think the queen is stretched too thin between losing her husband and son and this war." Ginnith sucked in her lip as she continued down the winding halls lit with glittering balls of fairy light.

"It's that bad? But the entire royal family are gold fae. Can't they protect the people — I mean they're so powerful."

Ginnith frowned. "They're royals. Look at what happened when the king went into battle. The general is the only one who should be fighting now that the line is at stake."

"They care more about lineage at a time like this? They should all be out there fighting. Innocents are dying, the US might stop taking people from Fairy, and it'll just get harder for them to find refuge."

"You don't understand war. Leave it to the experts; I trust the gold fae will lead us well. I just wish the queen would show her face to the people... they worry." She knocked on a plain wood door. "Your Majesty? I have news on your son."

"Enter," came a wavering voice. The door creaked open, and Freddie stepped inside.

The queen whipped around. She had Pelrin's turquoise eyes and straight nose, but her waist-length hair was brown and her face was much rounder. "You're — what are you doing here?"

"Your Majesty." Freddie gave a quick and awkward curtsy. "I was just with Pelrin — we were cursed, and then he was kidnapped by Mab."

She let out a little choked sob. "Then he is lost to us."

"No, I don't think he's dead. Maybe if you could just send —"

"Send? Send who? My army that is already stretched thin? My guards who are all that stand between Elessea and destruction? As much as I love my son, I need to be a queen. It's something someone like you wouldn't understand."

"But Pelrin—"

"Is a soldier of this realm. He knew the risks of war."

"But this palace is filled with gold fae. Just one of them could help save him." A siren blared through the walls. Freddie's chest tightened as she looked around for a window but saw nothing.

The queen's face fell. For a moment, terror replaced the fury in her eyes, then she turned her gaze back to Freddie. "The Dark Fae are at our doorstep, and we've lost our most powerful weapon against them. Our only hope is having enough gold fae to keep the city strong, and that still might not be enough." Her turquoise eyes blazed as she stared Freddie down.

Anger gathered in Freddie's chest. Even if the city was weak, surely one gold fairy wouldn't make the difference. She opened her mouth to retort but lost her thoughts as screams rang out.

The queen continued to stare out the window. "Ginnith, find some wing powder and send her home. I don't need any more deaths on my shadow."

"But—" Freddie's voice broke. She couldn't just leave Pelrin to die.

"Leave!" A flash of blue fire shot across the courtyard, and the queen gasped. Eyes wide, she turned to Ginnith. "He's here."

"How—" Freddie started. Could Aiden truly be here? But why?

"Ginnith, come with me. Freddie, you stay here until this is over." Another boom rocked the palace, followed by a cacophony of screams.

"But wait. What's happening?"

The queen spun on her heel with Ginnith following after. She turned as though to say something, but the queen slammed the door, followed by a loud click. Freddie pressed her lips together. If the Dark Fae were attacking the city, she needed to get to her friends. She tried the door—it was locked, but not magically. Freddie rolled her eyes and pulled a bobby pin from inside her braid. The lock came undone easily, and she slipped out into the hall. People were collapsing everywhere she looked.

For a moment, she thought they were dead, and her heart squeezed. Please no. But then, a loud snore erupted from a satyr, and she noticed the gentle rise and fall of the chests of the people she passed. If Aiden was here, had he done this? Or perhaps Mab and Oberon had found a way to curse Elessea too. She needed to get to Amanda, Raul, and Jefferson before it hit them. She ran through the halls to where people were still standing in line.

"Run, there's a curse behind me!"

Some of them just stared at her, others turned to each other with panicked voices; a few followed her down the hall.

As she rounded a corner, a woman dressed in a black cloak blocked her path. "What's a human doing in Summer?" she asked.

Freddie drew back. "There's no time! You've gotta get out of here—there's a curse coming."

She laughed, tossing back her dark braid. "You're the girl whose likeness is in the prince's room."

Was this woman a palace servant? How else would she know that detail? Freddie said nothing and tried to move past the woman, but she blocked her path.

The woman reached out a hand. "Follow me. I can help."

But Freddie moved out of her grasp. A tendril of smoke curled about her wrist and tightened around Freddie's arm. "Come along dear, I want you to meet some friends of mine." The woman grinned with sharpened teeth as the darkness around her grew. Freddie screamed as the woman yanked her forward, and the shadows swallowed them up.

CHAPTER 25

Aiden

Elessea had fallen. Summer was theirs, and yet Aiden couldn't help the unease pulsing through his body. Wyn was missing again, though perhaps she was back in the Human Realm. He needed to see her safe with his own eyes. Then… Then he'd give her up for good.

The thought made his throat tighten as he paced the halls waiting for Mare to return. With her back, their Majesties wouldn't notice him missing. The note with her parents' new address seemed to burn a hole in his pocket. He let out a sigh and pounded a fist against the icy wall.

Trooping up the steps, Aiden crossed to the doors of the throne room so he'd know as soon as Mare arrived. There was another pre-wedding revel that evening, and their Majesties, Tatiana, and the prince were all in attendance. Mare would surely stop there with any information before she sought him out or returned to her chambers. Aiden leaned against a pillar as a hag and yeti couple strode into the ballroom. He didn't need to show his face and have their Majesties humiliate him for their guest's enjoyment. Aiden slipped to the space between the pillar and the wall and peered out to spy on the party.

The prince was cuffed to the throne beside Tatiana; the poor girl, despite some frost fairy's best efforts, looked as miserable as the prince. She'd already picked apart the curls trailing down from her high bun. A pin was tucked along the neckline of her gown, no doubt a victim of her worrying fingers. She didn't deserve to be forced into a relationship with the prince—no one did. A dark thought nagged at the back of his mind. But did Wyn want that relationship? He shook it away; she pitied him for being cursed. Though even as a bear, he couldn't have been pleasant to be around.

Shadows rippled across the room, and Aiden's breath hitched. Finally.

Mare stepped out of the darkness dragging something... someone behind her. When the shadows receded, Aiden's eyes widened. No. Wyn struggled in Mare's grasp but froze when she saw the four royals staring at her.

"Your Majesties." Mare bowed low. "I thought some leverage might help encourage our friend a bit." Tatiana shot a glare at Mare, but Mare didn't meet her eyes.

Wyn's gaze flicked from the prince to Mab to Oberon, skipping over the less imposing Tatiana. Though she didn't speak, terror was written across her face. It took everything in him not to rush the ballroom and save her—it was his worst nightmare made real. Of course the prince would drag Wyn into this. Why couldn't he just keep her safe? Perhaps he didn't truly care for her. It was hard to imagine someone like him falling for the charms of a human, even someone like Wyn.

"Rise, Mare," Mab said. "What have you brought us?"

"This." Mare shoved Wyn's pack, nearly making her tumble forward. "Is the girl your prince passed his time with in the Southern palace. I found her in Summer pleading for aid to free him and thought she might be useful."

The prince let out a choked sound, but his features remained tight and tense. Aiden's lip curled—he didn't deserve to feel pain for Wyn's capture. She'd been in Summer because of him.

"My, my, dear, you're a long way from home," the queen said. "I'm Queen Mab, but you may call me Your Majesty. This is my husband, King Oberon. I'm sure, even in the Human Realm, you've heard of us?"

Wyn seemed to consider her words for a long while before responding. "Yes, but the media doesn't do you justice." Aiden let out a breath, at least she wasn't hurling insults as a first impression — there was hope.

"All good things, I hope. We're fighting for equality for the non-magical, including humans, like yourself. We're even adding some gold fae into our family to seal the peace." Mab smiled and gestured at Pelrin.

Wyn looked to the prince, seemed to pause for a moment, then her face crumpled. "Please, your Majesty. Return my love to me. I've come all this way."

Her love? Aiden's chest ached. No, it couldn't be true.

Mab laughed. "He is to marry my daughter. Isn't that right, son?"

The prince bowed his head. "I will do as you say so long as you don't hurt her." Bringing Wyn here had served its purpose. But how long could he stay obedient to Mab's whims?

"I would never hurt her." Mab placed a hand to her chest. "Come dear, let us find a way to send you back home."

Aiden shook his head. No. Where would Mab take her? He tensed, readying himself to follow after them. No matter the consequences, he wouldn't let them hurt her.

"Let Pelrin come with me. Please, I know he loves me and doesn't wish to marry another."

The prince's face softened when he looked at her. A tiny flame flared on Aiden's arm. With a breath it died down, and he pressed himself deeper into his hiding place.

"The prince loves my daughter. Do not stand here and insult us. I said I wouldn't harm you, but I said nothing about my pets."

Wyn looked behind her, and Aiden's heart lifted. Would Mab truly put him in charge of watching Wyn? Could he be so lucky?

The prince strained against his cuffs. "Please, you can't. He'll kill her. I'll do whatever you want."

Mab threw her head back and laughed. "You will do what I want regardless." She turned to Mare. "Take her to my pet's room and ensure she doesn't escape."

Mare bowed low. "Yes, your majesty." She gripped Freddie's arm and led her from the room.

Aiden's heart pounded in doubletime as they passed. Wyn was here, and soon they would be together, just the two of them. Then his stomach dropped—Wyn was here.

He waited several long minutes while the music started back up and chatter filled the ballroom once more. The prince flexed his hands, his hair curtaining his face. Something twinged in Aiden's chest, but he refused to spare pity on him when the gold fairy couldn't be bothered to return it.

Pushing himself out from behind the pillar, Aiden retraced his steps back to his room. Two guards stood watch outside his door and snickered as he approached.

"Leave," he snapped.

They looked at each other and took off back in the direction from where he'd come. "Enjoy your treat!" one of them called back. Aiden could've crisped him where he stood.

He opened the door and flicked a wrist to light the fairy orbs that bobbed in even intervals around the space. What would Wyn think of his singular crumpled bed and his scattering of belongings leaking out from beneath it? Her room was far more elegant than this.

He took a step inside and shut the door behind him. Something slammed into his face, and he stumbled back. Putting a hand to his head, he cried out as someone shoved him against the wall and the door flew open. Aiden reached out with his magic and shut it again. Blinking back the stars in his eyes, he rounded on his attacker.

Wyn stood in a ready stance; one of his human science books in both her hands. For a moment no sound passed between them. They stared at one another, chests heaving. Finally, Wyn's expression softened.

"Aiden? Is it really you?" She straightened, but her grip around the book remained firm.

"Wyn," he breathed. Rushing toward her, all thoughts of the prince, her words in the ballroom, his jealousy, everything was forgotten. He wrapped his arms around her, taking in the all too human scents of her. Wyn, in his arms.

"I'm so glad it's really you. I screwed up big time, and now I'm stuck here, and Pelrin, he's captured too, and I—I..." Wyn's hot tears pressed into his chest as he stroked her messy curls. He wanted to tell her it would be ok, that he'd help her get home and everything would be as it was—but he couldn't lie.

Guiding her to the bed, Aiden gestured for her to sit as he leaned against the wall. "How did you get here? Mare said you were in Summer, but your parents..."

"I was in Summer to tell Pelrin's parents that Mab had taken him. I thought they would help, but they didn't, and then everyone started collapsing, and I was captured before I could do anything." Wyn swiped at the tears falling down her cheeks and let her head fall into her hands. "It's all my fault Pelrin's here."

"Why would you risk yourself to help the prince?" Aiden said, his voice stiff. "Do you really think he's worth saving?"

Wyn's head snapped up, and she glared at him. "There is a lot about Pelrin I don't like, but I'm not going to just let him die. Besides, he'd do the same for me."

"Well, unfortunately their Majesties don't plan on killing him."

"You don't know that." She folded her arms. The weary look that had been tugging at her face vanished, replaced by anger. He looked away, pain pulsing through his chest. "I thought you were better than this. Just because you're enemies on the battlefield doesn't mean you have to condemn him to this fate."

"I—I didn't mean to upset you. But you do not know him as I do."

"I know Pelrin pretty well. I know he can be a downright ass, but I'd never wish him dead. I'd never wish anyone dead."

Aiden stared up at the ceiling, his lips moving as though counting. Silence washed between them like spring rain. Did he dare tell her? If she cared for the prince, would she defend him or see him for the monster he truly was? Putting a hand to his chest as though clutching at his heart, he looked to her, his voice trembling.

"You do not know what he has done to me. If you did, perhaps you wouldn't judge me so."

Her brow creased, and she inched to the edge of the bed so their feet were inches apart. "He's done some crappy things to me, too. Tell me how he hurt you." Her voice was soft and devoid of the anger it had just been filled with.

"He hurt you, too?" Sparks danced along his arms as he pushed from the wall to take a seat on the bed beside her.

She nodded. "Tell me first."

Aiden bit his lip, unsure of where to begin. "You may not know I am from Spring," he said. Freezing frosts. Why was this so hard? He'd been longing for someone to care enough to want to know his story for ages, but now…

"I passed through Spring on my way here. There was this blue fairy who wanted my—your ring." She held up her hand, letting the light catch in its grooves.

"You met Nona? How—Is she well?"

"Save for trying to hold my friends and I hostage in Spring, she's peachy."

"Right, she probably recognized the ring and wished to preserve it. She used to care for me when I was small. I miss her." He closed his eyes, pushing back the tears gathering in them. At least he wasn't the last of his kind, but how many years did Nona have left? She'd already started aging as though her end was approaching. He moved closer to Wyn, positioning himself just beside her legs. Pausing just before they touched, she nodded, and he pressed his lips against the back of her hand.

Wyn smiled. "Did Pelrin try to steal this or something? Is that why you hate him?"

"No. He took something much greater from me." Aiden flinched as Wyn moved her hand to lay atop his own. His breath hitched as he savored the warmth of her skin against his. Spreading his fingers, hers filled the spaces between each digit.

"When I was younger, after my parents passed, I was brought to Summer to be the guard to their prince. It was supposed to be an honor, serving beside a gold fairy, but…"

Wyn let out a soft, "ha."

He shrugged. "It is what I was told. However, it was no honor for me. I'd been raised to believe that fighting was wrong, and every training session for me with the realm's general was painful." Aiden bit his lip. A vision of the general's face pleading with him to return to Elessea pressed to the front of his mind. Aiden shook his head. "He wasn't a cruel man, but he would grow frustrated with me, and I wasn't used to such harsh criticism. Eventually my skill grew enough to spar with the prince. I'd never met him before, but had been made to believe that his skill was far beyond whatever mine could hope to be. And with blades they'd been right; I struggled for mere minutes before the prince defeated me — in none too kind a fashion. But with magic." Aiden's lip quirked. "I am a blue fairy, after all. His magic, no matter how powerful, couldn't come close to mine."

"I can't imagine Pelrin taking that well," Wyn said. Her fingers tightened around his.

"No. He didn't take it well. The prince and his gold fae cousins would torment me endlessly. With harsh words, sticks, and whatever else they could find, they'd never give me a moment's peace. It was so bad I pleaded with the general to let me go back to Spring and live on the streets. I hated Summer and all the stuck up courtiers who'd do nothing when they witnessed their prince's cruelties or, worse, would laugh. I thought it was the worst thing that could ever happen to me."

"I'm sorry he picked on you when you were little, but that's no reason to want him dead now. Aiden, I —"

"If it was just him challenging me as a child I could leave our feud on the battlefield. Clouds above, I've paid him back enough times for that alone." He ran a hand through his hair, his eyes catching in her intense stare.

"He's said as much." Wyn stared down at their hands, not moving, at least she didn't hate him for his anger, or at least wasn't showing it.

"The stronger I got, the angrier he grew. I begged the general every day to let me go home. And he worried that with the state of the prince's and my relationship we might never be the perfect pair of lord and guard the royals had hoped for."

"But that wasn't your fault," Wyn said. "Surely they could see how he treated you."

Aiden shook his head. "They either didn't believe me or blamed me for not being tough enough to endure it. I'm surprised you believe me, having loved the prince and all."

"I don't think I ever loved him. It was just infatuation."

Aiden's gaze flicked to hers. "You know he's like this and still you defended him at the castle."

"I know what he's like now. Pelrin can be the worst, but he's still my friend, and I can't just abandon him."

Aiden swallowed hard. Perhaps him being her friend was better than him being something more… still, it made his heart want to flee from his chest. "A year after I'd arrived, I tried to escape. I waited until the palace was sleeping and flew off into the night."

"You didn't wend?"

"I was too young." Aiden moved, shifting his weight as she moved so close their legs touched. "His highness and the others caught me. I guess they were sneaking out, too. They flew after me and dragged me down. I tried to fight them off, but this time the prince was strong enough to match me." He opened his mouth, but the words died in his throat.

Wyn slid her other hand over their interlocked fingers. "What? Had he practiced more?"

Aiden stared at her hand but couldn't keep from trembling. This story had been his secret for so long, and to share it with another — revealing such a raw part of himself — it scared him in a way nothing had before. "The prince had stolen his father's crown. He had his cousins hold me down to 'punish me for trying to fly away.'" Pausing, Aiden swallowed hard. "He took my wings." The tears finally escaped to run down his cheeks, and he bowed his head. "He used the crown and burned them off." He ground his teeth, tasting metal.

Wyn was quiet. What had he expected her to say? Her hand

clenched tight around his.

He raised his head to study her face. "If their Majesties hadn't found me, I would have died."

"Pelrin just left you? For dead?" She touched his shoulder briefly, then retracted her hand.

Aiden flinched and nodded. The memory reignited the sting of the burn along his back. He lowered his head again.

"He's done a lot of shitty stuff but — oh, Aiden, I'm so sorry."

"I've lost my home, my wings, my freedom. Tell me, what else do I have besides my vengeance?"

"You have me." She slid off the bed so their bodies pressed against one another.

"I do?" He looked up, and she met his gaze.

"Of course, Aiden." She placed a soft kiss on his cheek, and his face blazed.

A roaring heat stirred throughout his body. She cared for him. Even if she'd come all this way to save the prince, she still cared for him in a way the prince would have no part of. His heart pounded in his ears, and if she said anything else, he didn't hear it. He needed to distract himself from the clawing memories, and she was so close… Wyn looked at him sidelong, and the flame in his chest grew into a pounding need. "May I kiss you?" he rasped.

Wyn smiled. "Of course."

He cupped her face and pressed his lips to hers. It was as though he'd been stranded in the Rhydian desert and she was the first water he'd come upon in days. He breathed her in as she wrapped her hands about his neck. When she pulled back for air, Aiden panted.

"It's your turn. Tell me, when I'm full of more joy than rage, how did he hurt you?"

"Oh, well it's nothing like what he did to you. He just slept with another girl when he was supposed to be with me."

"What could he crave greater than you?" A lightness fluttered in his chest; yet another favor for him over the prince. But his heart sank. "I must find a way to get you home." He bit his lip, trying to put all images of what Mab would do to him for helping her escape out of his mind.

"You can't. What will they do to you when they find me gone? And besides, despite all he's done, I need to find a way to get Pelrin out of here. The people of Summer need him."

Aiden glared, fighting to keep the flames in his arms from springing to life. "You cannot stay, not for him. Their Majesties will not tolerate your presence here for too long."

"They'll hurt you too, if you take me home. Won't they?"

Aiden looked away.

"I'm not going anywhere," Wyn said. "Help me and maybe there's a way to free you, too. I can't just leave him, and there may be others, too. Students from the Human Realm that vampire and werewolf turned."

Aiden flexed his jaw. "They keep the new recruits in the rooms just beyond the dungeons. You must forget about them; they're unsavable."

"I can't." Her eyes turned glassy. "There has to be some way to save them. No one else will. And you —"

"None of this is your responsibility." He pressed his palms into his eyes and tried to think of a way this could all work out. "Wyn, there is no helping me. Their Majesties would have to die, and they long ago ordered me not to harm them. Someone else would have to do it, and you cannot."

Her face fell. "I'm sorry, Aiden. But if they have to hold you here by a life debt, how are they holding Pelrin? Couldn't he just wend out of here?"

"There are wards around this place. He's highly guarded; if he were able to get outside the palace, he could wend back to Summer, but their Majesties won't let that happen."

"So I just need to find a way to get him outside the palace, and maybe he can help me free the others." Wyn rubbed her chin and sat quietly.

Aiden watched her. He wanted to tell her there was no hope, to give up on Pelrin and let him take her home. But who was he to stop her? Who was he to let her die? "If you insist on staying, we must be careful to not let their Majesties find out about us." His cheeks heated.

"I can pretend to be in love with Pelrin. I can lie fairly well." She raised her chin as a yawn overtook her.

Aiden yawned too as he studied her face—she was set on being a savior. But she didn't know Mab like he did. When she was caught, it wouldn't be a fast death. If he could just steal some wing powder, he could take her home, even if it meant she'd hate him. But he could allow himself this moment at least; one last, perfect moment with her.

"I suppose it would be better than telling him the truth of your feelings… I'd love to see his expression though." A smirk tugged at Aiden's lips.

She smiled back. "We'll figure it out in the morning. I'm too tired to think."

Aiden looked at the clock on his wall—five minutes to midnight. He cringed. "Stay here. I'll be back later." Kissing her forehead, he rose and left. For the first time happiness bubbled in his heart as he headed to the study.

CHAPTER 26

Freddie

Freddie breathed in Aiden's scent of fresh rain as she woke. For a moment, she was back in her own bed, safe. He'd just come for a visit, and her mom was downstairs making breakfast. The only thing she had to worry about was how to explain his presence to her parents.

Then, reality slammed back into her. She wasn't in her own bed. She was in his, Mab and Oberon were holding her and Pelrin captive, and she had to find a way to escape with the students.

Aiden had his back turned toward her. His wing stubs twitched beneath his loose shirt as though he were dreaming of flying. A horrible pang ran through her. How could Pelrin have done that to him? The Pelrin she knew could never be so cruel, but Aiden's wings were gone, and he couldn't lie. Anger flashed through her sharp as broken ice. If it had been anyone else who'd hurt Aiden like that, would she wish them dead as well? Things couldn't be the same between her and Pelrin, even if she did save him. The thought of him lounging so casually in her dorm, with the knowledge of what he'd done. Did he even care? It was his fault Aiden was trapped here. And he spent his time trying to kill the fairy he'd bullied, maimed, and forced into an impossible situation. Perhaps she should just save the students and leave Pelrin here.

But if she didn't at least try to help, she'd regret it. Every time her friends would talk about Pelrin, she'd feel a pit in her stomach, not to mention Aiden would likely suffer for helping her — and she needed help.

He stirred and rolled over, his eyes scrunching before opening. She smiled and gazed at his impossibly beautiful face.

"Is it wrong for me to be happy to see you here?" He stretched and pushed himself into a sitting position.

Freddie smirked. "Perhaps a little." She sat up beside him. "I've been thinking. You should probably pretend to have made me miserable last night. Mab and Oberon might let me stay longer if they think I detest it."

Aiden pressed his lips tight. "I can try. Though, if they ask me a direct question I must be truthful."

"Well you did tell me a story which frightened me, and you did technically sleep with me."

Aiden flushed. "I — I suppose I could say that if it came up." Freddie bit her lip. Would that be going too far? It wasn't as though Mab and Oberon could spread rumors about her at school or tell her parents. Still…

"You made me question my friendship with Pelrin. And I'm afraid of what that will mean for the future. Pelrin's been a big part of my life since I met him, even after we broke up. It's been hard, but now… I won't be able to look at him without thinking about what he did to you."

Aiden pulled his lips tight. "I cannot say I'm sorry you care for him less than you did before."

She squeezed Aiden's hand and slipped out of the bed. Her clothes clung to her body and smelled of fear-sweat. She needed to feel somewhat fresh to tackle the long day ahead.

"Do you have somewhere I can wash up?" she asked. Aiden pointed to a small door, opposite the one leading to the hall. Making her way over to her pack, Freddie dug for a change of clothes.

Her hand brushed across something icy as she pulled out a fresh pair of jeans and the orb Aiden had given her for Christmas.

"Do you like it?" he asked, still watching her from the bed.

"It's beautiful. Is it magic, like the ring?"

Aiden nodded. "It's supposed to be very powerful, but only gold fae can use it. Please don't give it to him."

Freddie's hands trembled around the orb. "Maybe you should keep it."

"No, I—if I were found with it, I'm not sure their Majesties would be forgiving that I kept it from them. It'd be much safer in the Human Realm with you."

Freddie stared into the pearlescent ball—she could just make out what looked to be glittering snow falling within it. "I'll keep it safe then." Her heart pounded. The ring, this orb; she was just a human, and there was no way she could defend herself if a fae attacked to try and steal these. But if Aiden had faith in her, she'd do her best to keep them safe.

"Thank you," Aiden said.

Stomach twisting in knots, she hurried to the bathroom, took her time in the tiny shower, and struggled to change in the tight space. How did Aiden live like this? Even the showers at school were bigger. When she was done, Aiden was in his fighting leathers and waiting for her by the door.

"Ready?"

Freddie took a deep breath and nodded. He gripped her forcefully by the arm, casting a quick glance at her before tugging open the door.

"Let go of me. I'm fine walking." Freddie shook herself best she could but Aiden's grip remained firm. He didn't look at her as he led her back up the long flight of stairs and down a frosty hallway. This time they didn't take the turn toward the grand room with the thrones, but instead passed through a smaller set of double doors carved in an intricate pattern of ice creatures like the door to the dining room in the other palace.

Her legs felt like water as Aiden pushed her forward. Oberon sat at the head, Mab to his right, and Pelrin and their daughter were positioned across from each other on either side of the royals. Pelrin looked up as they entered, his dull face darkening into a glower as his gaze turned to Aiden.

Freddie swallowed down her disgust and struggled again. "Pelrin!" It near pained her to fake genuine concern into her voice — not after what he'd done to Aiden.

"Please, let her go." He looked, this time not to Aiden, but to Mab, who nodded.

Aiden's tight grip on Freddie's arm relaxed, and his arm dropped to his side. He walked around the table to Pelrin's side and bowed to Mab and then to Oberon.

"Come, child," Mab said. "Sit beside Tatiana." She gestured to her daughter, and Freddie made jerky movements forward, not taking her eyes off of Pelrin. She sat silently. There'd been countless stories about green fae who's escaped the wrath of the Dark Fae Army and their fearsome queen who played with people like a cat to mice. The true mystery was Oberon. He shared near the exact likeness of Oscar Fallus, save for his dull brown eyes and elaborate antlers sprouting from his head. Though perhaps the antlers were a glamour. Mr. Fallus had said his brother had been taken by the fae. Could Oberon be his true brother? Perhaps rotten ran in the family, for Oscar shared none of the bravado as the other two men.

Mab beckoned and something moved in the corner of Freddie's vision. Suddenly a girl was by her side with a steaming plate of food.

Freddie's eyes widened as she set the food down. Freya.

The girl gave a nod so slight, Freddie was scarce sure she saw it, before zipping out of sight.

"Oh, I forgot that was the servant girl we sent to attend to you," Mab said. "We, of course, wished you to have every luxury while the prince ensnared you in his little game."

"It wasn't my game," Pelrin said. He reached for Freddie, but a look from Mab made his hand drop. Freddie was almost grateful for it.

"We wish you to be comfortable here, too, but we can't just have you lazing about the castle. You must have a job to do." The queen tapped her chin with one perfectly manicured nail.

"Please, haven't you put her through enough with a night with him?" Pelrin's blue eyes widened. How was it he could be so caring with her and so evil to Aiden? Then again, he had betrayed and kidnapped her — she couldn't forget.

"I'm sure my pet was a perfect gentleman, isn't that right?"

"Yes, Your Majesty." Aiden bowed his head.

"See? Tell me pet, what did you do with her last night?"

Aiden's eyes flicked between her, Mab, and Pelrin. His expression looked pained as he choked out his answer. "We slept together." The words came out so fast Freddie thought for a moment she'd misheard.

Her stomach sank when she saw Pelrin's red face, a snarl painted on his lips. "I vow, when I am free of this place, I'll make your death slow."

Aiden met his eyes and tightened his jaw but said nothing. Although she'd told Aiden to say that, she hadn't thought of the consequences Pelrin might cause him. What if Aiden was caught? What if Pelrin managed to set Elessea free of the curse and defeat the Dark Fae? She shrank back in her chair, trying to shove back images of Aiden, lying bloody or as a pile of ash at Pelrin's feet.

Oberon jerked his head, calling Aiden over. "Enough of these games," he said. "We have a battle to plan. Summer is weakest now; one final assault on Shell Bay should bring them down."

"No!" Pelrin struggled against Mab who was twirling bright blue ribbons of magic around him, binding him to his chair. His face was twisted in agony as he stared at Aiden and Oberon. The king rose from his seat and led Aiden towards the door, then paused, returning to the table. Plucking an apple from the bowl of fruit in the center, he tossed it to Aiden. "You'll need all your strength to carry out this next attack."

Aiden's lips pulled into a thin line. "Thank you, Your Majesty." He bit into the apple and followed Oberon from the room.

Freddie swallowed hard, staring down at the baked fish, bread, and bowl of some type of hot cereal sitting on her plate. She poked at it with her fork, waiting for Mab to say some new horrible thing.

"Now let's think of what we can have you do," she said as

though nothing had happened.

Freddie said nothing as a shudder ran through her. Pelrin had told her about the enslaved people of Autumn and Winter forced into the cold to build up the Dark Fae stronghold or serving the brutal courtiers. Would she join them?

"I need a handmaid," Tatiana said. Freddie blinked. The girl, set to be Pelrin's bride, hadn't spoken a word since Freddie arrived. Maybe she was saving some horrible revenge for Freddie trying to steal her future husband.

Mab cleared her throat. "That seems —"

"She can do my hair and polish my shoes, stitch the pearls on my dresses. I need someone dedicated to do those things, not just random servants."

Freddie stopped herself from saying she was terrible at doing hair, she'd never polished anything before, and sewing was more of an exercise in pricking her fingers than stitching anything.

"If you insist, dear." Mab's face was tight. It seemed whatever she'd had in store for Freddie, it likely wasn't as pleasant as being a handmaid to Pelrin's bride-to-be.

"I do." Tatiana looked to Freddie. "Are you going to eat at all?" Her voice sounded almost kind — not what the daughter of Mab should sound like.

Freddie shook her head.

"Then let's go to my room. We are having my engagement ball tonight, and I want to look my best."

Good luck. Although, admittedly, the girl wasn't ugly. Maybe a bit plain, especially for a fae and compared to Mab's beauty, but if Oberon was the real Oscar Fallus, that meant Tatiana was half human.

Across the table, Mab cocked her head, looking at her daughter, her brow crinkled. "Yes, do get ready. You'll want to impress the prince." She glanced sharply at Pelrin, who glared back.

Freddie got up from her seat. She needed to get away from the tension and the disgust she couldn't shake for Pelrin. Tatiana rose too and led her towards the dining room door.

"I'm sorry," Pelrin said as she passed his chair. "I wish there was something I could've done."

She nodded stiffly and left the room with Tatiana. They walked in silence for a while, pausing every so often for Tatiana to greet one of the troll guards. Freddie could scarcely believe she knew them all by name, and their cold demeanor melted as they met their princess. When they reached a hallway with two ice doors opposite each other, Tatiana pushed one open, and they entered.

Careful to keep her head slightly bowed, Freddie took in the room. Books lined the room on floor-to-ceiling shelves in a rainbow pattern. She spotted several vinyl dolls of anime characters decorating them. There was a desk off to one side covered in crafting supplies and a large circular bed taking up the majority of the space made up with white furs. Was this truly the room of Mab and Oberon's daughter?

The girl closed the door behind Freddie and leaned against it. "I'm so sorry about Aiden. He's usually really nice." She paused and flushed. "You don't want to hear that. What I meant is — oh crap, I suck at this."

"He didn't do anything — it was just sleeping. You don't need to pity me." The words tumbled out; Tatiana seemed so sincere. She couldn't let the girl go on pitying her… but perhaps it was a tactic to get Freddie to spill her secrets. Would Aiden get in trouble for his half truth?

"Oh… well, that's… good, but he doesn't even know you. I figured he'd at least give you the bed or something."

Freddie shrugged. "So do you want me to clean or something?"

"No," Tatiana said. "I want you to help me find a way out of this marriage so you and that stupid — sorry — prince can go home."

Freddie narrowed her eyes. She couldn't detect a lie in the girl's voice, but maybe she was just really cunning. "You want to help me? Why?"

Pushing herself off the wall, Tatiana crossed the room and sank down on her bed. "I don't love him. Besides, I'm not even into boys."

"Do your parents know?" Freddie gave the girl a half smile.

She didn't deserve to be stuck with Pelrin.

Tatiana nodded. "My mom says I don't have to be faithful, but…"

"Pelrin's an ass and the idea of being stuck with him for life makes you gag?"

"I thought you loved him. You came all this way."

"He's more of a friend, ish. I feel obligated to save him. What I can't figure out is why you're being so nice. Couldn't you just kill him to get out of this?"

She laughed. "I pretty much grew up in the Human Realm and before that in the Winter mountains with my grandfather. I'm not quite used to this place; I don't think I could kill anyone. Sometimes I feel like I hardly know my parents anymore."

Freddie nodded. "My parents and I have different views, too. Though it must be hard to be constantly surrounded by it. I go to boarding school, so at least —"

"I go to boarding school, too! Or at least I used to go. Is it terrible that I'm glad you're here?"

Freddie shook her head. "I get it. And I'll help drag Pelrin away from you. If you don't get him out fast he'll just get worse, trust me." Tatiana laughed, and Freddie joined in, but it quickly turned to silence.

"So… How do you think we actually get him out of here? My parents are going to make him wear the iron crown tonight so he can't attack the guests or fly away. And I, um, heard my Mom saying you're not long-term leverage. Sorry."

Freddie shrugged. "I'm not planning on being here long term."

"We could cause a distraction. A big one. That way we could break the prince out during the chaos, and once he's free he can protect you, right?"

The sparks of a terrible idea lit Freddie's mind. "What if we start a fire? Everyone would be too busy trying to put it out, and maybe they'd call the guards."

"Yeah, but how would we do that? Starting a fire in an ice castle isn't easy." Tatiana lay back on her bed and drummed her fingers against her stomach.

"I have some travel hairspray in my bag," Freddie said. "Do you have a lighter?"

"No, we typically use magic to start fires. Or at least my parents do."

"Too bad Pelrin can't do it. He has a ton of fire power."

"What about Aiden? He has those blue flames. He might help if we ask."

Freddie bit her lip. She didn't want Aiden to get hurt either. No, he couldn't be involved in their plans... or at least he couldn't know about them. Mab and Oberon might corner him in a lie, and he wouldn't be able to escape it. "Maybe we could find some way to get your parents to order him to light something on fire and use the hairspray to spread it."

"He'll do whatever my parents tell him to do for sure. But won't you get hurt? Have you ever used hairspray on a fire?"

Freddie frowned. "No... But if I point it away from myself, how bad could it be?"

"Not really a good plan," Tatiana said. "So many things could go wrong. How would you even get my parents to order him to start a fire?"

"We could make them really angry at something when Aiden's nearby. They might do it."

Tatiana pursed her lips. "Maybe if you flirted with the prince, but then one of you might get hurt."

Freddie frowned. It was dangerous, but if she did nothing, that was even more dangerous. "Well, Pelrin heals fast and I—I can dodge or something until there's enough of a distraction. We could get Pelrin out tonight, so you won't have to worry about marrying him, and I won't have to worry about your mom killing me."

Tatiana bit her lip. "Just make sure no one gets hurt. I know my parents can be a pain, but they are still my parents."

Freddie nodded. "Of course. We'll just have to be ready to get people out."

"Let's go find a good spot to ignite, and we can go and get your hairspray." Tatiana got to her feet. "And let's hope we don't burn this place to the ground."

Freddie grinned. She could make no promises to that.

CHAPTER 27

Aiden

Aiden faced Oberon in the throne room. It was empty but for the few green fae servants prepping for the evening's festivities. He needed to find a way to get Wyn home before the prince married Tatiana. She'd be useless to Mab after that, if not an annoyance. His thoughts raced through the possibilities. After his briefing with Oberon, perhaps he could steal some wing powder and send her home. She might hate him for it, but it was her life at stake.

"Are you paying attention?" Oberon's brow creased into a frown, and Aiden blinked hard and bowed his head. At least Oberon wasn't as sadistic as Mab. It was doubtful he, at least, would punish him for his momentary distraction. "As I was saying, the remnants of Summer must fall quickly if we are to use the prince to our advantage. If his people see he's allied himself with us, the rebels will be less motivated."

Aiden nodded. It was a fair plan. The Summertons might not rebel against them if they were loyal to their prince, but the general was still a strong leader. And with him and the small army holding Shell Bay they might see the prince as a traitor or a captive, and the marriage would serve to fuel their determination to take back their realm.

"When do you wish for us to carry this out?" He needed time to save Wyn.

"After the engagement ceremony tonight. You will have three days to take Shell Bay before the wedding. It should be more than enough time with the fall of the capital," Oberon said.

Three days was hardly any time to defeat the realm they'd been battling for years. The general was still alive, and though Aiden's magic was stronger, the general had decades of practice. It would be no simple feat.

"I understand. It will be done, Your Majesty." He cleared his throat. If he did manage to bring Summer down, perhaps their Majesties might grant him a boon, and he could take Wyn home without consequence. Though it was doubtful; they hadn't granted him such a favor when Autumn and Winter fell.

"Good. Now, for this evening. I expect you to attend just in case the prince tries anything he shouldn't. We'll keep you far enough away that his crown won't impact you, but if something should happen, you will get close."

Aiden pulled his lips tight. Pity was not something he ever wished to feel for the prince, but the thought of being forced to wear an iron crown, for hours, turned his stomach.

"Will the human girl be in attendance?" Aiden asked, trying to keep his words neutral. If one of the courtiers tried toying with Wyn, he'd be at her side in moments to dissuade them.

A smile crept across Oberon's face. "Enjoyed her last night, did you?" Aiden swallowed back the rush of emotions threatening to betray his feelings for Wyn. Oberon was a father to a half human daughter. How could he find any hint Aiden did something nonconsensual with Wyn amusing? After several seconds of Aiden not responding, the king continued. "I believe she is still useful leverage with the prince. And my wife mentioned something about having her renounce her relationship for the court. Perhaps if you're successful in Summer, I'll let you keep her after the wedding."

Adien's heart lifted. A way out for Wyn that wouldn't end in pain for him, at least not until he forced Wyn home. She'd likely want nothing to do with him, but perhaps it was for the best. Even with Summer vanquished, he was still indebted and had nothing to offer her. Just being with her endangered her from both sides of the war, but he'd wanted to be selfish. He couldn't put her at risk anymore, not after he got her back.

"Thank you, Your Majesty." He bowed, and Oberon waved a hand, dismissing him.

Suppressing a run, Aiden left the room. He needed to find Wyn to tell her of the way out. She wouldn't be happy, but it'd be worse if he simply dragged her off with wing powder. He hurried down the hall but stopped himself, remembering Wyn was with Tatiana. At the revel then, after she renounced her love for that monster.

When evening fell and Aiden entered the ballroom, it was filled with people. Brown fae wearing an assortment of fashions from fur-made suits to gowns of earth and twigs. Even a few red fae dotted among their midst: vampires with remnants of their meals around their mouths to look fierce and partially transformed werewolves despite the gibbous moon.

Their Majesties were on their thrones, sipping pale wine and smiling out at the festivities. Mare stood behind Tatiana's empty seat dressed in her typical silky black gown while beside her the new throne built for the prince was empty as well.

Where could they be? The revel was underway — should not the guests of honor be early? Shouldn't Wyn be here? He bit his lip and rocked on his heels. They'd ordered him not far from the dais on Mab's side in front of one of the sets of dramatic black curtains that hung in intervals throughout the room.

"Welcome friends!" Mab called out, and a hush fell over the crowd. Something tingled in the back of Aiden's throat as though discouraging him from speaking. Power wafted from the queen's hand. Did her people truly respect her so little she needed to enchant them while she spoke, or was this a product of her own insecurities? "Tonight, we celebrate our daughter, Tatiana. Finally, home again."

Applause filled the room, and a bright light shone at the top of the stairs. Tatiana stood in a gown of the finest silk decorated with snowflakes which clung to her skin and hair as well. She looked pretty, though far from the overwhelming beauty of her mother's glamour if she'd donned similar attire. Or if Wyn wore such a gown—Aiden's face burned at the thought. Wyn hovered several paces behind the Dark Fae princess and didn't look as though she were attending a revel. She still wore the jeans and red hoodie from that morning, her pack slung over her shoulder. Did Tatiana not permit her to leave it in her room? Or perhaps Wyn didn't trust going anywhere without it.

The two descended the staircase heading for the throne. A guard held Wyn back from the dais as Tatiana took her seat. Aiden's heartbeat in his throat as Wyn's face wrinkled in confusion. They were not going to kill her tonight; he had time. Oberon had even promised him Wyn after the wedding. He could take her home, and everything would be fine.

Mab waved at the crowd again to quiet them. "Let me introduce you all to my daughter and her future husband, Prince Pelrin of Summer." The crowd went wild with applause, which devolved into laughter as the prince was escorted out.

Guards stood on either side of him, half dragging him to the throne. His face was contorted with pain as the iron crown sat atop his head. Even at his distance, a dull ache gnawed at the back of Aiden's neck. The prince must be in utter agony.

They sat him beside Tatiana, and Mab's gaze honed in on Wyn. "The prince has unfortunately arrived here with some baggage that we will now relieve him of." She smiled and beckoned Wyn forward.

Wyn stepped up to the dais, her face pale and eyes darting around the room. Aiden grit his teeth; he should be with her, comforting her. When Wyn found his stare, their eyes locked for one brief moment before Mab grabbed her by the arm.

"Now, child, renounce your claim on the prince and pass your blessing onto my daughter."

Wyn's eyes narrowed as she struggled to shake herself free.

"Will not. Why are you trying to force this? He doesn't love her."

Aiden's heart sank. Couldn't she just pretend to act as though she feared Mab? They just needed to get through the next few days, and everything would be all right.

"You forget yourself, girl. Do as you're commanded or else."

"Or else what? You'll kidnap me? Hold me hostage? I'm here, and you've done it."

"P-please," the prince groaned. Mab looked at him, her violet eyes flaming. The court surrounding her was silent, though their collectively held breaths were nearly enough to make the room tremble with tension.

"You wish to know what I'm capable of, little girl?" The queen smiled—it was too sweet. Silver in puddles and splattering the walls, the knife… No, Wyn wouldn't survive something like that. "Pet!"

No. Aiden took a trembling step toward the queen. Wyn twisted and pulled a canister out of her bag and pointed it at Mab. Courtiers gasped, but Oberon let out a chuckle as Wyn forced Mab back toward the curtain.

"My dear, it is just what the humans use to hold their hair in place without magic. Fear it not."

Mab smirked as her eyes blazed. A snarl curled its way across her lips. "Burn her!"

"No," the prince shouted as he twisted in his throne. He tried to stand but collapsed to his knees. "Don't hurt her, please."

Aiden's hands trembled as he tried to resist the command. Not Wyn, he couldn't do this to her. Maybe if he just gave her a small burn. If he could fulfill the order and frighten Wyn into becoming more passive.

"Burn hands so she might never try to raise a weapon against me, now." The queen raised her chin. Her pale skin against the black backdrop seemed to glow.

Swallowing his pain, Aiden raised his arm and pointed at Wyn. She struggled free of Mab's grasp and rolled out of the way just as the small blue jet hit the curtains. Flames licked their way up to the icy ceiling. She tossed the canister over her head into the fire.

A beat passed where everything was silent, then the compulsion to burn overtook Aiden again. He raised his hand, but there was an explosion, and Mab screamed. "Wait, stop!"

He did, but it was too late for the queen. Hungry fire climbed up her dress and dripped from the curtain into her hair — she flailed and fell into the blaze with a scream.

"Mom!" Tatiana shouted, as Oberon pulled her back from the fire. The flames were now on a path of destruction throughout the ballroom.

Screams fell against dull ears as Aiden looked from his hand to the place where Mab fell. Dead. Half of his freedom obtained, and likely to be cursed by the other half. He looked to Wyn, who was staring at where Mab had stood her mouth open. If it hadn't been for her, this murder might not have happened.

How could she use him like that? But no, she wouldn't — it had to have been an accident. Still, anger, confusion, and despair all burrowed into his bones as he tried to push through the fog and clear his head. Gold flashed at the side of his vision, and he turned. If not for the Summer Prince, he wouldn't have been forced to serve Mab and Oberon in the first place. And now he was weak and couldn't fight back. There was no one to stop him from finally getting his revenge.

A smile tugged at Aiden's lips as he rounded on the prince, blue flame blazing in his hand.

CHAPTER 28

Freddie

Freddie's heart thundered as Aiden turned from her. Green fae servants raced to the door as flames caught on banners and other bits of drapery that hung around the throne room. She looked around — where was Pelrin?

From across the flames, Tatiana stared at her, her jaw tight and her eyes glassy. "What did you do?" she screamed.

Freddie shook her head, staring at the spot Mab had stood — now a charred skeleton. "I — I didn't mean to, I just —" Murderer. But Mab had been so close, and she'd ordered Aiden… and Freddie had moved in the wrong direction. Tears filled her eyes as she searched for any sort of forgiveness in Tatiana's horrified gaze as a sea of people rushed towards the exit.

"We need to get out of here." A cold hand gripped her arm, and Freddie blinked back her tears to meet Freya's panicked gaze.

A streak of blue flame made Freddie turn. Aiden stared down Pelrin as the prince clutched his head, crawling behind the throne. The crown; it was hurting him — he wouldn't be able to flee like that. And they needed to get out of there before Oberon or any of the guards organized enough to turn on them.

"I need to save him!"

Freya nodded and swooped an arm beneath Freddie's legs,

lifting her with ease. Fast as a breeze, they were beside Pelrin.

"What are you—" Aiden began.

Freddie yanked the crown from Pelrin's head, along with several strands of hair. He groaned as Freddie tossed it deep into the crowd. "Come on, Pel, we have to go."

"Not before I take care of him." Turquoise eyes blazing, flames lit in Pelrin's hand.

Aiden glowered. "I'd like to see you try." Blue flames raced down his arms.

Pelrin growled and hurled his fire at Aiden, who shot forth his own blast. Their magic met in the middle with a loud boom. Freddie shielded her face from the intense heat wafting off them. Ducking under the jet of fire, Aiden raced toward the exit leading to the hall, Pelrin half flying after him. A puddle remained in the ice where they'd stood, and something cool dripped onto Freddie's shoulder. She jerked and sniffed the damp spot on her sweatshirt. Water?

As though to answer her question, one of the pillars that lined the ballroom crumbled away from the ceiling to come crashing down on an escaping frost fairy. Their scream was cut short as they disappeared beneath the stampede headed toward the main entrance.

Freddie looked back toward the door where Pelrin and Aiden had gone. "I need to find the other students. Just tell me where they are, and you can go save yourself."

"What do you mean, 'go'? I'm not just leaving you. If this is supposed to be a rescue mission, I want in. They've held all of us captive for so long, and I'm willing to risk myself." Her voice was choked as she struggled to get out the words. "I have no one back home who'd accept me like this."

"You have me and Raul. Possibly even Pelrin…" Though she hated the thought, Pelrin might be the only one of them who could truly help Freya. Her parents would never take in a vampire, and neither Raul nor his family had the space or money to assist her.

Freya shook her head. "Raul? The guy I went on a date with once? I doubt he even remembers me." She fiddled with the end of her hair as another pillar hit the ground, shaking the ballroom floor.

She gasped and pulled Freddie back through the door Pelrin and Aiden had left through.

"I'm pretty sure he remembers you. Just tell me where we need to go, and we can talk about boys after."

Freya bit her lip and nodded. "The others are here. Daniel and everyone else they took are under the palace. They won't have heard the commotion."

Freddie scanned the ballroom; if they didn't leave soon, they'd be trapped in the destruction. But she'd come to rescue everyone. Pelrin had chosen to fly off, and if the other students were here, she couldn't just abandon them. No investigative journalist would leave innocents to die; they'd call the police. But the police weren't here, so it was up to her. A headline flashed in her mind, and she shoved it back. These were real people in real danger — the article could come after they saved them.

"Let's hurry. I don't know how long this place will hold. Not if those two morons keep it up," Freddie said.

Freya led the way into a long hallway. Everything looked so familiar, as though tracing steps she'd followed in a half-remembered dream. The portraits were different; images of jovial elves and blue-skinned giants lined the walls rather than the snow women and yetis from the Southern Palace. But the layout was roughly the same as they raced down multiple flights of stairs — none of which moved.

They finally came to an area where the stairs let out into a large atrium. Green light reflected against the shiny ice walls, and the metallic scent of blood filled the air. Freddie's breath hitched as she followed Freya into a darkened section of the room. Something stirred, and a pair of golden eyes flashed.

"Freya, what took you so long? Training starts in just a couple minutes. Were their Majesties having you play servant again?" A boy limped out from the shadows — his left leg gone, replaced by a wooden appendage.

"Daniel, there's no time. We have to gather the others and get out. The palace is falling apart."

"What? You're joking. The guards aren't going to believe

that."

Freya shook her head, and Freddie stepped up alongside her. "Daniel? What happened to you?"

He grunted. "Freddie? How are you here?" He frowned.

"That doesn't matter. Your leg, though, did they do that to you?"

"I broke the rules," he said solemnly. "Freya's just lucky vampires heal better than weres do."

"I'm so, so sorry. When we get back to school, I promise to make amends to you guys." Guilt sliced through Freddie's torso like a knife. She'd been so obsessed with chasing her story. How could she forget the cruelties the Dark Fae would inflict on Daniel and Freya if she got them into trouble.

"Guys, we're running out of time!" Freya tugged Freddie deeper into the darkness, and Daniel limped after them.

"Our trainers won't like this," he said.

"There's more of us than there are of them. Even if there's nowhere to go once we get outside, it'll be better than dying or being trapped down here forever," Freya said.

"And the Summer Prince is here. He can get you back home... I think." Freddie bit her lip. "But we have to go now."

Daniel let out a breath and followed them down an unlit passageway. It was likely designed to invoke fear into the new red fae who joined and heighten their senses. Freddie's heart pounded, and just breathing took more concentration than usual as she stumbled through the dark.

At the end of the passage, Freya hauled aside a sliding door. Light poured out, momentarily blinding Freddie. She blinked away the white spots and made out what looked like a large gymnasium. The floor was still covered in frost, and the walls of ice, but it was open with no decorations and large crates surrounding the edges.

Several people her own age and perhaps a few years older gathered in rows, waiting — all of them with glowing eyes. A few of them frowned as they entered; one girl sniffed and wrinkled her nose. She zipped over to Freya, her inhuman beauty giving her away as a vampire.

"Is she… still human?" The girl pointed at Freddie.

"Yes, and we're here to get you out," Freddie said.

The girl blinked. "How?"

Freddie pushed past her and stepped forward. More of the werewolves and vampires stared at her as she did. Likely they all smelled the human on her now. "We have to run. The palace is collapsing. We'll be trapped in here if we don't."

A deep laugh sounded from behind her, and Freddie turned to see a muscular man with gray, leather-like skin and a face only a mother could love. He grinned, revealing a set of teeth that looked more like rocks than dentin.

"No one is going anywhere," he said in a voice like stone falling down a mountain. Freddie had never seen a fae like him, but there was no mistaking a rock troll for anything else.

"We have to go," Freya shouted. "There are more of us than guards. This might be our only chance to get home. It's either that or die down here."

Voices rang throughout the crowd as Freddie tried to side step the troll.

"I agree," Daniel said. "This isn't our war. Let the Fairy folk kill each other. It's none of our concern."

Freddie screamed inwardly. She'd wanted to get them to safety, not turn them against all fae, but if it convinced the others to move, it was good enough for now. Freya exchanged looks with the other vampire girl, and they faced Freddie. Swallowing hard, she took a step back. Before she could take a second step, the girls sprang, Freya landing on the troll's shoulders while her companion went for his legs. He let out a short, sharp cry as Freya twisted his neck, and with a sickening crack, his head fell to the ground.

Feet thundered from other directions — more guards.

"Run, everyone!" Freya screamed as she hoisted Freddie onto her back and raced back towards the sliding door.

It'd closed again. The other vampire girl dragged it open, leaving dents in the metal. They were greeted by two more guards. Daniel lunged, his hands transforming into claws and swiping them across the chest of one the goblin guards before he could react.

The other guard quickly fell to the vampire girl's deadly bite.

Freddie's jaw hung open. Could Raul transform his hands into claws? She'd never seen him do it. But he'd also been born a werewolf rather than turned — perhaps it was different. Nor had he ever been trained for battle.

Screams erupted behind them as the girl smeared the goblin's black blood from her mouth. Armored guards chased them into the dark passage as the remaining students joined their flight. Goblins, centaurs, and other brown fae roared as they clashed with the students. But the red fae had the advantage; werewolves and vampires, all blessed with the ability to move faster than the brown fae, were perfectly equipped to flee, even if they were ill-trained fighters.

They raced back through the atrium and up the stairs. Around them the palace crumbled. It now seemed the guards were more interested in preserving their own lives than holding them back.

Flames blazed before them, and Freya let out a squeak as she stumbled to a halt and Freddie fell off her back. Pelrin and Aiden were still at it, shooting bursts of flame at one another — their eyes ablaze with hate. Chunks of the ceiling lay in cracked shambles on the floor, revealing the black sky.

The others continued to race past the battling fairies as though they'd hardly seen them. Freddie winced as ice shards fell from above and pierced and crushed some of the people ahead. Yet still both courtiers and captives plowed ahead.

Pelrin jumped into the air, hurling a ball of orange fire at Aiden. He ducked, and it burned a crater in the floor. Aiden's returning blast smashed the wall behind Pelrin, leaving a gaping hole. They needed to get to the front door — and fast.

"Come on. While they're away from the ballroom." Freya gripped her wrist and dragged her towards the crowd.

Freddie screamed as a large piece of the ceiling fell and pierced Freya through her neck. A pillar fell before them, and Freddie stumbled back as half of Freya's body was crushed beneath it. A scream tore from her lungs as she stared at her fallen friend. "Freya? Please get up. It's only wood that can kill vampires, right?" But

Freya lay still, her eyes wide and fixed at the ceiling, no longer glowing. "Freya, please."

Once, in class, Freddie had learned that while vampires had extraordinary healing abilities, they couldn't survive a beheading. She swallowed hard, but Freya's head was still on. It was just her neck. No. A rasping breath stuttered from her chest. This was all her fault. If she hadn't dragged Freya to get the others, if she'd only insisted she could do it herself, Freya would still be alive. Maybe even if she'd snooped less, then Freya might have been able to leave with her and Raul back at the palace.

Tears streamed down her face. There was nowhere to go now; the fallen pillar blocked the only way out. She'd killed Tatiana's mom, killed so many by destroying the palace, and now Freya. What had she done? Everything she'd ever done was supposed to be to help people, but this… This was just the opposite.

Freddie looked back at Aiden and Pelrin, and her heart squeezed. They were still fighting, causing more and more ice to fall from the ceiling. She huddled by the pillar, praying one of them would notice her and stop this madness. Aiden had said he truly cared for her, but his hatred of Pelrin seemed to have taken over his senses, not that she could blame him.

A crumbling noise from overhead made her look up, and she screamed. Suddenly, strong arms were around her, and a loud crash sounded as ice smashed to the ground in the place she'd been. Freddie stared back at it wide-eyed as air brushed her mess of curls across her face.

"Unhand her, or I swear —" a voice called, but it seemed so far away.

She brushed back the hair in her face to see the hole in the wall, the twinkling stars, and the snow beyond as they grew ever closer.

Then she was out, weightless, into the dark night.

CHAPTER 29

Aiden

Aiden curled his body around Wyn as they hit the snow with a wet thump. Thank the sweet rain, it was soft. Still, she sobbed into his chest. Pulling her back, he searched her face.

"Are you hurt?"

She shook her head. "I killed them." Her eyes were fixed back on the palace. "I killed them all."

"You didn't destroy the palace." Guilt twinged in his chest. He'd killed them, every last one of them, from his selfish battle with the prince. Even Mab… though she'd driven him to it. He gritted his teeth as she shivered into him. With a breath, a warm breeze rushed over them both. Their first outing together he'd done the same for her, but it had barely been as cold as this.

Exhaustion pulsed through his bones. His battle had worn him through, though he still had just enough to protect them should the prince give chase.

The castle looked as though it were sagging. Its bright green lights dimmed as water ran down its sides. Above them, the northern lights shimmered, unperturbed by the magical chaos beneath. Those in the Air Realm were so lucky to be free of such problems.

What would Oberon do to him? Aiden had destroyed the palace, murdered Mab. He'd never faced the king's wrath before, though the man had never stayed his wife's hand. A shudder ran through him, and he glanced back at Wyn. How could she have been so rude to Mab? Why couldn't she have just pretended to renounce her love and give Tatiana her blessing? A tiny voice in the back of his mind whispered, what if she did it on purpose? But Wyn wouldn't do that; she knew how he felt. She'd never put him in a situation where he'd be forced to hurt her. She wouldn't.

"Well, at least Mab's gone now. You're half free, right?" She looked up at him, her eyes glittering with unspilled tears.

"Did you do that on purpose?"

Wyn tensed. "What? I was just trying to make a distraction, I didn't mean for Mab to…" Her face crumpled, and she took an unsteady breath. "But at least it's a good thing, for you at least."

"You made me a murderer, and you think that's a good thing." Aiden shoved her back, leaving her crouched in the snow. His head pounded with the sharp realization.

"I—I needed a way to get out. She wanted me dead, Aiden. There was no way she was going to keep me around after Tatiana and Pelrin married." Her dark eyes glittered, reflecting the snow glowing from the moonlight.

"You could've told me, but instead you used me!" Aiden's heart squeezed as though there was a fist around it. "You're like everyone else. I am just another weapon to you." He could scarcely breathe, scarcely think with the roaring betrayal in his ears.

She shook her head, not meeting his eyes. "No, of course not. I needed a distraction, so we could run. It was the only way. But—"

"The only way for you to save him, you mean. I could've saved you, but of course he is more important to you."

Wyn clenched her fingers into fists as she got to her feet. "Mab was a monster, and you expect me to be sorry she's dead. You should be happy. Once Oberon's gone, you'll be free."

"And shall I let you use me again to kill him? Does my soul need to be stained by more people who force me to kill?"

Tears glistened in her eyes. "It was an accident. I never meant for you to kill her."

Aiden rocked his jaw back and forth. No. Pain wracked his body. He'd trusted her, and she'd used him to destroy everything. Flashes of the dark room, the glint of the knife, the pain, the silver splattering the wall. Aiden closed his eyes. Would Oberon demand more of his flesh?

"I knew this was a bad idea. We should've never…" He trailed off. Why had he agreed to meet her at that tower? Why had he showed up? Nothing good could've come from caring for someone, but he'd craved for some sliver of happiness.

"What are you saying? I swear to you, Aiden, I didn't mean for Mab to die."

Another flash of anger raced through him, tinged with despair. Every time he'd hoped, his happiness was ripped away. "Then maybe you shouldn't have used me." Aiden turned his back to her. "Goodbye, Wyn."

"Aiden!"

He glanced at her one last time, the knot in his throat stretching to his heart. She thought of him as merely something to use. Her heart belonged with the prince. Swallowing hard past the lump, Aiden wended, leaving the snowdrift behind.

CHAPTER 30

Freddie

Sinking to her knees, Freddie let tears fall into the snow with soft pats. How could he just leave her? She could easily die out here. A gust of wind blew past, biting through her sweatshirt to raise goosebumps across her skin. Her teeth chattered as she gripped her knees. It'd been an accident; a horrible, horrible accident. She should've told him — he was right to be angry. Freya and all those people were dead because of her, and now she'd lost Aiden, too. A sob tore its way from her throat as she buried her face in her hands.

"Freddie!"

She looked up; a golden light sped toward her.

"Oh Freddie, I'm so glad you're alright. Where is he?" Pelrin wrapped her in an embrace.

She leaned into him, soaking in the warmth coming from his blazing skin. "He's gone." Her voice cracked, sounding just like the pathetic human Pelrin knew her to be.

"Well, let's get gone, too, before he comes back." Pelrin leapt into the air, catching her legs up into his arms. Freddie cringed against him as they flew. She used to enjoy this, she told herself. But nothing seemed particularly enjoyable now, not with Pelrin, not anything she could imagine.

He touched down on the other side of the melting castle. A group of green fae gathered around as he let Freddie down. She steadied herself on the hardened ice and looked to where the guards gathered on the other side of the bridge.

"What now?"

Pelrin's jaw stiffened as a growing number of the Dark Fae guards crossed the bridge towards them. It would be mere minutes until they reached the group of escapees. Freddie looked up at Pelrin. Could he take all the soldiers on his own? His haggard face and weary stance hinted that he was low on magic.

"They outnumber our fighters, and some of the people here cannot remain in this cold much longer. If only we had some wing powder I might be able to get everyone out, so long as he doesn't make another appearance," Pelrin said.

"I think—I have wing powder." Freddie turned to dig in her bag from the dead Winter queen. Please be enough. Her fingers brushed something cold and hard, and she pulled it out and stared at the pearlescent ball. Her throat tightened as she closed her fingers around it, pushing thoughts of Aiden aside. He wanted her to protect it, to not give it to Pelrin, but with the soldiers so close, they couldn't take chances. She'd killed so many—the least she could do was save those who remained.

"What's that?" Pelrin knelt beside her. "That's not wing powder but… may I see it?"

She showed it to him, not letting go.

"Where did you get this?" he asked.

"Does it matter?" She went back to digging in her bag and held out the wing powder.

Pelrin took it. Some of the soldiers had made it across the bridge—they were only yards away. Freddie's heart pounded. If Pelrin could use this ball of magic, now was the time. She passed it to him.

"I can feel its power. Hmmm…" He held the orb in the direction of the soldiers, his breath coming out in hard puffs.

"Stand back." He waved a hand over it, and the orb glowed bright. A flurry of snow formed in Pelrin's palm. He pointed at the

Dark Fae Army, and the snow in front of them picked up, swirling across the ice bridge and pushing back the guards in front of them. Screams and howls of the Dark Fae were lost in the wind as the flakes increased in volume.

Pelrin lowered his hand, and the flakes died down. No longer were there any Dark Fae on the ice bridge; they all stood on the other side. She could just make out a figure, blue flames twisting down his arms staring back at her.

She forced her features neutral—God, she'd messed up. "Take me home, Pel."

He reached a hand into the bag of wing powder. "Let's go."

###

If she had drank ten glasses of fairy wine, Freddie doubted her head would pound as much as it did. She lay in her bed, tossing and turning through her nightmares.

Something tugged at her satin bonnet, and she batted it away. Her body craved sleep, but the horrific images of Mab and Freya refused to leave her mind. Someone knocked at her door, and she flinched.

"Hey, it's just me." Pelrin knelt beside her bed. A pang shot through Freddie's heart. Amanda and Raul should be here, but instead they were stuck in enchanted sleep in Summer.

"I'm fine, Pel. What do you want?" Freddie sat up suddenly, but vertigo kicked in, and she promptly fell back.

"Just checking to make sure you're ok. It's been a long night." He leaned against her bed and closed his eyes. "I managed to get Raul and Amanda to Shell Bay, but I couldn't find my mother." He let out a sigh as dark circles clung beneath his eyes.

"We have to find a way to break this curse. Amanda and Raul—this is all my fault."

He reached up a hand and stroked her cheek. "They're not harmed, and I promise I'll find a way to break the spell. Just think about all the people you did save."

Freddie closed her eyes, remembering all the no longer missing students rushing into the police station to call their parents. Headlines for potential articles swirled in her mind.

What happened to the students after the kidnappings, The forgotten history of the South Pole, and Fairy Civil War Status: The Fall of Winter.

But what was the point? Her investigation had come at too high of a cost. Perhaps her parents were right; this was too dangerous of a career path.

She closed her eyes as tears trickled down her face. Everything was ruined—maybe she shouldn't ever have tried.

CHAPTER 31

Aiden

Aiden stumbled out of his wend onto the damp ice before the remains of the Winter Palace. A field of soldiers stood watching the last of their base melt away. Many more were trapped inside—crushed by the falling ice or drowned in meltwater. He'd be blamed for this; Oberon would be beyond understanding after today. What would he do to him? The thought sent sickening shudders through his body.

It wasn't his fault all this was happening. It was the prince's and… Wyn's. What was he doing? Standing here and feeling sorry for himself while Wyn was freezing on the tundra. He should know better than to leave a human to die in this weather. Cursing himself, Aiden turned to wend when someone called his name. Tatiana ran toward him waving one hand in the air.

"Aiden! Have you seen Mare?" She puffed as she ran, causing her breath to cloud before her.

"No, I haven't." He bit the inside of his lip. Wyn needed him. He wouldn't be able to live with himself if he were the reason she died. "I'll go look for her."

"Take me with you! Please, it's my fault she's gone." Tatiana grabbed hold of his arm. Images of Wyn's lips slowly turning blue flashed in his mind. How long did it take for humans to freeze out here?

"I can't. I don't know how, but I promise I'll find her."

"You don't understand. I was going to go back for some of the servants in the lower parts of the palace, but she said it was too dangerous. I insisted, and she said she'd go instead. What if she's trapped in there?"

"I was in the lower parts of the palace. I saw no one there — she must have gotten out." He'd fought the prince there, the two of them destroying everything in sight. Was Wyn truly to blame for this, or was it his own thirst for vengeance? She said she didn't care for the prince, not in the same way she cared for him, but why then would she risk everything to save him? He shook his head. Saving her came before placing blame.

"Let's go look. It'll at the very least keep you away from my dad. I know — I know what happened with my mom. I know that wasn't your fault. That girl tricked her, and you were just following orders." Tatiana wiped her nose on the sleeve of her jacket.

"Let me go, just for a second. I promise I'll be right back." He slipped his arm out of her grip and wended back to the snow drift. "Wyn!"

The howling wind was all who answered him.

"Wyn!" he tried again. Yet still there was nothing.

Aiden kicked his way through the snow searching for her footprints, her fallen body, some hint of her, but there was nothing. Perhaps she found her way out, found her way to the other side of the bridge. Unlikely.

A hand clasped his shoulder, and he jerked. "I've been looking everywhere for you. Oberon is incensed, but he's not blaming everything on you. He mostly blames that human girl." Mare stood behind him, her loose dark hair flying like a nymph's wild vines around her head. "Come back with me."

He looked up and swallowed. "Tatiana is worried about you; she's right by the entrance."

"Then let's go to her. It'll probably be best if the three of us approach him together anyway."

Scanning the drift and the tundra beyond, Aiden winced at the ache in his heart — screaming at him to stay. "Does Oberon have the human?"

"He'd be a lot happier if he did. No, no one's seen her. They think she's with the prince."

Her words punched him in the gut. Everything between them was so thoroughly ruined. She didn't deserve to be left to die, and with the prince's cruel words in her ear, she'd no doubt hate him for eternity.

Clenching his jaw, he turned to Mare. "Let's return to Tatiana then."

He wended as shadows creeped up Mare's body, and they stepped back to where Tatiana stood shivering.

"You found her!" Tatiana rushed to Mare and wrapped her arms around her neck. "I was so worried."

Mare stumbled back a step. "You needn't worry so much about me. I'm fine, I'm always fine." Their eyes lingered on one another, Tatiana's cheeks turning a deeper red in the midst of their embrace. Mare pulled her closer and shot Aiden a look as though he were intruding in their private moment.

He took a step back and stared up at the green-streaked sky, amazed again at how it could remain so unchanged despite the chaos below. Thoughts of Wyn came back, and he swallowed hard. She'd just been fighting for her life, but she still should've told him of her plans. He'd almost killed her. What if she hadn't gotten out of the way in time? She hadn't thought of what something like that would do to him.

Around them, the remaining guards and courtiers gathered close. Some shivering against the cold. Others, cloaked or covered in fur, stood silently watching the castle crumble. He turned to look across the ice bridge where the escaped green fae stood. Several Dark Fae soldiers were crossing the ice bridge, approaching them.

Gold shimmered amongst the huddling mass of fae, then white exploded before them, pushing the Dark Fae attackers into the ravine. Aiden's eyes widened. No. She couldn't have given the orb to him. She'd promised to keep it safe. His vision turned glassy as he shot up an invisible shield to protect the remaining fae from the blizzard. Her life was at stake. The Dark Fae soldiers would have killed her, or worse, brought her back here if they'd gotten to her. At least now he knew she was with the prince, safe. His heart stung at the thought of them together.

The blizzard died down, and he lowered the shield. There was no one on the other side. Had they somehow gotten a hold of wing powder? But how?

"At least we survived this," Tatiana said, placing a hand on his shoulder.

Aiden nodded as they merged into the larger group.

Mare pressed against his other side. "Don't worry, we'll get through this. Elessea is still under your curse, there is no one to claim back Autumn, and the Summer army is reduced to hiding in Shell Bay. Oberon can't be too mad when this war is nearly won."

As though summoned by Mare's words, the crowd parted, allowing Oberon to pass through—the Crown of Flames glinting on his brow. His face was stoic as he stared directly at Aiden. "Come."

A tug pulled at his chest, and he wended to the ground to kneel before Oberon. When the king stepped forward, Aiden rose to follow him.

Tatiana stepped forward. "Dad, it wasn't his fault. Mom…" She choked on a sob. "He didn't—"

Oberon held up his hand, and his daughter fell silent.

Head bowed, Aiden balled his hands into fists to keep them from trembling. Would Oberon kill him, or would he act as his wife had and sentence Aiden to a fate worse than death? The crowd moved aside as Oberon led them beyond the chunks of ice that were once the palace. They continued walking in silence until they were both out of sight and earshot of the Dark Fae.

Oberon turned to him. The king's face was stern but not full of the rage Aiden had feared. "I should be furious with you for destroying my palace, releasing our most valuable prisoner, and killing my wife, but I'm not… yet."

"Th-thank you, Your Majesty." Aiden bowed and caught sight of red blood seeping through gashes on the king's sleeves. His clothes, like many of the others, were covered in burns. But it was strange; he'd been with Tatiana, and she was free from any such marks.

"By ridding me of my wife, there is more power I can take for myself, and for that I am pleased. But I warn you, should you fail me, even in the slightest, again, I will make you regret ever taking breath. Do I make myself clear?" A ball of blue flame appeared in the king's palm, and Aiden swallowed. What would it be like to be burned by his own flames? Was it even possible? He didn't want to find out.

"Yes, Your Majesty."

"Kneel." Oberon reached into his coat and produced the crystal wand.

Aiden sank to the ground, dread filling his stomach as Oberon held the tip to his forehead.

"When you wake, you will meet us at the Autumn stronghold. I don't intend to let that girl seek peace in the Human Realm for long. It's about time the humans remember why they should fear us," the king said.

Before Aiden could fully process the man's words, pain exploded from the tip of his head and raked through his body. He cried out as it gnawed into his bones and made his arms and legs give way. The world swam before him as what felt like the last of his magic drained away.

When Aiden woke, his body was stiff from laying in the snow. He tried to move and winced as he made it to his knees. Never before had he been so cold, his body violently shivering against the harsh Winter wind.

He'd lost everything — again. Just when he'd thought Summer could take no more. They'd even driven him to temporary madness, fighting the prince despite Wyn needing his help. And then ignoring reason and blaming her for the mess the prince had caused. His fury against Summer had led him to sabotage the only bit of happiness in his life. Now she too was turned against him. It was better not to feel; he was nothing more than his orders, a weapon for Oberon to do with as he willed.

A figure cloaked in shadow stepped in front of him. Aiden didn't look up. His body was too cold for him to raise his head from being tucked against his chest.

"I-I'm f-fine, Mare," he said through chattering teeth.

"Close, but not quite." Mare's mom knelt before him, her sharp teeth gleaming as she looked him over. "Your misery smells..." She inhaled deeply. "Delicious."

Aiden forced his head up, his eyes pleading with her. He couldn't collapse in the snow again — he wasn't strong enough to withstand it. "Please." His voice scraped out as no more than a whisper.

She hummed a laugh. "You made the painful choice, and now your last hope has been snuffed out. Have you so soon forgotten our bargain?"

"Let me just get somewhere warmer and heal a bit. Then you can —" His jaw stiffened, more from fear than the frigid weather. "Feed."

"No, I prefer to dine now."

Pain shot through Aiden as though he were being run through the chest with a white hot blade. There was screaming, though he feared it was his own, and the gluttonous laughter of Mare's mom. It felt as though hours had passed as she fed, then it finally subsided and he crouched in the snow, panting.

"Thank you for the delicious meal. Now, we shall see what you do without your tasty misery." Shadows clouded around her, and she vanished, leaving him alone again.

Aiden blinked. The pain was gone, but it was as though she'd taken a heavy burden from his shoulders — his doubt, fear, and despair were all gone. Trembling, he got to his feet and looked around. Winter had fallen, just like it had for his mother, but she'd found happiness again after its fall, and so would he.

Wyn was right; his freedom was half won. And he would find his way to rid himself of the other half and finally be able to live his life. He'd prove himself to Wyn again. Though anger tinged his thoughts of her, he couldn't fight the overwhelming desire to be by her side. Perhaps it hadn't been complete betrayal; she'd hid her plan from him, but she'd said killing Mab hadn't been part of it. She hadn't willingly used him to murder.

He let out a breath. For the first time since he met Wyn his hope won out against his misery. Revenge had gotten him nowhere — perhaps the owl lady was right. He needed to choose a different path.

Getting to his feet, Aiden summoned his magic to conjure a warm wind to defrost him before he returned to Oberon. There had to be a way to gain his freedom despite Oberon's direct order not to harm him. Wyn had found the loophole with Mab — now it was his turn. A smile crept across his face as he pictured a life with Wyn, free and in the Human Realm. If Oberon was going after the humans next, Aiden would find a way to stop him. After all, with all the human weaponry taking on the now weakened army, it'd be the perfect opportunity to fail to protect the imposter king.

Then, and only then, could he finally be free to pursue the girl he loved.

BONUS STORY

Aiden

Tall grass crumpled beneath Aiden's new boots. Sweat soaked through the crisp black shirt and leather jerkin that made up his new uniform adding to the prickling feeling along the back of his neck. A small village lay ahead, it reminded him of home—no more than twenty buildings surrounding an open park with a cheery fountain at its heart. Fruit trees, heavily laden with peaches and pears, bowed around the shady space filling the air with their ripe fragrance.

Aiden's stomach growled as he watched a young, fairy girl flit to a nearby branch and pluck a peach causing the leaves to rain down on a laughing woman—no doubt her mother. He gritted his teeth and glowered at the child as her translucent wings reflected the sun's rainbows. Other children ran past her, boys not yet in their teens, like himself. They were fighting a mock battle, unaware of the danger that watched them.

A band of faun musicians played at one end of the square. Red-haired nymphs twirled and leaped around them; wide smiles stretched across their faces. Aiden clenched his fist and took a step back. Something solid blocked his path. He looked up. Oberon loomed over him, watching the dancers, with a fierce hunger in his eyes. Running a hand through his thinning brown hair, he pulled his withering lips into a straight line. Not for the first time did Aiden wonder what manner of fae he was.

"You know what you have to do." The tone of his voice was sharp enough to cut glass. Aiden swallowed hard and nodded.

"These people aren't soldiers, though. They're not a threat." His palms turned clammy, and the words stuck to his throat. Joyous shouts rang out from the boys, still locked in their pretend battle, making him flinch.

"Your parents weren't soldiers either, but that didn't stop our enemies from murdering them. Now did it?" Oberon let out a dark chuckle and placed a hand on Aiden's shoulder. He shuddered at the contact but stayed silent, unable to pull away.

His parents wouldn't want him to do this. They'd always taught him to be kind and respect all creatures no matter what type of fae or non-fae they were. But they were dead, murdered, without even a chance to fight or flee. He blinked back tears.

"I don't think I can do this," Aiden mumbled.

"I am not asking boy," Oberon said. "You owe me your life and you will obey. Now go!"

Before he could stop himself a torrent of blue flames shot down his arm. Aiden jumped in surprise and then hurled the blaze at the nearest house. The straw roof was instantly devoured by the intensity of his fire. Tears ran down his cheeks as he desperately tried to block out the sounds of the eruption of screams. Again and again, he launched flames at the town until every building was on fire. Now, the villagers took notice of him. A small band of fae marched toward him; several fairies, two undines, and a satyr.

Oberon bent low to whisper in his ear. "No survivors."

Aiden wiped the tears on his sleeve and then hurled a jet of blue at one of the fairies. She shrieked as one of the undines frantically tried to get her out of the way. The other fairies attempted to swarm him, but he was too fast. Their ashes hit the ground before they were in arm's reach.

"It's just a child!" the satyr called out before he too was

engulfed in fire and disintegrated into gray dust.

The remaining undine stared at him, wide-eyed and open-mouthed. The blue-skinned fae tried to shield himself with a fountain of water. Aiden closed his eyes, as flame flew from his hands and the man released an animalistic howl as the blaze hit the water and the steam surrounded him.

Scents of burning wood and flesh made him gag as Aiden approached the town. His legs wobbled and tears blurred his vision. People ran and screamed in all directions, buildings crashed to the ground, and water pounded against the roaring flames. Hands raised; Aiden pushed flames toward the fountain. It boiled and hissed in a cloud of searing vapor. He pivoted, targeting the undines, who were busy extinguishing the fires that had now devoured half the town. Ensuring nothing stopped his destruction, Aiden hurled a wave of blue fire at them.

Several times one of the brave, or foolish, villagers would try to attack him. Each time his flames would shoot them down. These were farmers—not soldiers—they had no experience defending themselves from anyone more threatening than a troupe of wandering bandits. Aiden lost himself in the haze of fire, screams, and the burning town clogging the air with thick, black smoke. Sobbing, he looked around at the remains of the village around him. Nothing moved. Half burnt corpses lay scattered in the streets and flame-charred bones stuck out amongst the rubble of buildings.

He passed the park, his eyes scanning for any sign of life. *No survivors.* Something crunched beneath his boot. He stumbled and looked down. The brittle remains of an arm stuck out from beneath his foot. The body was only half burnt—a tiny hand clutched the remains of a squashed peach. Aiden sucked in a gasping breath.

The shuffling of fallen wood made him jump and turn. A boy, roughly his own age trembled in the rubble of what once must have been his home. His knees were pulled against his chest, a wooden sword clutched in his hands. A strange force compelled Aiden forward, he fought to keep his arms from shaking. The boy looked up. His eyes widened in horror as he took in Aiden's unscathed form.

"Did you do this?" the boy croaked. He got to his feet, a wooden sword trembling in his hand.

Aiden nodded and continued walking toward the boy.

"Why? What did we ever do to you?" The boy's eyes were filled with tears — sobbing through his words.

"I'm sorry." Aiden avoided meeting the boy's horrified gaze and held up his hand.

"Wait! Are you going to kill me too?" The boy pointed the sword at Aiden. Aiden just stared back at him. "Please."

"I'm sorry." Tears ran in rivers down Aiden's face, pooling in the crook of his neck.

Blue flames shot from his palm engulfing the boy in their searing heat. Aiden clenched his teeth as the boy let out something between a howl and a scream. It was over in a matter of seconds that felt like an eternity. The boy's blackened corpse crumpled onto the rubble.

Now the village was silent.

Ann Dayleview

Ann Dayleview writes fantasy novels which aim to transport the reader to worlds unlike any other. She reads any young adult and middle grade fantasy novel she can get her hands on. Her writing is often inspired by the wild assortment of music she listens to. Everything from classical to pop and beyond!

In addition to writing, Ann loves spending time with her two dogs, baking all the sweet things, and bringing awareness about taking care of your mental health. She lives in Pennsylvania with her ever-rotating collection of books she lugs from place to place.

Visit her online:

www.anndayleview.com

Social: @anndayleview

Glossary

Fairy – The land separated from the Human Realm by invisible borders accessible in specific locations in the Human Realm. Fairy is the homeland of the green, brown, and gold fae.

The Dark Fae Army (Dark Fae) – These rebel forces led by Mab and Oberon who've crowned themselves Queen and King of the brown fae. They seek to overthrow the gold fae rulers of the Seasonal Realms.

The Seasonal Realms – Summer, Winter, Autumn, and Spring are the four Seasonal Realms that make up Fairy.

The Sea Realm – The Sea Realm encompasses all of the magic of the oceans. It expands between Fairy and the Human Realm.

The Air Realm – Similar to the Sea Realm, the Air Realm encompasses everything in the sky. It is also said to be home to dragons.

The Human Realm – This is home to the humans and red fae. It borders Fairy and polices the crossing locations.

The Nightmare Plains – A place of darkness and evil creatures, where the Realms send their worst criminals.

Blue Fae – The mythical and most powerful of all the fae. They are marked by their blue wings and have been known to grant the wishes of humans.

Gold Fae – Rulers of Fairy, the gold fae are incredibly powerful. They are marked by their gold wings.

Green Fae – These are magic-using natives of Fairy. Some examples include genies, fairies, and leprechauns.

Brown Fae – Non-magic-using natives of Fairy. Some examples include dwarves, goblins, and fauns.

Red Fae – These are closely related to humans but are supernatural in nature. Some examples include vampires, werewolves, and banshees.

Nightmare – A shapeshifting creature native to the Nightmare Plains. It preys on the minds of its victims, showing them their worst nightmares before devouring them.

Sundiva – A type of green fae who have immense power over fire. They have large feathered wings and are rumored to have lava instead of blood.

Drekavac – Derived from Slavic mythology, these brown fae are humanoid with disproportionally large, bald heads and are thought to be the souls of dead children.

Undine – These green fae are derived from the writings of Paracelsus. Also known as water nymphs, undines call the Sea Realm home.

Mare – Derived from Germanic folklore, this green fae is traditionally a creature who rides on people's chests and brings them nightmares.

Anansi – These rare red fae live in Fairy. They are half spider and half human and are said to feed on "flesh".

Satyr – A bipedal green fae with the torso of a human and the lower half of a goat. They also have large ram's horns and pointed ears. Satyrs can use their magic flute to compel people to follow them.

Faun – These are brown fae, similar to satyrs, but with much smaller horns and no magical abilities.

Minotaur – Inspired by Greek mythology, these brown fae have the head of a bull and the body of a human.

Garuda – Inspired by Hindu mythology these brown fae are native to the Air Realm and have a mix of human and eagle features.

Naga – Inspired by Hindu mythology, these brown fae have the tail of a snake and the torso and head of a human.

Marid – Inspired by Islamic mythology, these green fae are humanoid with blue skin and power over water.

Anubis – Inspired by the Egyptian god, these rare red fae have the heads of jackals and the bodies of humans. They give off an energy preventing people from lying in their presence.

Wili- Inspired by Russian folklore, these red fae are veiled, graceful women. They are spirits with a reputation for dragging philandering men to watery graves.

Ifrits – Inspired by Islamic folklore, these green fae have power over fire, though often not as powerful as sundivas.